SUPER MARIO ADVENTURES ™

Art by
CHARLIE NOZAWA

Story by
KENTARO TAKEKUMA

Translation by
LESLIE SWAN

Super Mario Adventures

Art by
Charlie Nozawa

Story by
Kentaro Takekuma

Super Mario Adventures
TM & © 1993 Nintendo. All Rights Reserved.

SUPER MARIO ADVENTURES MARIO NO DAIBOKEN
by Charlie NOZAWA, Kentaro TAKEKUMA
Book planning and editing: APE/Shigesato ITOI
© 1993 Charlie NOZAWA, Kentaro TAKEKUMA
All rights reserved.
Original Japanese edition published by SHOGAKUKAN.
English translation rights in the United States of America, Canada,
the United Kingdom, Ireland, Australia and New Zealand
arranged with SHOGAKUKAN.

Translation / Leslie Swan
Cover & Interior Design / Sam Elzway
Editor / Elizabeth Kawasaki

Printed in the U.S.A.

Published by VIZ Media, LLC
1355 Market St., Suite 200
San Francisco, CA 94103

10 9 8 7
First printing, October 2016
Seventh printing, November 2018

SKA-LOP
YOU'VE BEEN A GOOD BROTHER, MARIO...
SKA-LOP

TABLE OF CONTENTS

GOBBLE GOBBLE
....

MUNCH. MUNCH. MUNCH.

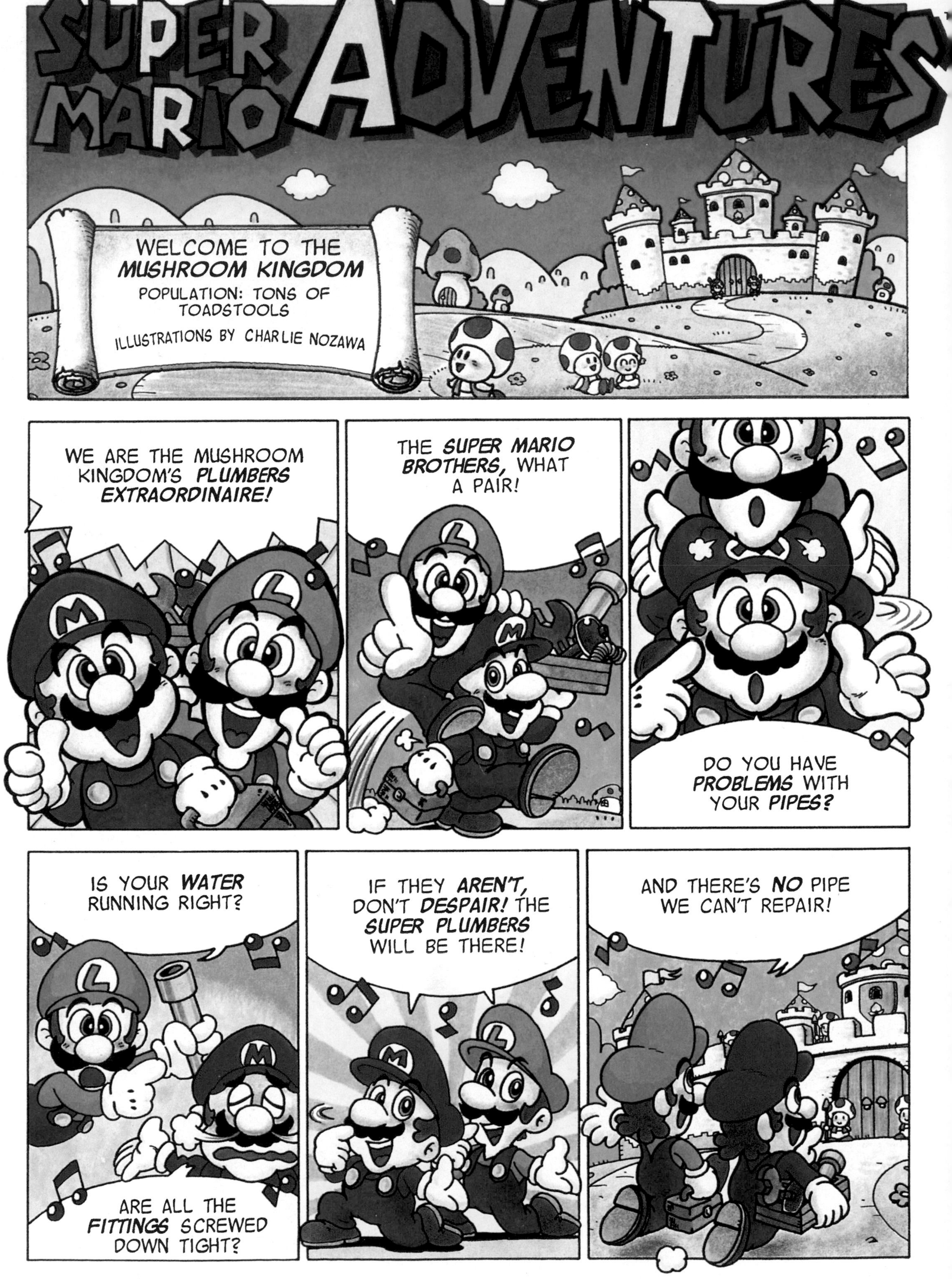
SUPER MARIO ADVENTURES
WELCOME TO THE *MUSHROOM KINGDOM*
POPULATION: TONS OF TOADSTOOLS
ILLUSTRATIONS BY CHARLIE NOZAWA
WE ARE THE MUSHROOM KINGDOM'S *PLUMBERS EXTRAORDINAIRE!*
THE *SUPER MARIO BROTHERS,* WHAT A PAIR!
DO YOU HAVE *PROBLEMS* WITH YOUR *PIPES?*
IS YOUR *WATER* RUNNING RIGHT?
ARE ALL THE *FITTINGS* SCREWED DOWN TIGHT?
IF THEY *AREN'T,* DON'T *DESPAIR!* THE *SUPER PLUMBERS* WILL BE THERE!
AND THERE'S *NO* PIPE WE CAN'T REPAIR!

CIAO!

PUT DOWN YOUR PLUMBER'S HELPER! LET THE *PROS* AT THE PALACE *PIPES*.

FINALLY! THERE'S NO TIME TO *MONKEY AROUND*!

IT'S A ROYAL *MESS*--AND THE PRINCESS' PARTY IS *TONIGHT*!

NO *SWEAT*!

HAVE WRENCH, WILL TRAVEL.

EGAD!

MAMA MIA, WHAT A MESS!

AND I HAVE A PERSNICKETY, PARTY-PLANNING *PRINCESS* EXPECTING PLUMBING-- BY *TONIGHT*!

EH, NO PROBLEMO!

A PIPELINE JOB BY *TONIGHT*? I CAN'T START A JOB *THIS* BIG ON AN *EMPTY STOMACH*.

YOU JUST HAD *BREAKFAST*! NOW PUT DOWN THE *PASTA* AND PICK UP A *WRENCH*.

WE'LL FASTEN THESE FITTINGS IN *NO TIME*!

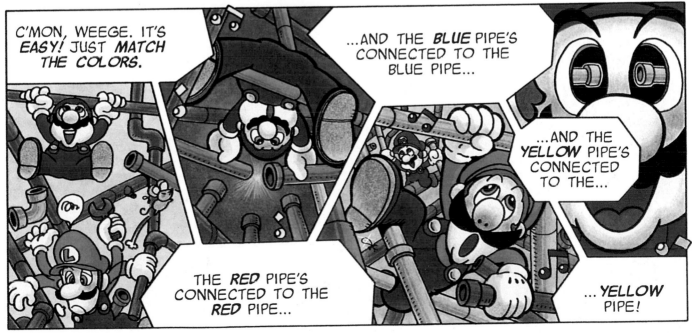

C'MON, WEEGE. IT'S *EASY*! JUST *MATCH THE COLORS*.

THE *RED* PIPE'S CONNECTED TO THE *RED* PIPE...

...AND THE *BLUE* PIPE'S CONNECTED TO THE BLUE PIPE...

...AND THE *YELLOW* PIPE'S CONNECTED TO THE...

...*YELLOW* PIPE!

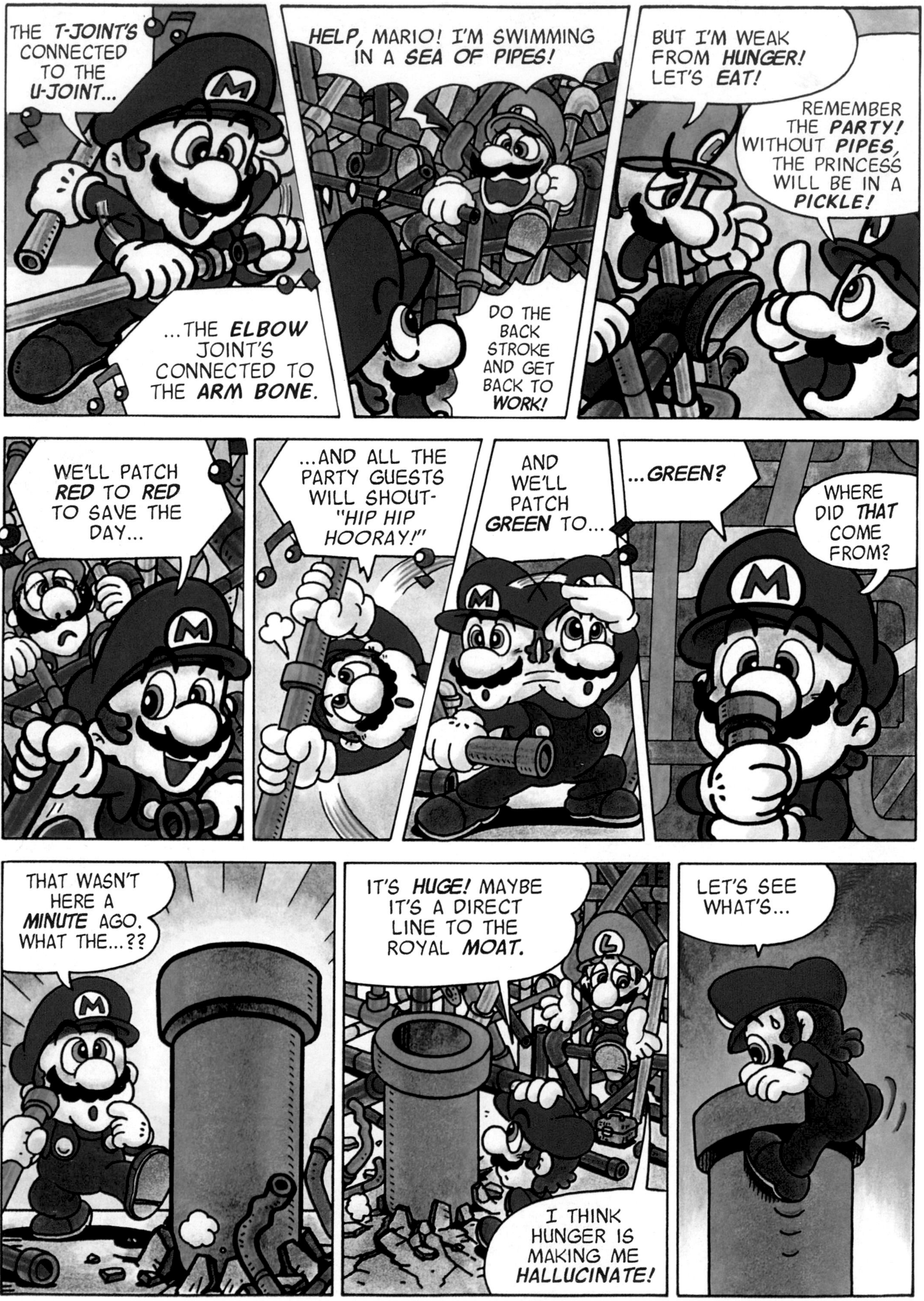

THE T-JOINT'S CONNECTED TO THE U-JOINT...
...THE ELBOW JOINT'S CONNECTED TO THE ARM BONE.
HELP, MARIO! I'M SWIMMING IN A SEA OF PIPES!
DO THE BACK STROKE AND GET BACK TO WORK!
BUT I'M WEAK FROM HUNGER! LET'S EAT!
REMEMBER THE PARTY! WITHOUT PIPES, THE PRINCESS WILL BE IN A PICKLE!
WE'LL PATCH RED TO RED TO SAVE THE DAY...
...AND ALL THE PARTY GUESTS WILL SHOUT- "HIP HIP HOORAY!"
AND WE'LL PATCH GREEN TO...
...GREEN?
WHERE DID THAT COME FROM?
THAT WASN'T HERE A MINUTE AGO. WHAT THE...??
IT'S HUGE! MAYBE IT'S A DIRECT LINE TO THE ROYAL MOAT.
I THINK HUNGER IS MAKING ME HALLUCINATE!
LET'S SEE WHAT'S...

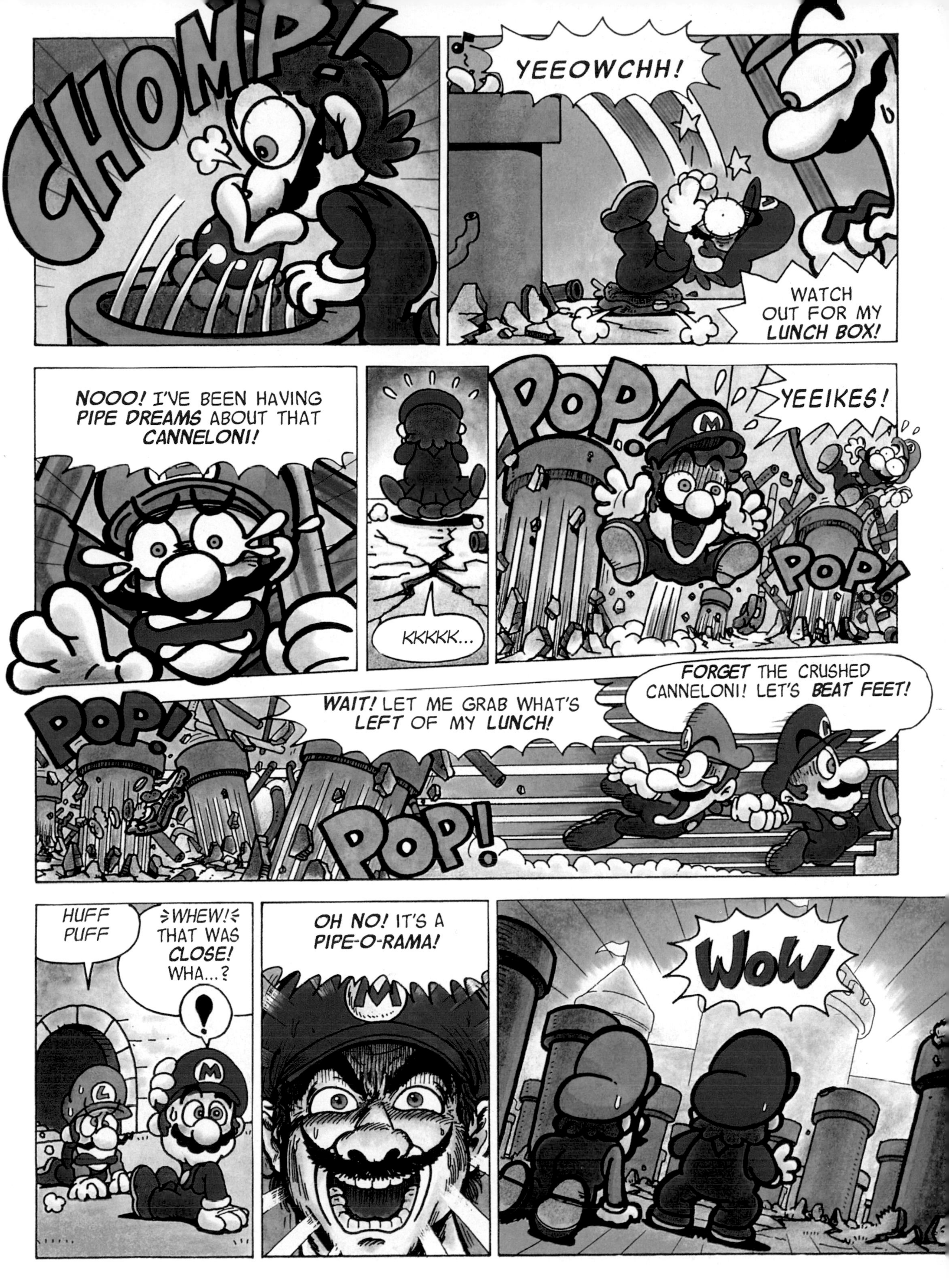
CHOMP!
YEEOWCHH!
WATCH OUT FOR MY LUNCH BOX!
NOOO! I'VE BEEN HAVING PIPE DREAMS ABOUT THAT CANNELONI!
KKKKK...
POP!
YEEIKES!
POP!
POP!
WAIT! LET ME GRAB WHAT'S LEFT OF MY LUNCH!
FORGET THE CRUSHED CANNELONI! LET'S BEAT FEET!
POP!
HUFF PUFF
WHEW! THAT WAS CLOSE! WHA...?
!
OH NO! IT'S A PIPE-O-RAMA!
WOW

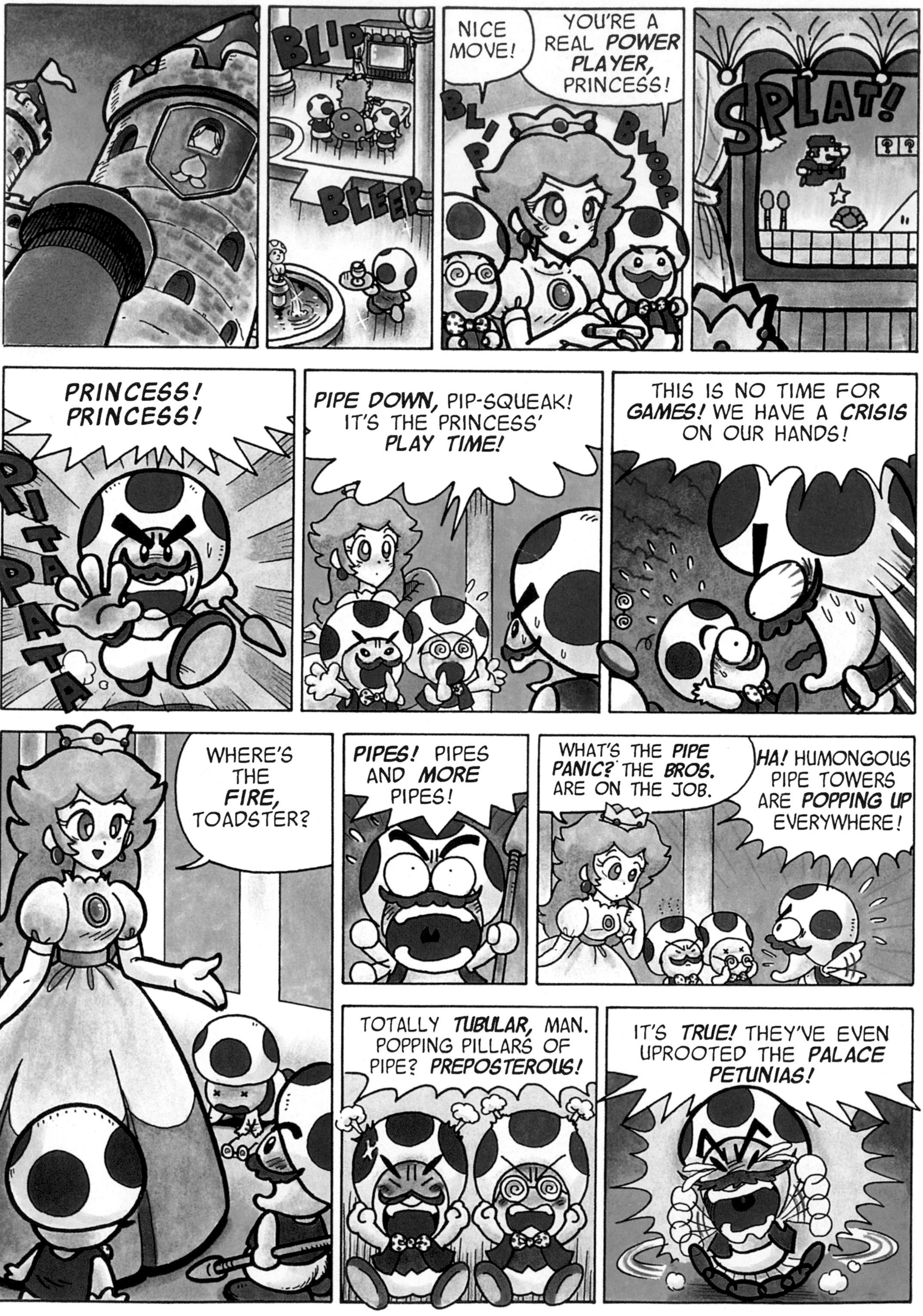
BLIP
BLEEP
NICE MOVE!
YOU'RE A REAL POWER PLAYER, PRINCESS!
BLIP
BLOOP
SPLAT!
PRINCESS! PRINCESS!
PITA PATA
PIPE DOWN, PIP-SQUEAK! IT'S THE PRINCESS' PLAY TIME!
THIS IS NO TIME FOR GAMES! WE HAVE A CRISIS ON OUR HANDS!
WHERE'S THE FIRE, TOADSTER?
PIPES! PIPES AND MORE PIPES!
WHAT'S THE PIPE PANIC? THE BROS. ARE ON THE JOB.
HA! HUMONGOUS PIPE TOWERS ARE POPPING UP EVERYWHERE!
TOTALLY TUBULAR, MAN. POPPING PILLARS OF PIPE? PREPOSTEROUS!
IT'S TRUE! THEY'VE EVEN UPROOTED THE PALACE PETUNIAS!

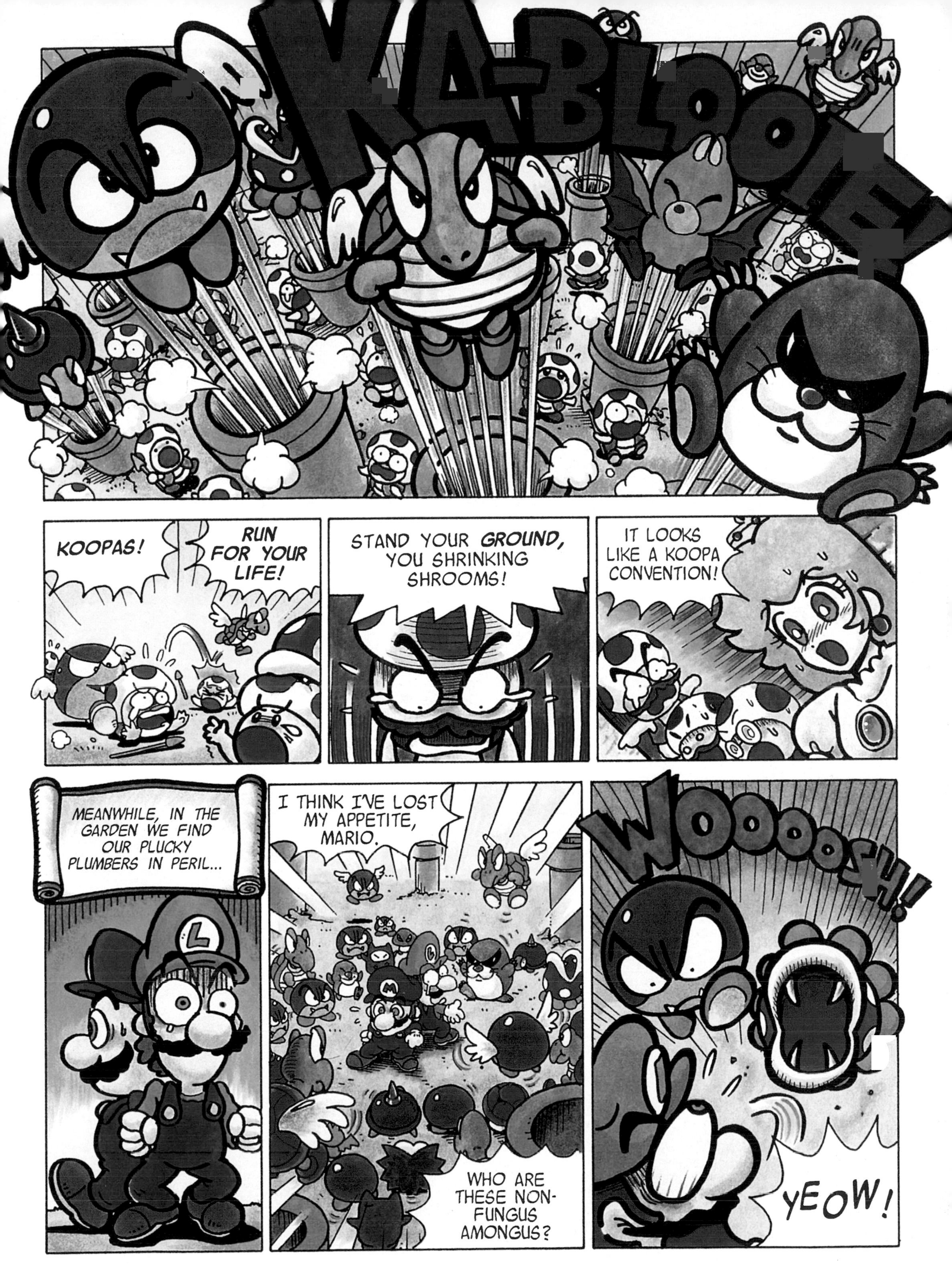
KA-BLOOIE!
KOOPAS!
RUN FOR YOUR LIFE!
STAND YOUR *GROUND,* YOU SHRINKING SHROOMS!
IT LOOKS LIKE A KOOPA CONVENTION!
MEANWHILE, IN THE GARDEN WE FIND OUR PLUCKY PLUMBERS IN PERIL...
I THINK I'VE LOST MY APPETITE, MARIO.
WHO ARE THESE NON-FUNGUS AMONGUS?
WOOOOSH!!
YEOW!

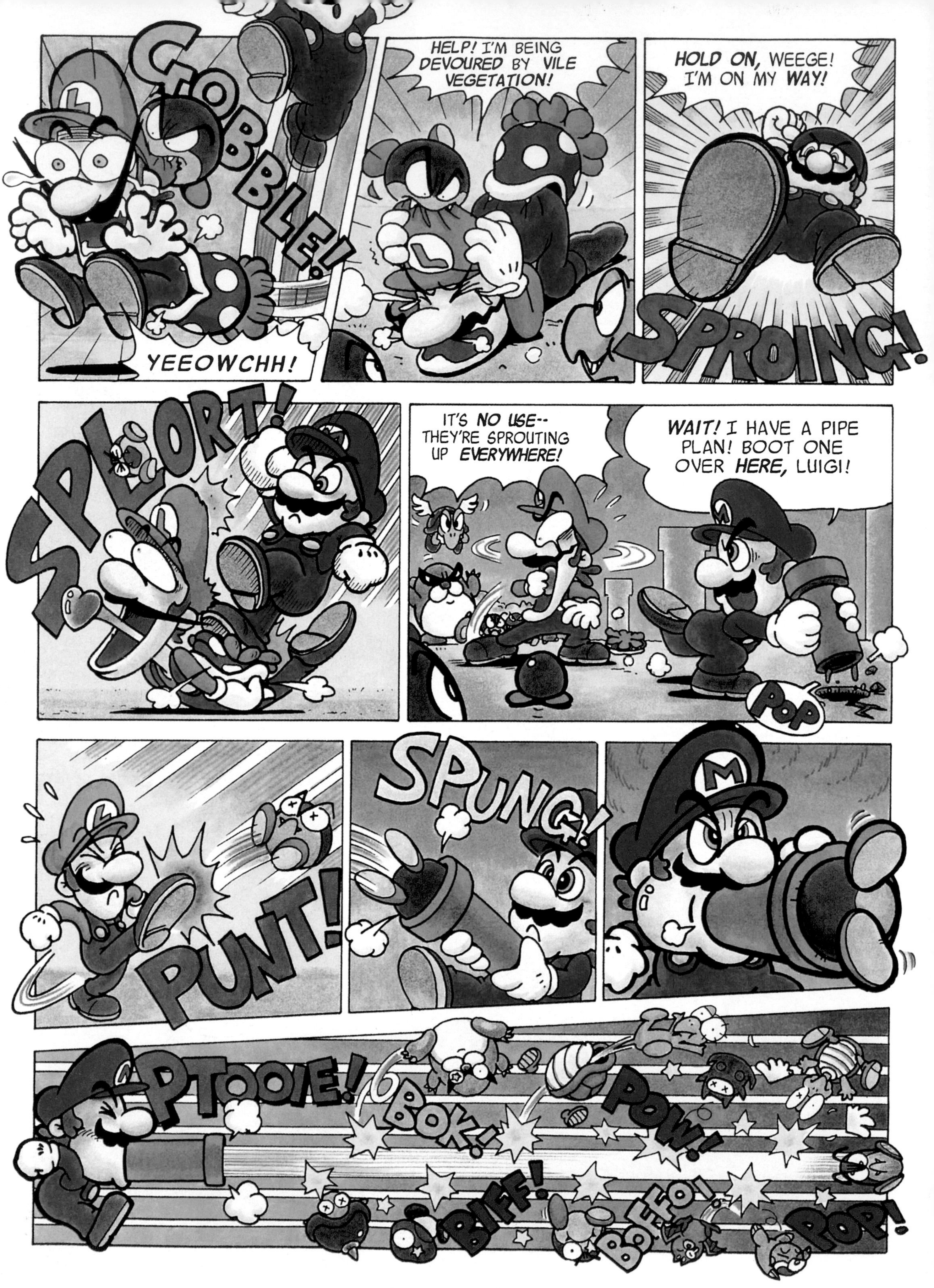
GOBBLE!
YEEOWCHH!
HELP! I'M BEING DEVOURED BY VILE VEGETATION!
HOLD ON, WEEGE! I'M ON MY WAY!
SPROING!
SPLORT!
IT'S NO USE-- THEY'RE SPROUTING UP EVERYWHERE!
WAIT! I HAVE A PIPE PLAN! BOOT ONE OVER HERE, LUIGI!
POP
PUNT!
SPUNG!
PTOOIE!
BOK!
POW!
BIFF!
BOFO!
POP!

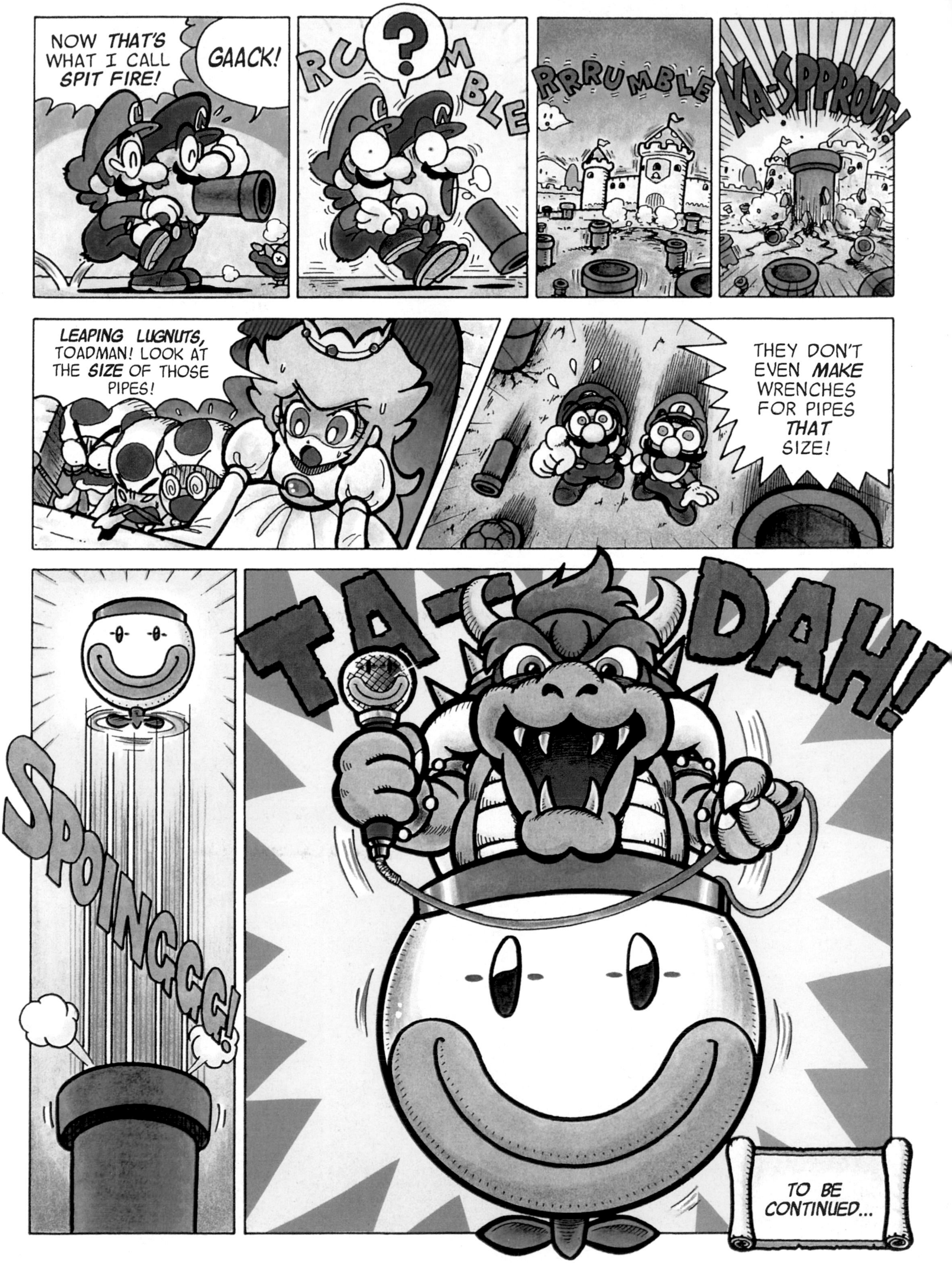

NOW THAT'S WHAT I CALL SPIT FIRE!
GAACK!
RUMBLE
?
RRRUMBLE
KA-SPPROUT!
LEAPING LUGNUTS, TOADMAN! LOOK AT THE SIZE OF THOSE PIPES!
THEY DON'T EVEN MAKE WRENCHES FOR PIPES THAT SIZE!
SPOINGGG!
TA-DAH!
TO BE CONTINUED...

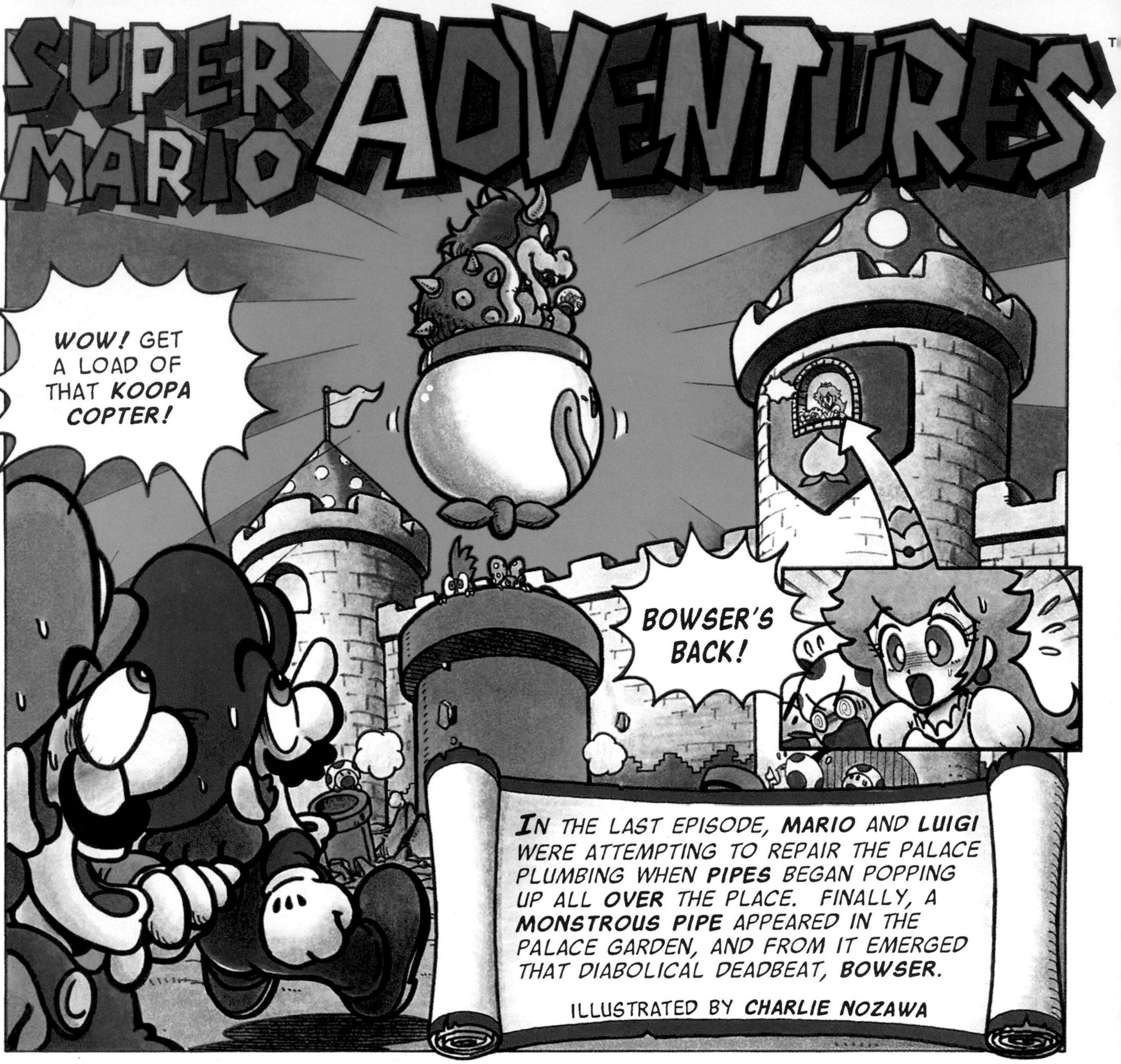
SUPER MARIO ADVENTURES™
WOW! GET A LOAD OF THAT KOOPA COPTER!
BOWSER'S BACK!
IN THE LAST EPISODE, MARIO AND LUIGI WERE ATTEMPTING TO REPAIR THE PALACE PLUMBING WHEN PIPES BEGAN POPPING UP ALL OVER THE PLACE. FINALLY, A MONSTROUS PIPE APPEARED IN THE PALACE GARDEN, AND FROM IT EMERGED THAT DIABOLICAL DEADBEAT, BOWSER.
ILLUSTRATED BY CHARLIE NOZAWA

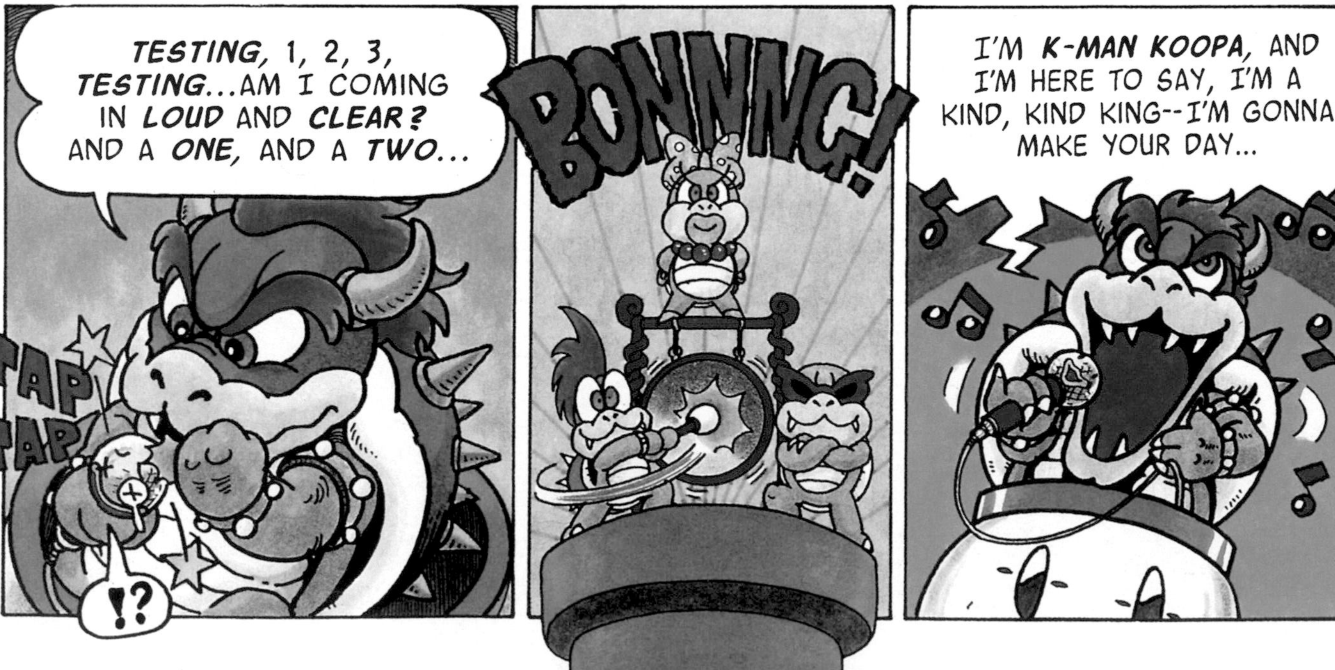
TESTING, 1, 2, 3, TESTING...AM I COMING IN LOUD AND CLEAR? AND A ONE, AND A TWO...
TAP TAP
!?
BONNNG!
I'M K-MAN KOOPA, AND I'M HERE TO SAY, I'M A KIND, KIND KING--I'M GONNA MAKE YOUR DAY...

THE K-MAN HAS A **BIG SURPRISE**, SO **LISTEN UP**, SHROOMS, AND **PEEL** YOUR **EYES!**

MOUNTAINS HIGH...

TO **VALLEYS** LOW...

K-MAN KOOPA IS **IN CONTROL!**

I RULE 'MOST ALL THE LAND YOU SEE, BUT THAT'S STILL NOT **ENOUGH** FOR ME...

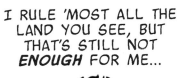

I WANT TO RULE **THIS** KINGDOM, TOO, AND THAT'S **JUST** WHAT I PLAN TO **DO.**

THUMBS UP, K-MAN, HERE'S TO **YOU!**

CUT THE **RAP,** KOOPA CREEP. WHAT'S YOUR **SCAM?**

CHILL OUT, AND LEND AN EAR: I HAVE A **PRO-POSAL** FOR YOU, MY DEAR.

IF WE WANT TO LIVE IN **HAR-MO-NY,** YOU'RE GOING TO HAVE TO **MARRY ME!**

IN YOUR **DREAMS** -- AND IN **MY NIGHTMARES!**

COME ON, SWEETCAKES, WE'LL MAKE A **GREAT** PAIR! **I** CAN DO THE **RULING** WHILE **YOU** STYLE YOUR **HAIR!**

I'LL BE **BACK** FOR YOUR **ANSWER** BUT BEFORE I **GO...**

...JUST REMEM-BER THAT IF THE **ANSWER** IS "NO"...

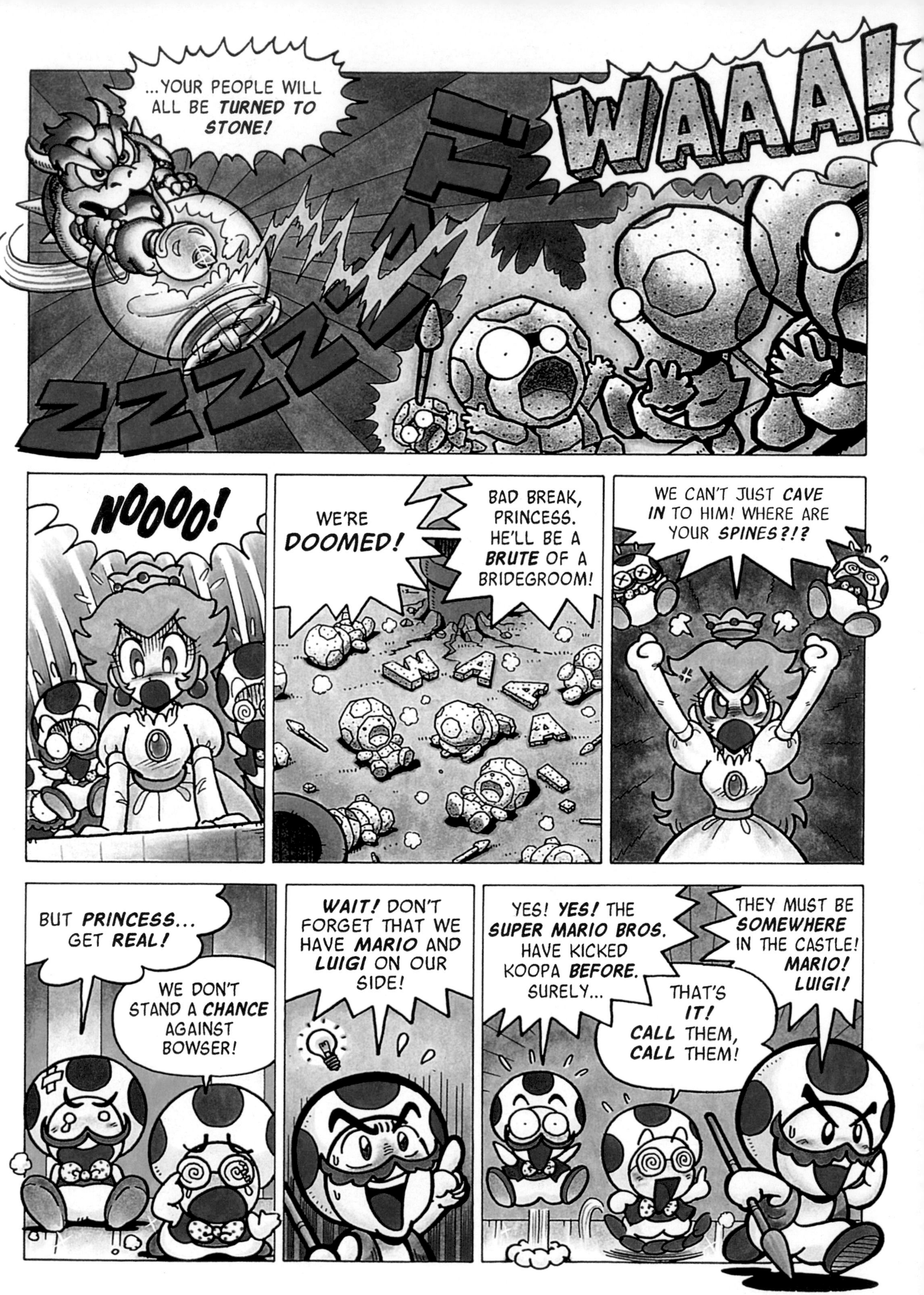
...YOUR PEOPLE WILL ALL BE TURNED TO STONE!
DOZZZZ
WAAAA!
NOOOO!
WE'RE DOOMED!
BAD BREAK, PRINCESS. HE'LL BE A BRUTE OF A BRIDEGROOM!
WE CAN'T JUST CAVE IN TO HIM! WHERE ARE YOUR SPINES?!?
BUT PRINCESS... GET REAL!
WE DON'T STAND A CHANCE AGAINST BOWSER!
WAIT! DON'T FORGET THAT WE HAVE MARIO AND LUIGI ON OUR SIDE!
YES! YES! THE SUPER MARIO BROS. HAVE KICKED KOOPA BEFORE. SURELY...
THAT'S IT! CALL THEM, CALL THEM!
THEY MUST BE SOMEWHERE IN THE CASTLE! MARIO! LUIGI!

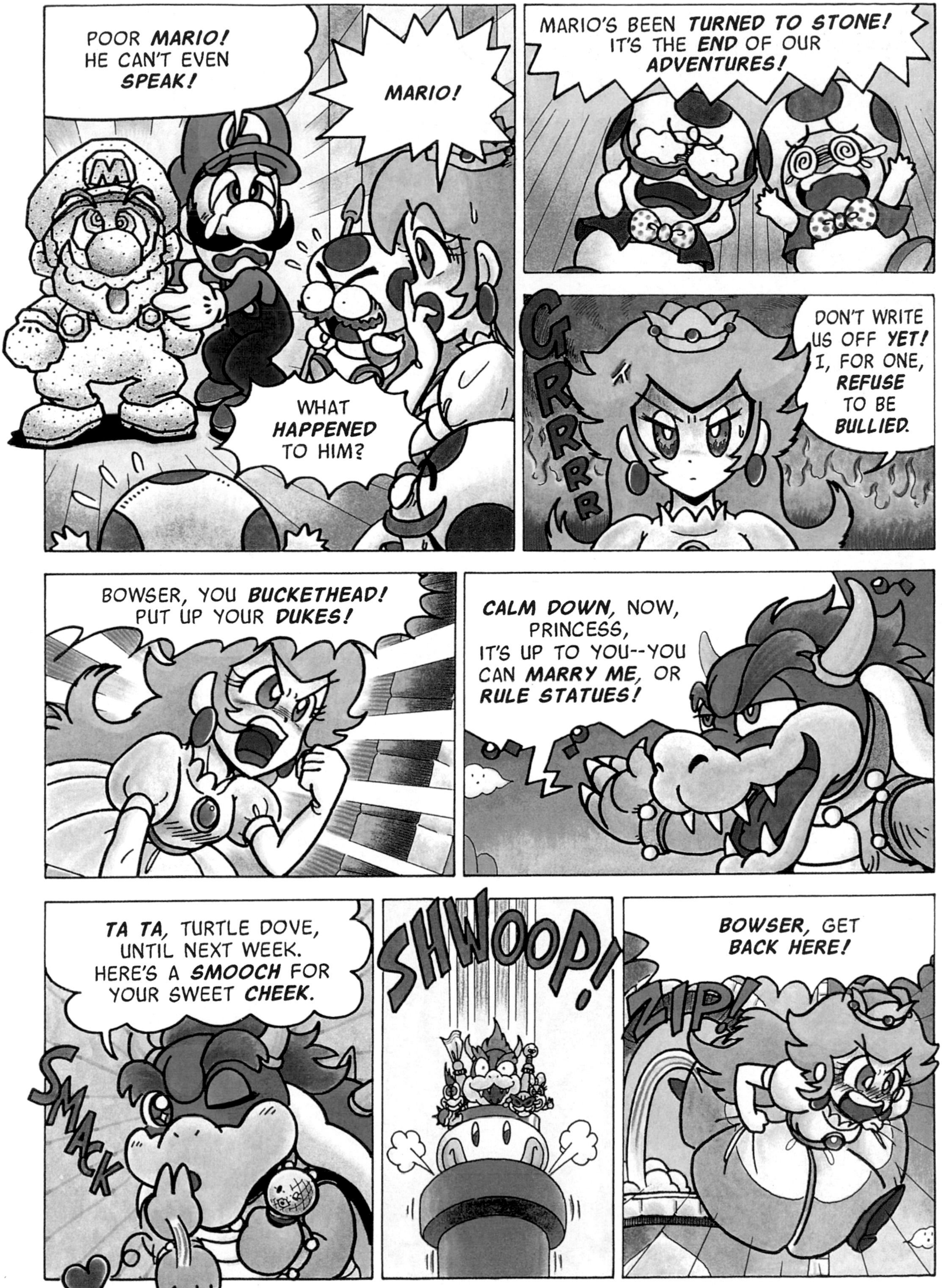
POOR MARIO! HE CAN'T EVEN SPEAK!
MARIO!
WHAT HAPPENED TO HIM?
MARIO'S BEEN TURNED TO STONE! IT'S THE END OF OUR ADVENTURES!
GRRRRR
DON'T WRITE US OFF YET! I, FOR ONE, REFUSE TO BE BULLIED.
BOWSER, YOU BUCKETHEAD! PUT UP YOUR DUKES!
CALM DOWN, NOW, PRINCESS, IT'S UP TO YOU--YOU CAN MARRY ME, OR RULE STATUES!
TA TA, TURTLE DOVE, UNTIL NEXT WEEK. HERE'S A SMOOCH FOR YOUR SWEET CHEEK.
SMACK
SHWOOP!
BOWSER, GET BACK HERE!
ZIP!

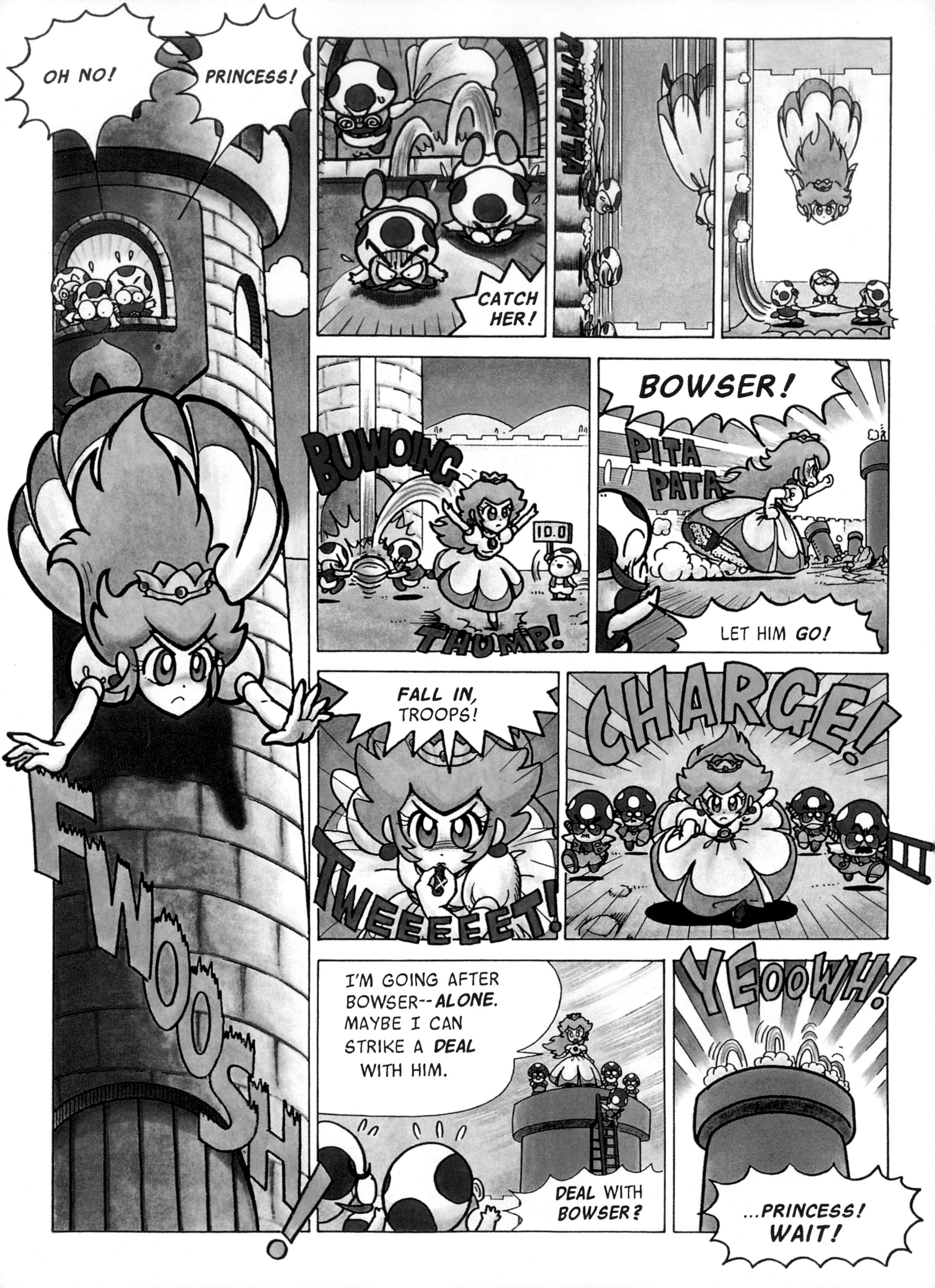
OH NO!
PRINCESS!
FWOOSH!
CATCH HER!
PITAPATA
BUWOING
10.0
THUMP!
BOWSER!
PITA PATA
LET HIM GO!
FALL IN, TROOPS!
TWEEEEEET!
CHARGE!
I'M GOING AFTER BOWSER--ALONE. MAYBE I CAN STRIKE A DEAL WITH HIM.
DEAL WITH BOWSER?
YEOOWH!
...PRINCESS! WAIT!

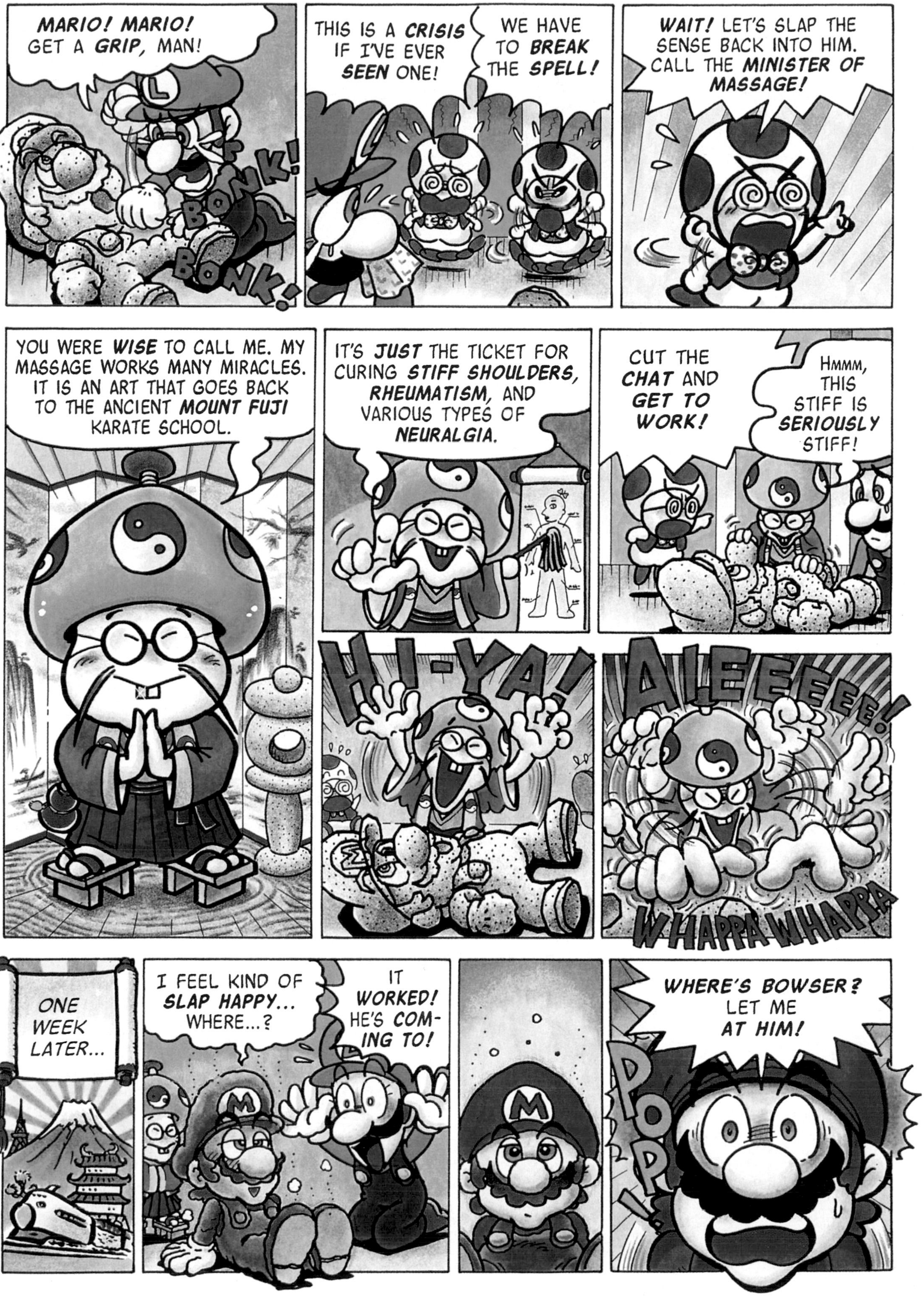
MARIO! MARIO! GET A GRIP, MAN!
BONK!
BONK!
THIS IS A CRISIS IF I'VE EVER SEEN ONE!
WE HAVE TO BREAK THE SPELL!
WAIT! LET'S SLAP THE SENSE BACK INTO HIM. CALL THE MINISTER OF MASSAGE!
YOU WERE WISE TO CALL ME. MY MASSAGE WORKS MANY MIRACLES. IT IS AN ART THAT GOES BACK TO THE ANCIENT MOUNT FUJI KARATE SCHOOL.
IT'S JUST THE TICKET FOR CURING STIFF SHOULDERS, RHEUMATISM, AND VARIOUS TYPES OF NEURALGIA.
CUT THE CHAT AND GET TO WORK!
HMMM, THIS STIFF IS SERIOUSLY STIFF!
HI-YA!
AIEEEEE!
WHAPPA WHAPPA
ONE WEEK LATER...
I FEEL KIND OF SLAP HAPPY... WHERE...?
IT WORKED! HE'S COMING TO!
WHERE'S BOWSER? LET ME AT HIM!
POP!

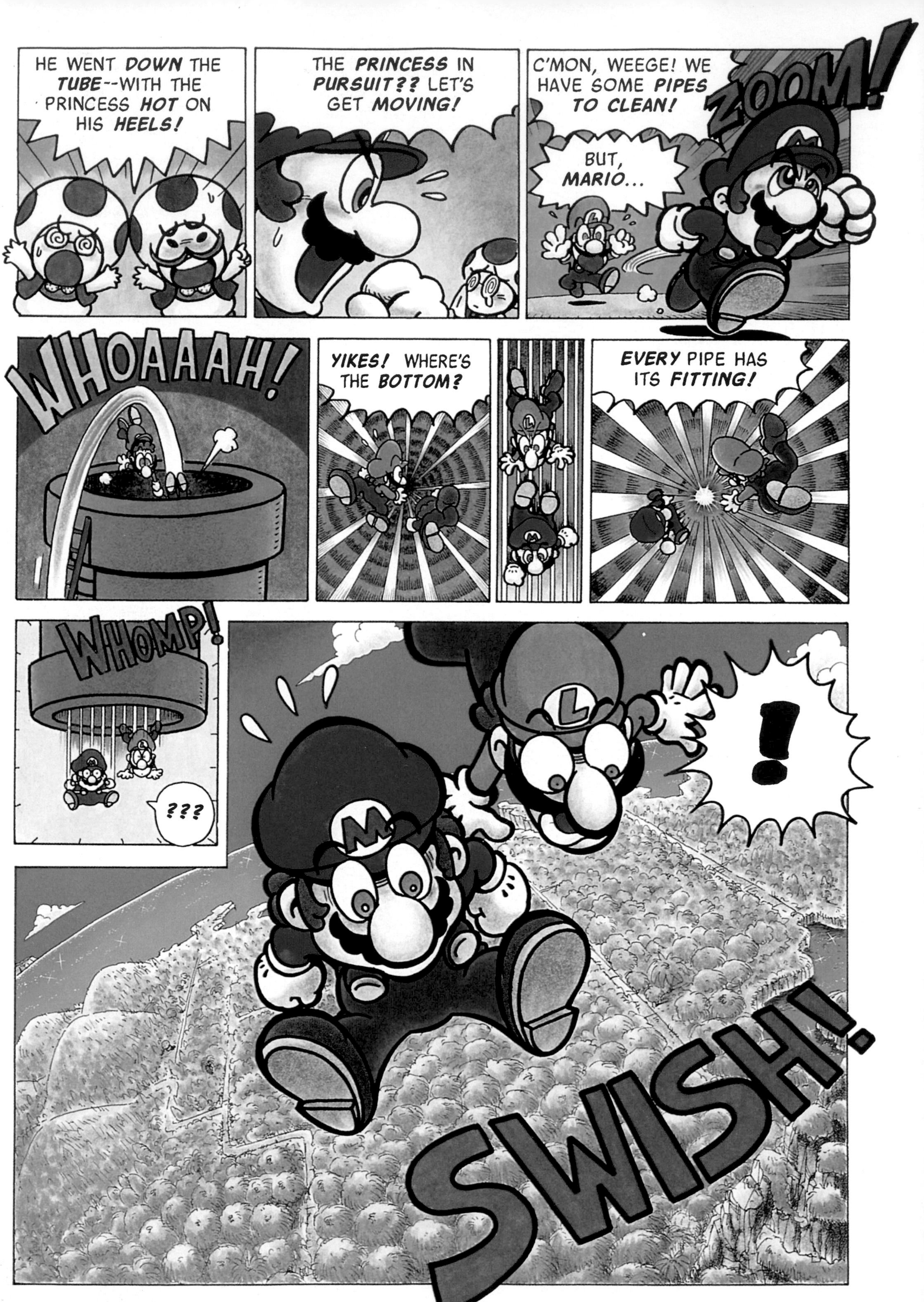
HE WENT DOWN THE TUBE--WITH THE PRINCESS HOT ON HIS HEELS!
THE PRINCESS IN PURSUIT?? LET'S GET MOVING!
C'MON, WEEGE! WE HAVE SOME PIPES TO CLEAN!
ZOOM!
BUT, MARIO...
WHOAAAAH!
YIKES! WHERE'S THE BOTTOM?
EVERY PIPE HAS ITS FITTING!
WHOMP!
???
!
SWISH!

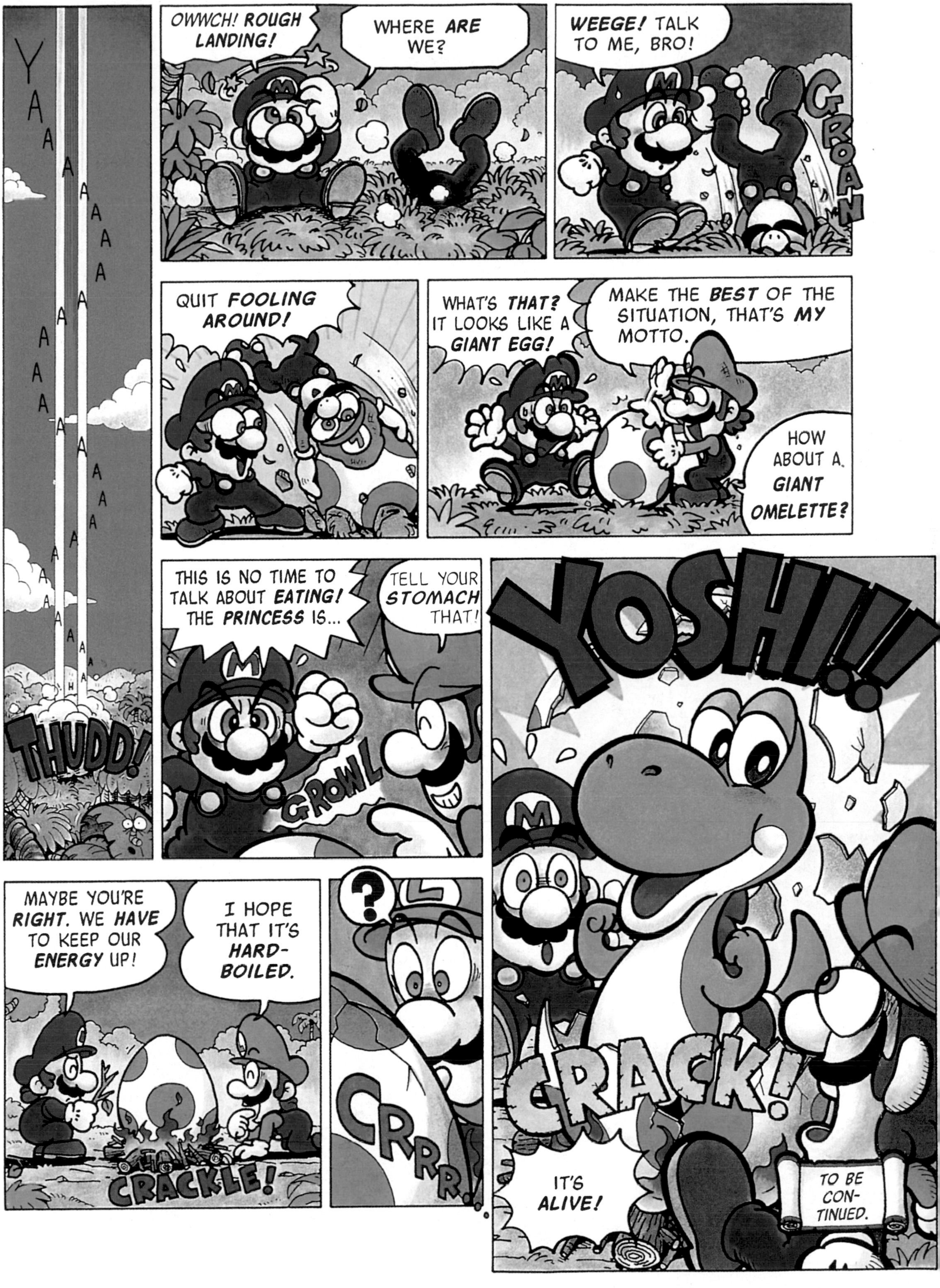

YAAAAAAAAAAAAAAAAAAAAAAAAH
THUDD!
OWWCH! ROUGH LANDING!
WHERE ARE WE?
WEEGE! TALK TO ME, BRO!
GROAN
QUIT FOOLING AROUND!
WHAT'S THAT? IT LOOKS LIKE A GIANT EGG!
MAKE THE BEST OF THE SITUATION, THAT'S MY MOTTO.
HOW ABOUT A GIANT OMELETTE?
THIS IS NO TIME TO TALK ABOUT EATING! THE PRINCESS IS...
TELL YOUR STOMACH THAT!
GROWL
MAYBE YOU'RE RIGHT. WE HAVE TO KEEP OUR ENERGY UP!
I HOPE THAT IT'S HARD-BOILED.
CRACKLE!
?
CRRRR...
YOSHI!!!...
CRACK!
IT'S ALIVE!
TO BE CONTINUED.

SUPER MARIO ADVENTURES™

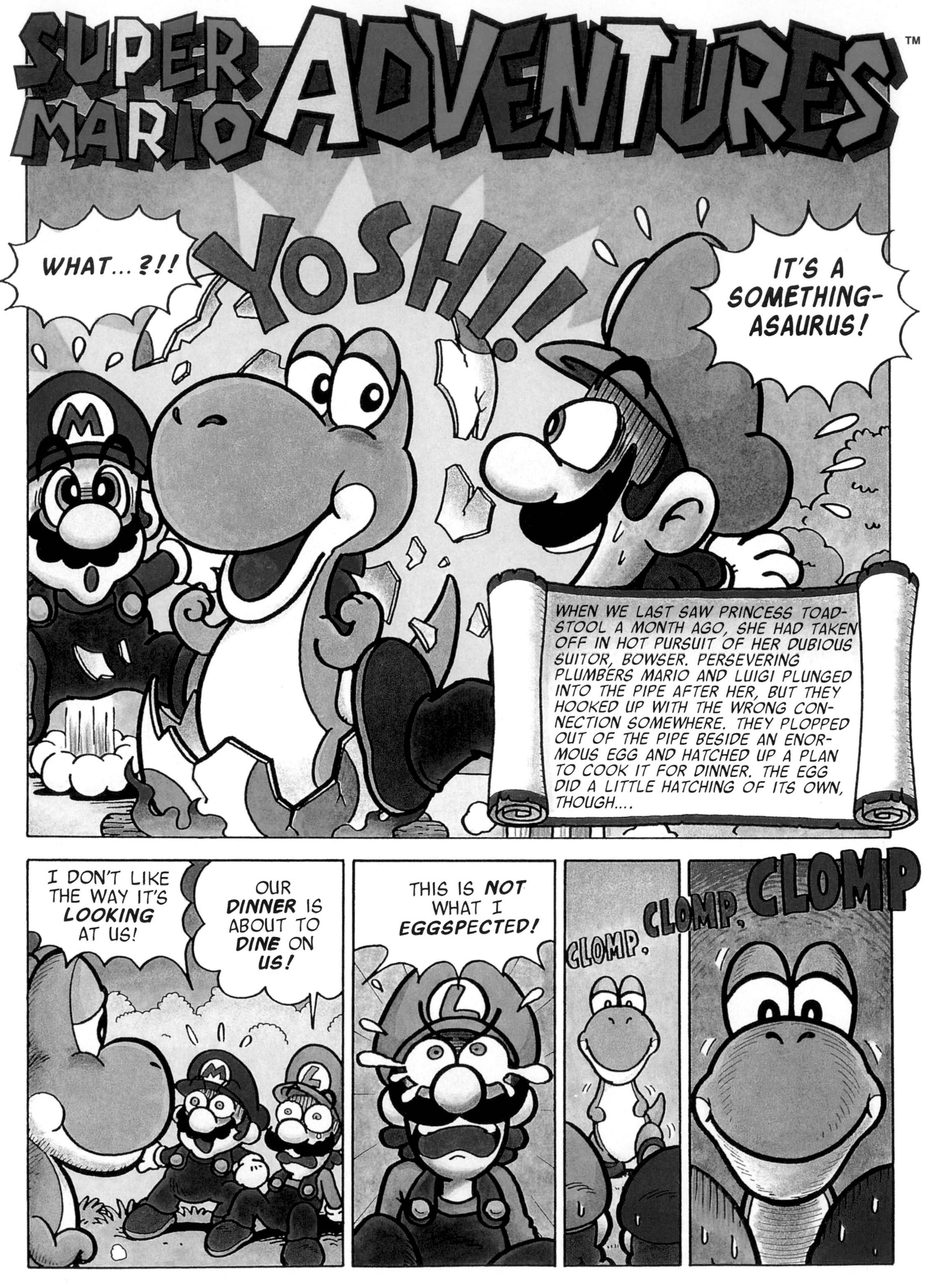

WHAT...?!!
YOSHI!!
IT'S A SOMETHING-ASAURUS!
WHEN WE LAST SAW PRINCESS TOADSTOOL A MONTH AGO, SHE HAD TAKEN OFF IN HOT PURSUIT OF HER DUBIOUS SUITOR, BOWSER. PERSEVERING PLUMBERS MARIO AND LUIGI PLUNGED INTO THE PIPE AFTER HER, BUT THEY HOOKED UP WITH THE WRONG CONNECTION SOMEWHERE. THEY PLOPPED OUT OF THE PIPE BESIDE AN ENORMOUS EGG AND HATCHED UP A PLAN TO COOK IT FOR DINNER. THE EGG DID A LITTLE HATCHING OF ITS OWN, THOUGH....
I DON'T LIKE THE WAY IT'S LOOKING AT US!
OUR DINNER IS ABOUT TO DINE ON US!
THIS IS NOT WHAT I EGGSPECTED!
CLOMP, CLOMP, CLOMP

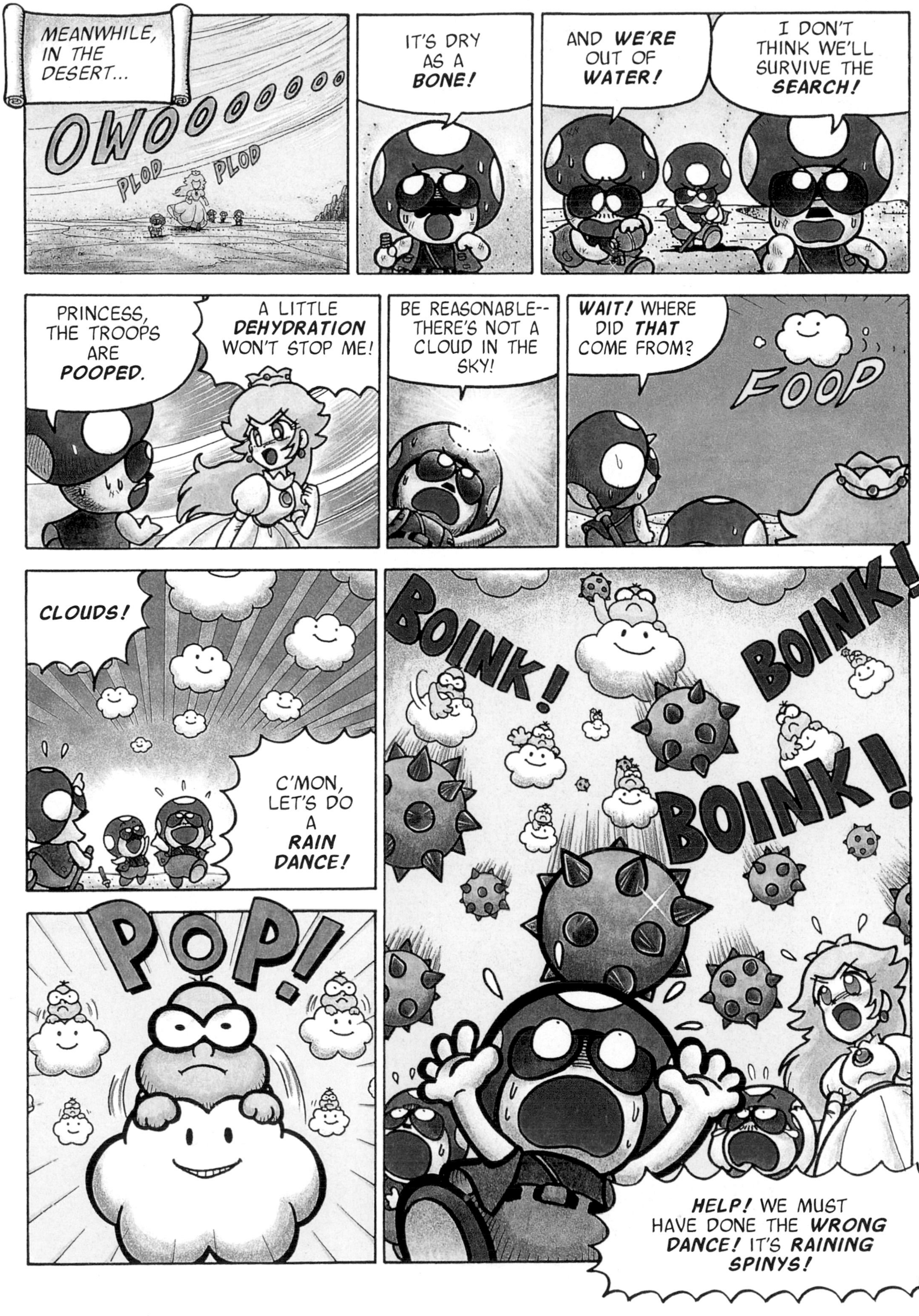
MEANWHILE, IN THE DESERT...
OWOOOOOOOOO
PLOD PLOD
IT'S DRY AS A BONE!
AND WE'RE OUT OF WATER!
I DON'T THINK WE'LL SURVIVE THE SEARCH!
PRINCESS, THE TROOPS ARE POOPED.
A LITTLE DEHYDRATION WON'T STOP ME!
BE REASONABLE-- THERE'S NOT A CLOUD IN THE SKY!
WAIT! WHERE DID THAT COME FROM?
FOOP
CLOUDS!
C'MON, LET'S DO A RAIN DANCE!
POP!
BOINK!
BOINK!
BOINK!
HELP! WE MUST HAVE DONE THE WRONG DANCE! IT'S RAINING SPINYS!

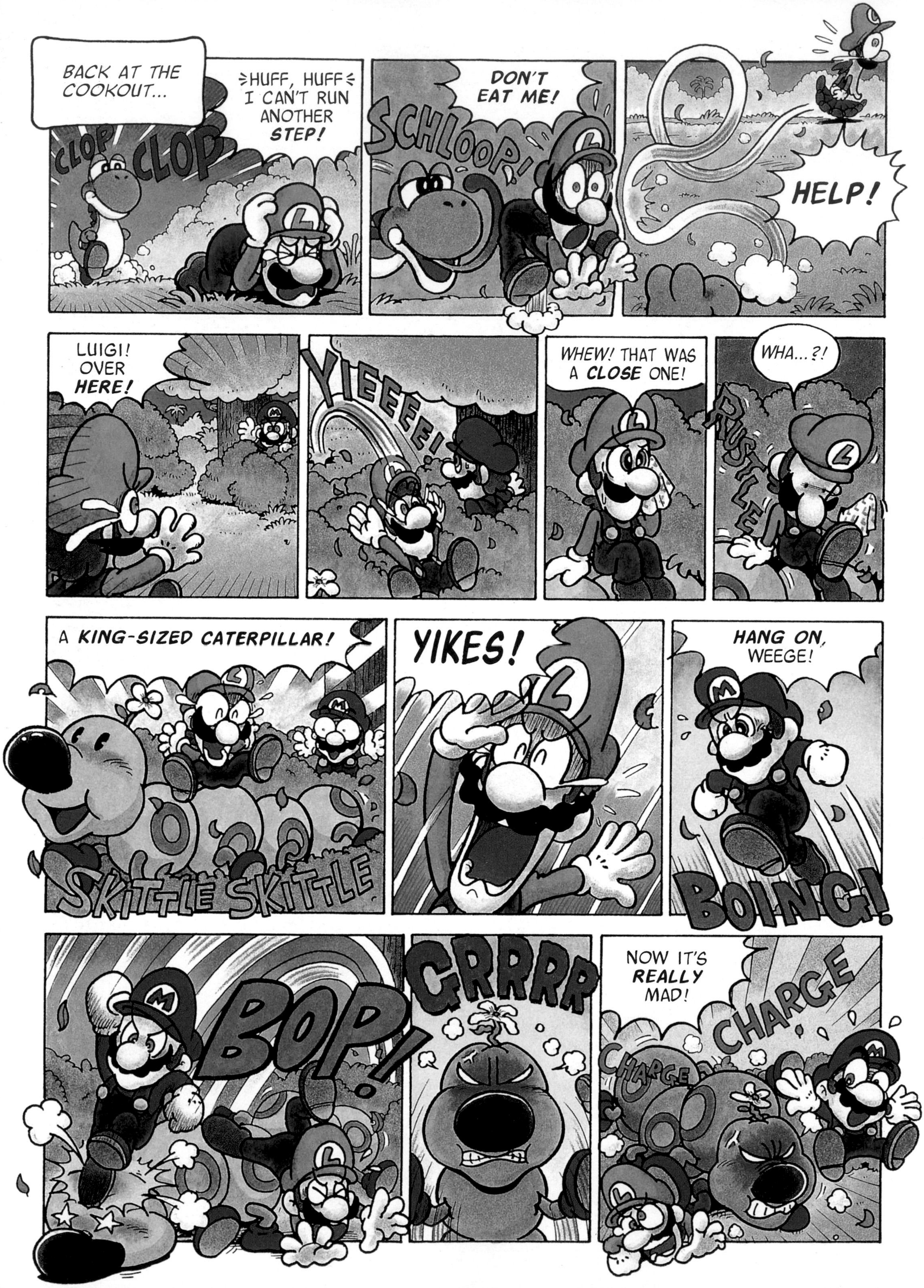

BACK AT THE COOKOUT...
CLOP CLOP
HUFF, HUFF I CAN'T RUN ANOTHER STEP!
SCHLOOP!
DON'T EAT ME!
HELP!
LUIGI! OVER HERE!
YIEEEEE!
WHEW! THAT WAS A CLOSE ONE!
RUSTLE
WHA...?!
A KING-SIZED CATERPILLAR!
SKITTLE SKITTLE
YIKES!
HANG ON, WEEGE!
BOING!
BOP!
GRRRRR
NOW IT'S REALLY MAD!
CHARGE
CHARGE

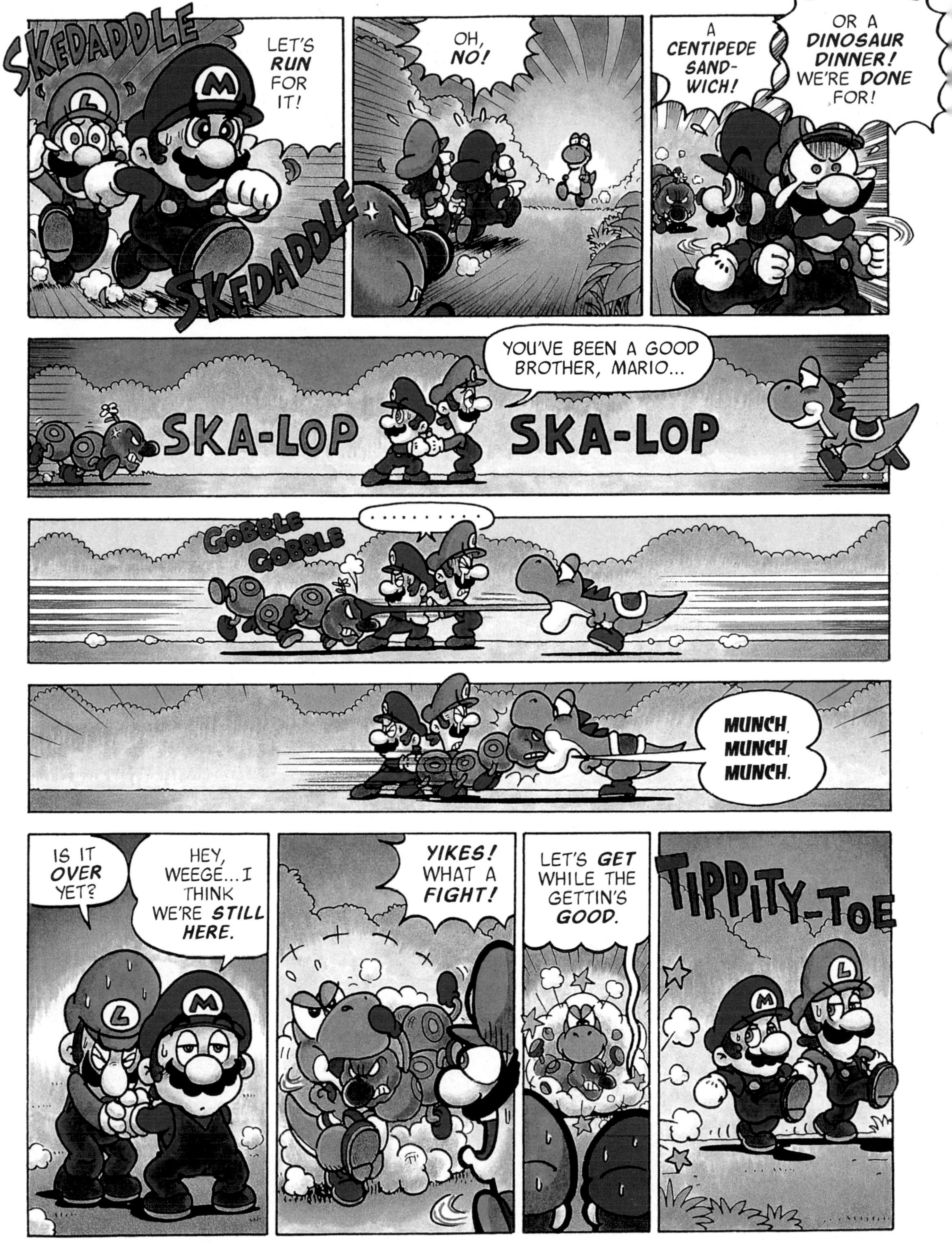
SKEDADDLE
LET'S RUN FOR IT!
SKEDADDLE
OH, NO!
A CENTIPEDE SANDWICH!
OR A DINOSAUR DINNER! WE'RE DONE FOR!
SKA-LOP
YOU'VE BEEN A GOOD BROTHER, MARIO...
SKA-LOP
GOBBLE GOBBLE
....
MUNCH. MUNCH. MUNCH.
IS IT OVER YET?
HEY, WEEGE... I THINK WE'RE STILL HERE.
YIKES! WHAT A FIGHT!
LET'S GET WHILE THE GETTIN'S GOOD.
TIPPITY-TOE

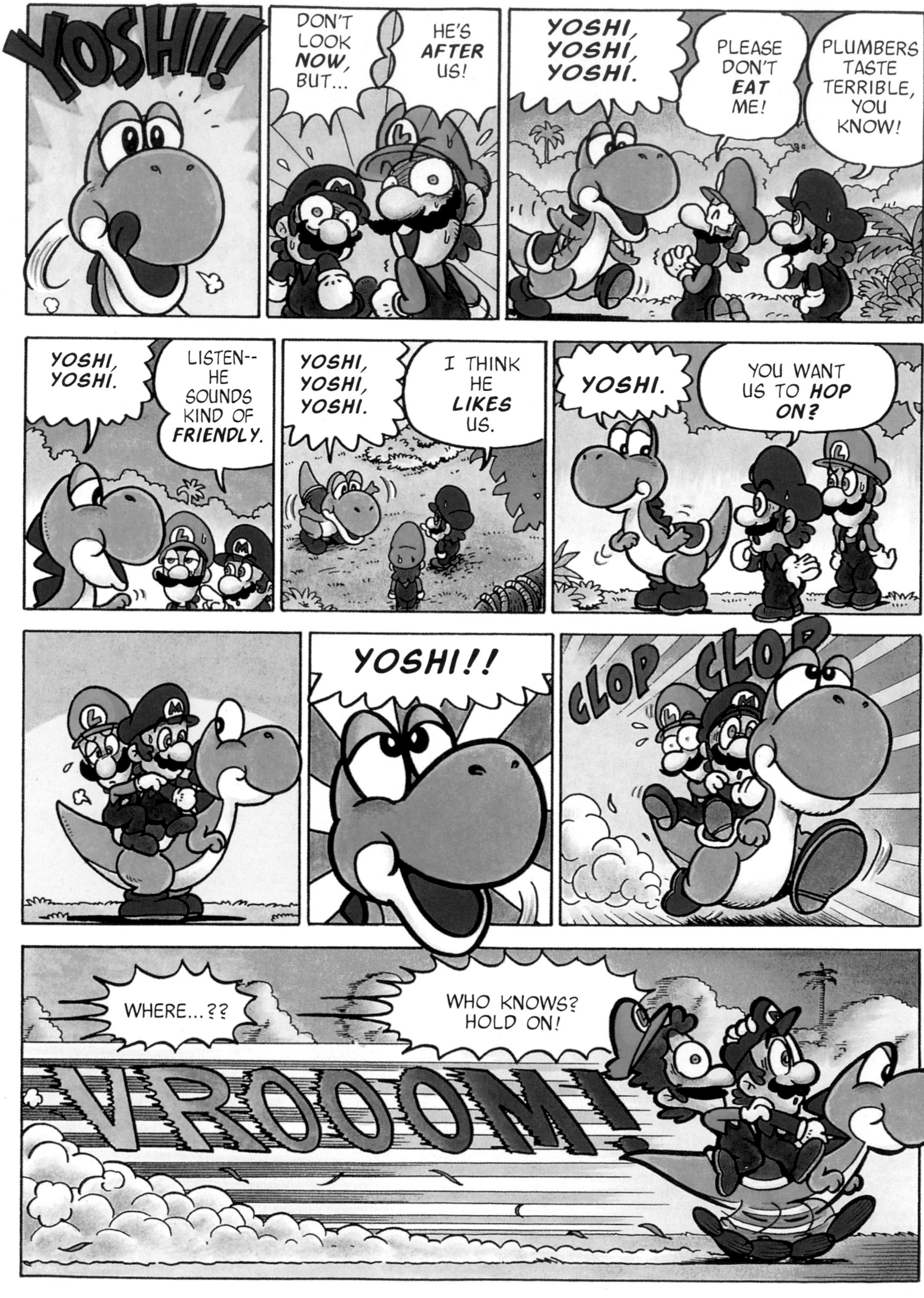
YOSHI!!
DON'T LOOK NOW, BUT...
HE'S AFTER US!
YOSHI, YOSHI, YOSHI.
PLEASE DON'T EAT ME!
PLUMBERS TASTE TERRIBLE, YOU KNOW!
YOSHI, YOSHI.
LISTEN-- HE SOUNDS KIND OF FRIENDLY.
YOSHI, YOSHI, YOSHI.
I THINK HE LIKES US.
YOSHI.
YOU WANT US TO HOP ON?
YOSHI!!
CLOP CLOP
WHERE...??
WHO KNOWS? HOLD ON!
VROOOM!

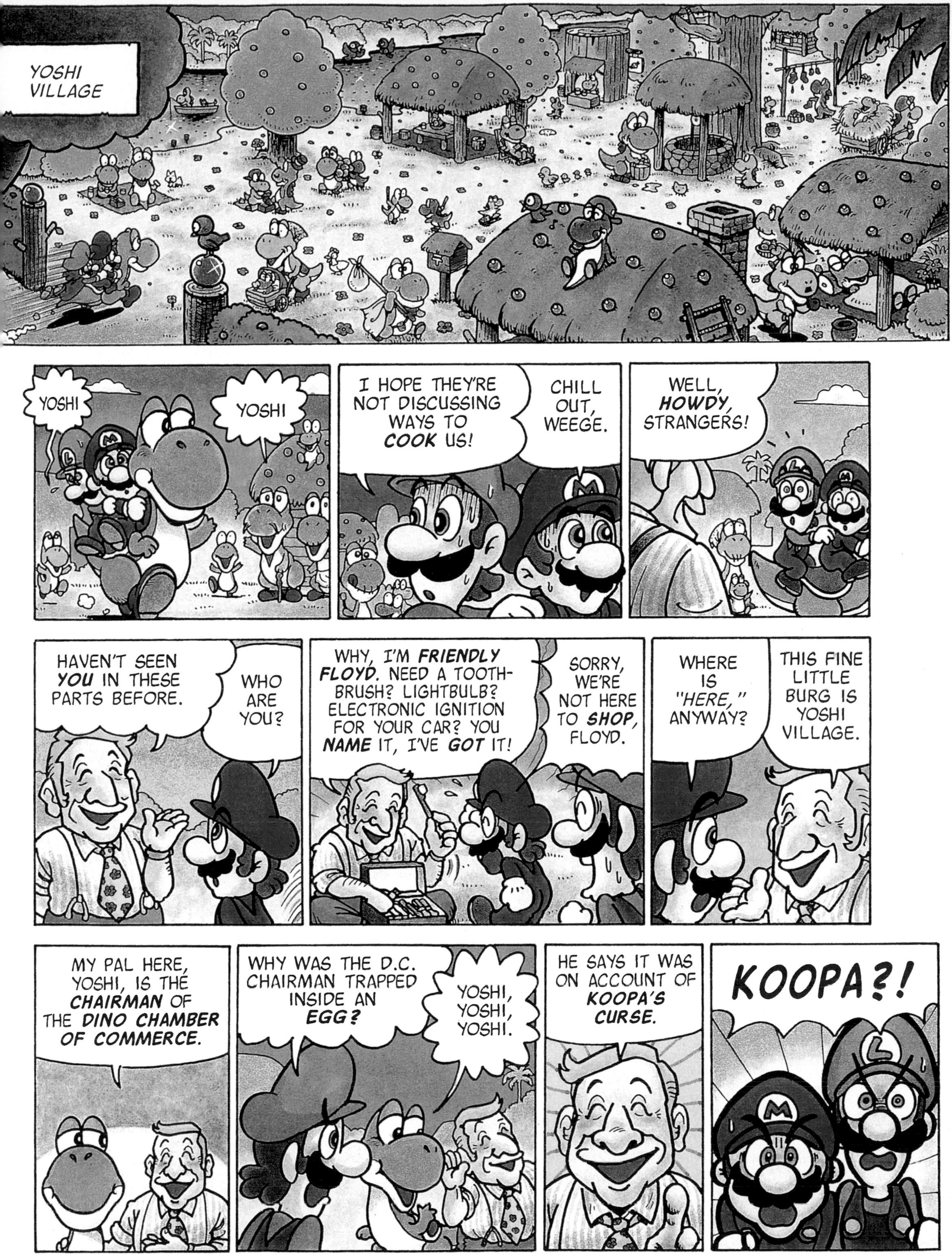
YOSHI VILLAGE
YOSHI
YOSHI
I HOPE THEY'RE NOT DISCUSSING WAYS TO COOK US!
CHILL OUT, WEEGE.
WELL, HOWDY, STRANGERS!
HAVEN'T SEEN YOU IN THESE PARTS BEFORE.
WHO ARE YOU?
WHY, I'M FRIENDLY FLOYD. NEED A TOOTH-BRUSH? LIGHTBULB? ELECTRONIC IGNITION FOR YOUR CAR? YOU NAME IT, I'VE GOT IT!
SORRY, WE'RE NOT HERE TO SHOP, FLOYD.
WHERE IS "HERE," ANYWAY?
THIS FINE LITTLE BURG IS YOSHI VILLAGE.
MY PAL HERE, YOSHI, IS THE CHAIRMAN OF THE DINO CHAMBER OF COMMERCE.
WHY WAS THE D.C. CHAIRMAN TRAPPED INSIDE AN EGG?
YOSHI, YOSHI, YOSHI.
HE SAYS IT WAS ON ACCOUNT OF KOOPA'S CURSE.
KOOPA?!

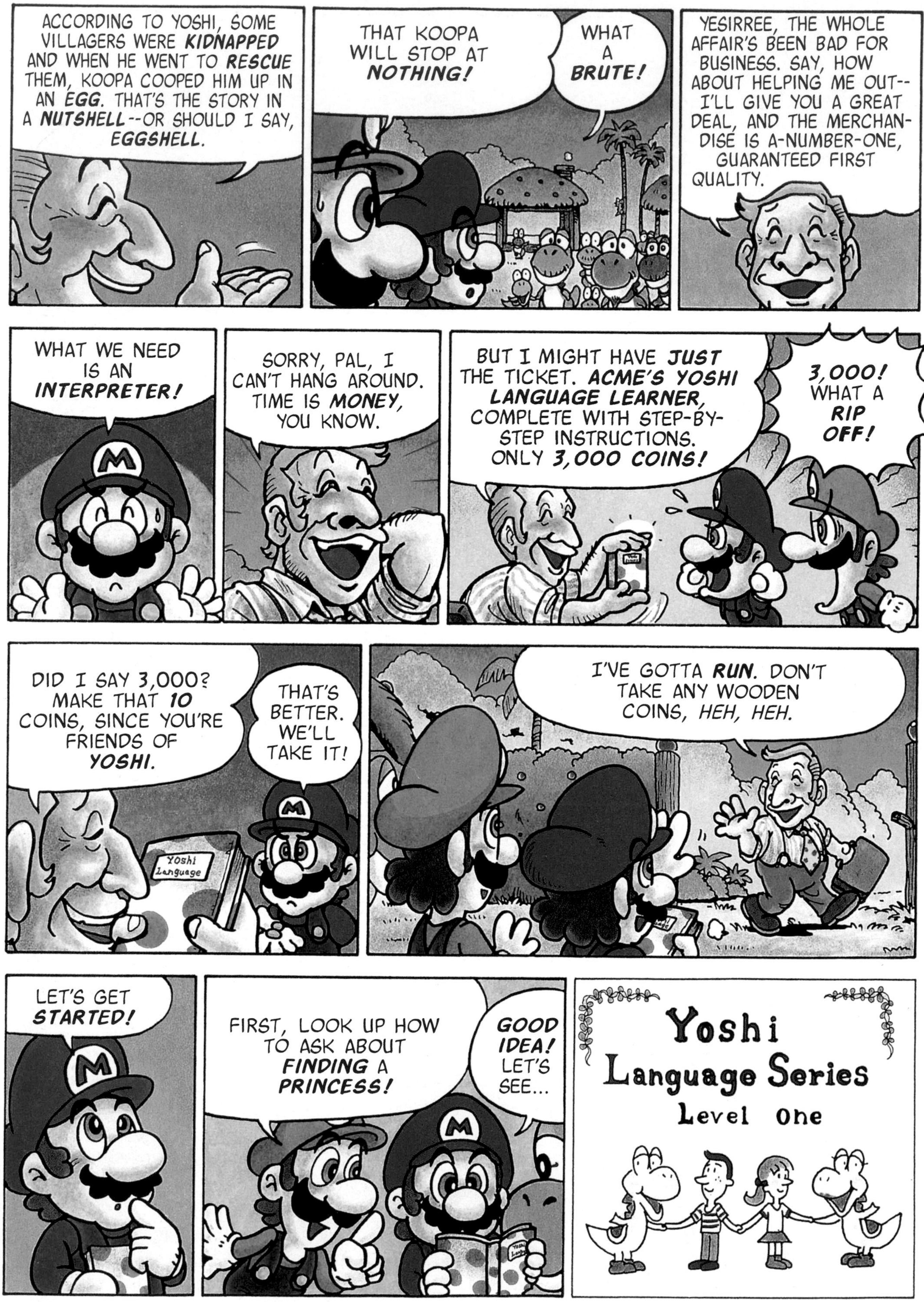
ACCORDING TO YOSHI, SOME VILLAGERS WERE KIDNAPPED AND WHEN HE WENT TO RESCUE THEM, KOOPA COOPED HIM UP IN AN EGG. THAT'S THE STORY IN A NUTSHELL--OR SHOULD I SAY, EGGSHELL.
THAT KOOPA WILL STOP AT NOTHING!
WHAT A BRUTE!
YESIRREE, THE WHOLE AFFAIR'S BEEN BAD FOR BUSINESS. SAY, HOW ABOUT HELPING ME OUT-- I'LL GIVE YOU A GREAT DEAL, AND THE MERCHANDISE IS A-NUMBER-ONE, GUARANTEED FIRST QUALITY.
WHAT WE NEED IS AN INTERPRETER!
SORRY, PAL, I CAN'T HANG AROUND. TIME IS MONEY, YOU KNOW.
BUT I MIGHT HAVE JUST THE TICKET. ACME'S YOSHI LANGUAGE LEARNER, COMPLETE WITH STEP-BY-STEP INSTRUCTIONS. ONLY 3,000 COINS!
3,000! WHAT A RIP OFF!
DID I SAY 3,000? MAKE THAT 10 COINS, SINCE YOU'RE FRIENDS OF YOSHI.
THAT'S BETTER. WE'LL TAKE IT!
Yoshi Language
I'VE GOTTA RUN. DON'T TAKE ANY WOODEN COINS, HEH, HEH.
LET'S GET STARTED!
FIRST, LOOK UP HOW TO ASK ABOUT FINDING A PRINCESS!
GOOD IDEA! LET'S SEE...
Yoshi
Language Series
Level One

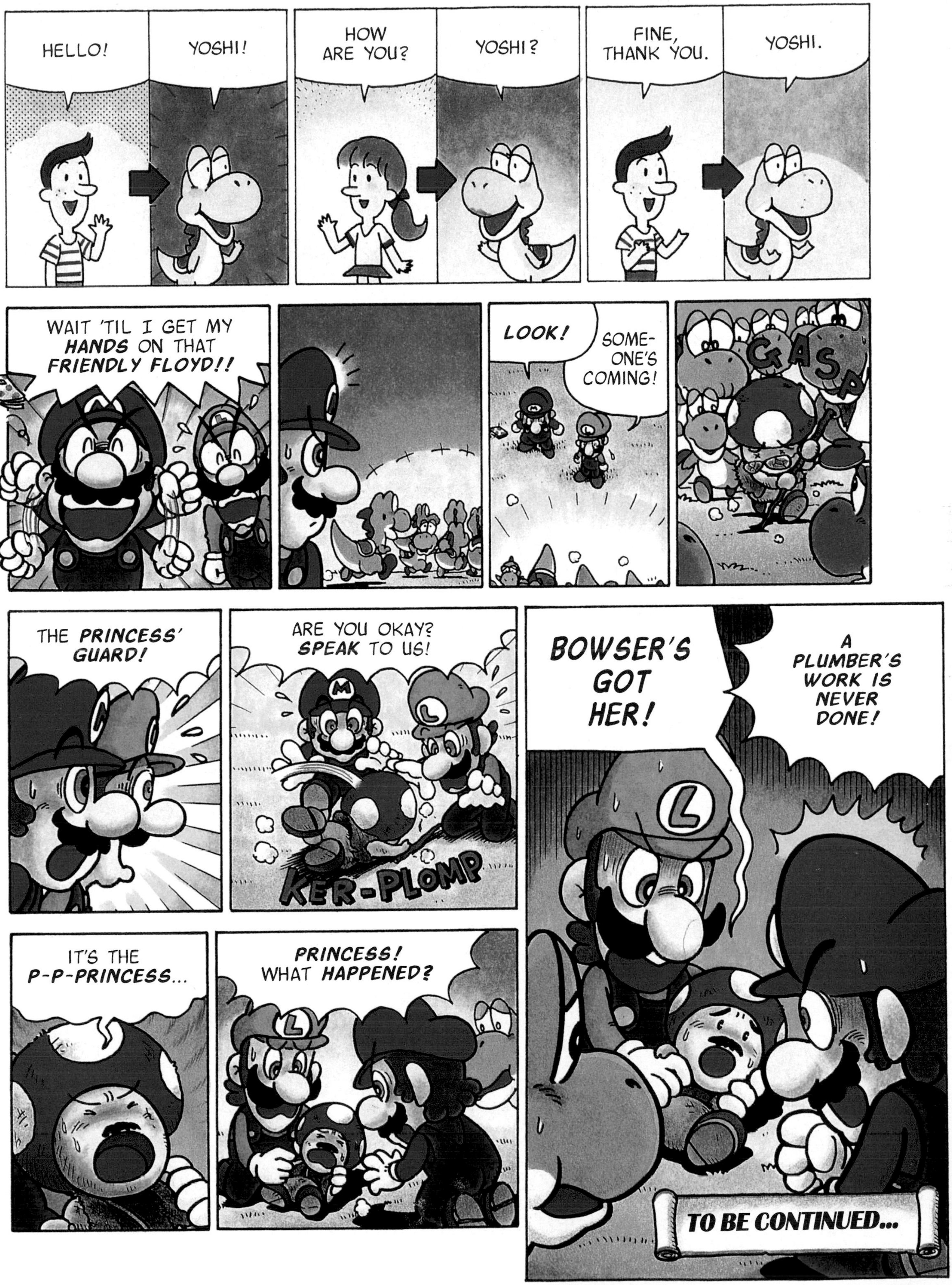
HELLO!
YOSHI!
HOW ARE YOU?
YOSHI?
FINE, THANK YOU.
YOSHI.
WAIT 'TIL I GET MY HANDS ON THAT FRIENDLY FLOYD!!
LOOK!
SOME-ONE'S COMING!
GASP
THE PRINCESS' GUARD!
ARE YOU OKAY? SPEAK TO US!
KER-PLOMP
BOWSER'S GOT HER!
A PLUMBER'S WORK IS NEVER DONE!
IT'S THE P-P-PRINCESS...
PRINCESS! WHAT HAPPENED?
TO BE CONTINUED...

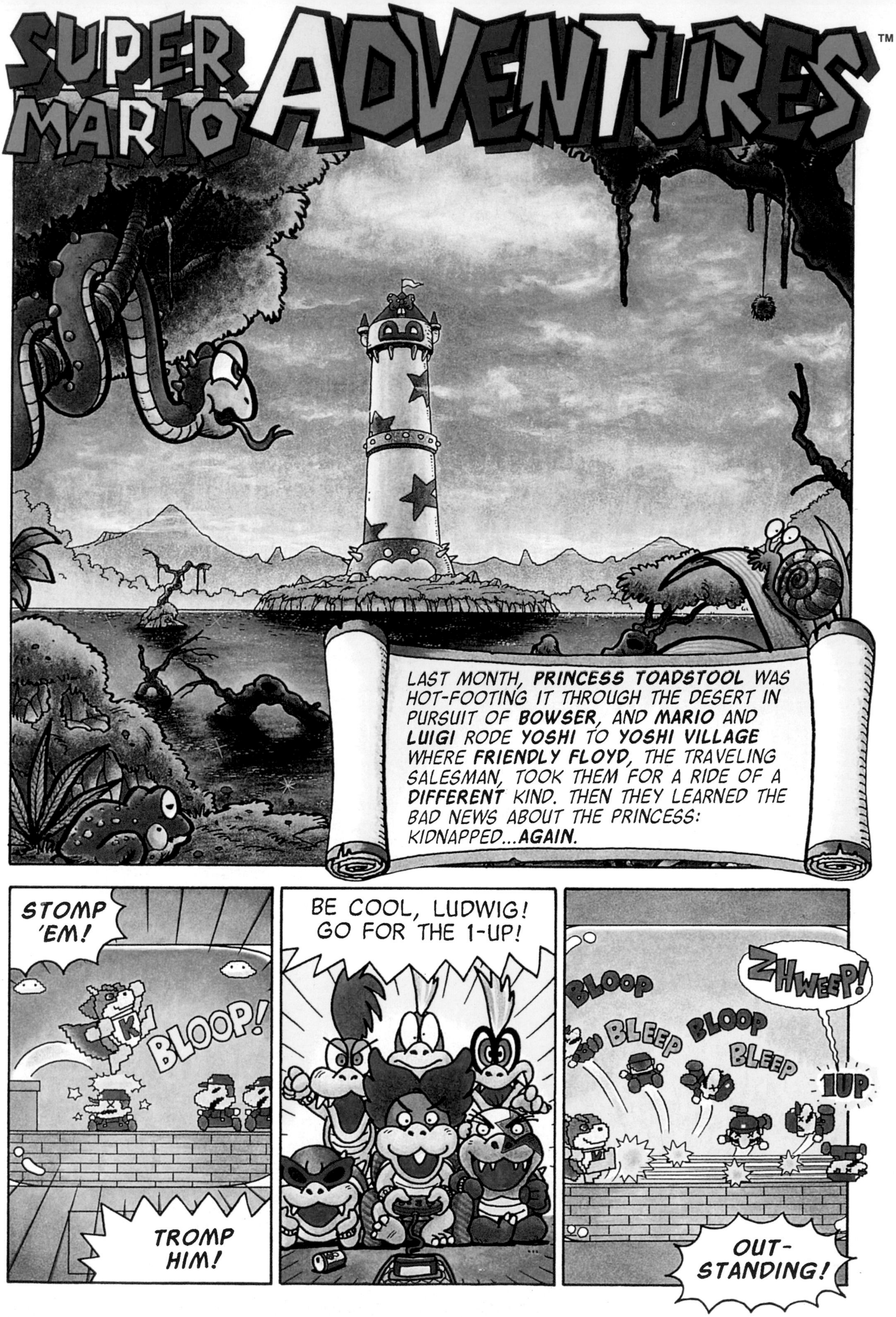
SUPER MARIO ADVENTURES™
LAST MONTH, PRINCESS TOADSTOOL WAS HOT-FOOTING IT THROUGH THE DESERT IN PURSUIT OF BOWSER, AND MARIO AND LUIGI RODE YOSHI TO YOSHI VILLAGE WHERE FRIENDLY FLOYD, THE TRAVELING SALESMAN, TOOK THEM FOR A RIDE OF A DIFFERENT KIND. THEN THEY LEARNED THE BAD NEWS ABOUT THE PRINCESS: KIDNAPPED...AGAIN.
STOMP 'EM!
BLOOP!
TROMP HIM!
BE COOL, LUDWIG! GO FOR THE 1-UP!
BLOOP
ZHWEEP!
BLEEP
BLOOP
BLEEP
1UP
OUT-STANDING!

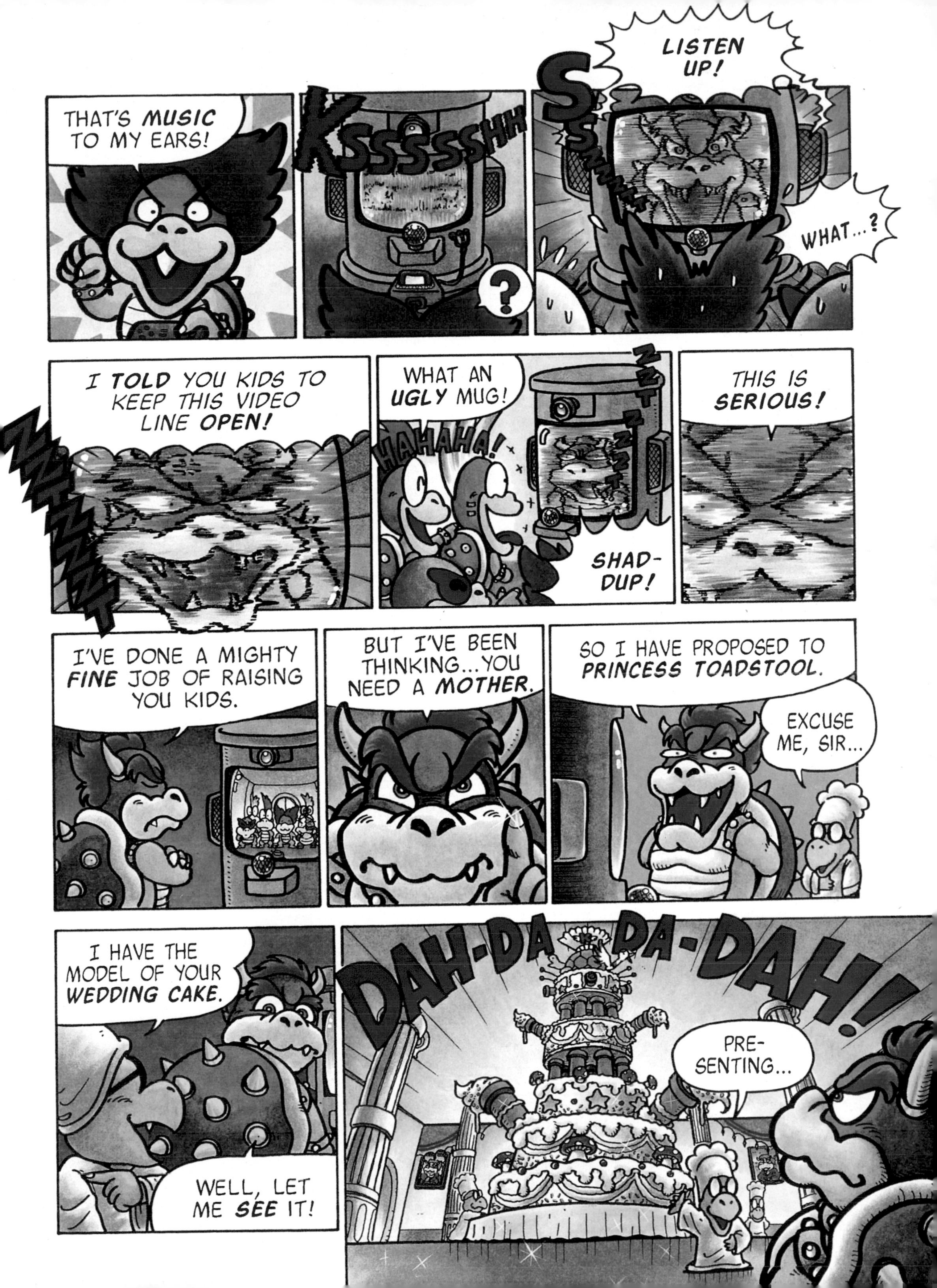
THAT'S MUSIC TO MY EARS!
KSSSSSSHH
?
S SHHHH
LISTEN UP!
WHAT...?
NNNNNNT
I TOLD YOU KIDS TO KEEP THIS VIDEO LINE OPEN!
WHAT AN UGLY MUG!
HAHAHA!
ZZZT
SHAD-DUP!
THIS IS SERIOUS!
I'VE DONE A MIGHTY FINE JOB OF RAISING YOU KIDS.
BUT I'VE BEEN THINKING... YOU NEED A MOTHER.
SO I HAVE PROPOSED TO PRINCESS TOADSTOOL.
EXCUSE ME, SIR...
I HAVE THE MODEL OF YOUR WEDDING CAKE.
WELL, LET ME SEE IT!
DAH-DA DA-DAH!
PRE-SENTING...

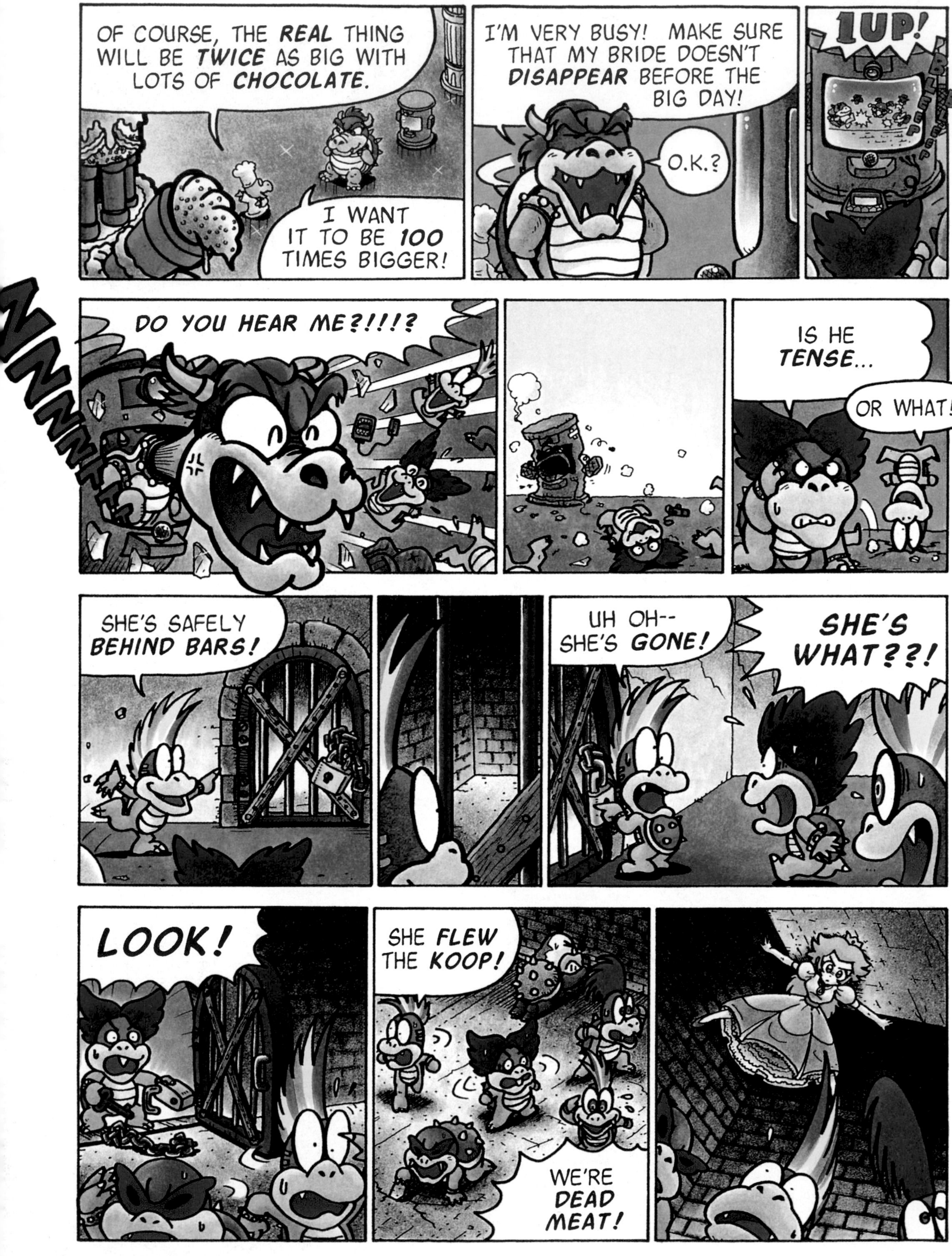

OF COURSE, THE REAL THING WILL BE TWICE AS BIG WITH LOTS OF CHOCOLATE.
I WANT IT TO BE 100 TIMES BIGGER!
I'M VERY BUSY! MAKE SURE THAT MY BRIDE DOESN'T DISAPPEAR BEFORE THE BIG DAY!
O.K.?
1UP!
DO YOU HEAR ME?!!!?
IS HE TENSE...
OR WHAT!
SHE'S SAFELY BEHIND BARS!
UH OH-- SHE'S GONE!
SHE'S WHAT??!
LOOK!
SHE FLEW THE KOOP!
WE'RE DEAD MEAT!

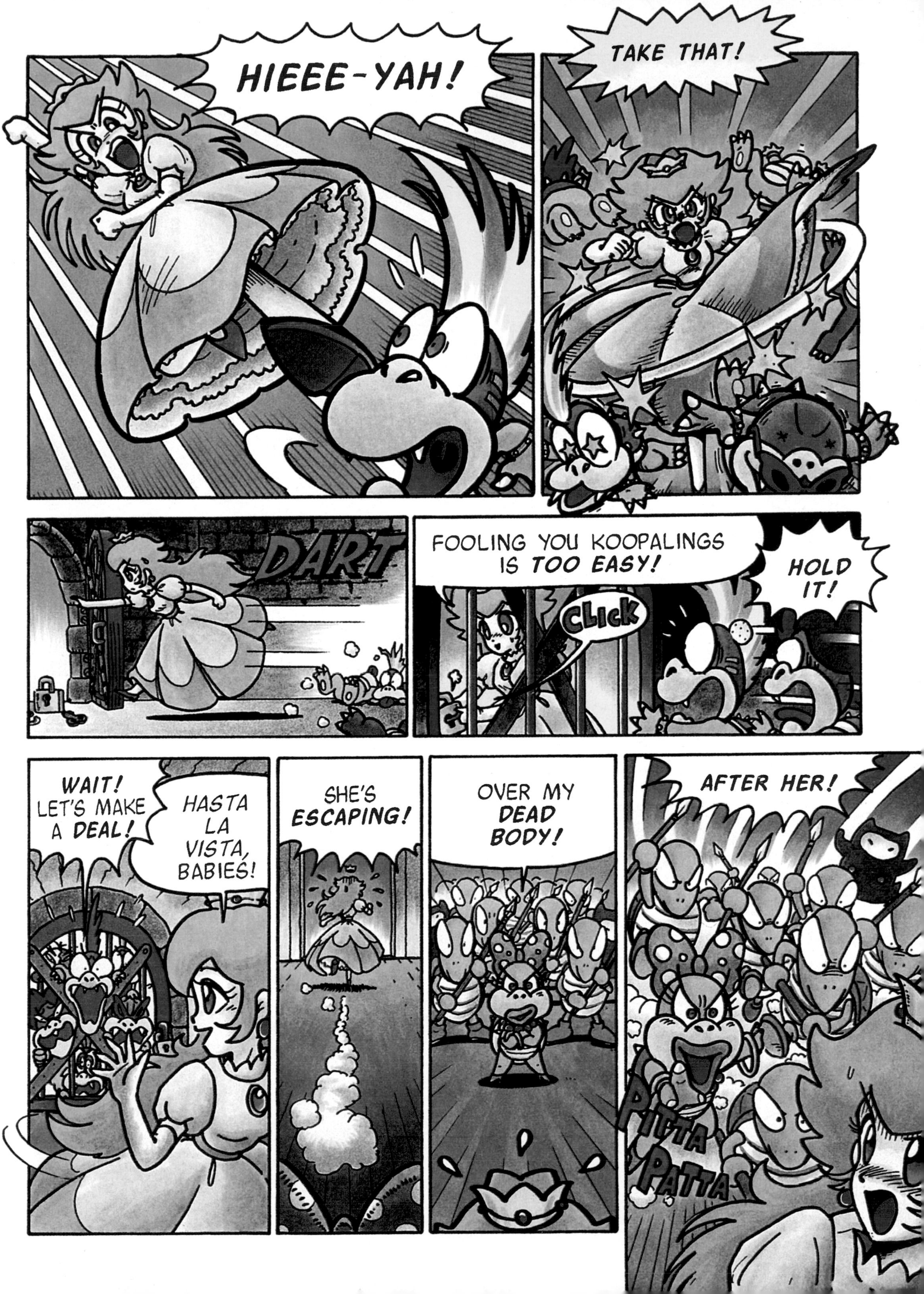
HIEEE-YAH!
TAKE THAT!
DART
FOOLING YOU KOOPALINGS IS TOO EASY!
CLICK
HOLD IT!
WAIT! LET'S MAKE A DEAL!
HASTA LA VISTA, BABIES!
SHE'S ESCAPING!
OVER MY DEAD BODY!
AFTER HER!
PITTA PATTA

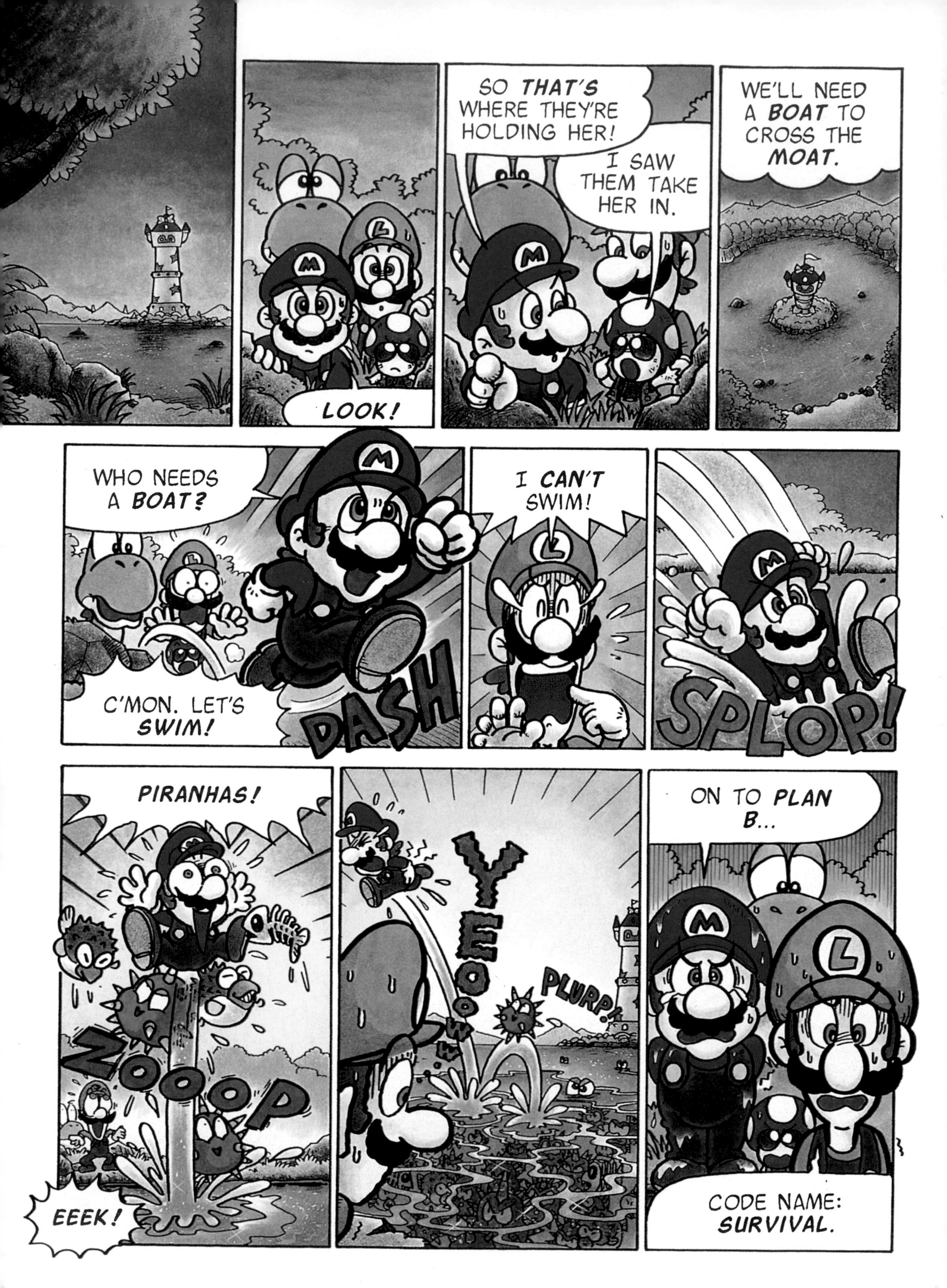
LOOK!
SO THAT'S WHERE THEY'RE HOLDING HER!
I SAW THEM TAKE HER IN.
WE'LL NEED A BOAT TO CROSS THE MOAT.
WHO NEEDS A BOAT?
C'MON. LET'S SWIM!
DASH
I CAN'T SWIM!
SPLOP!
PIRANHAS!
ZOOOOP
EEEK!
YEOOOW
PLURP!
ON TO PLAN B...
CODE NAME: SURVIVAL.

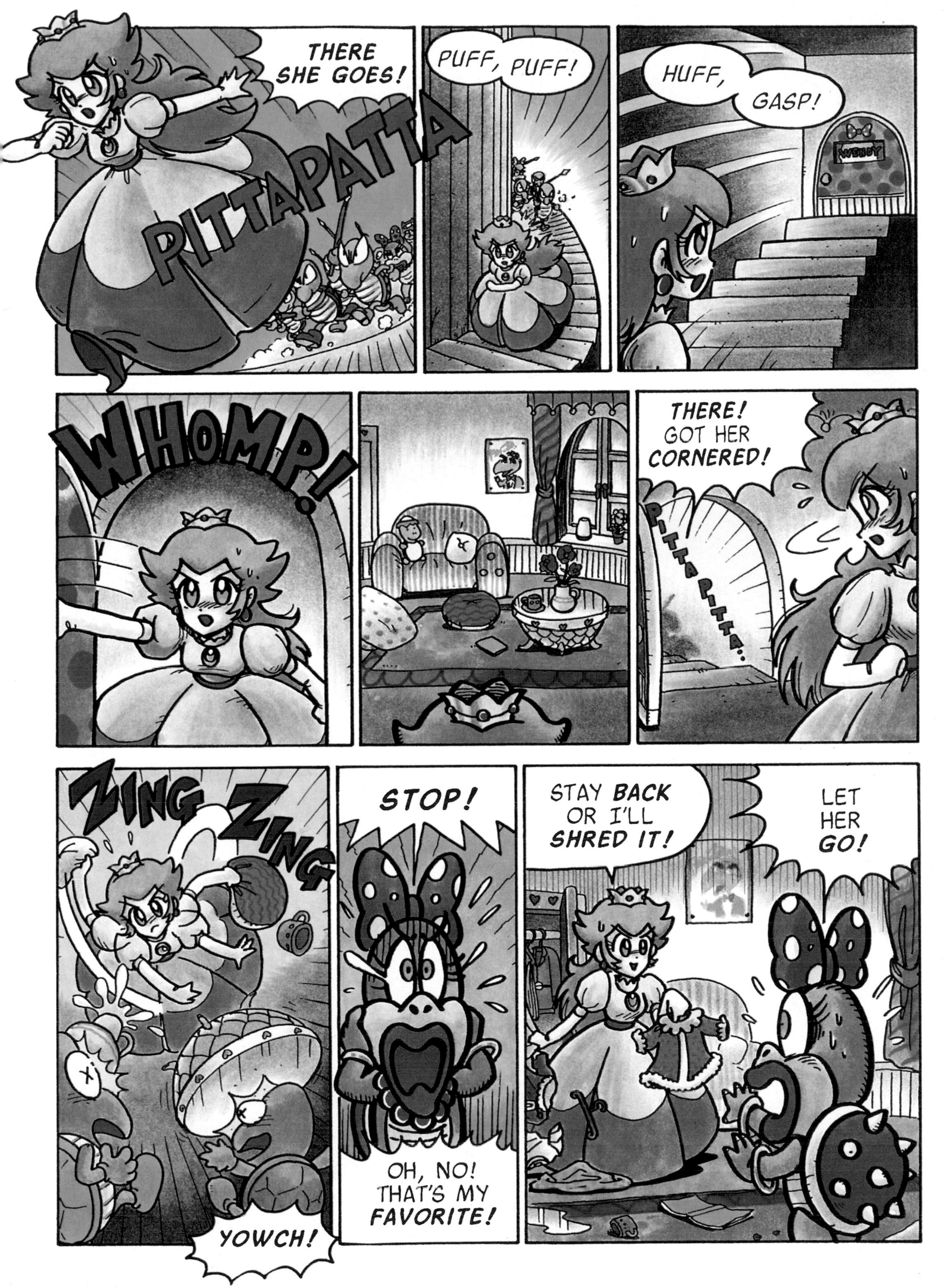
THERE SHE GOES!
PITTAPATTA
PUFF, PUFF!
HUFF,
GASP!
WENDY
WHOMP!
THERE! GOT HER CORNERED!
PITTA PITTA...
ZING ZING
YOWCH!
STOP!
OH, NO! THAT'S MY FAVORITE!
STAY BACK OR I'LL SHRED IT!
LET HER GO!

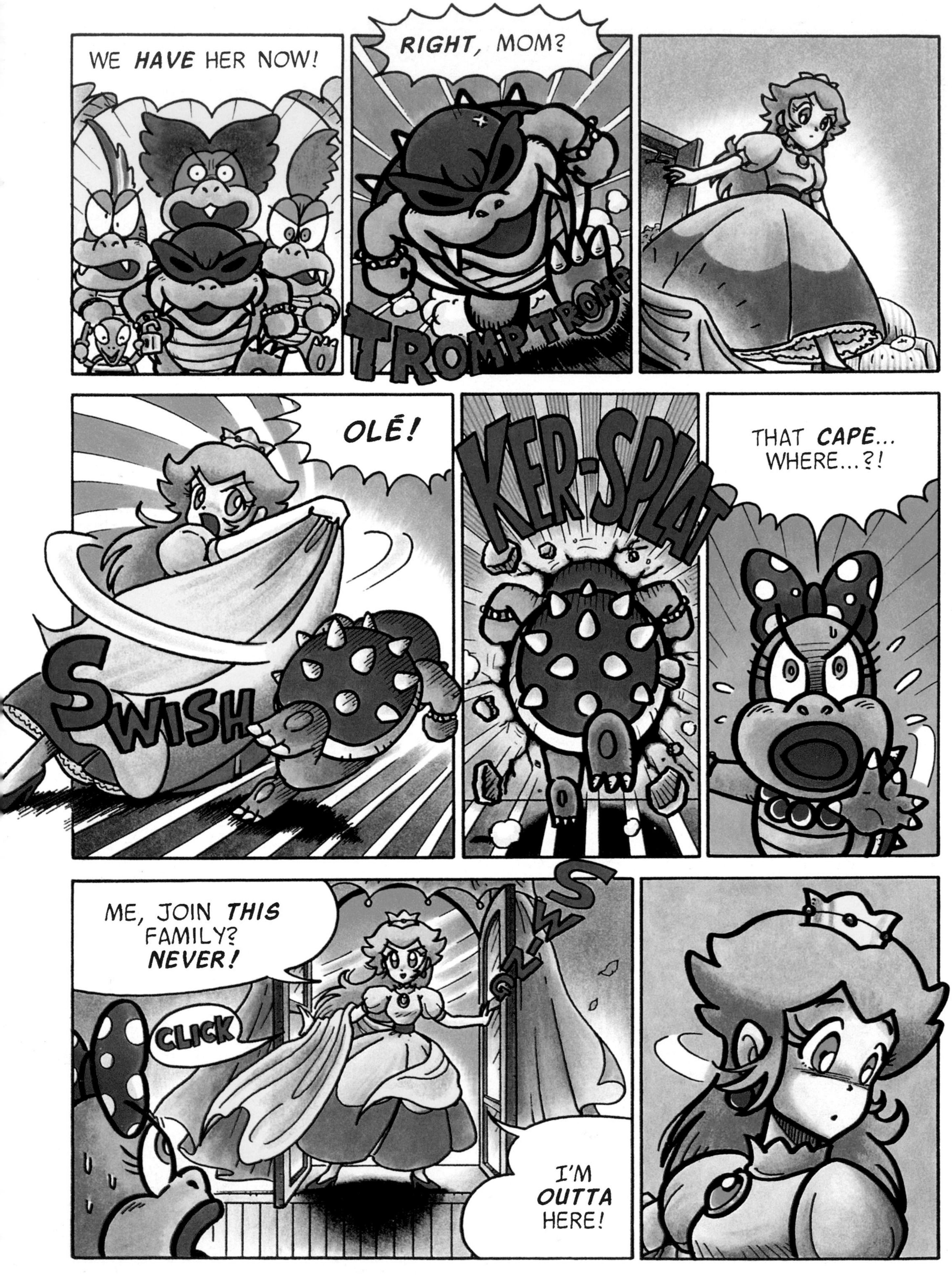
WE HAVE HER NOW!
RIGHT, MOM?
TROMP TROMP
OLÉ!
SWISH
KER-SPLAT
THAT CAPE... WHERE...?!
ME, JOIN THIS FAMILY? NEVER!
CLICK
SWISH
I'M OUTTA HERE!

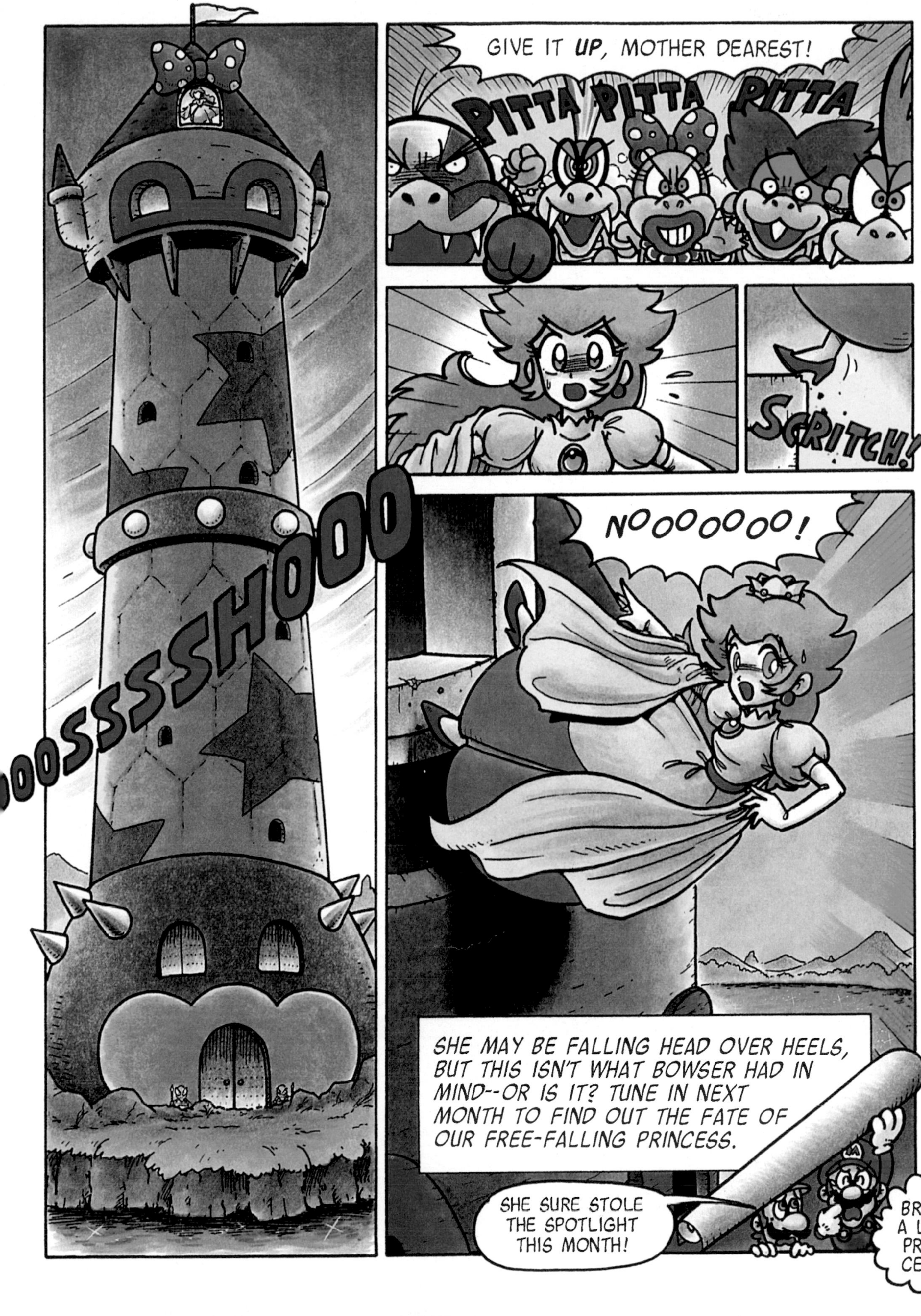
OOSSSSSHOOO
GIVE IT *UP*, MOTHER DEAREST!
PITTA PITTA PITTA
SCRITCH!
NOOOOOOO!
SHE MAY BE FALLING HEAD OVER HEELS, BUT THIS ISN'T WHAT BOWSER HAD IN MIND--OR IS IT? TUNE IN NEXT MONTH TO FIND OUT THE FATE OF OUR FREE-FALLING PRINCESS.
SHE SURE STOLE THE SPOTLIGHT THIS MONTH!
BREAK A LEG, PRIN-CESS!

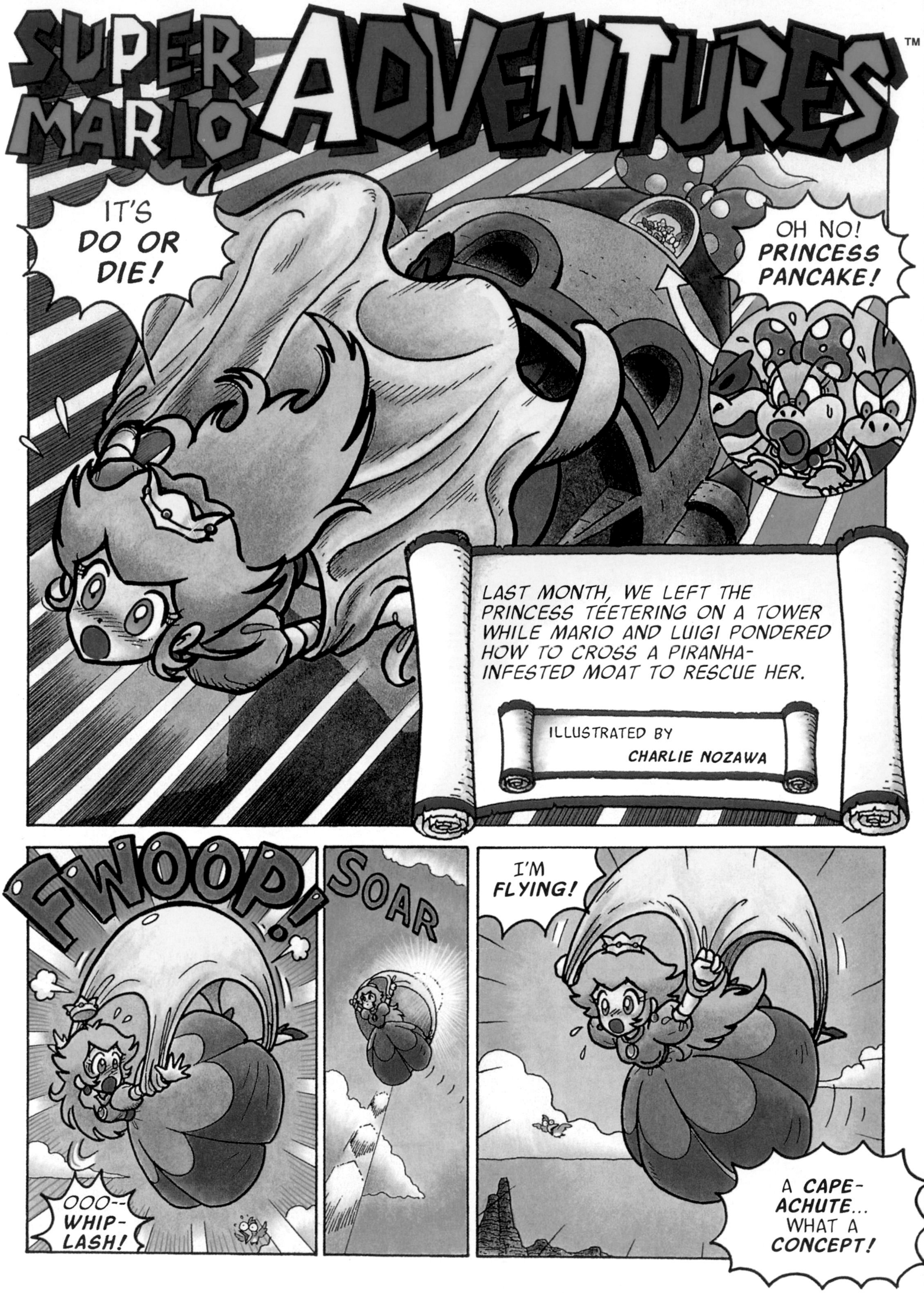
SUPER MARIO ADVENTURES™
IT'S DO OR DIE!
OH NO! PRINCESS PANCAKE!
LAST MONTH, WE LEFT THE PRINCESS TEETERING ON A TOWER WHILE MARIO AND LUIGI PONDERED HOW TO CROSS A PIRANHA-INFESTED MOAT TO RESCUE HER.
ILLUSTRATED BY CHARLIE NOZAWA
FWOOP!
OOO-- WHIP-LASH!
SOAR
I'M FLYING!
A CAPE-ACHUTE... WHAT A CONCEPT!

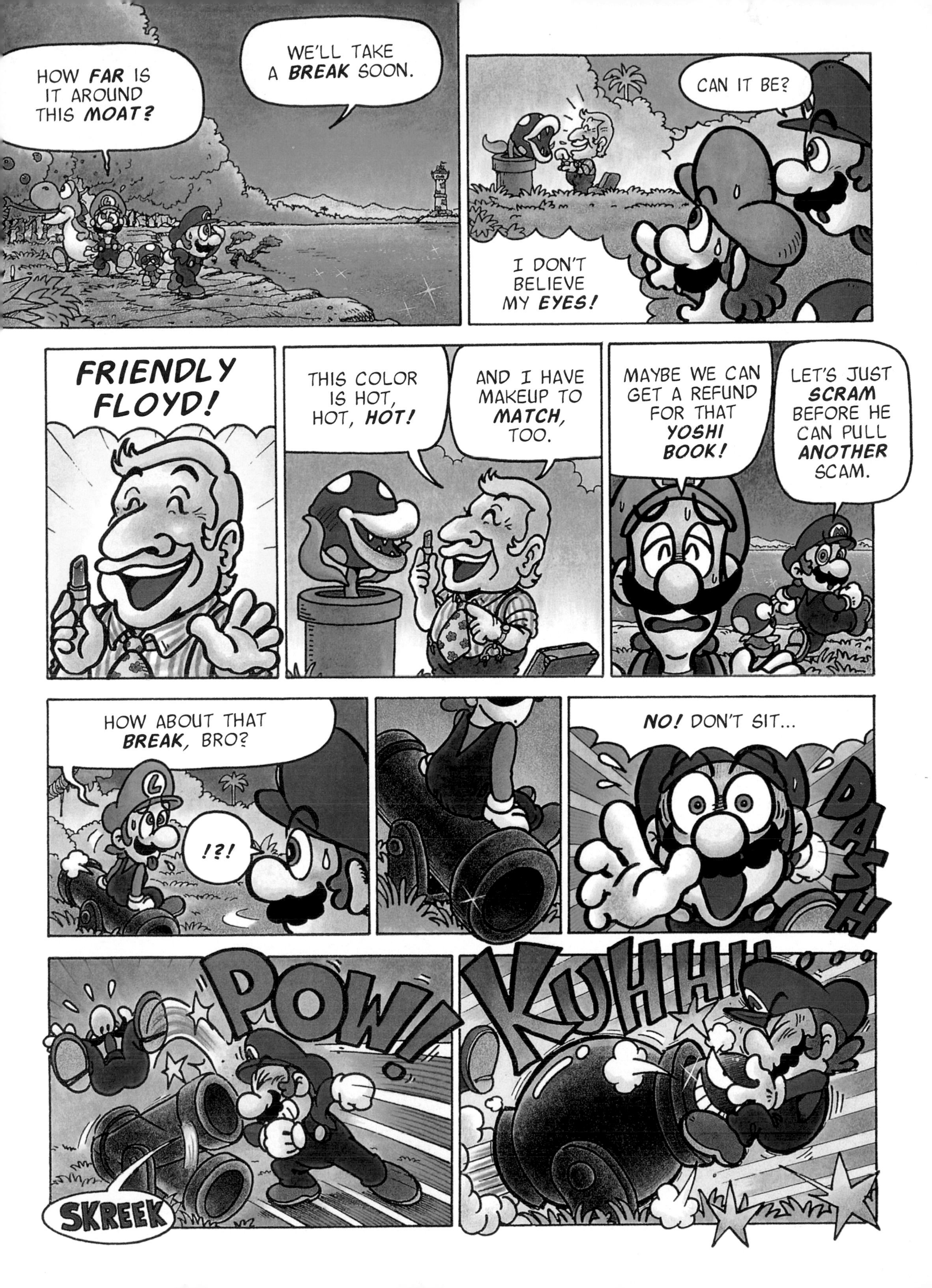
HOW FAR IS IT AROUND THIS MOAT?
WE'LL TAKE A BREAK SOON.
CAN IT BE?
I DON'T BELIEVE MY EYES!
FRIENDLY FLOYD!
THIS COLOR IS HOT, HOT, HOT!
AND I HAVE MAKEUP TO MATCH, TOO.
MAYBE WE CAN GET A REFUND FOR THAT YOSHI BOOK!
LET'S JUST SCRAM BEFORE HE CAN PULL ANOTHER SCAM.
HOW ABOUT THAT BREAK, BRO?
!?!
NO! DON'T SIT...
DASH
POW!!
SKREEK
KUHHH!!

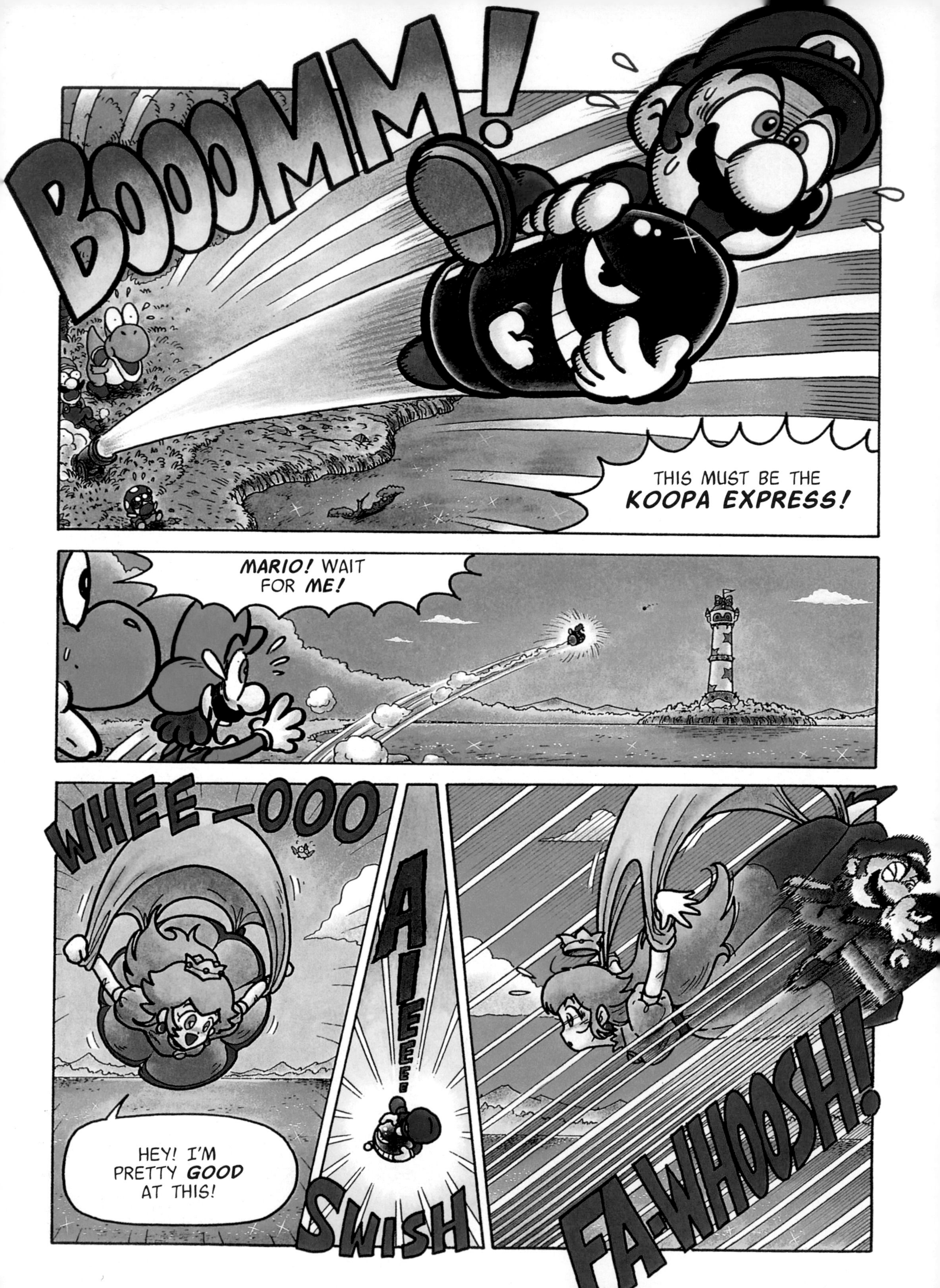
BOOOMM!
THIS MUST BE THE KOOPA EXPRESS!
MARIO! WAIT FOR ME!
WHEE-OOO
HEY! I'M PRETTY GOOD AT THIS!
AIIEEEE!
SWISH
FA-WHOOSH!

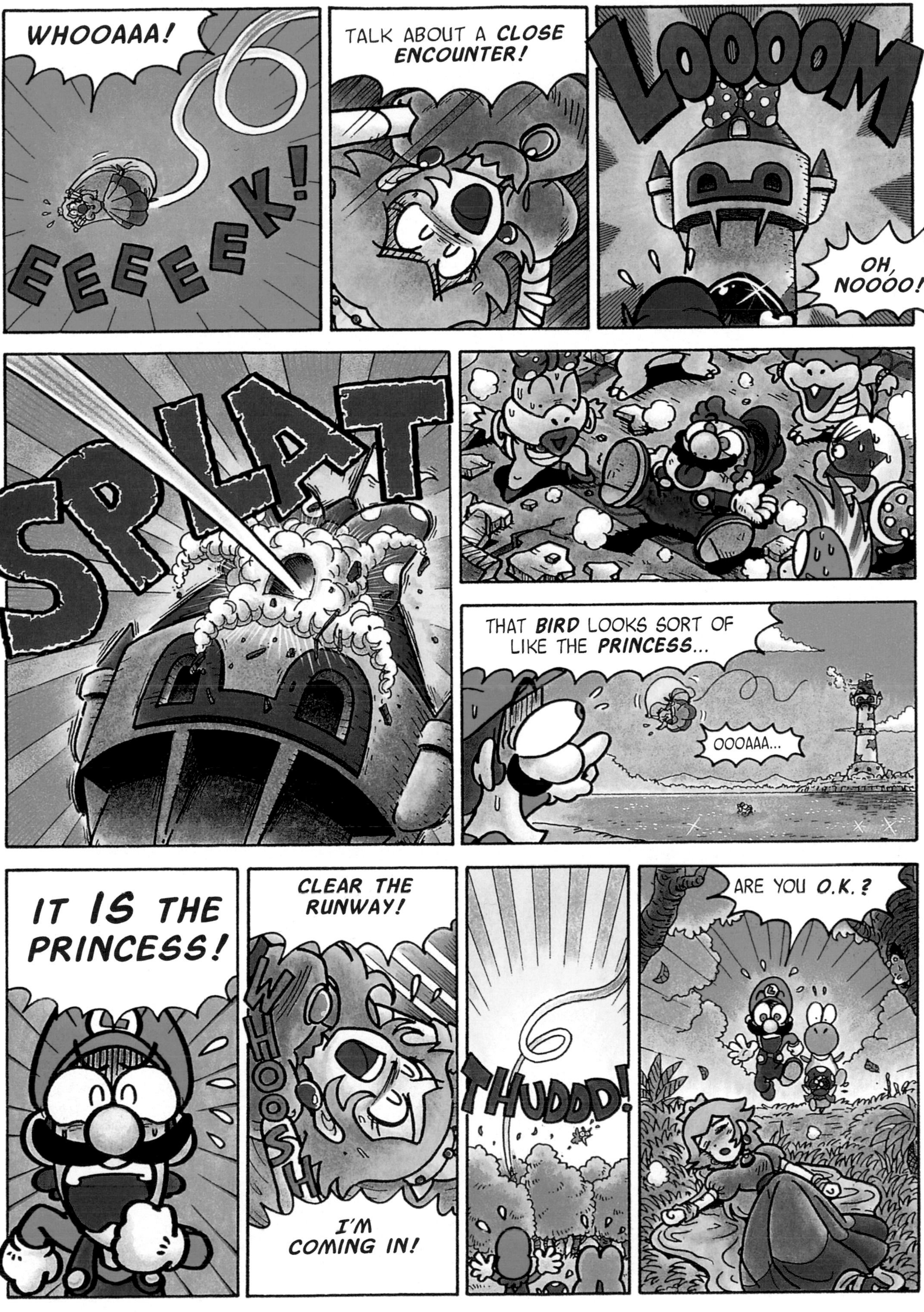

WHOOAAA!
EEEEEK!
TALK ABOUT A CLOSE ENCOUNTER!
LOOOOM
OH, NOOOO!
SPLAT
THAT BIRD LOOKS SORT OF LIKE THE PRINCESS...
OOOAAA...
IT IS THE PRINCESS!
CLEAR THE RUNWAY!
WHOOOSH
I'M COMING IN!
THUDDD!
ARE YOU O.K.?

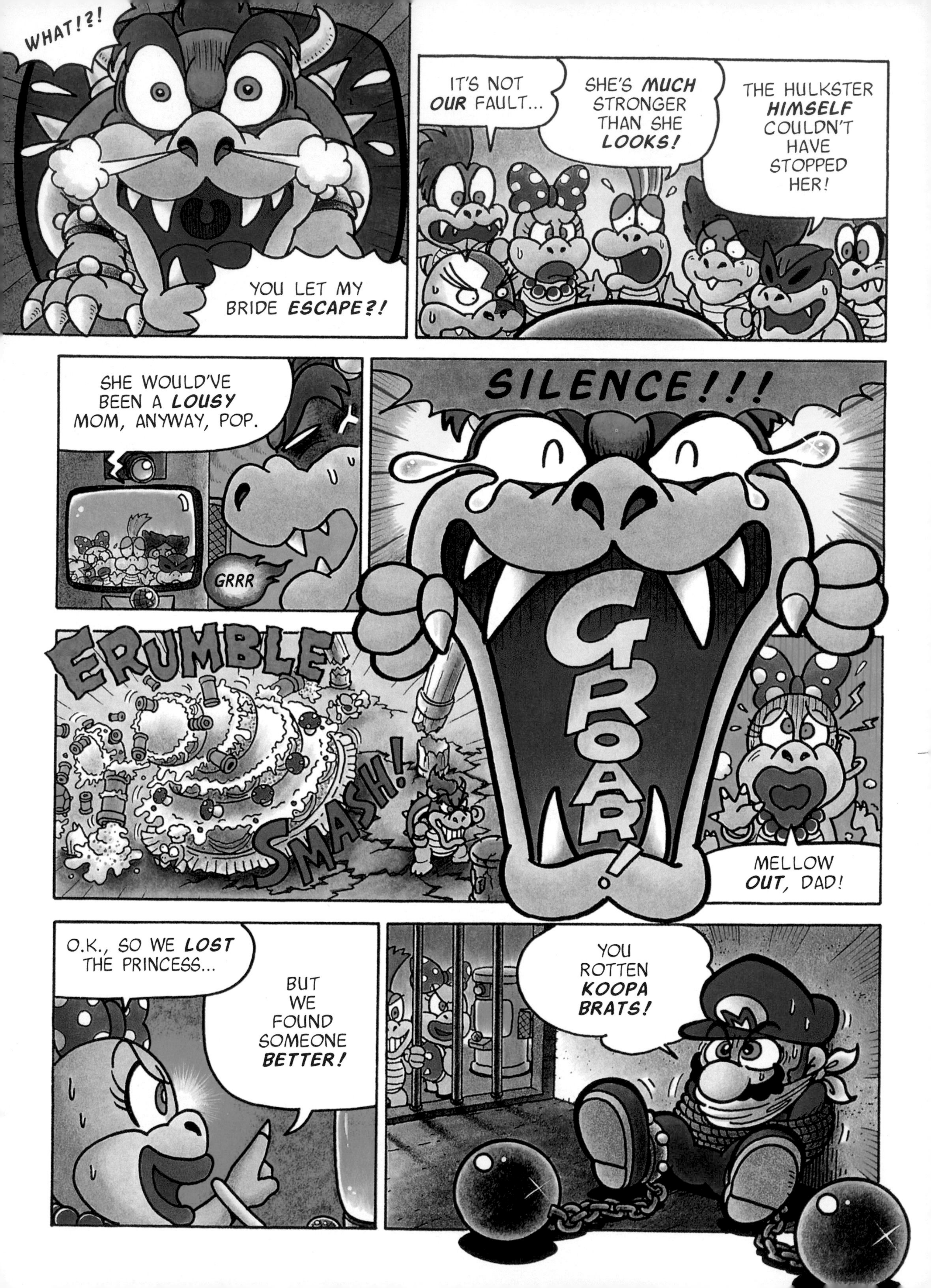
WHAT!?!
YOU LET MY BRIDE ESCAPE?!
IT'S NOT OUR FAULT...
SHE'S MUCH STRONGER THAN SHE LOOKS!
THE HULKSTER HIMSELF COULDN'T HAVE STOPPED HER!
SHE WOULD'VE BEEN A LOUSY MOM, ANYWAY, POP.
GRRR
SILENCE!!!
GROAR!
ERUMBLE
SMASH!
MELLOW OUT, DAD!
O.K., SO WE LOST THE PRINCESS...
BUT WE FOUND SOMEONE BETTER!
YOU ROTTEN KOOPA BRATS!

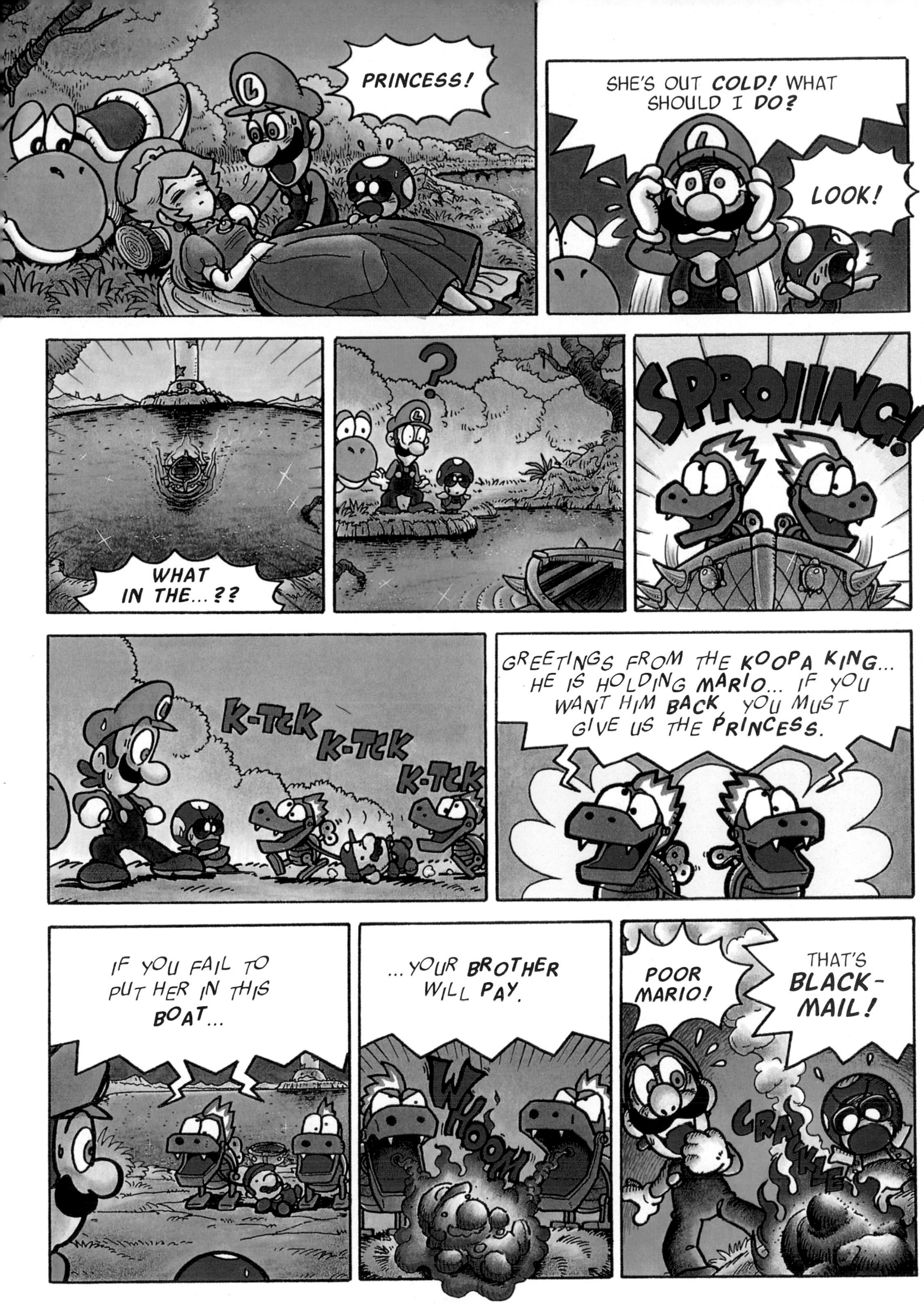
PRINCESS!
SHE'S OUT COLD! WHAT SHOULD I DO?
LOOK!
WHAT IN THE...??
?
SPROIING!
K-TCK
K-TCK
K-TCK
GREETINGS FROM THE KOOPA KING... HE IS HOLDING MARIO... IF YOU WANT HIM BACK, YOU MUST GIVE US THE PRINCESS.
IF YOU FAIL TO PUT HER IN THIS BOAT...
...YOUR BROTHER WILL PAY.
WHOOM
POOR MARIO!
THAT'S BLACK-MAIL!
CRACKLE

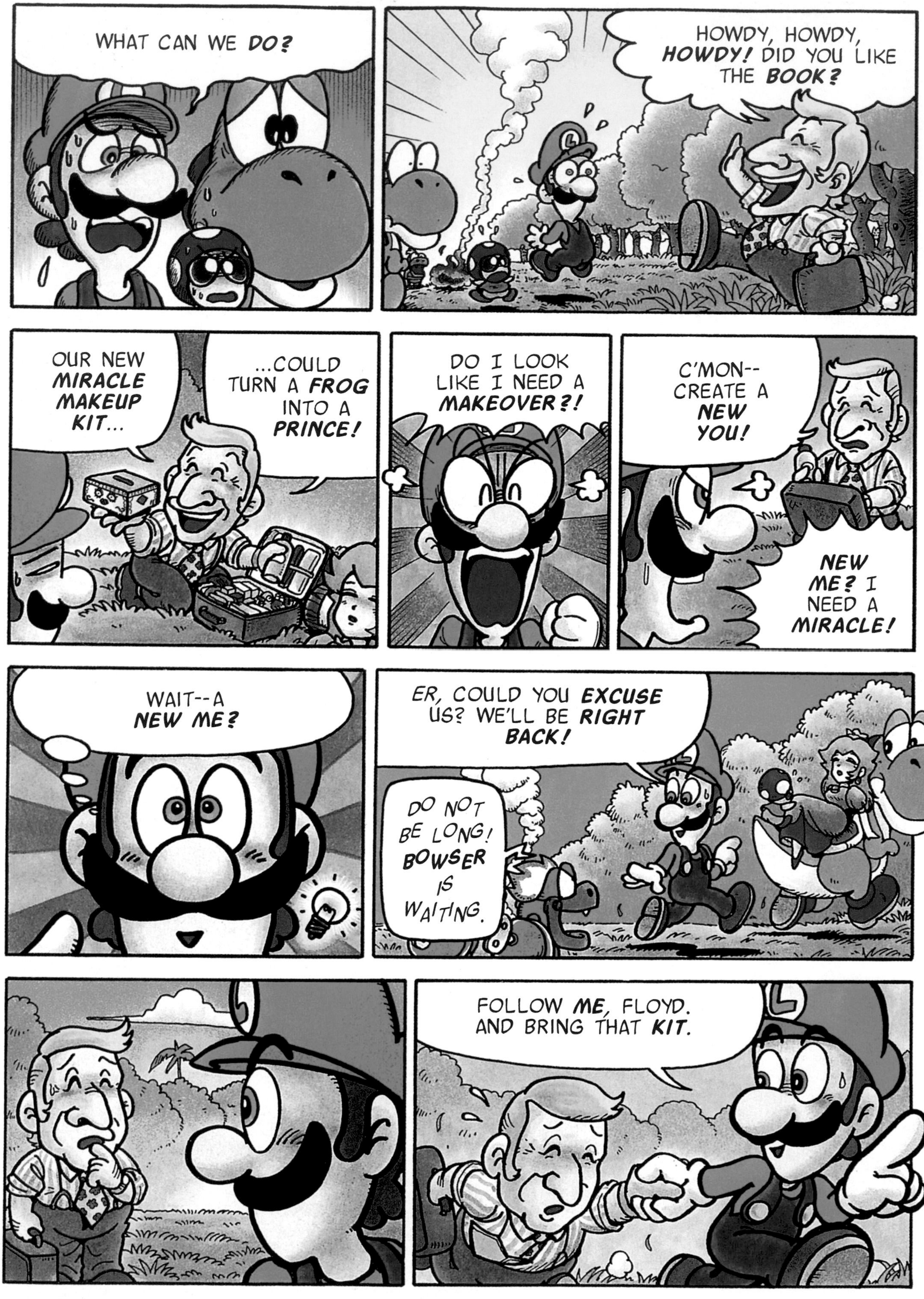
WHAT CAN WE DO?
HOWDY, HOWDY, HOWDY! DID YOU LIKE THE BOOK?
OUR NEW MIRACLE MAKEUP KIT...
...COULD TURN A FROG INTO A PRINCE!
DO I LOOK LIKE I NEED A MAKEOVER?!
C'MON--CREATE A NEW YOU!
NEW ME? I NEED A MIRACLE!
WAIT--A NEW ME?
ER, COULD YOU EXCUSE US? WE'LL BE RIGHT BACK!
DO NOT BE LONG! BOWSER IS WAITING.
FOLLOW ME, FLOYD. AND BRING THAT KIT.

HOW DO I **LOOK?**

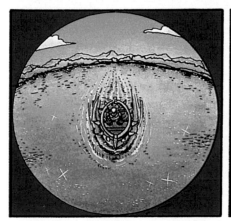

SHE'S ON HER WAY! IT **WORKED!**

KER-REEK

GRAB HER!

FLOYD, YOU'D BETTER COME **THROUGH** THIS TIME!

TO BE CONTINUED...

SUPER MARIO ADVENTURES ™

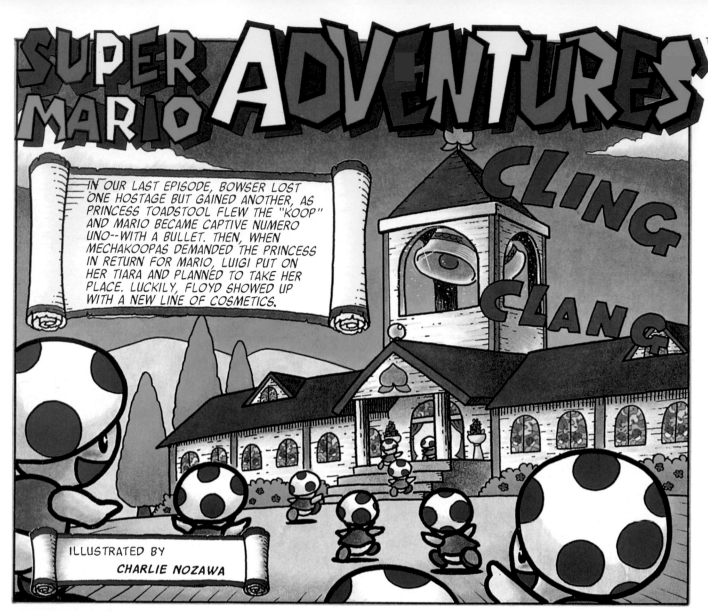

IN OUR LAST EPISODE, BOWSER LOST ONE HOSTAGE BUT GAINED ANOTHER, AS PRINCESS TOADSTOOL FLEW THE "KOOP" AND MARIO BECAME CAPTIVE NUMERO UNO--WITH A BULLET. THEN, WHEN MECHAKOOPAS DEMANDED THE PRINCESS IN RETURN FOR MARIO, LUIGI PUT ON HER TIARA AND PLANNED TO TAKE HER PLACE. LUCKILY, FLOYD SHOWED UP WITH A NEW LINE OF COSMETICS.

CLING

CLANG

ILLUSTRATED BY
CHARLIE NOZAWA

MARIO, DO YOU TAKE THIS WOMAN TO BE YOUR LAWFULLY WEDDED WIFE, FOR RICHER OR POORER, IN SICKNESS AND IN HEALTH, AS LONG AS YOU BOTH SHALL LIVE?

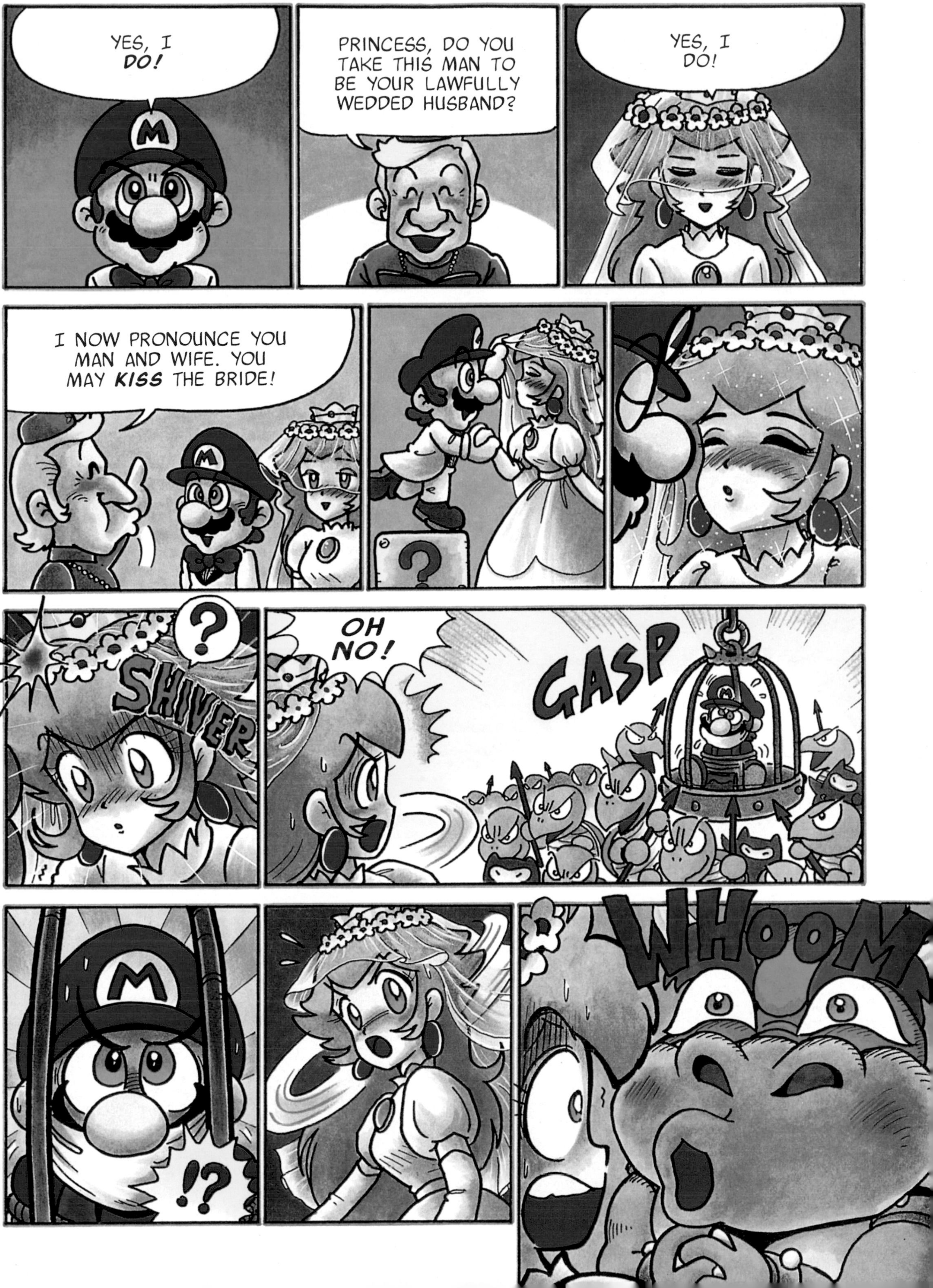
YES, I DO!
PRINCESS, DO YOU TAKE THIS MAN TO BE YOUR LAWFULLY WEDDED HUSBAND?
YES, I DO!
I NOW PRONOUNCE YOU MAN AND WIFE. YOU MAY KISS THE BRIDE!
SHIVER
?
OH NO!
GASP
!?
WHOOM

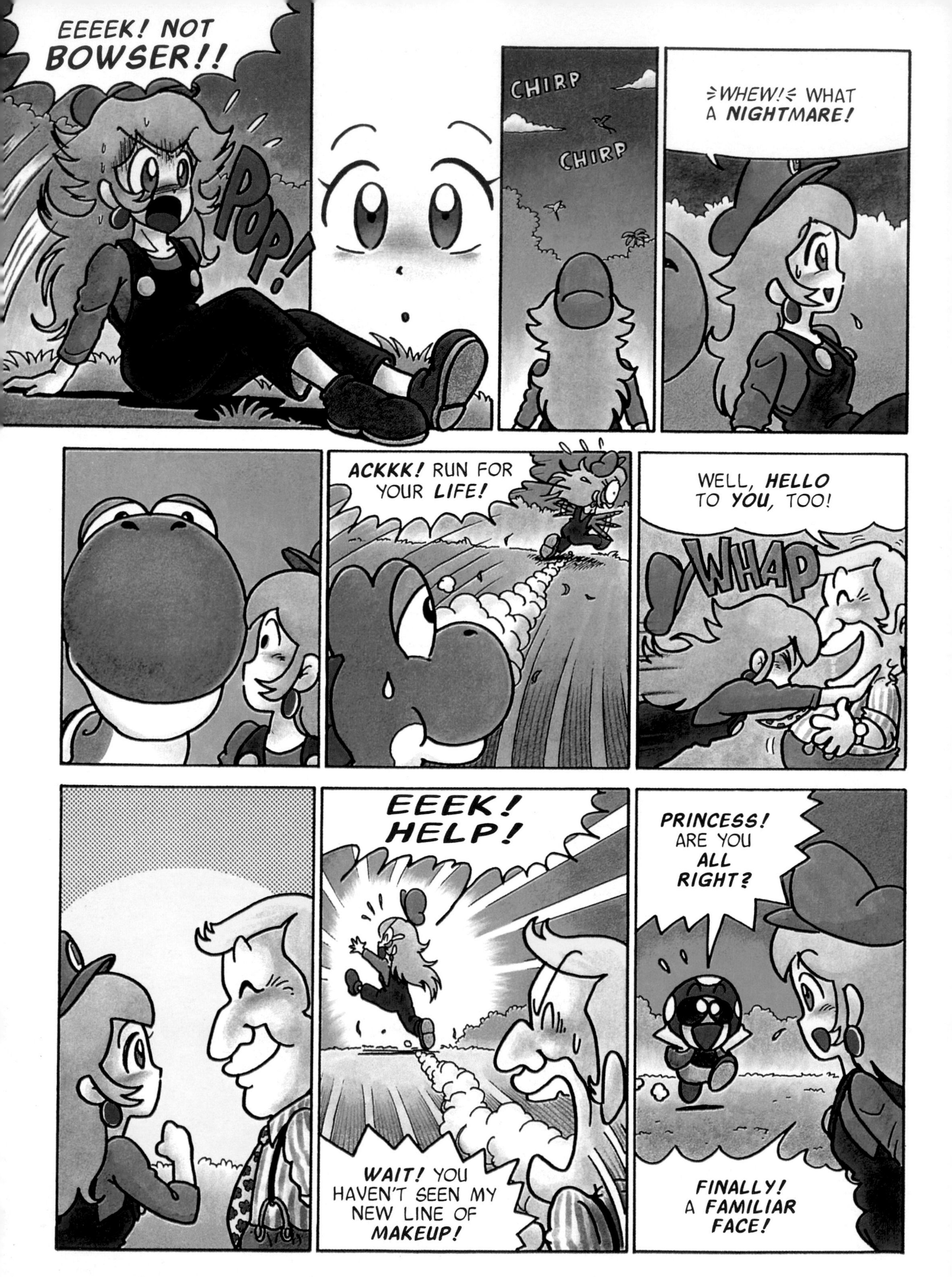
EEEEK! NOT BOWSER!!
POP!
CHIRP
CHIRP
WHEW! WHAT A NIGHTMARE!
ACKKK! RUN FOR YOUR LIFE!
WELL, HELLO TO YOU, TOO!
WHAP
EEEK! HELP!
WAIT! YOU HAVEN'T SEEN MY NEW LINE OF MAKEUP!
PRINCESS! ARE YOU ALL RIGHT?
FINALLY! A FAMILIAR FACE!

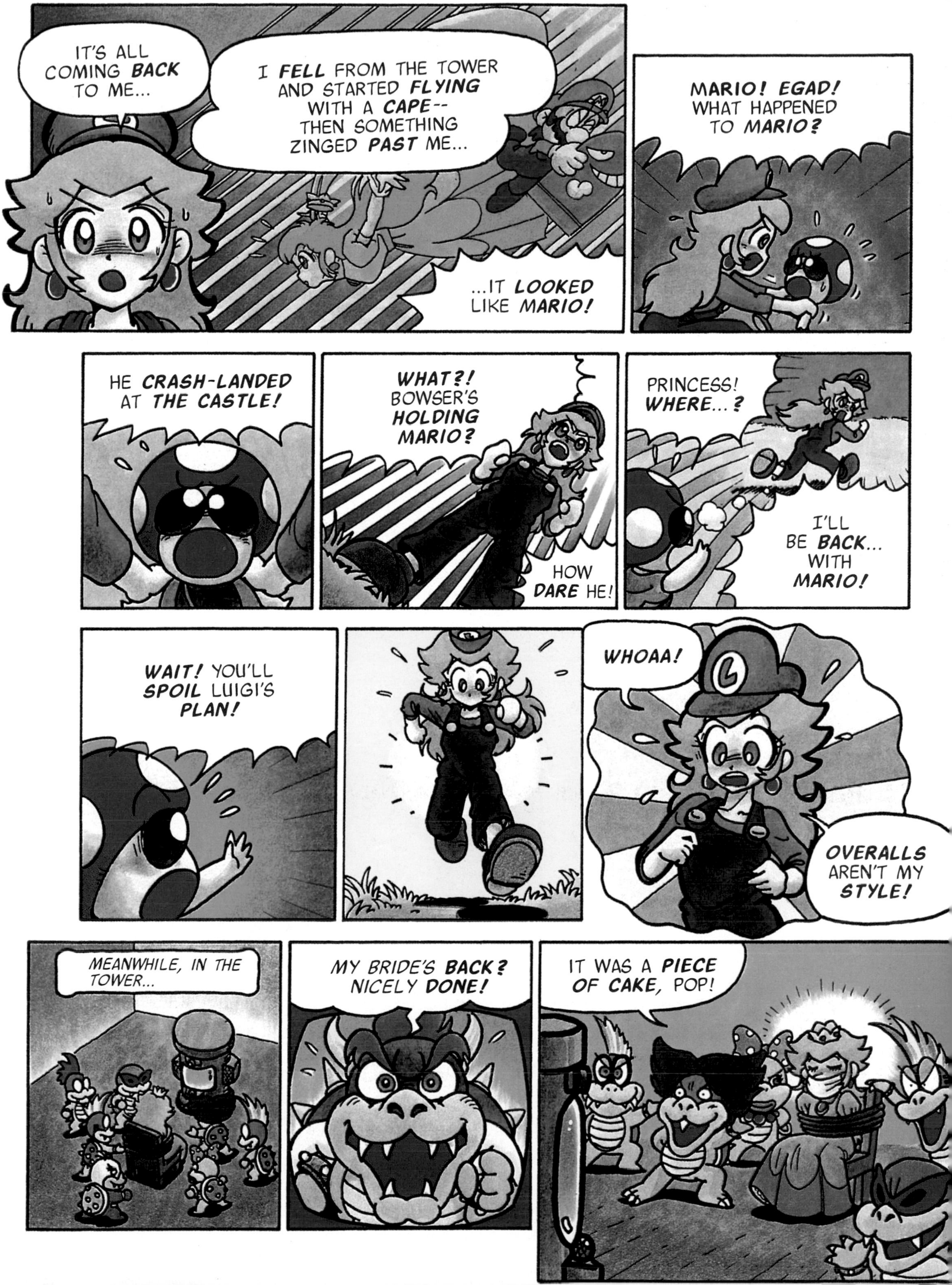
IT'S ALL COMING BACK TO ME...
I FELL FROM THE TOWER AND STARTED FLYING WITH A CAPE-- THEN SOMETHING ZINGED PAST ME...
...IT LOOKED LIKE MARIO!
MARIO! EGAD! WHAT HAPPENED TO MARIO?
HE CRASH-LANDED AT THE CASTLE!
WHAT?! BOWSER'S HOLDING MARIO?
HOW DARE HE!
PRINCESS! WHERE...?
I'LL BE BACK... WITH MARIO!
WAIT! YOU'LL SPOIL LUIGI'S PLAN!
WHOAA!
OVERALLS AREN'T MY STYLE!
MEANWHILE, IN THE TOWER...
MY BRIDE'S BACK? NICELY DONE!
IT WAS A PIECE OF CAKE, POP!

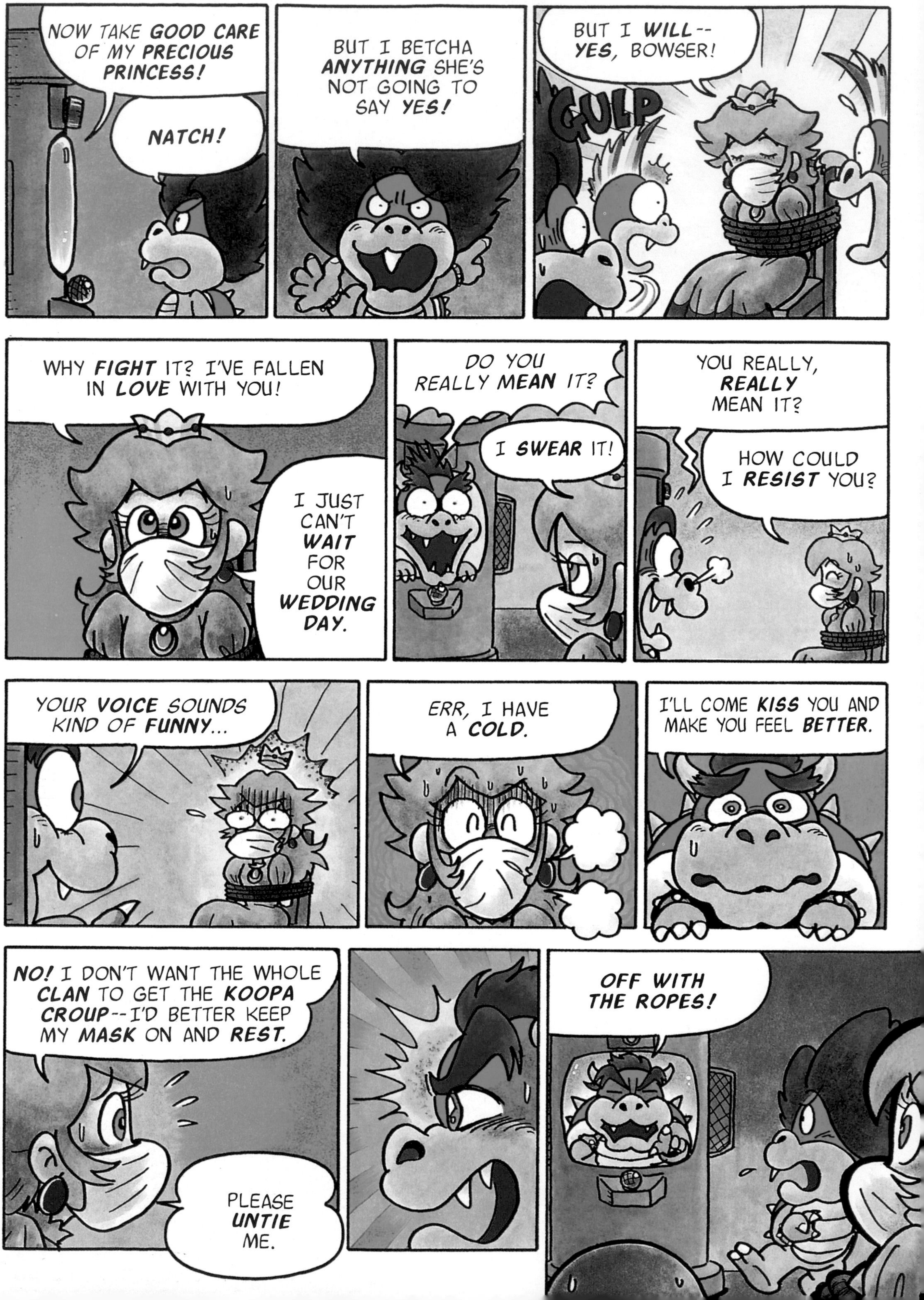

NOW TAKE GOOD CARE OF MY PRECIOUS PRINCESS!
NATCH!
BUT I BETCHA ANYTHING SHE'S NOT GOING TO SAY YES!
BUT I WILL-- YES, BOWSER!
GULP
WHY FIGHT IT? I'VE FALLEN IN LOVE WITH YOU!
I JUST CAN'T WAIT FOR OUR WEDDING DAY.
DO YOU REALLY MEAN IT?
I SWEAR IT!
YOU REALLY, REALLY MEAN IT?
HOW COULD I RESIST YOU?
YOUR VOICE SOUNDS KIND OF FUNNY...
ERR, I HAVE A COLD.
I'LL COME KISS YOU AND MAKE YOU FEEL BETTER.
NO! I DON'T WANT THE WHOLE CLAN TO GET THE KOOPA CROUP--I'D BETTER KEEP MY MASK ON AND REST.
PLEASE UNTIE ME.
OFF WITH THE ROPES!

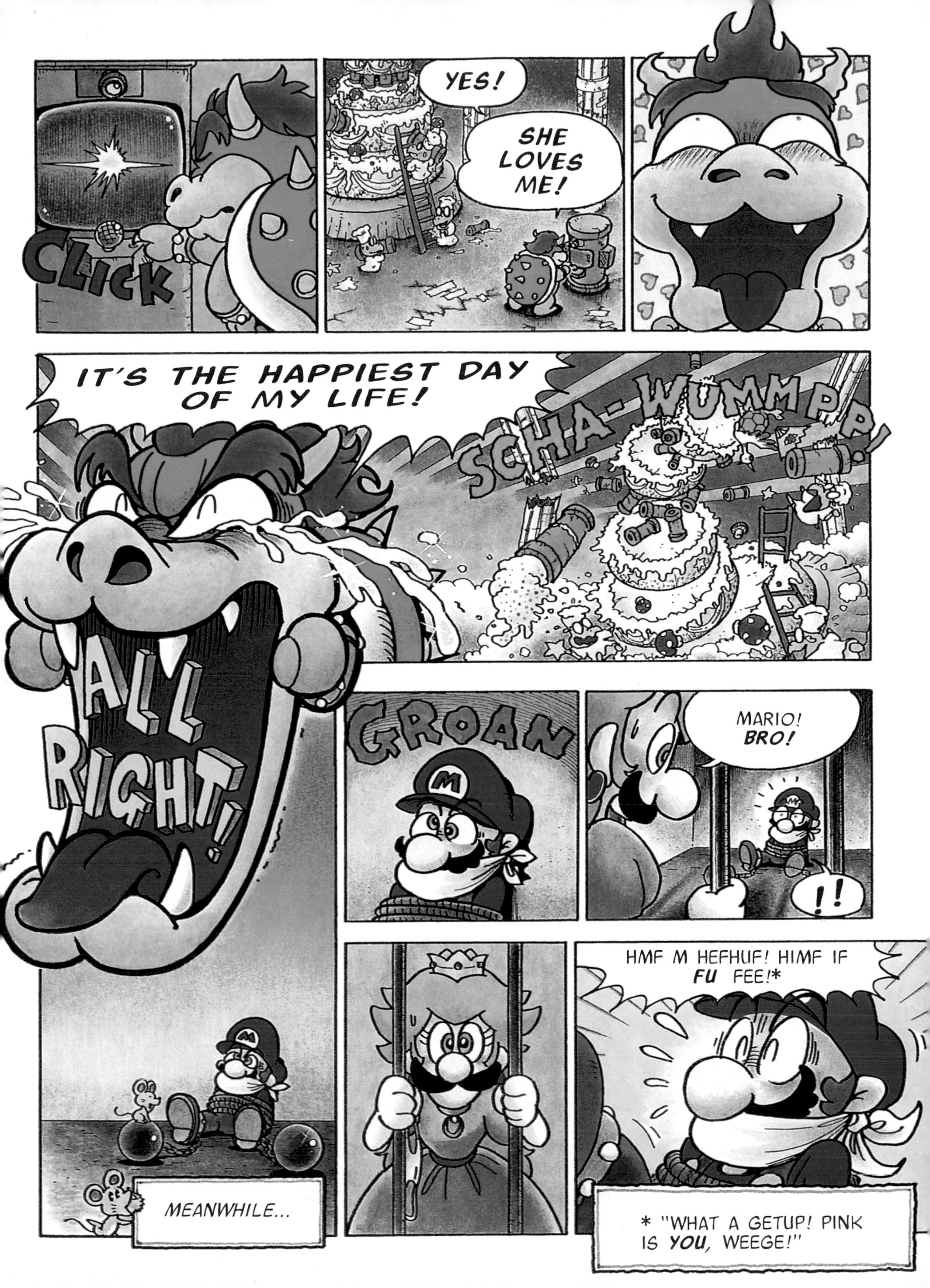
CLICK
YES!
SHE LOVES ME!
IT'S THE HAPPIEST DAY OF MY LIFE!
SCHA-WUMMPP!
ALL RIGHT!
MEANWHILE...
GROAN
MARIO! **BRO!**
!!
HMF M HEFHUF! HIMF IF ***FU*** FEE!*
* "WHAT A GETUP! PINK IS ***YOU,*** WEEGE!"

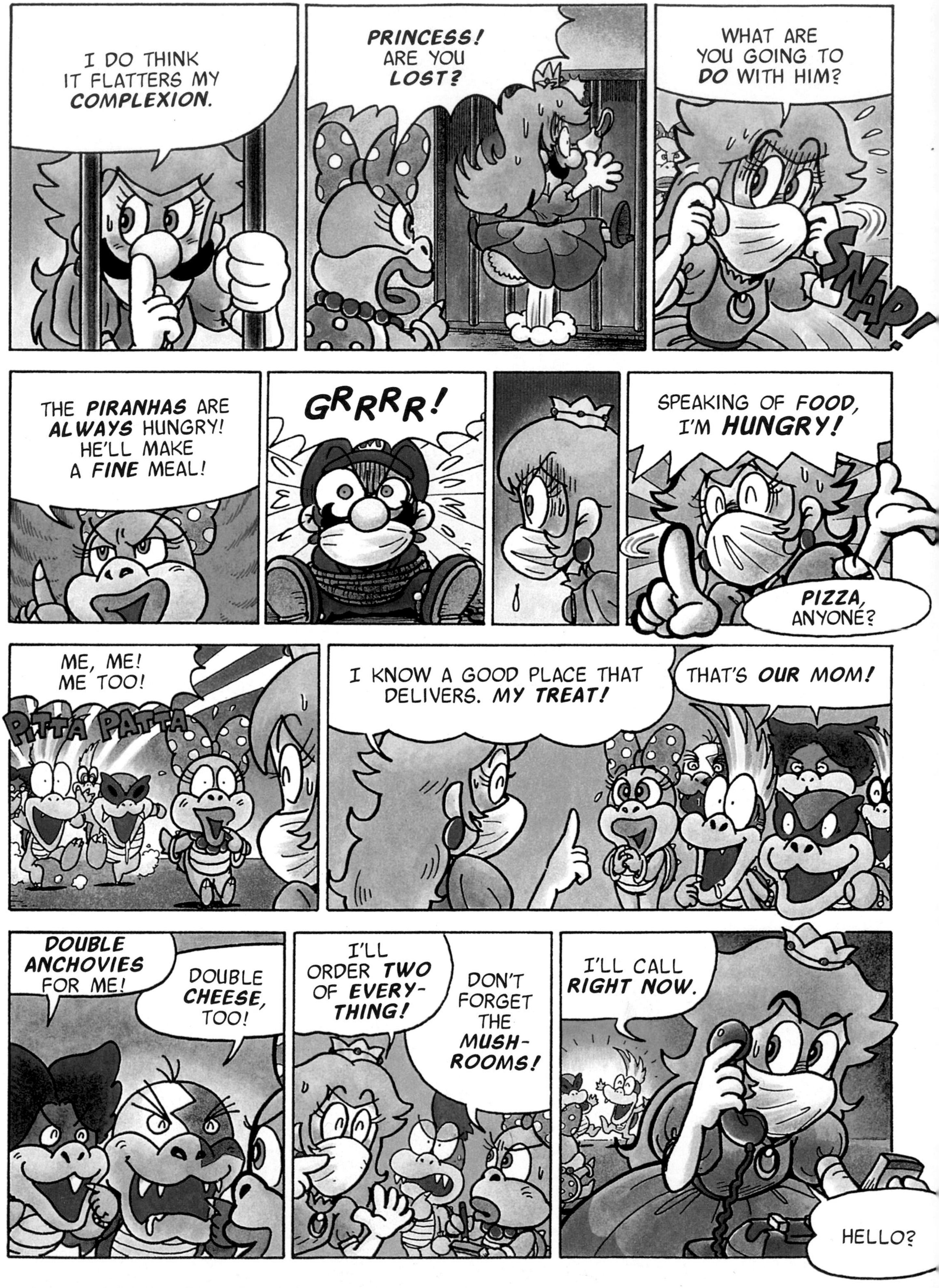

I DO THINK IT FLATTERS MY COMPLEXION.
PRINCESS! ARE YOU LOST?
WHAT ARE YOU GOING TO DO WITH HIM?
SNAP!
THE PIRANHAS ARE ALWAYS HUNGRY! HE'LL MAKE A FINE MEAL!
GRRRR!
SPEAKING OF FOOD, I'M HUNGRY!
PIZZA, ANYONE?
ME, ME! ME TOO!
PITTA PATTA
I KNOW A GOOD PLACE THAT DELIVERS. MY TREAT!
THAT'S OUR MOM!
DOUBLE ANCHOVIES FOR ME!
DOUBLE CHEESE, TOO!
I'LL ORDER TWO OF EVERY-THING!
DON'T FORGET THE MUSH-ROOMS!
I'LL CALL RIGHT NOW.
HELLO?

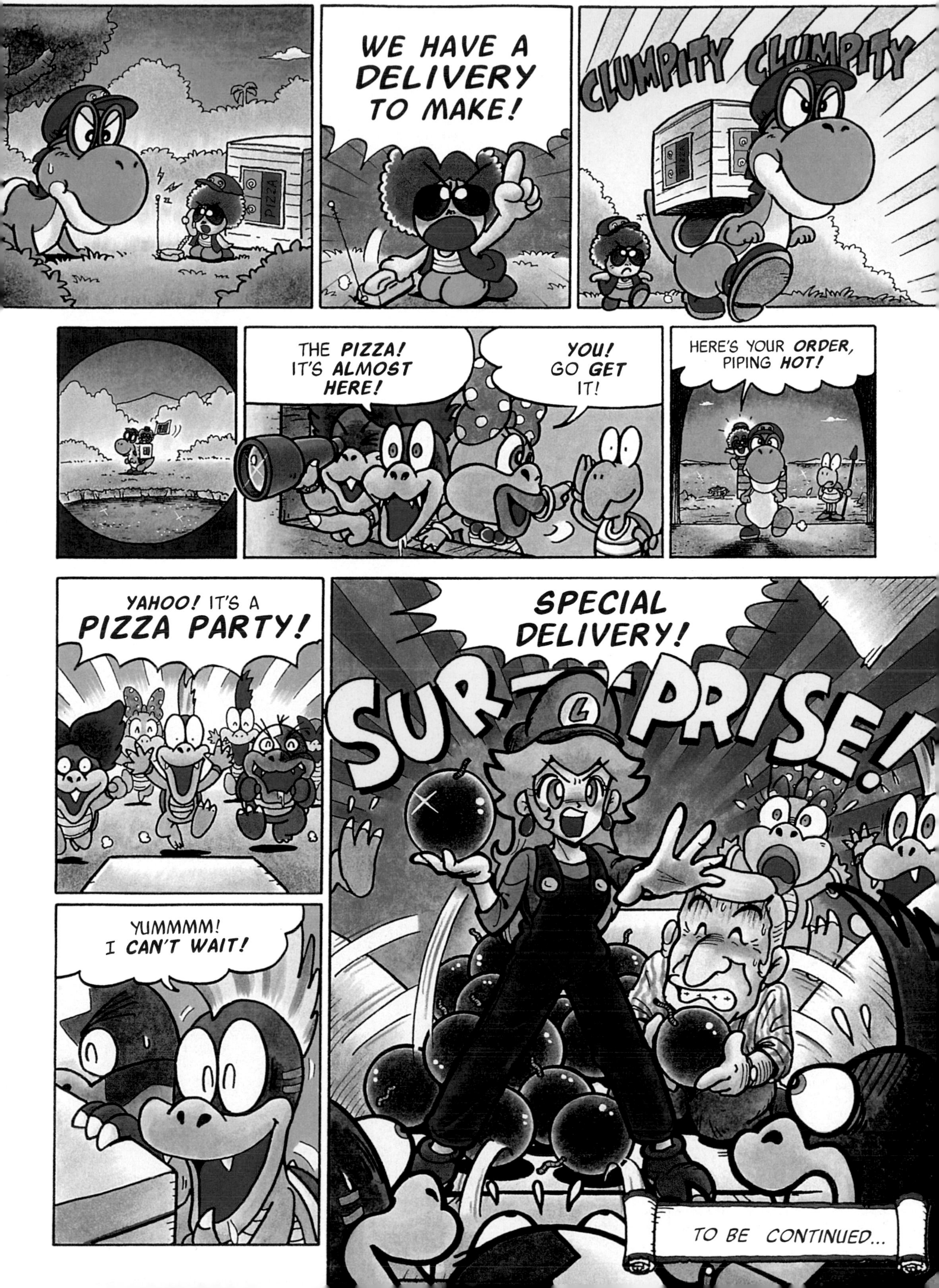
WE HAVE A DELIVERY TO MAKE!
CLUMPITY CLUMPITY
THE PIZZA! IT'S ALMOST HERE!
YOU! GO GET IT!
HERE'S YOUR ORDER, PIPING HOT!
YAHOO! IT'S A PIZZA PARTY!
YUMMMM! I CAN'T WAIT!
SPECIAL DELIVERY!
SUR-PRISE!
TO BE CONTINUED...

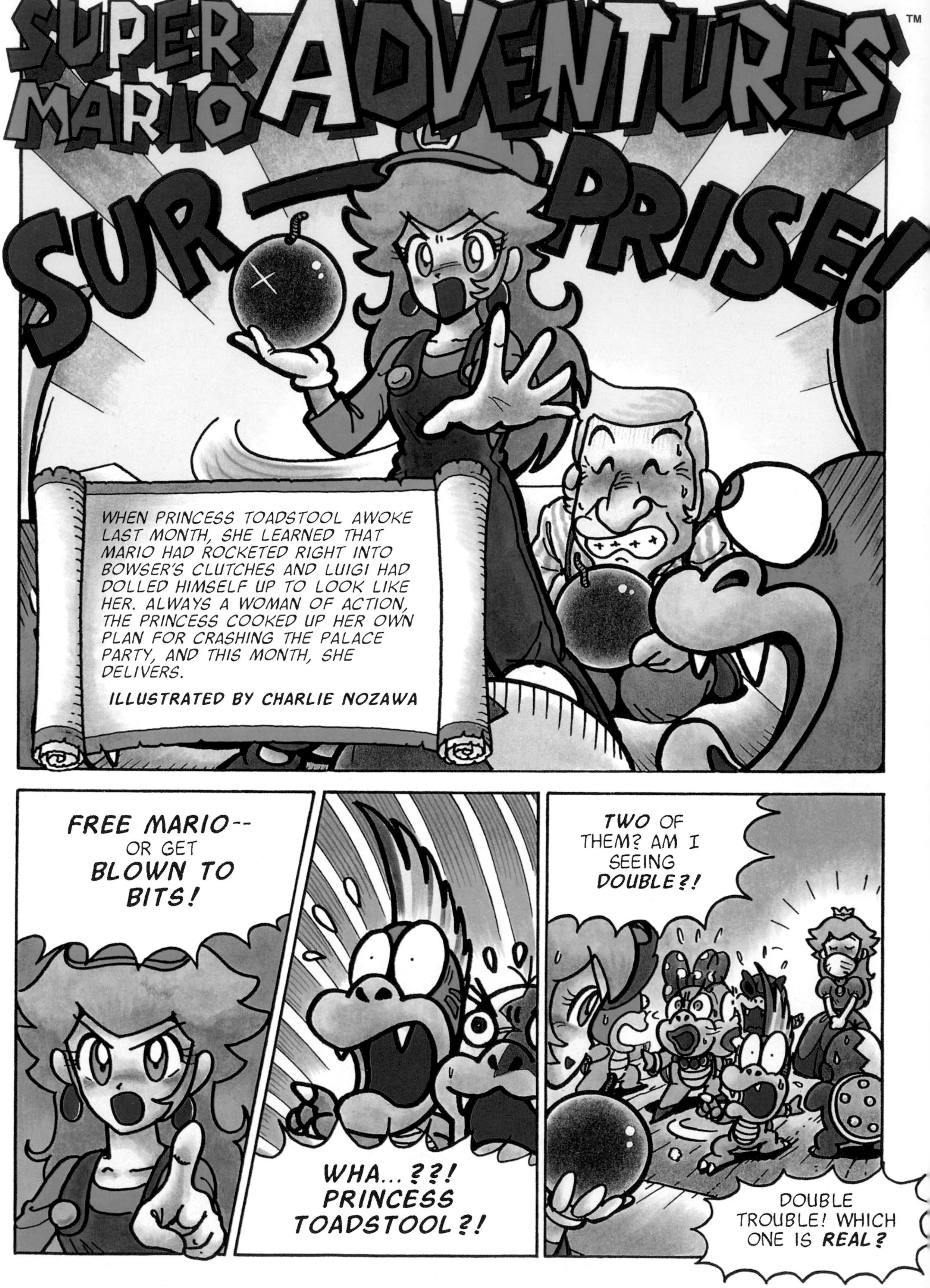
SUPER MARIO ADVENTURES™
SUR—PRISE!
WHEN PRINCESS TOADSTOOL AWOKE LAST MONTH, SHE LEARNED THAT MARIO HAD ROCKETED RIGHT INTO BOWSER'S CLUTCHES AND LUIGI HAD DOLLED HIMSELF UP TO LOOK LIKE HER. ALWAYS A WOMAN OF ACTION, THE PRINCESS COOKED UP HER OWN PLAN FOR CRASHING THE PALACE PARTY, AND THIS MONTH, SHE DELIVERS.
ILLUSTRATED BY CHARLIE NOZAWA
FREE MARIO-- OR GET BLOWN TO BITS!
WHA...??! PRINCESS TOADSTOOL?!
TWO OF THEM? AM I SEEING DOUBLE?!
DOUBLE TROUBLE! WHICH ONE IS REAL?

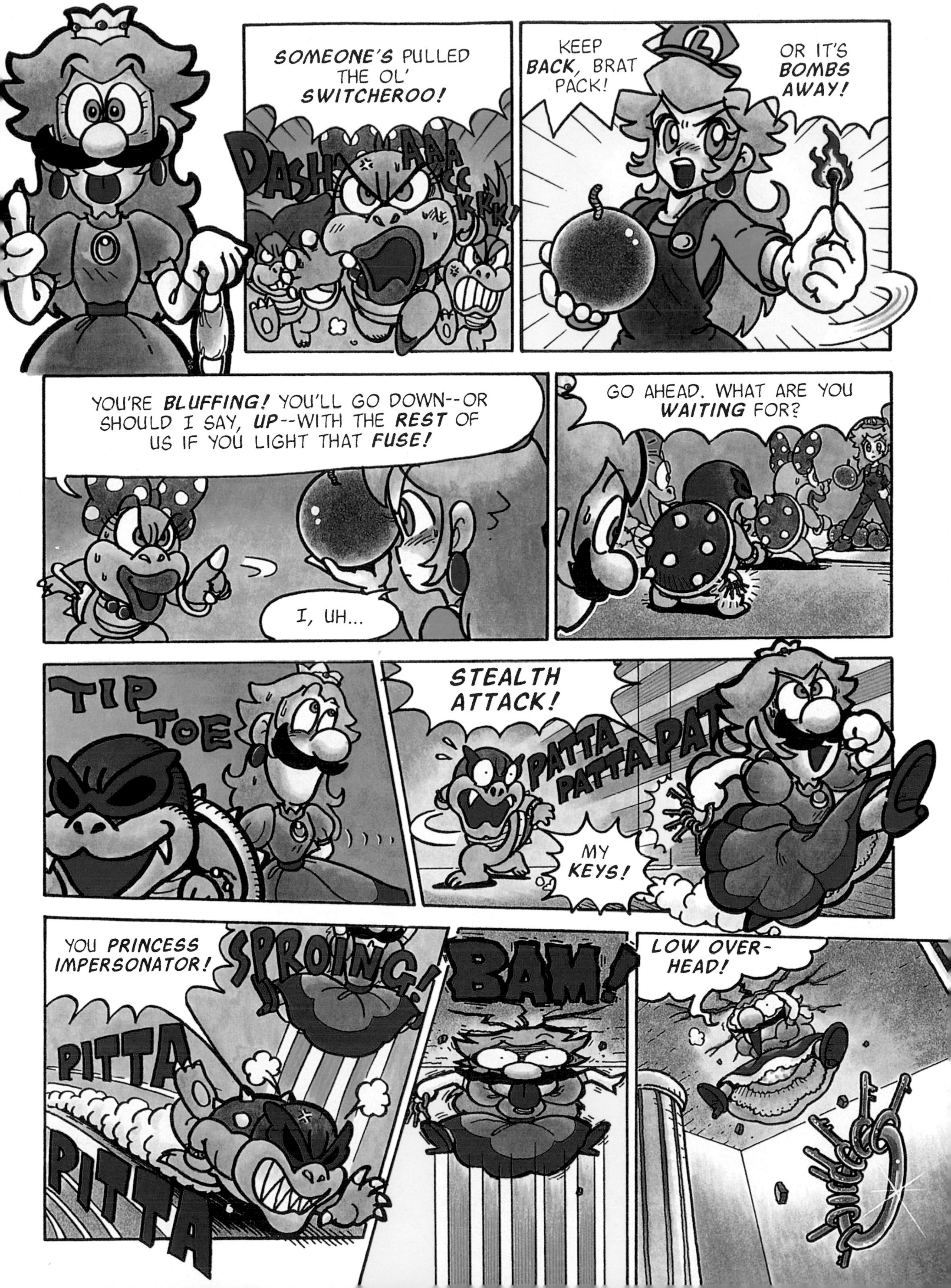
SOMEONE'S PULLED THE OL' SWITCHEROO!
DASH
AAACCKKK!
KEEP BACK, BRAT PACK!
OR IT'S BOMBS AWAY!
YOU'RE BLUFFING! YOU'LL GO DOWN--OR SHOULD I SAY, UP--WITH THE REST OF US IF YOU LIGHT THAT FUSE!
I, UH...
GO AHEAD. WHAT ARE YOU WAITING FOR?
TIP TOE
STEALTH ATTACK!
PATTA PATTA PAT
MY KEYS!
YOU PRINCESS IMPERSONATOR!
SPROING!
PITTA
PITTA
BAM!
LOW OVER-HEAD!

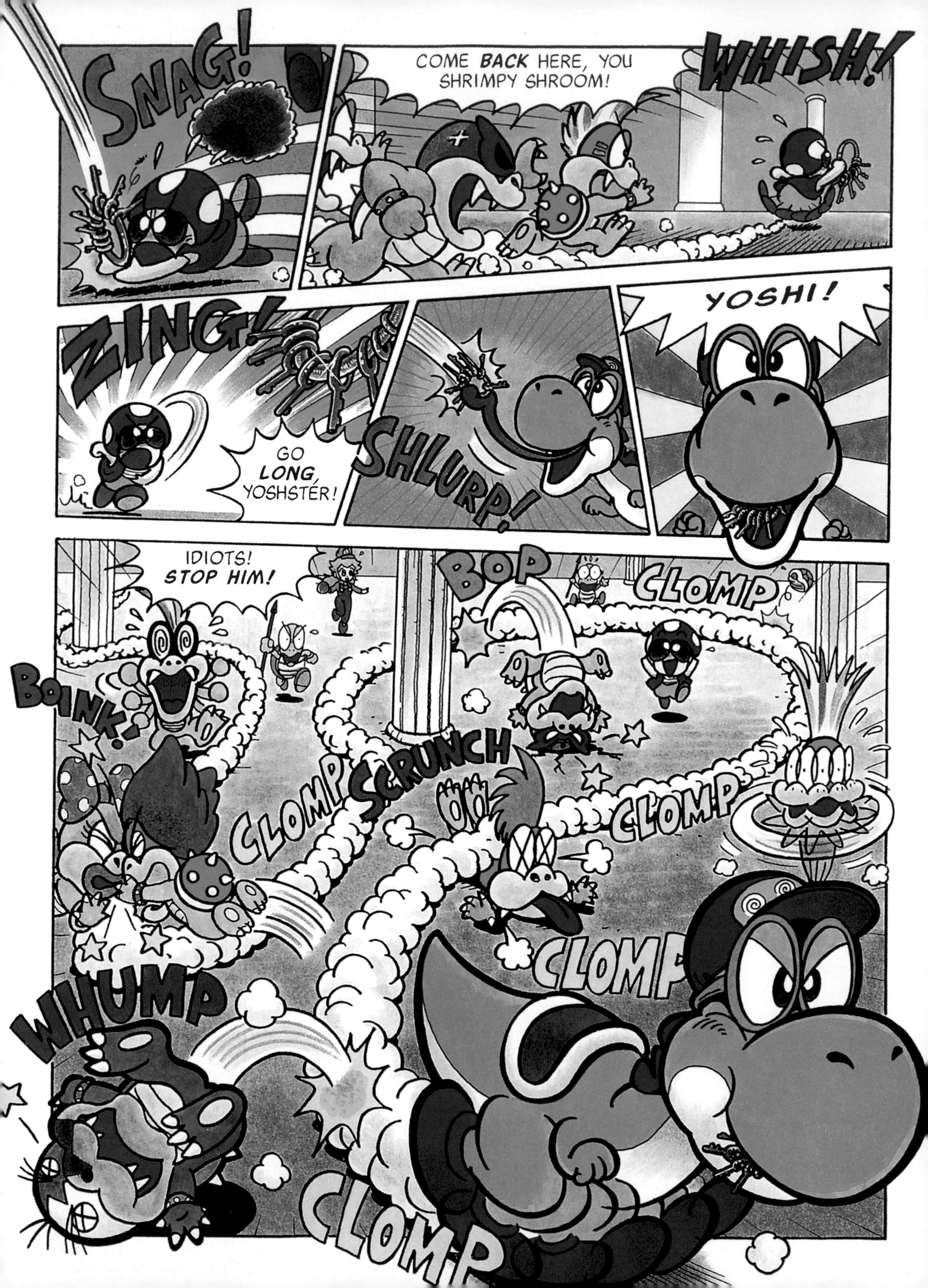
SNAG!
COME BACK HERE, YOU SHRIMPY SHROOM!
WHISH!
ZING!
GO LONG, YOSHSTER!
SHLURP!
YOSHI!
IDIOTS! STOP HIM!
BOP
CLOMP
BOINK!
CLOMP
SCRUNCH
CLOMP
CLOMP
WHUMP
CLOMP

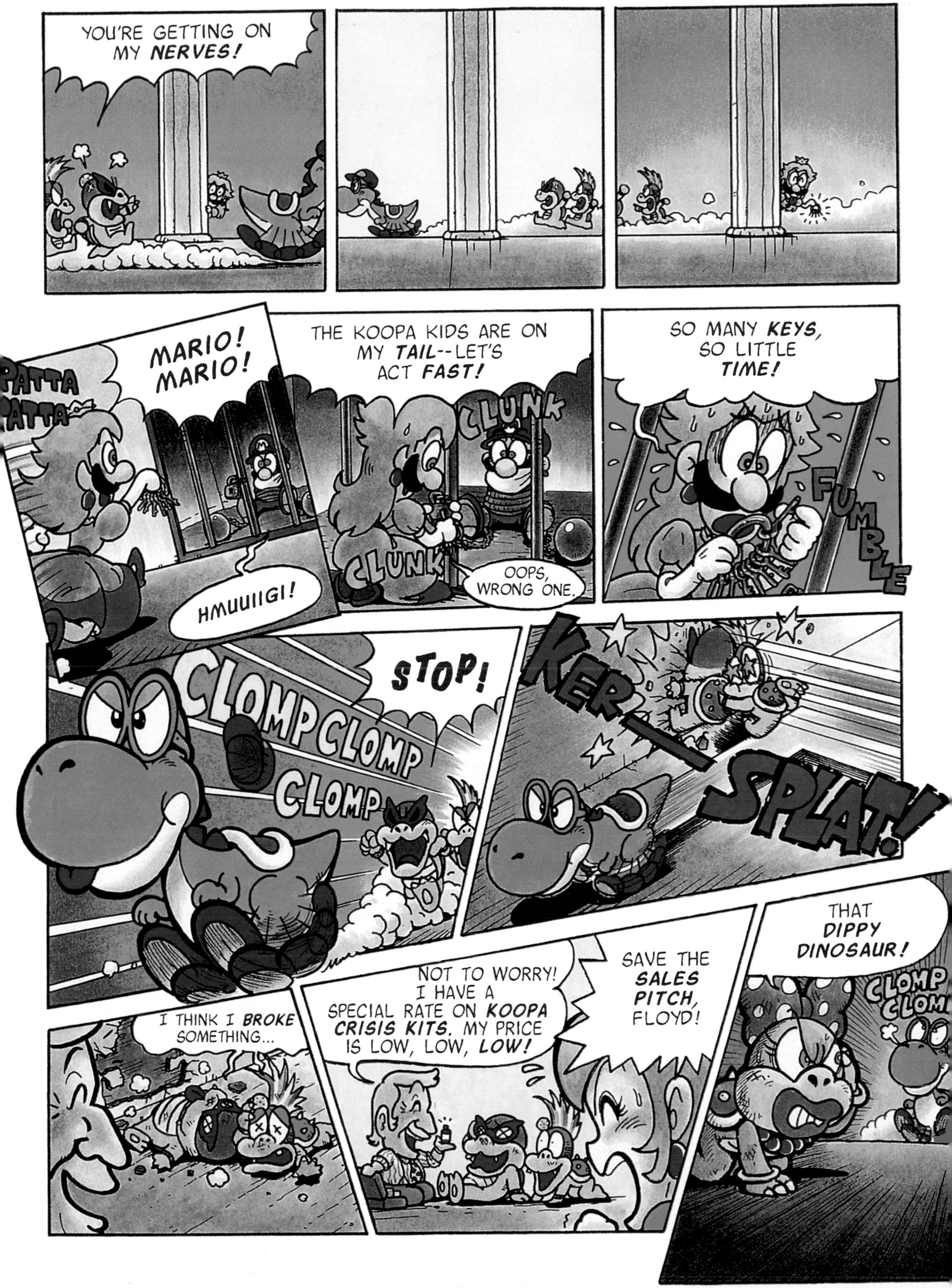
YOU'RE GETTING ON MY NERVES!
PATTA PATTA
MARIO! MARIO!
HMUUIIGI!
THE KOOPA KIDS ARE ON MY TAIL--LET'S ACT FAST!
CLUNK
CLUNK
OOPS, WRONG ONE.
SO MANY KEYS, SO LITTLE TIME!
FUMBLE
CLOMPCLOMP
CLOMP
CLOMP
STOP!
KER--
SPLAT!
I THINK I BROKE SOMETHING...
NOT TO WORRY! I HAVE A SPECIAL RATE ON KOOPA CRISIS KITS. MY PRICE IS LOW, LOW, LOW!
SAVE THE SALES PITCH, FLOYD!
THAT DIPPY DINOSAUR!
CLOMP CLOMP

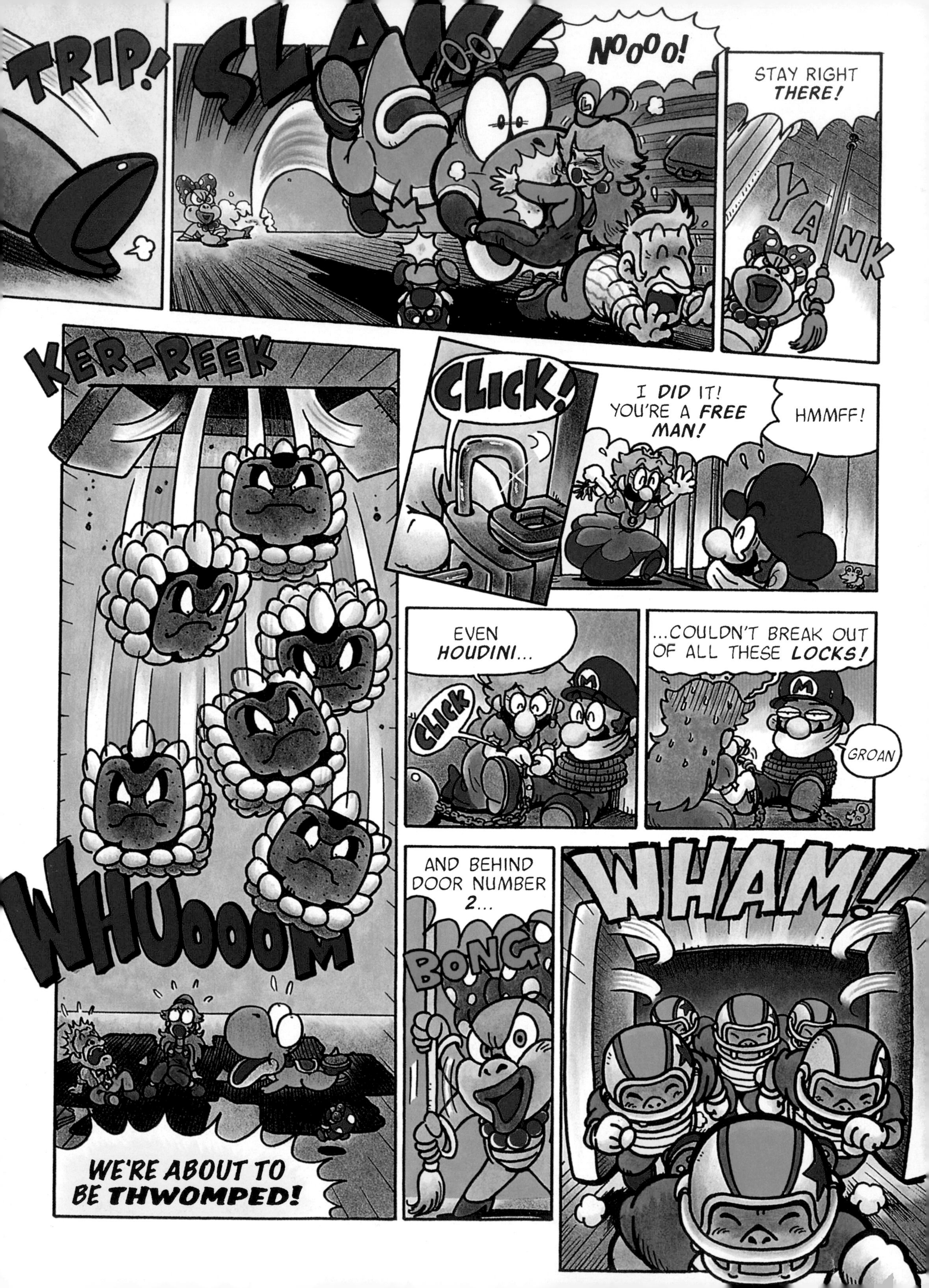
TRIP!
SLAM!
NOOOO!
STAY RIGHT THERE!
YANK
KER-REEK
WHUOOOOM
WE'RE ABOUT TO BE THWOMPED!
CLICK!
I DID IT! YOU'RE A FREE MAN!
HMMFF!
EVEN HOUDINI...
CLICK
...COULDN'T BREAK OUT OF ALL THESE LOCKS!
GROAN
AND BEHIND DOOR NUMBER 2...
BONG
WHAM!

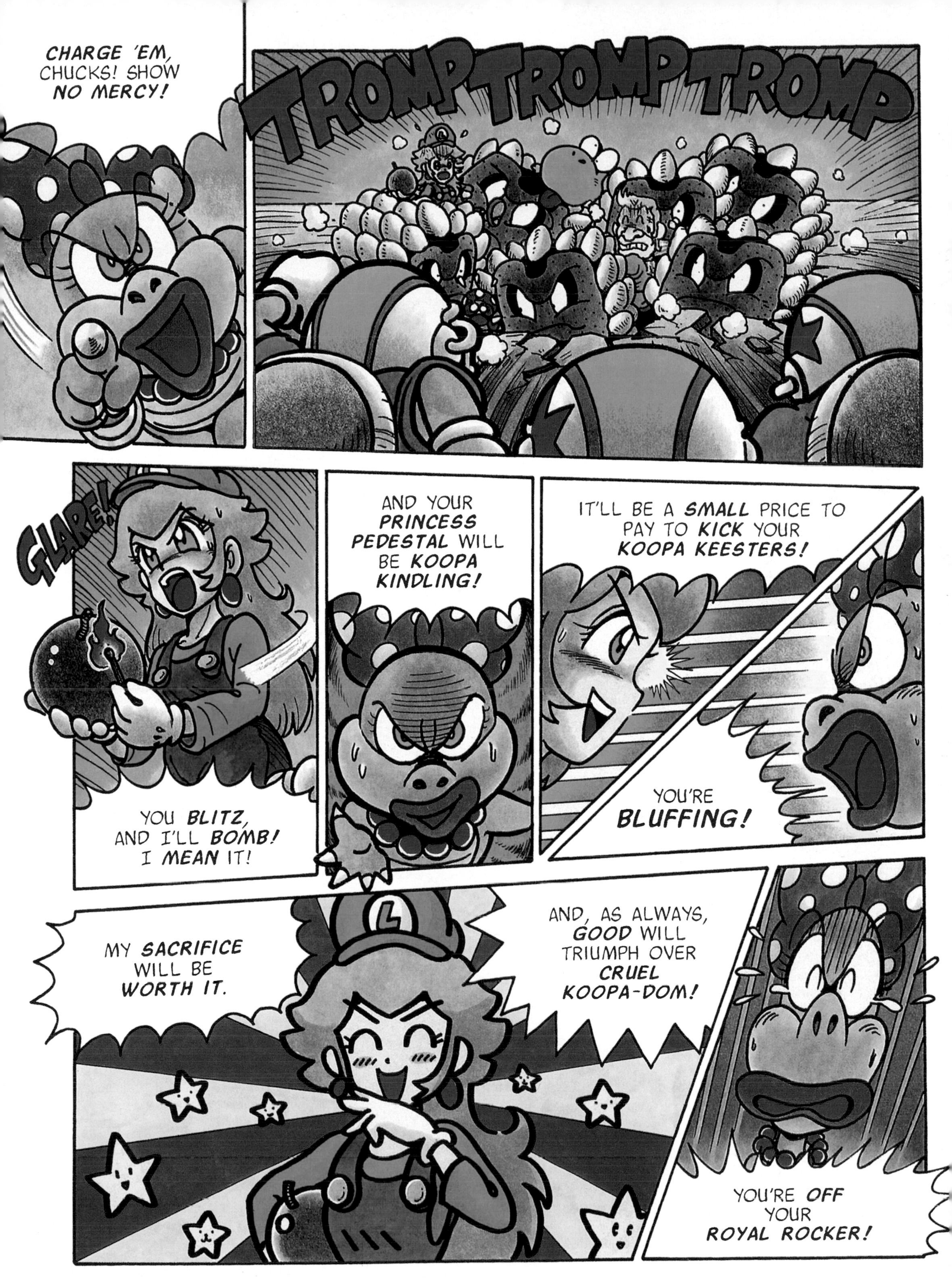
CHARGE 'EM, CHUCKS! SHOW NO MERCY!
TROMP TROMP TROMP
GLARE!
YOU BLITZ, AND I'LL BOMB! I MEAN IT!
AND YOUR PRINCESS PEDESTAL WILL BE KOOPA KINDLING!
IT'LL BE A SMALL PRICE TO PAY TO KICK YOUR KOOPA KEESTERS!
YOU'RE BLUFFING!
MY SACRIFICE WILL BE WORTH IT.
AND, AS ALWAYS, GOOD WILL TRIUMPH OVER CRUEL KOOPA-DOM!
YOU'RE OFF YOUR ROYAL ROCKER!

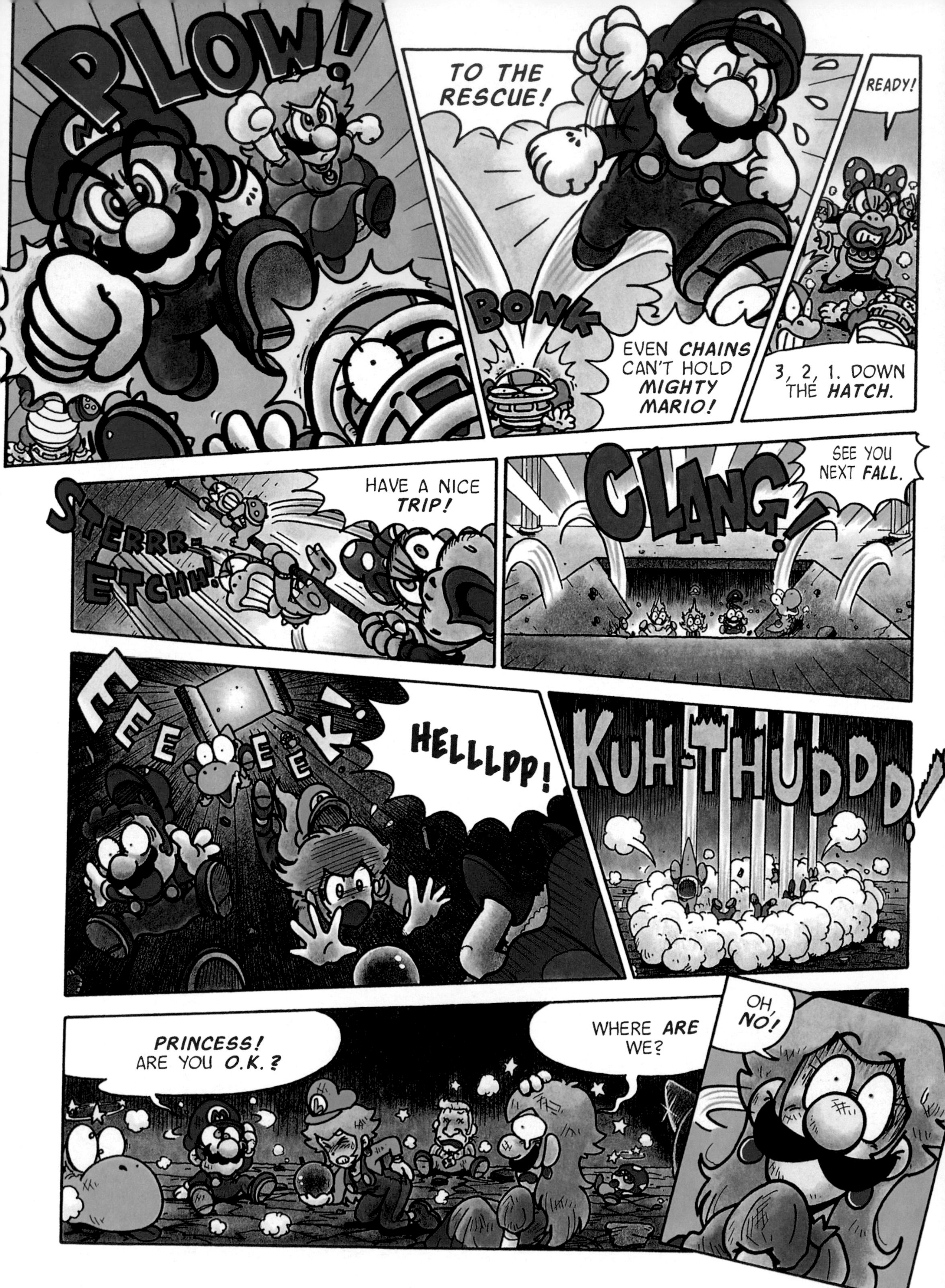
PLOW!
TO THE RESCUE!
BONK
EVEN CHAINS CAN'T HOLD MIGHTY MARIO!
READY!
3, 2, 1. DOWN THE HATCH.
STERRR-ETCHH!
HAVE A NICE TRIP!
CLANG!
SEE YOU NEXT FALL.
EEEEEEK!
HELLLPP!
KUH-THUDDD!
PRINCESS! ARE YOU O.K.?
WHERE ARE WE?
OH, NO!

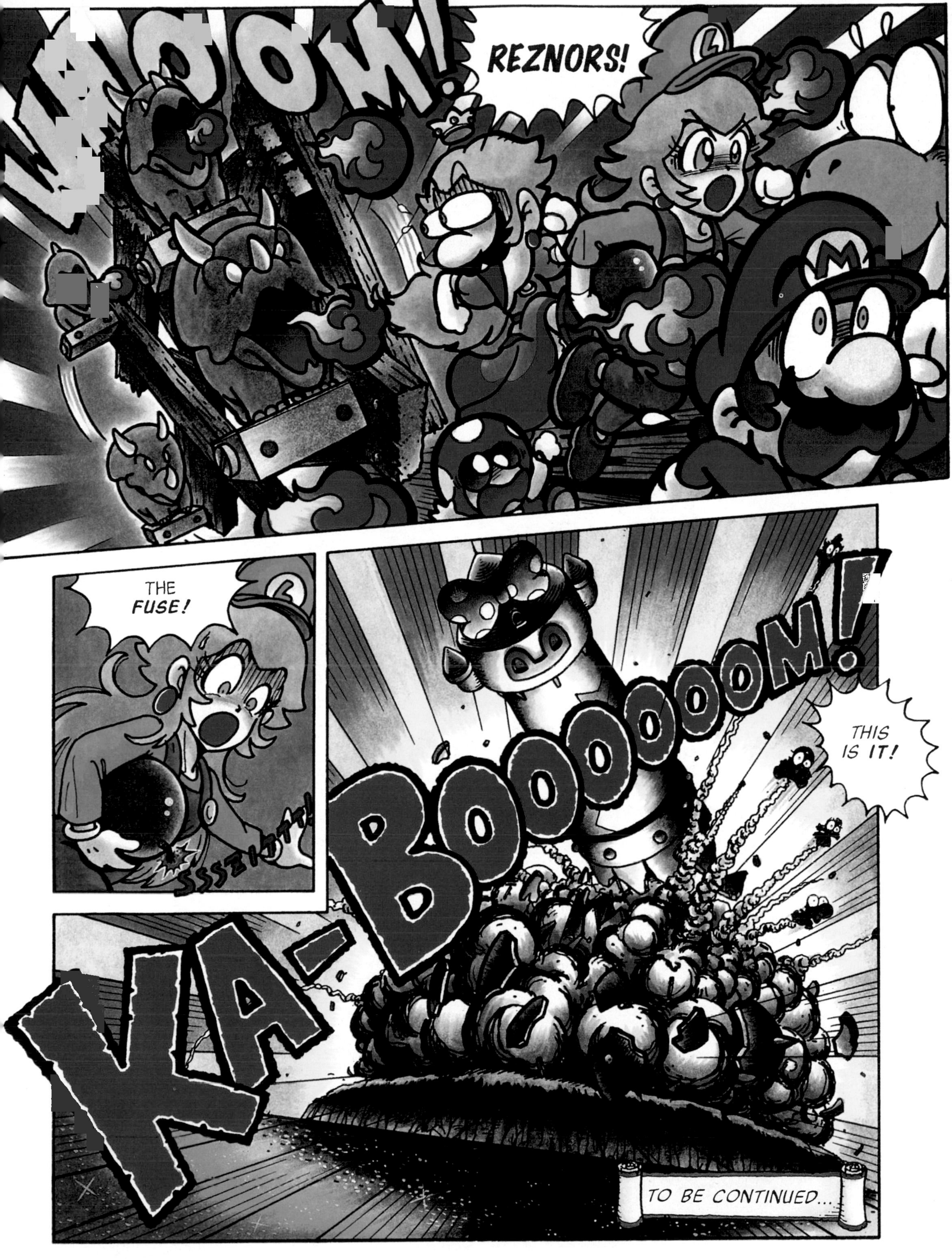
REZNORS!
THE FUSE!
KA-BOOOOOOOM!
THIS IS IT!
TO BE CONTINUED...

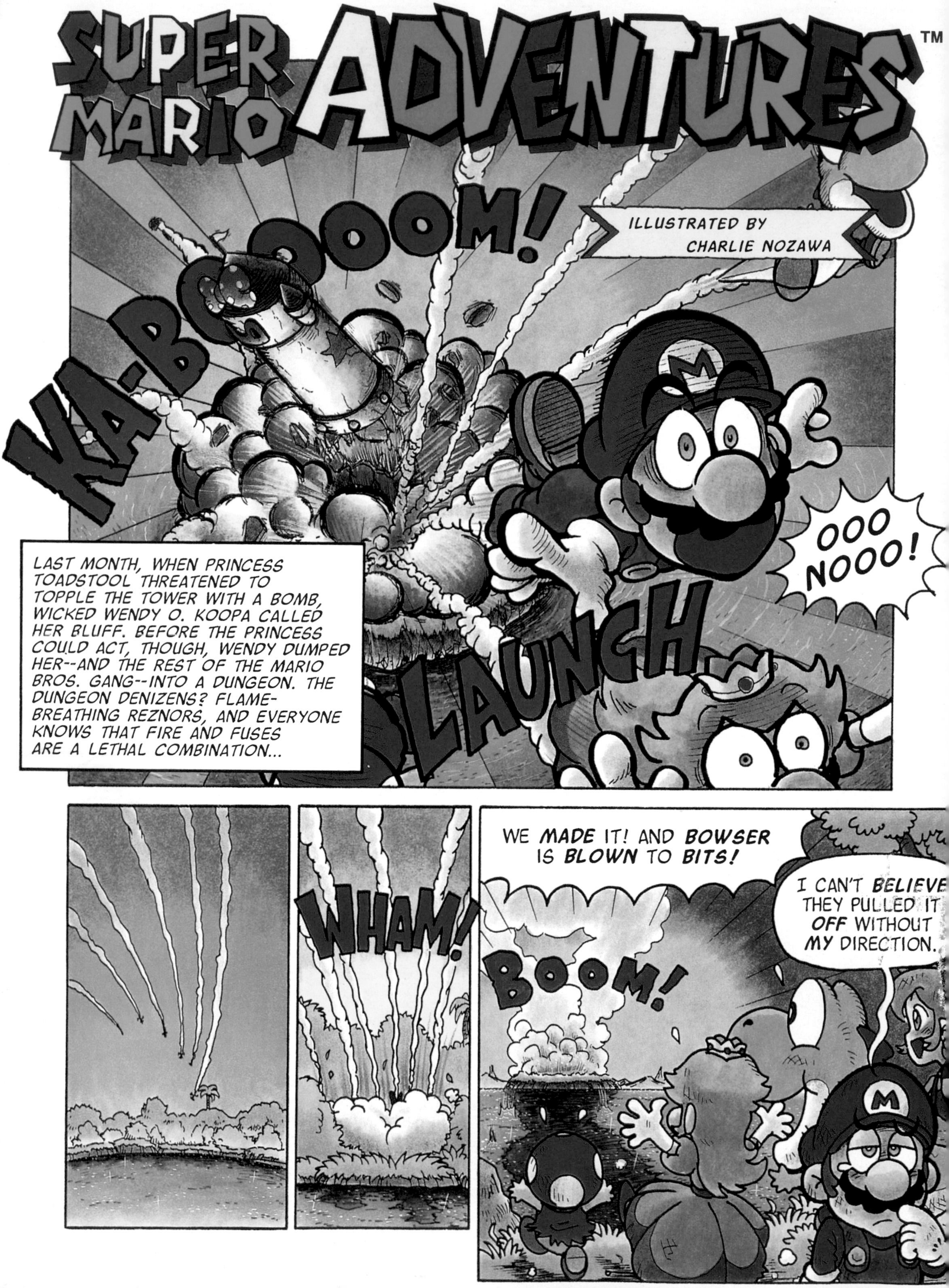
SUPER MARIO ADVENTURES™
ILLUSTRATED BY CHARLIE NOZAWA
KA-BOOOOOM!
LAST MONTH, WHEN PRINCESS TOADSTOOL THREATENED TO TOPPLE THE TOWER WITH A BOMB, WICKED WENDY O. KOOPA CALLED HER BLUFF. BEFORE THE PRINCESS COULD ACT, THOUGH, WENDY DUMPED HER--AND THE REST OF THE MARIO BROS. GANG--INTO A DUNGEON. THE DUNGEON DENIZENS? FLAME-BREATHING REZNORS, AND EVERYONE KNOWS THAT FIRE AND FUSES ARE A LETHAL COMBINATION...
OOO NOOO!
LAUNCH
WHAM!
WE MADE IT! AND BOWSER IS BLOWN TO BITS!
BOOM!
I CAN'T BELIEVE THEY PULLED IT OFF WITHOUT MY DIRECTION.

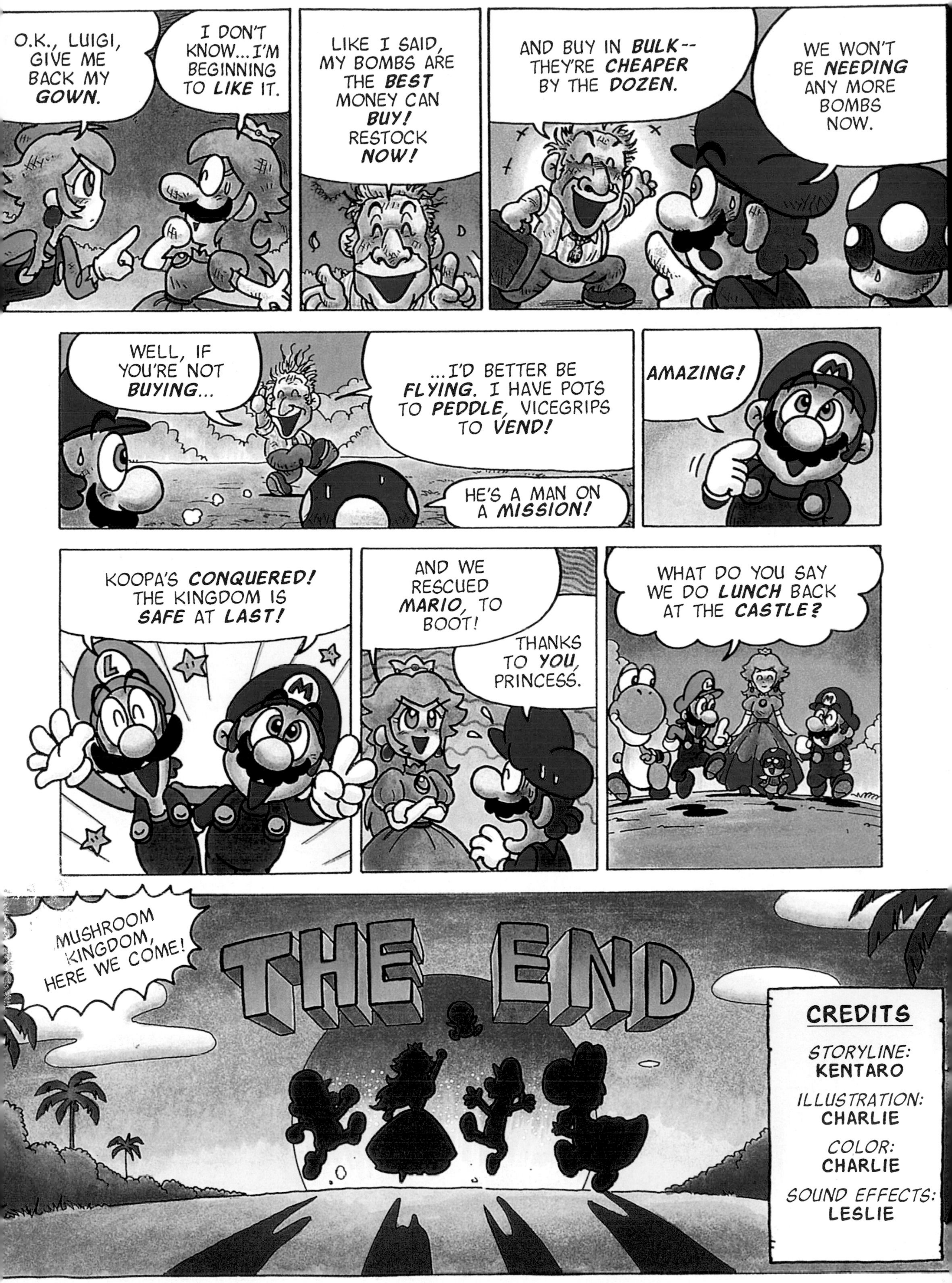

O.K., LUIGI, GIVE ME BACK MY GOWN.
I DON'T KNOW...I'M BEGINNING TO LIKE IT.
LIKE I SAID, MY BOMBS ARE THE BEST MONEY CAN BUY! RESTOCK NOW!
AND BUY IN BULK-- THEY'RE CHEAPER BY THE DOZEN.
WE WON'T BE NEEDING ANY MORE BOMBS NOW.
WELL, IF YOU'RE NOT BUYING...
...I'D BETTER BE FLYING. I HAVE POTS TO PEDDLE, VICEGRIPS TO VEND!
HE'S A MAN ON A MISSION!
AMAZING!
KOOPA'S CONQUERED! THE KINGDOM IS SAFE AT LAST!
AND WE RESCUED MARIO, TO BOOT!
THANKS TO YOU, PRINCESS.
WHAT DO YOU SAY WE DO LUNCH BACK AT THE CASTLE?
MUSHROOM KINGDOM, HERE WE COME!
THE END
CREDITS
STORYLINE: KENTARO
ILLUSTRATION: CHARLIE
COLOR: CHARLIE
SOUND EFFECTS: LESLIE

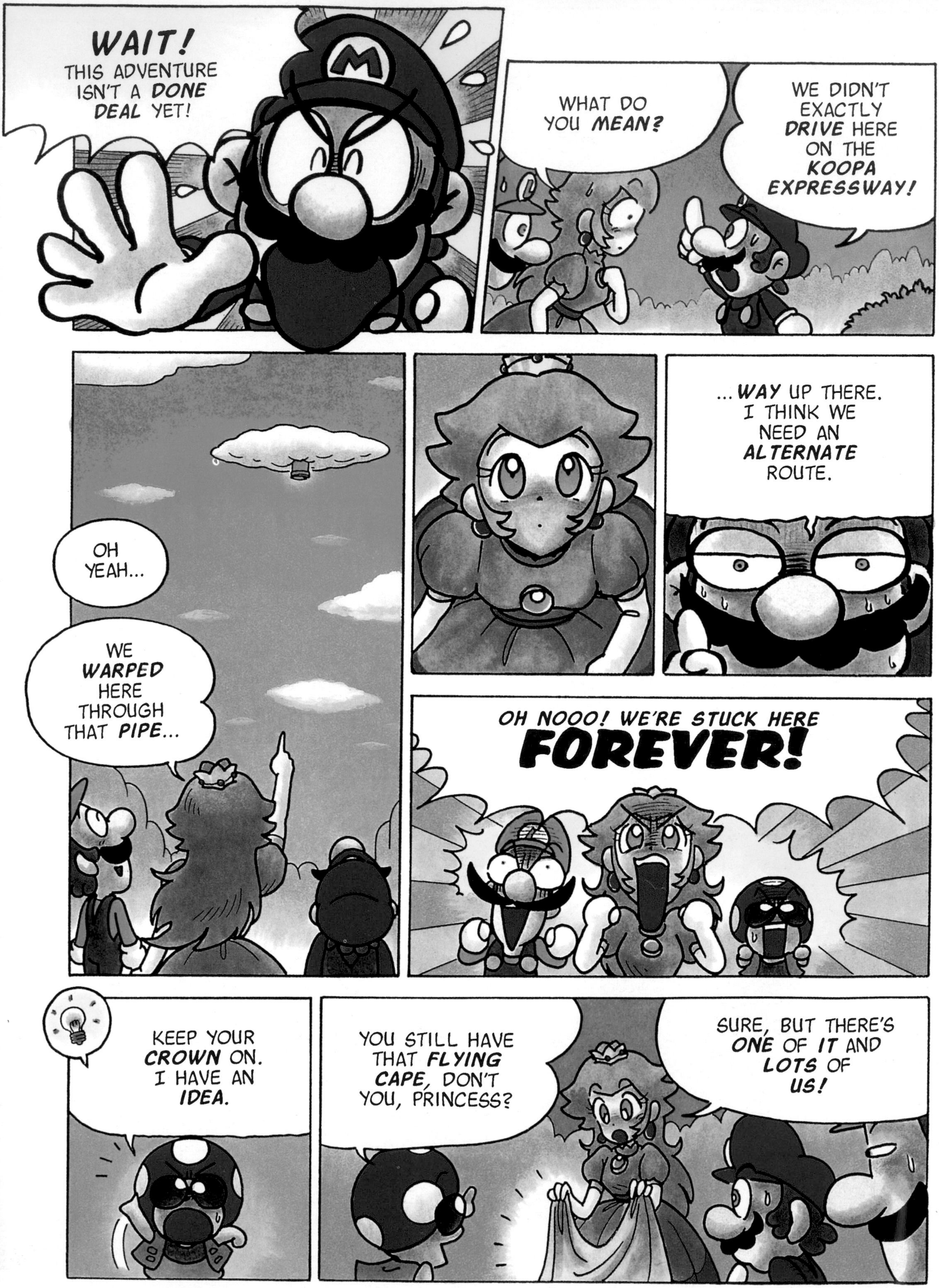

WAIT! THIS ADVENTURE ISN'T A DONE DEAL YET!
WHAT DO YOU MEAN?
WE DIDN'T EXACTLY DRIVE HERE ON THE KOOPA EXPRESSWAY!
OH YEAH...
WE WARPED HERE THROUGH THAT PIPE...
...WAY UP THERE. I THINK WE NEED AN ALTERNATE ROUTE.
OH NOOO! WE'RE STUCK HERE FOREVER!
KEEP YOUR CROWN ON. I HAVE AN IDEA.
YOU STILL HAVE THAT FLYING CAPE, DON'T YOU, PRINCESS?
SURE, BUT THERE'S ONE OF IT AND LOTS OF US!

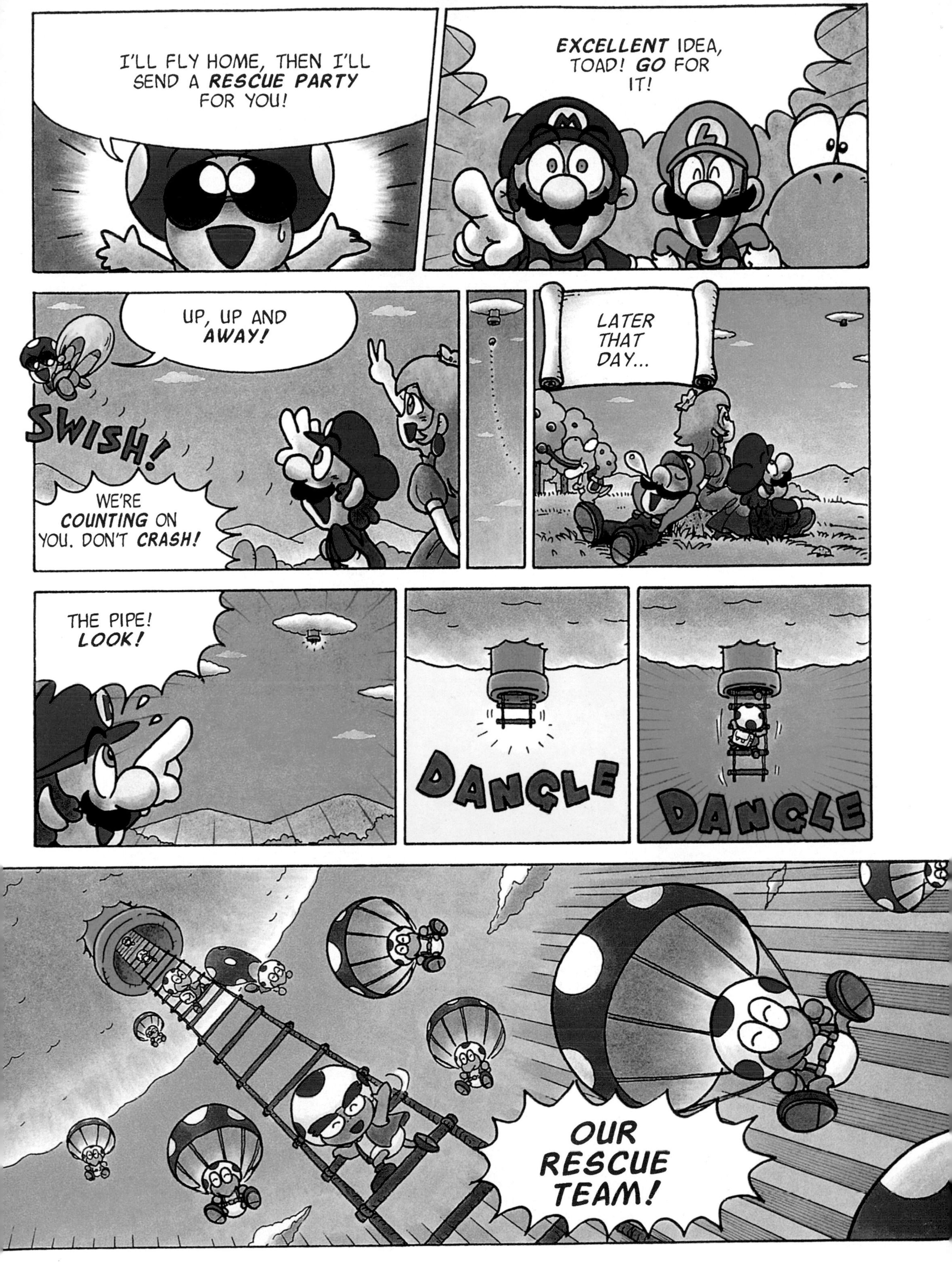
I'LL FLY HOME, THEN I'LL SEND A RESCUE PARTY FOR YOU!
EXCELLENT IDEA, TOAD! GO FOR IT!
UP, UP AND AWAY!
SWISH!
WE'RE COUNTING ON YOU. DON'T CRASH!
LATER THAT DAY...
THE PIPE! LOOK!
DANGLE
DANGLE
OUR RESCUE TEAM!

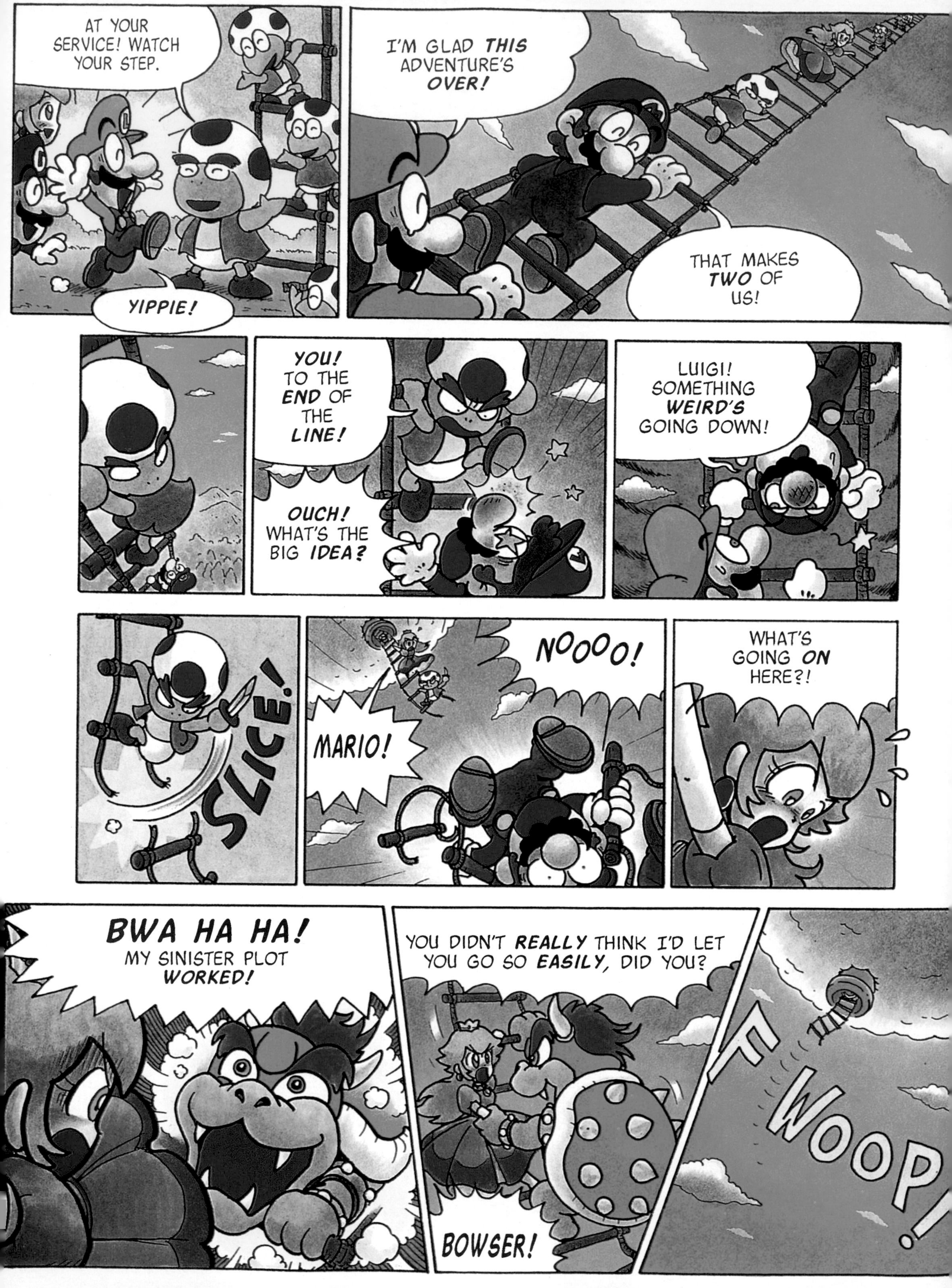
AT YOUR SERVICE! WATCH YOUR STEP.
YIPPIE!
I'M GLAD THIS ADVENTURE'S OVER!
THAT MAKES TWO OF US!
YOU! TO THE END OF THE LINE!
OUCH! WHAT'S THE BIG IDEA?
LUIGI! SOMETHING WEIRD'S GOING DOWN!
SLICE!
NOOOO!
MARIO!
WHAT'S GOING ON HERE?!
BWA HA HA! MY SINISTER PLOT WORKED!
YOU DIDN'T REALLY THINK I'D LET YOU GO SO EASILY, DID YOU?
BOWSER!
FWOOP!

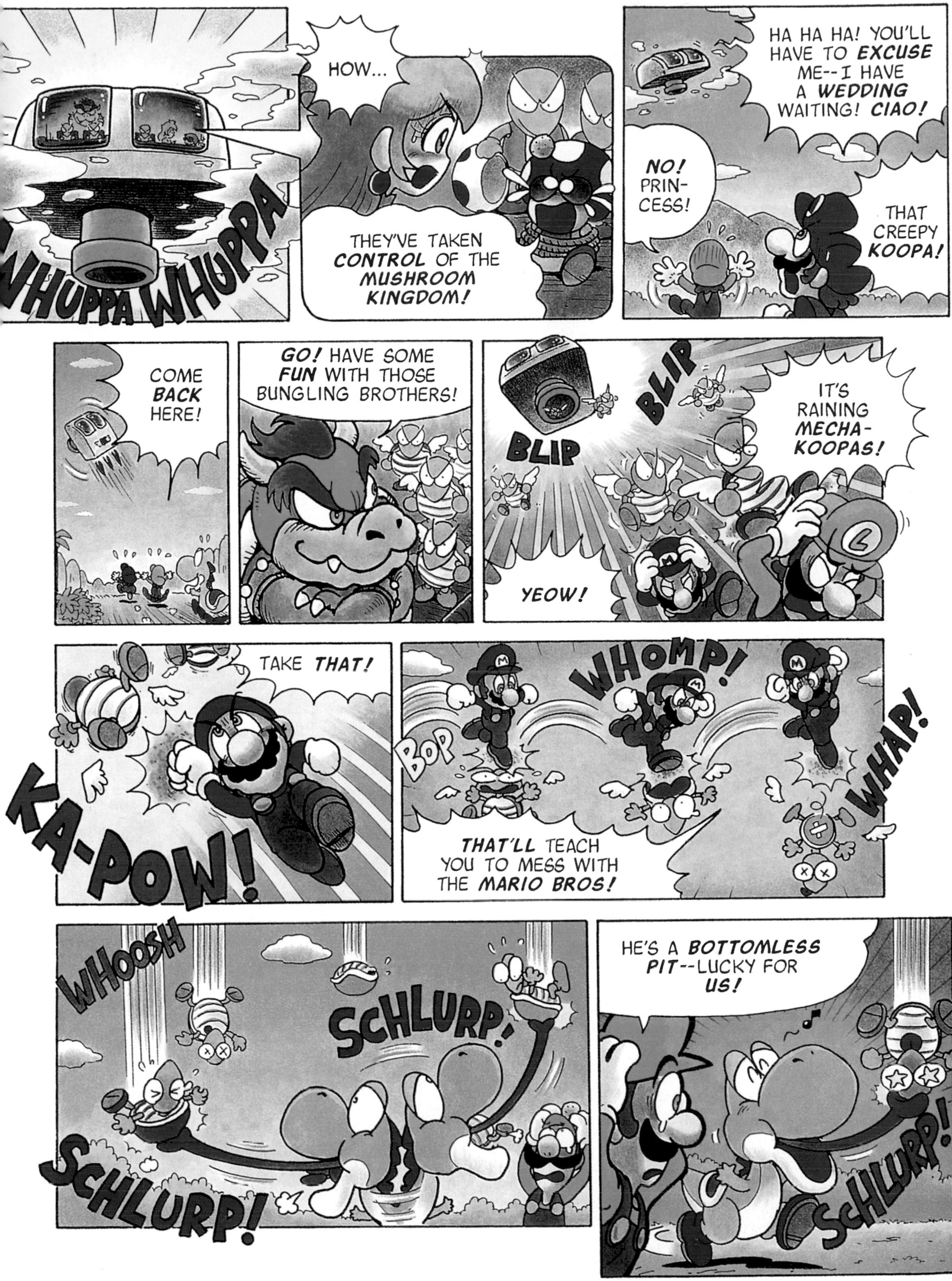
WHUPPA WHUPPA
HOW...
THEY'VE TAKEN CONTROL OF THE MUSHROOM KINGDOM!
HA HA HA! YOU'LL HAVE TO EXCUSE ME--I HAVE A WEDDING WAITING! CIAO!
NO! PRINCESS!
THAT CREEPY KOOPA!
COME BACK HERE!
GO! HAVE SOME FUN WITH THOSE BUNGLING BROTHERS!
BLIP
BLIP
IT'S RAINING MECHA-KOOPAS!
YEOW!
TAKE THAT!
KA-POW!
BOP
WHOMP!
WHAP!
THAT'LL TEACH YOU TO MESS WITH THE MARIO BROS!
WHOOSH
SCHLURP!
SCHLURP!
HE'S A BOTTOMLESS PIT--LUCKY FOR US!
SCHLURP!

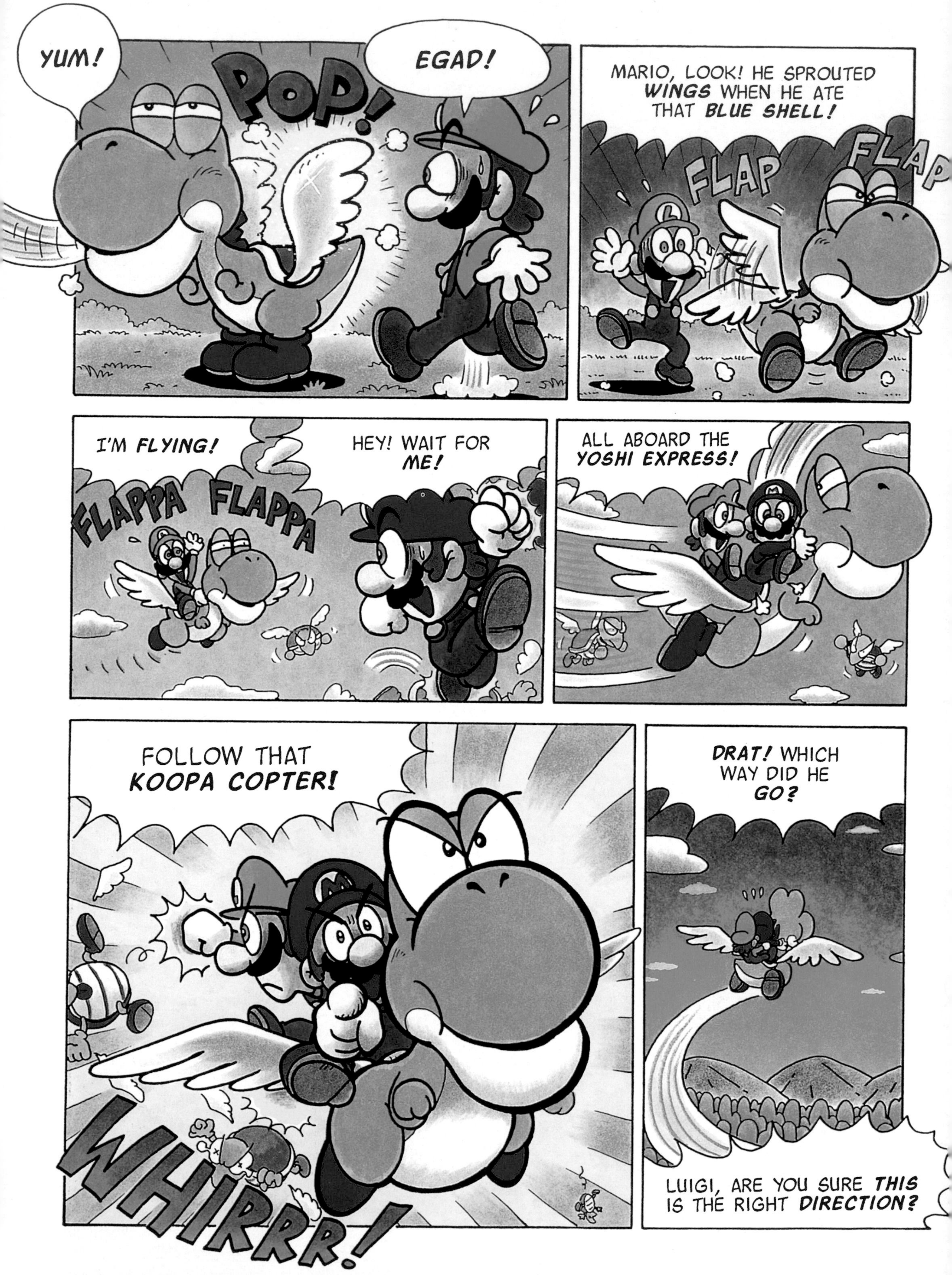
YUM!
POP!
EGAD!
MARIO, LOOK! HE SPROUTED WINGS WHEN HE ATE THAT BLUE SHELL!
FLAP
FLAP
I'M FLYING!
FLAPPA FLAPPA
HEY! WAIT FOR ME!
ALL ABOARD THE YOSHI EXPRESS!
FOLLOW THAT KOOPA COPTER!
WHIRRR!
DRAT! WHICH WAY DID HE GO?
LUIGI, ARE YOU SURE THIS IS THE RIGHT DIRECTION?

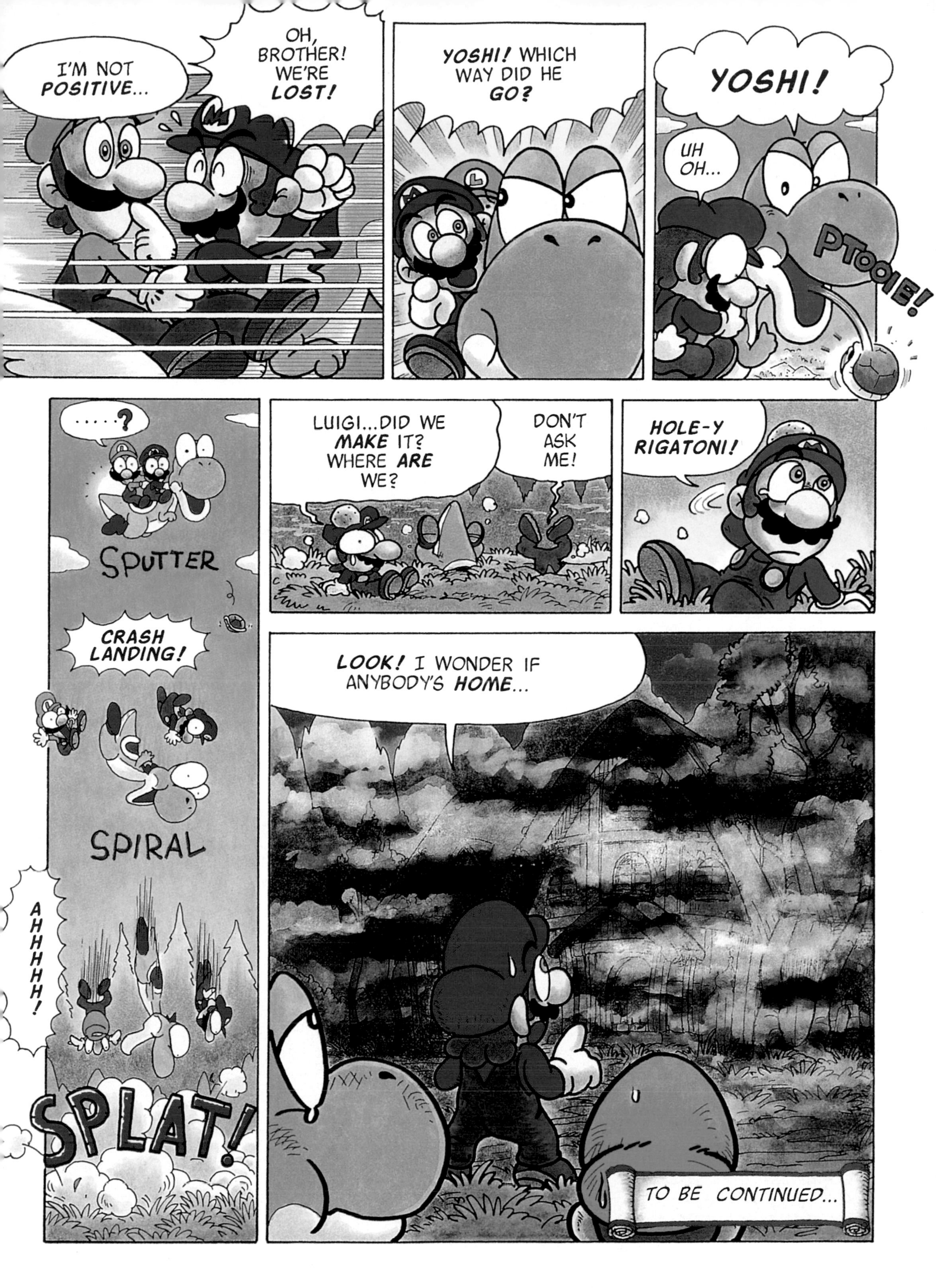

I'M NOT POSITIVE...
OH, BROTHER! WE'RE LOST!
YOSHI! WHICH WAY DID HE GO?
YOSHI!
UH OH...
PTOOIE!
.....?
SPUTTER
CRASH LANDING!
SPIRAL
AHHHHHH!
SPLAT!
LUIGI...DID WE MAKE IT? WHERE ARE WE?
DON'T ASK ME!
HOLE-Y RIGATONI!
LOOK! I WONDER IF ANYBODY'S HOME...
TO BE CONTINUED...

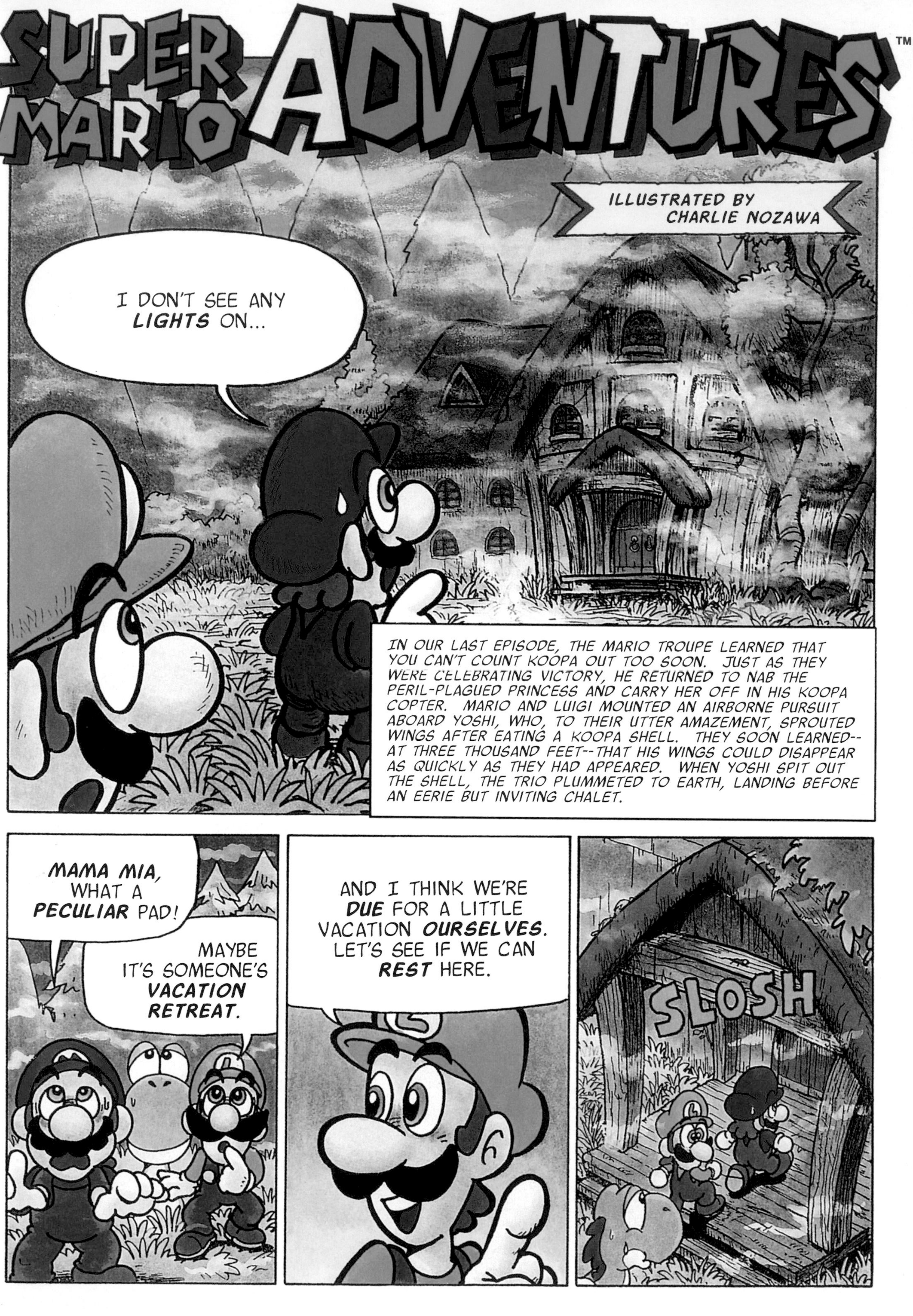

SUPER MARIO ADVENTURES™
ILLUSTRATED BY CHARLIE NOZAWA
I DON'T SEE ANY ***LIGHTS*** ON...
IN OUR LAST EPISODE, THE MARIO TROUPE LEARNED THAT YOU CAN'T COUNT KOOPA OUT TOO SOON. JUST AS THEY WERE CELEBRATING VICTORY, HE RETURNED TO NAB THE PERIL-PLAGUED PRINCESS AND CARRY HER OFF IN HIS KOOPA COPTER. MARIO AND LUIGI MOUNTED AN AIRBORNE PURSUIT ABOARD YOSHI, WHO, TO THEIR UTTER AMAZEMENT, SPROUTED WINGS AFTER EATING A KOOPA SHELL. THEY SOON LEARNED--AT THREE THOUSAND FEET--THAT HIS WINGS COULD DISAPPEAR AS QUICKLY AS THEY HAD APPEARED. WHEN YOSHI SPIT OUT THE SHELL, THE TRIO PLUMMETED TO EARTH, LANDING BEFORE AN EERIE BUT INVITING CHALET.
MAMA MIA, WHAT A ***PECULIAR*** PAD!
MAYBE IT'S SOMEONE'S ***VACATION RETREAT.***
AND I THINK WE'RE ***DUE*** FOR A LITTLE VACATION ***OURSELVES.*** LET'S SEE IF WE CAN ***REST*** HERE.
SLOSH

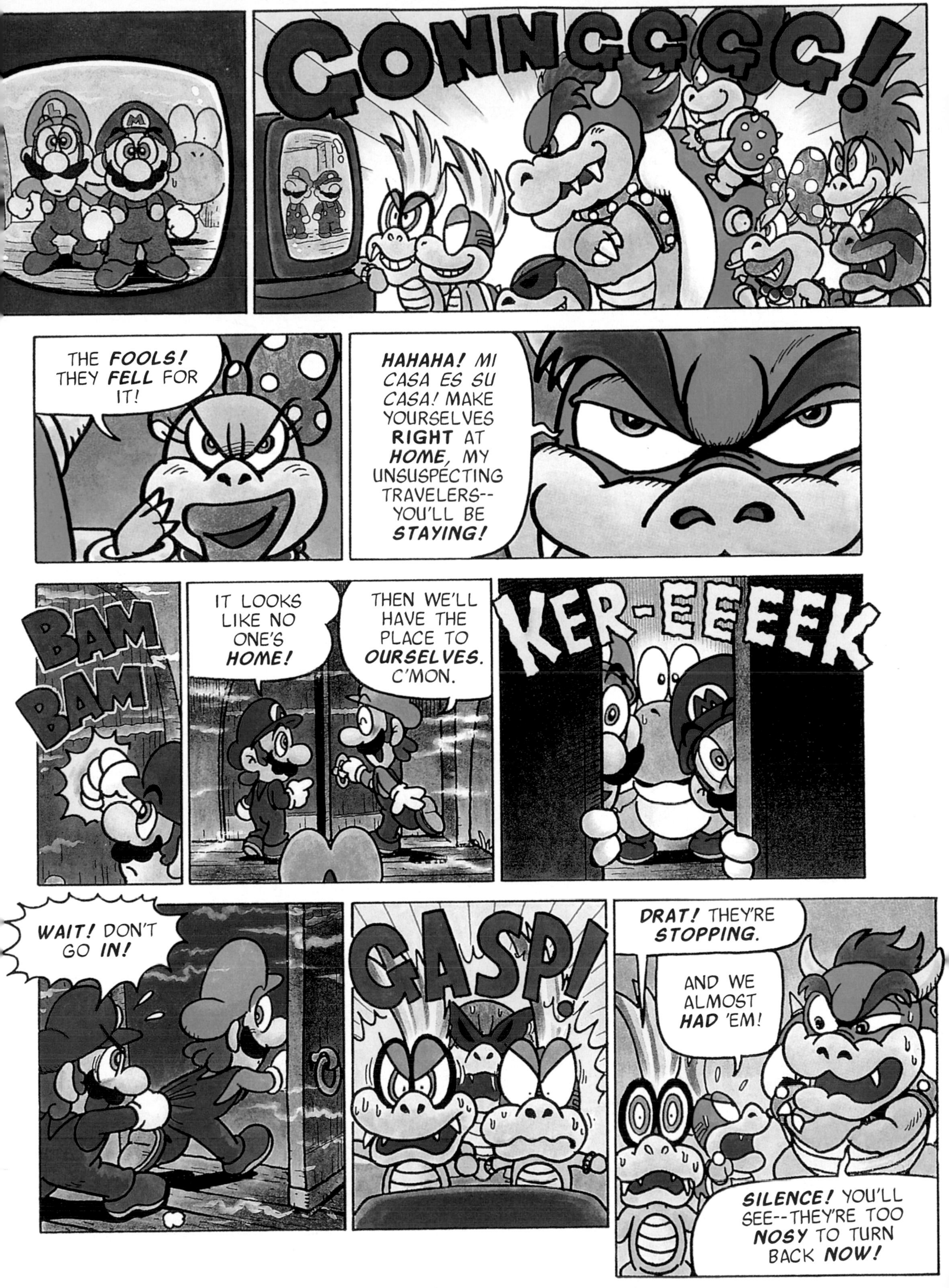
GONNGGGG!
THE FOOLS! THEY FELL FOR IT!
HAHAHA! MI CASA ES SU CASA! MAKE YOURSELVES RIGHT AT HOME, MY UNSUSPECTING TRAVELERS-- YOU'LL BE STAYING!
BAM BAM
IT LOOKS LIKE NO ONE'S HOME!
THEN WE'LL HAVE THE PLACE TO OURSELVES. C'MON.
KER-EEEEK
WAIT! DON'T GO IN!
GASP!
DRAT! THEY'RE STOPPING.
AND WE ALMOST HAD 'EM!
SILENCE! YOU'LL SEE--THEY'RE TOO NOSY TO TURN BACK NOW!

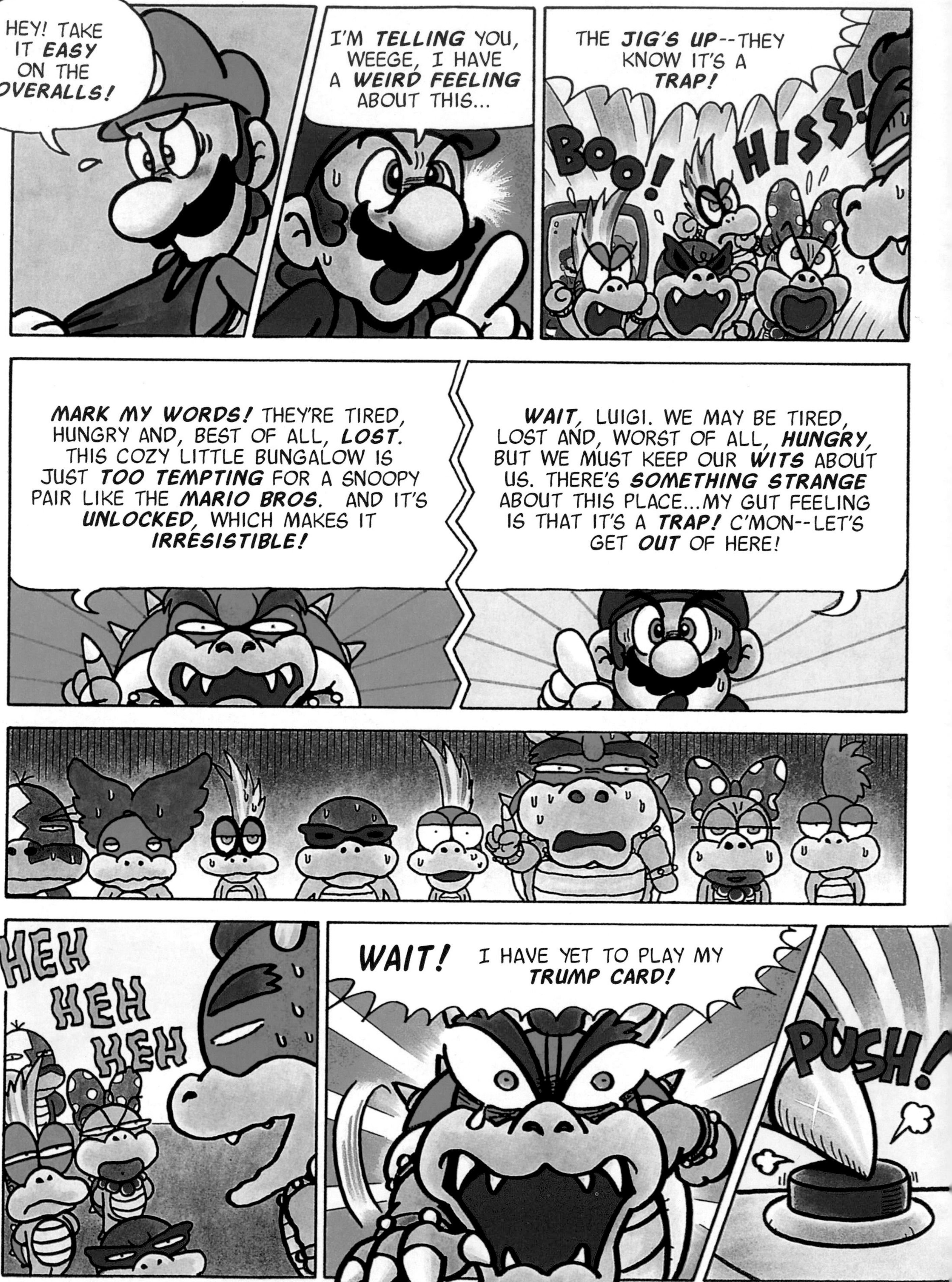
HEY! TAKE IT EASY ON THE OVERALLS!
I'M TELLING YOU, WEEGE, I HAVE A WEIRD FEELING ABOUT THIS...
THE JIG'S UP--THEY KNOW IT'S A TRAP!
BOO!
HISS!
MARK MY WORDS! THEY'RE TIRED, HUNGRY AND, BEST OF ALL, LOST. THIS COZY LITTLE BUNGALOW IS JUST TOO TEMPTING FOR A SNOOPY PAIR LIKE THE MARIO BROS. AND IT'S UNLOCKED, WHICH MAKES IT IRRESISTIBLE!
WAIT, LUIGI. WE MAY BE TIRED, LOST AND, WORST OF ALL, HUNGRY, BUT WE MUST KEEP OUR WITS ABOUT US. THERE'S SOMETHING STRANGE ABOUT THIS PLACE...MY GUT FEELING IS THAT IT'S A TRAP! C'MON--LET'S GET OUT OF HERE!
HEH HEH HEH
WAIT! I HAVE YET TO PLAY MY TRUMP CARD!
PUSH!

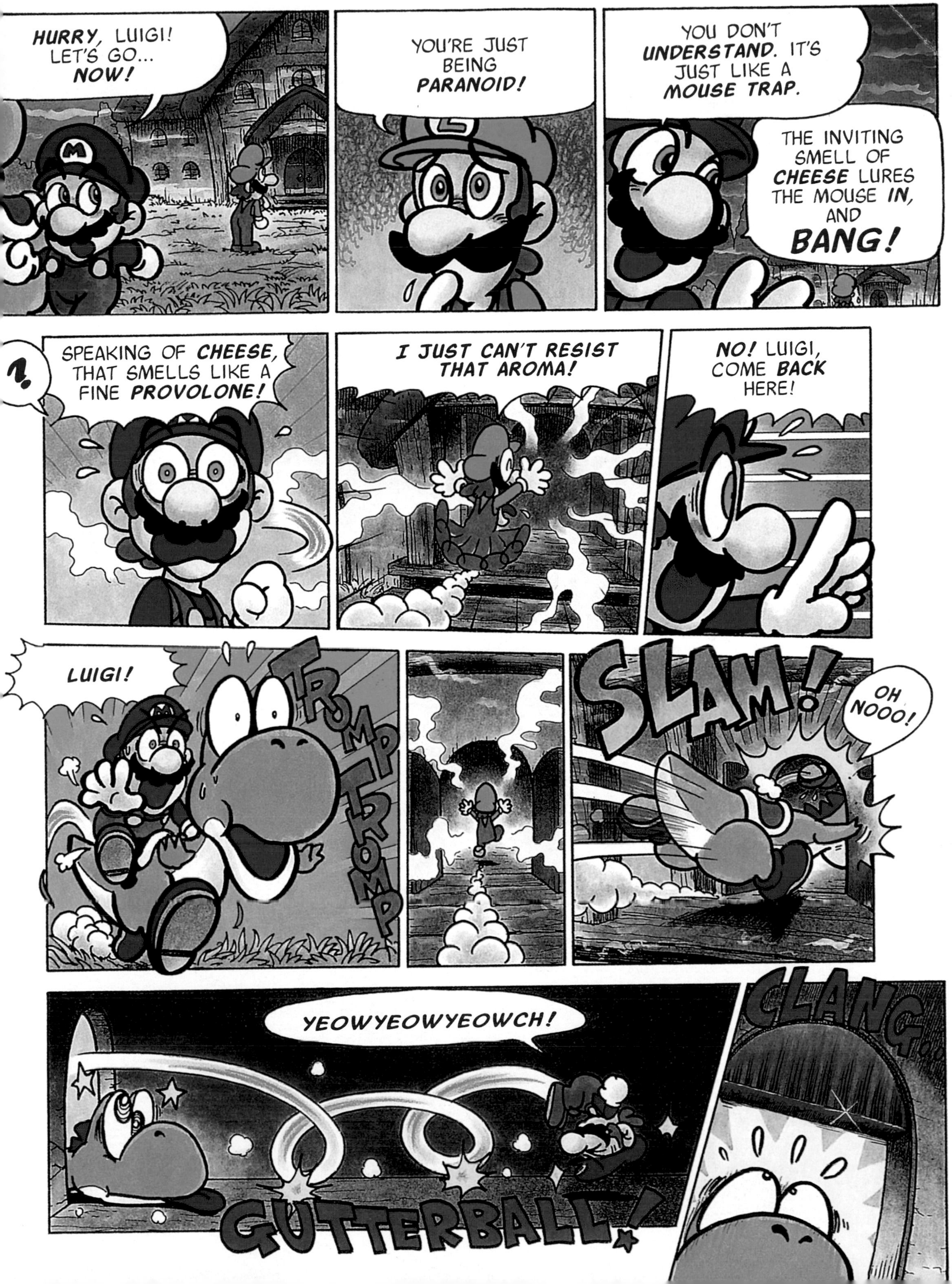
HURRY, LUIGI! LET'S GO... NOW!
YOU'RE JUST BEING PARANOID!
YOU DON'T UNDERSTAND. IT'S JUST LIKE A MOUSE TRAP.
THE INVITING SMELL OF CHEESE LURES THE MOUSE IN, AND BANG!
SPEAKING OF CHEESE, THAT SMELLS LIKE A FINE PROVOLONE!
I JUST CAN'T RESIST THAT AROMA!
NO! LUIGI, COME BACK HERE!
LUIGI!
TROMP TROMP TROMP
SLAM!
OH NOOO!
YEOWYEOWYEOWCH!
CLANG.
GUTTERBALL!

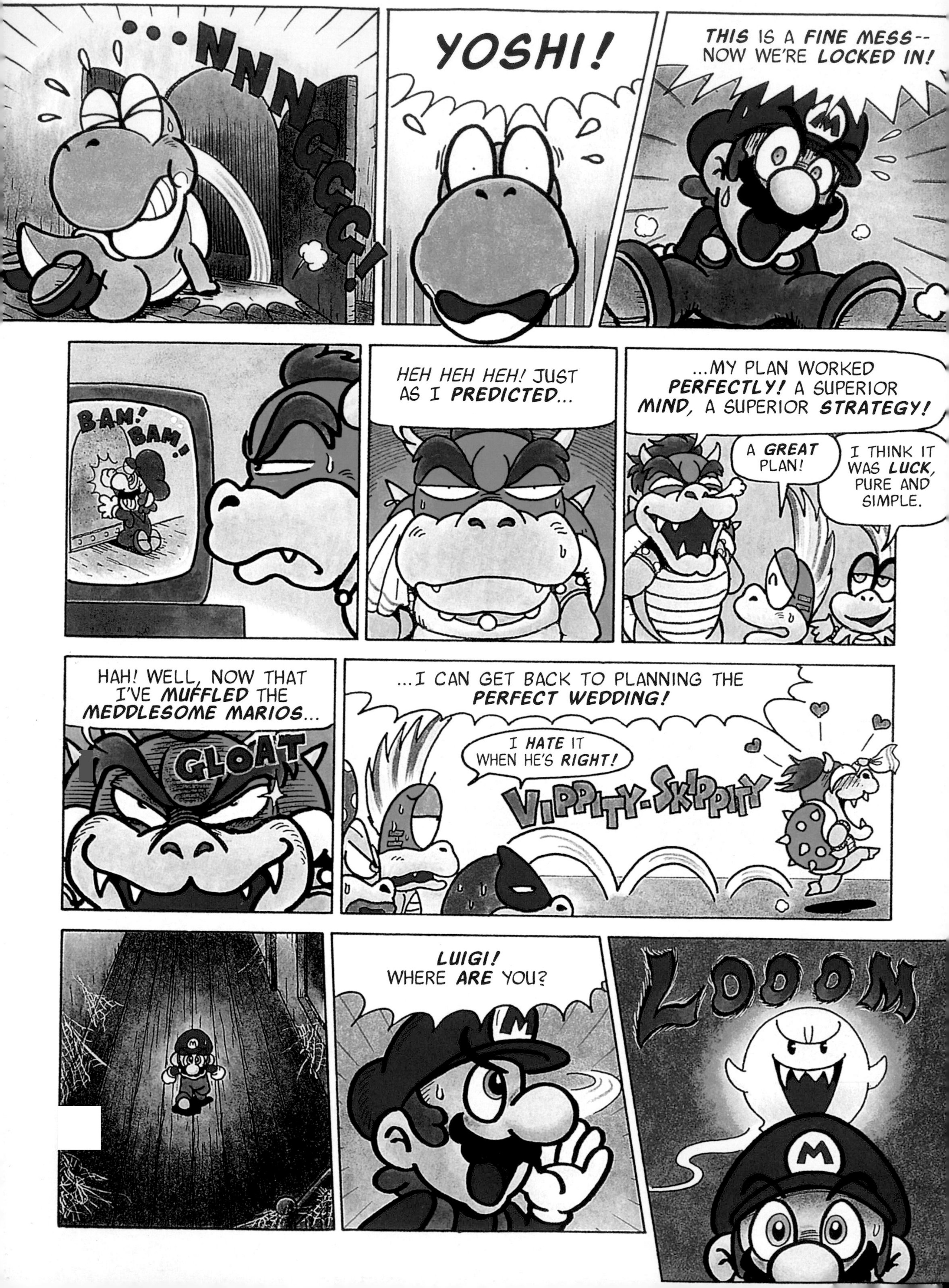
...NNNGGG!
YOSHI!
THIS IS A FINE MESS-- NOW WE'RE LOCKED IN!
BAM! BAM!
HEH HEH HEH! JUST AS I PREDICTED...
...MY PLAN WORKED PERFECTLY! A SUPERIOR MIND, A SUPERIOR STRATEGY!
A GREAT PLAN!
I THINK IT WAS LUCK, PURE AND SIMPLE.
HAH! WELL, NOW THAT I'VE MUFFLED THE MEDDLESOME MARIOS...
GLOAT
...I CAN GET BACK TO PLANNING THE PERFECT WEDDING!
I HATE IT WHEN HE'S RIGHT!
VIPPITY-SKIPPITY
LUIGI! WHERE ARE YOU?
LOOOM

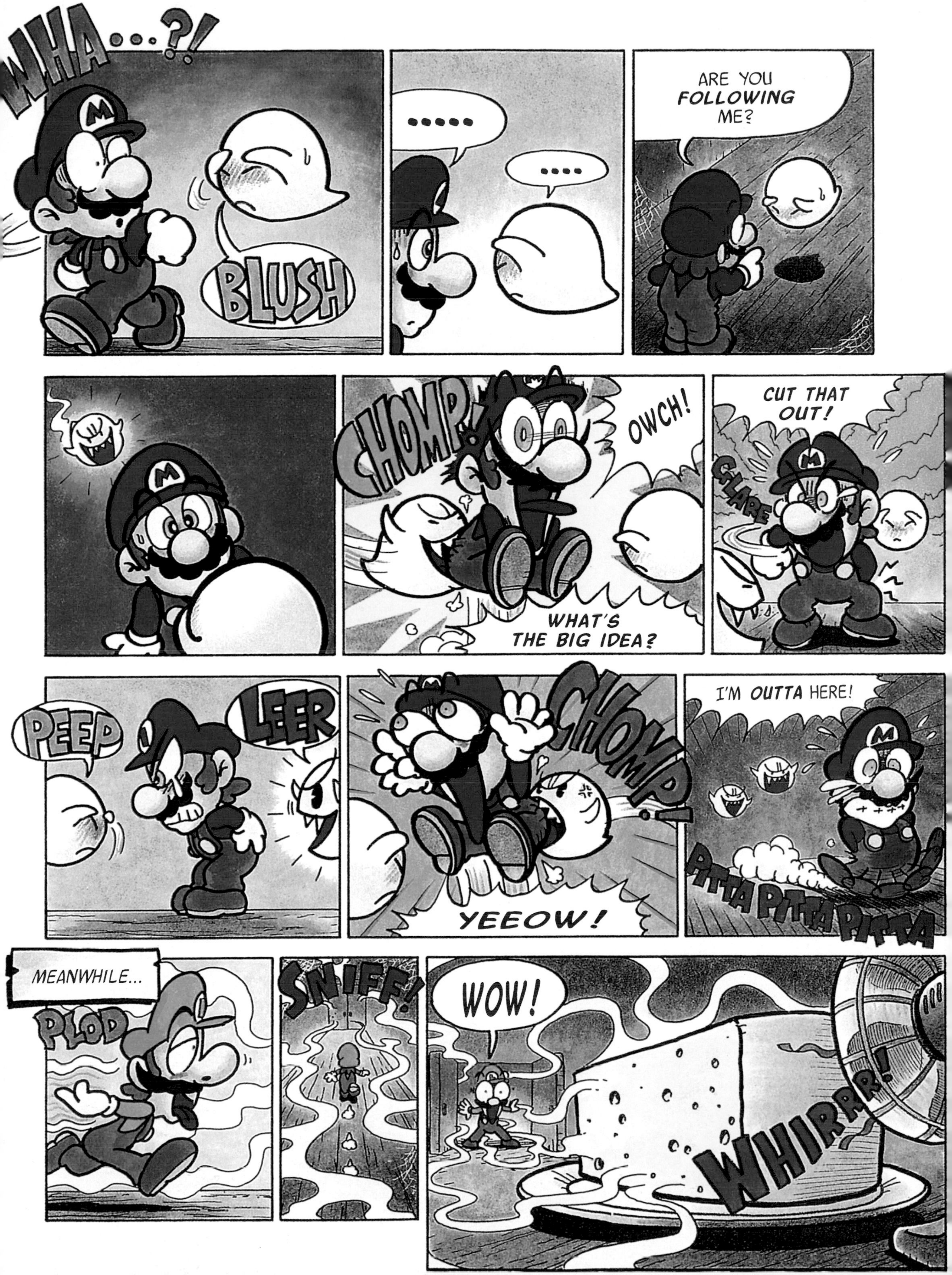
WHA...?!
BLUSH
.....
....
ARE YOU FOLLOWING ME?
CHOMP!
OWCH!
WHAT'S THE BIG IDEA?
CUT THAT OUT!
GLARE
PEEP
LEER
CHOMP!
YEEOW!
I'M OUTTA HERE!
PITTA PITTA PITTA PITTA
MEANWHILE...
PLOD
SNIFF!
WOW!
WHIRRR!

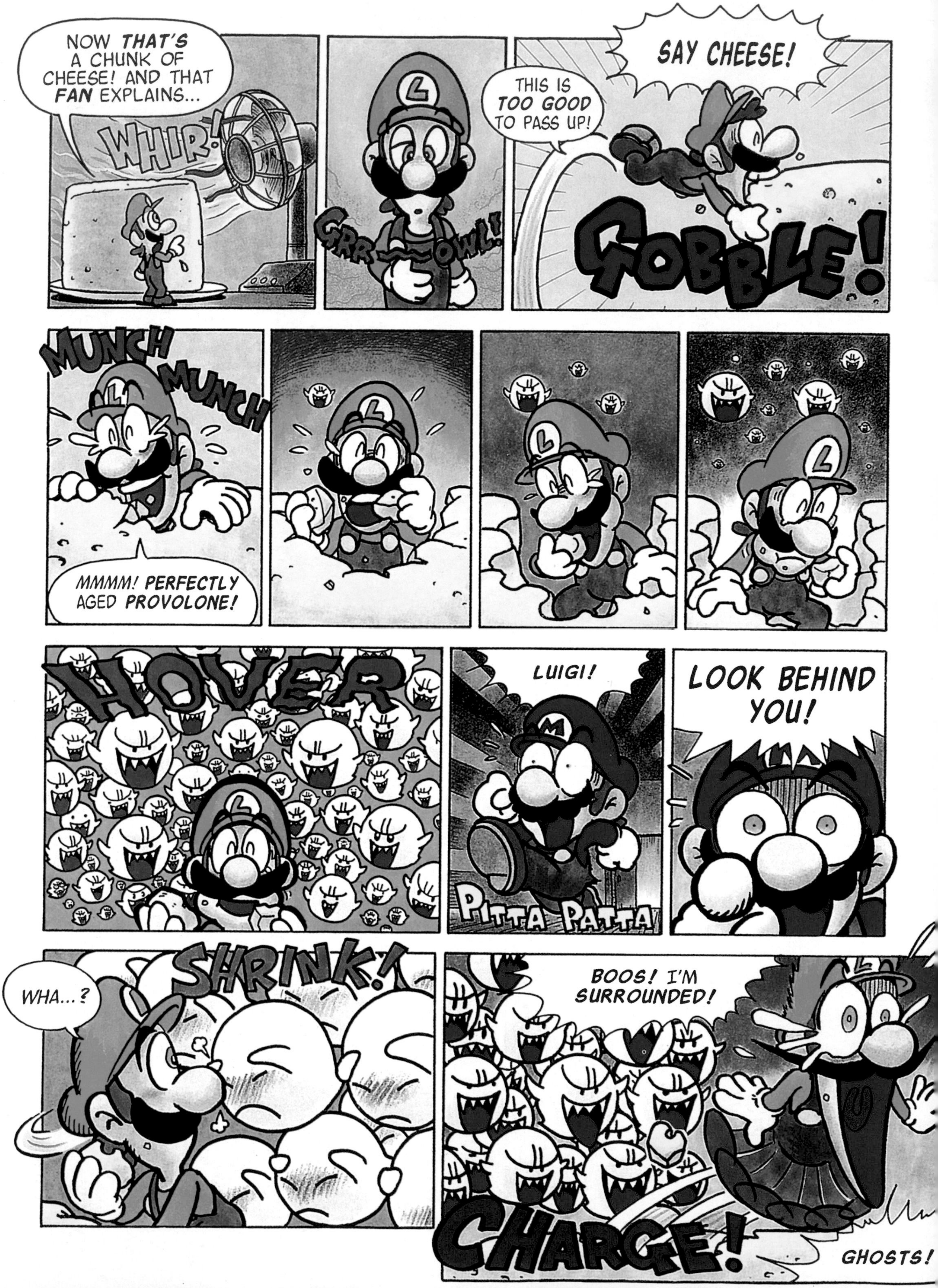
NOW THAT'S A CHUNK OF CHEESE! AND THAT FAN EXPLAINS...
WHIR!
GRR~~OWL!
THIS IS TOO GOOD TO PASS UP!
SAY CHEESE!
GOBBLE!
MUNCH MUNCH
MMMM! PERFECTLY AGED PROVOLONE!
HOVER
LUIGI!
PITTA PATTA
LOOK BEHIND YOU!
WHA...?
SHRINK!
BOOS! I'M SURROUNDED!
CHARGE!
GHOSTS!

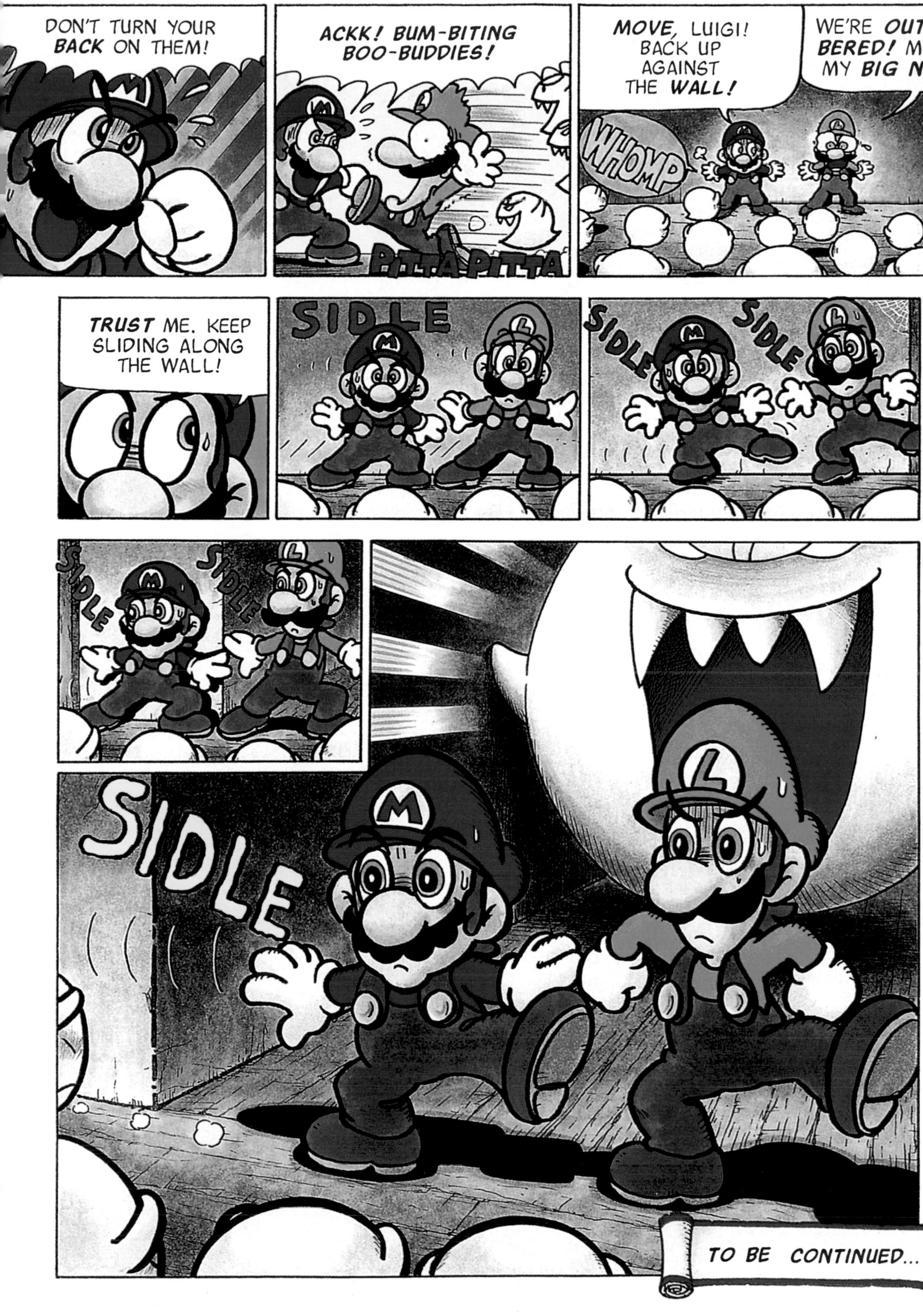
DON'T TURN YOUR BACK ON THEM!
ACKK! BUM-BITING BOO-BUDDIES!
PITTA PITTA
MOVE, LUIGI! BACK UP AGAINST THE WALL!
WE'RE OUTNUMBERED! ME AND MY BIG NOSE!
WHOMP
TRUST ME. KEEP SLIDING ALONG THE WALL!
SIDLE
SIDLE
SIDLE
SIDLE
SIDLE
SIDLE
TO BE CONTINUED...

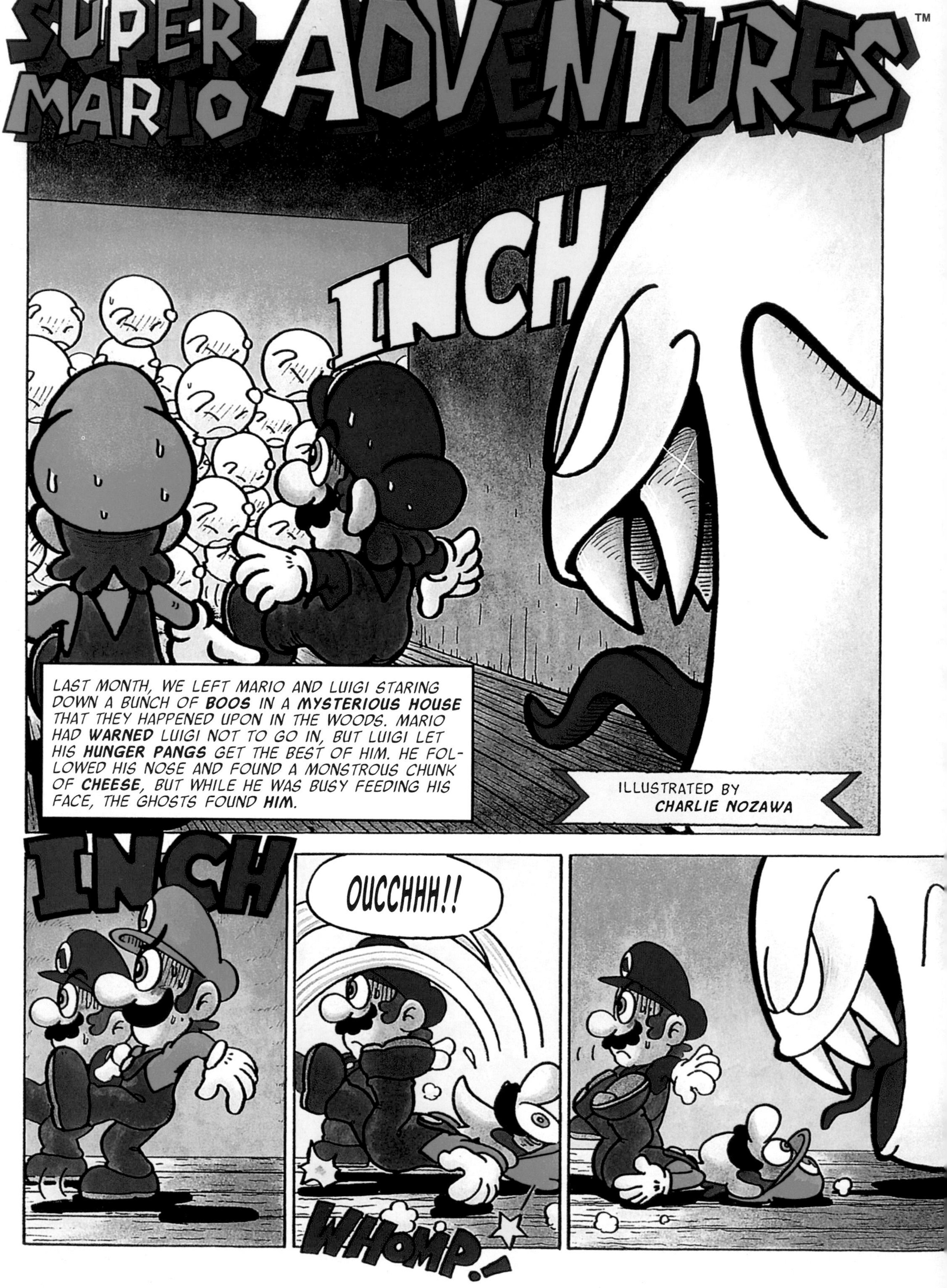

SUPER MARIO ADVENTURES™
INCH
LAST MONTH, WE LEFT MARIO AND LUIGI STARING DOWN A BUNCH OF **BOOS** IN A **MYSTERIOUS HOUSE** THAT THEY HAPPENED UPON IN THE WOODS. MARIO HAD **WARNED** LUIGI NOT TO GO IN, BUT LUIGI LET HIS **HUNGER PANGS** GET THE BEST OF HIM. HE FOLLOWED HIS NOSE AND FOUND A MONSTROUS CHUNK OF **CHEESE**, BUT WHILE HE WAS BUSY FEEDING HIS FACE, THE GHOSTS FOUND **HIM**.
ILLUSTRATED BY CHARLIE NOZAWA
INCH
OUCCHHH!!
WHOMP!

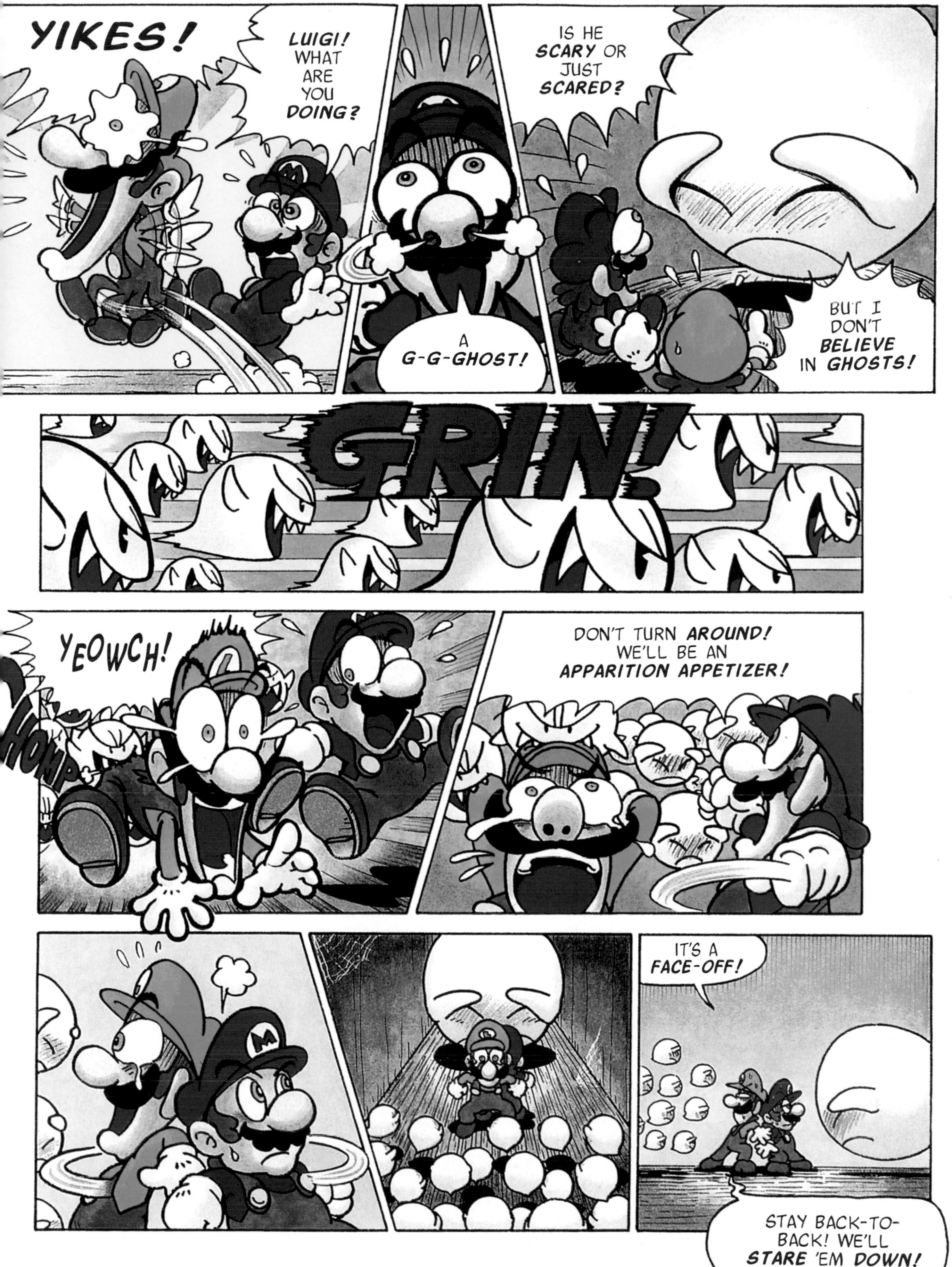
YIKES!
LUIGI! WHAT ARE YOU DOING?
A G-G-GHOST!
IS HE SCARY OR JUST SCARED?
BUT I DON'T BELIEVE IN GHOSTS!
GRIN!
YEOWCH!
CHOMP
DON'T TURN AROUND! WE'LL BE AN APPARITION APPETIZER!
IT'S A FACE-OFF!
STAY BACK-TO-BACK! WE'LL STARE 'EM DOWN!

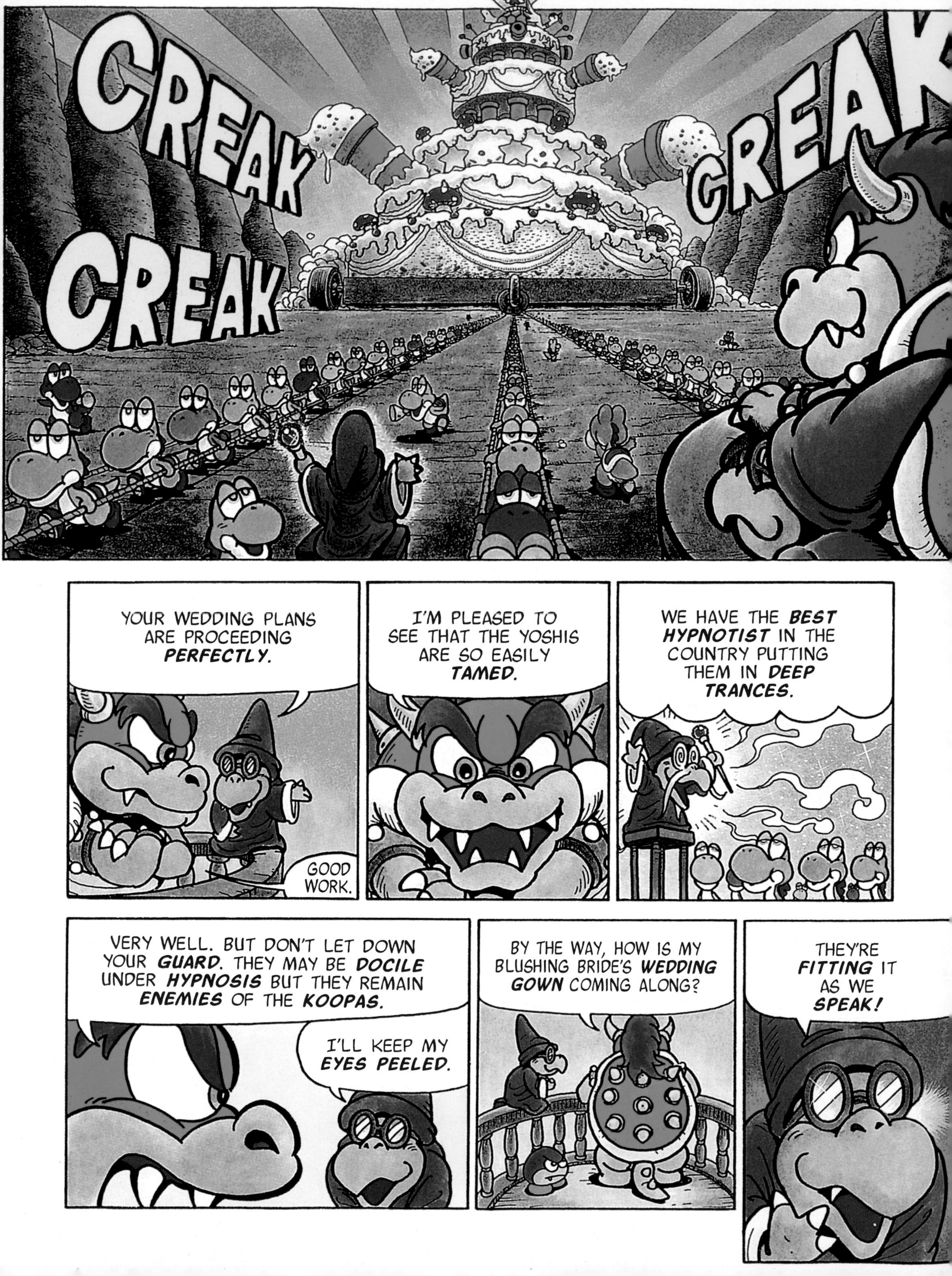
CREAK
CREAK
CREAK
YOUR WEDDING PLANS ARE PROCEEDING PERFECTLY.
GOOD WORK.
I'M PLEASED TO SEE THAT THE YOSHIS ARE SO EASILY TAMED.
WE HAVE THE BEST HYPNOTIST IN THE COUNTRY PUTTING THEM IN DEEP TRANCES.
VERY WELL. BUT DON'T LET DOWN YOUR GUARD. THEY MAY BE DOCILE UNDER HYPNOSIS BUT THEY REMAIN ENEMIES OF THE KOOPAS.
I'LL KEEP MY EYES PEELED.
BY THE WAY, HOW IS MY BLUSHING BRIDE'S WEDDING GOWN COMING ALONG?
THEY'RE FITTING IT AS WE SPEAK!

I CAN'T **WAIT** UNTIL THE WEDDING! I'M GOING TO SNEAK A **PEEK** AT THE **DRESS**!

SKIPPITY

SKIPPITY

WAIT! IT'S **BAD LUCK**!

HE'S A **BAD** ONE.

I HOPE THAT **MARRIAGE** DOESN'T **CHANGE** HIM.

HOURS LATER...

I'M GETTING **DIZZY** STARING AT ALL THESE **BLUSHING FACES**.

FOR BEING **PAINFULLY SHY**, THEY SURE ARE **PERSISTENT**.

STAGGER

SHY...BLUSHING... FEAR OF BLUSHING...

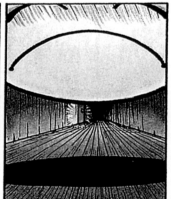

LUIGI! I HAVE A **PLAN!** FOLLOW ME INTO THAT **ROOM**!

WHAT GOOD WILL **THAT** DO?

JUST DO IT!

LET'S GO!

DASH

AIEEEE!

PITTA PITTAPITTA

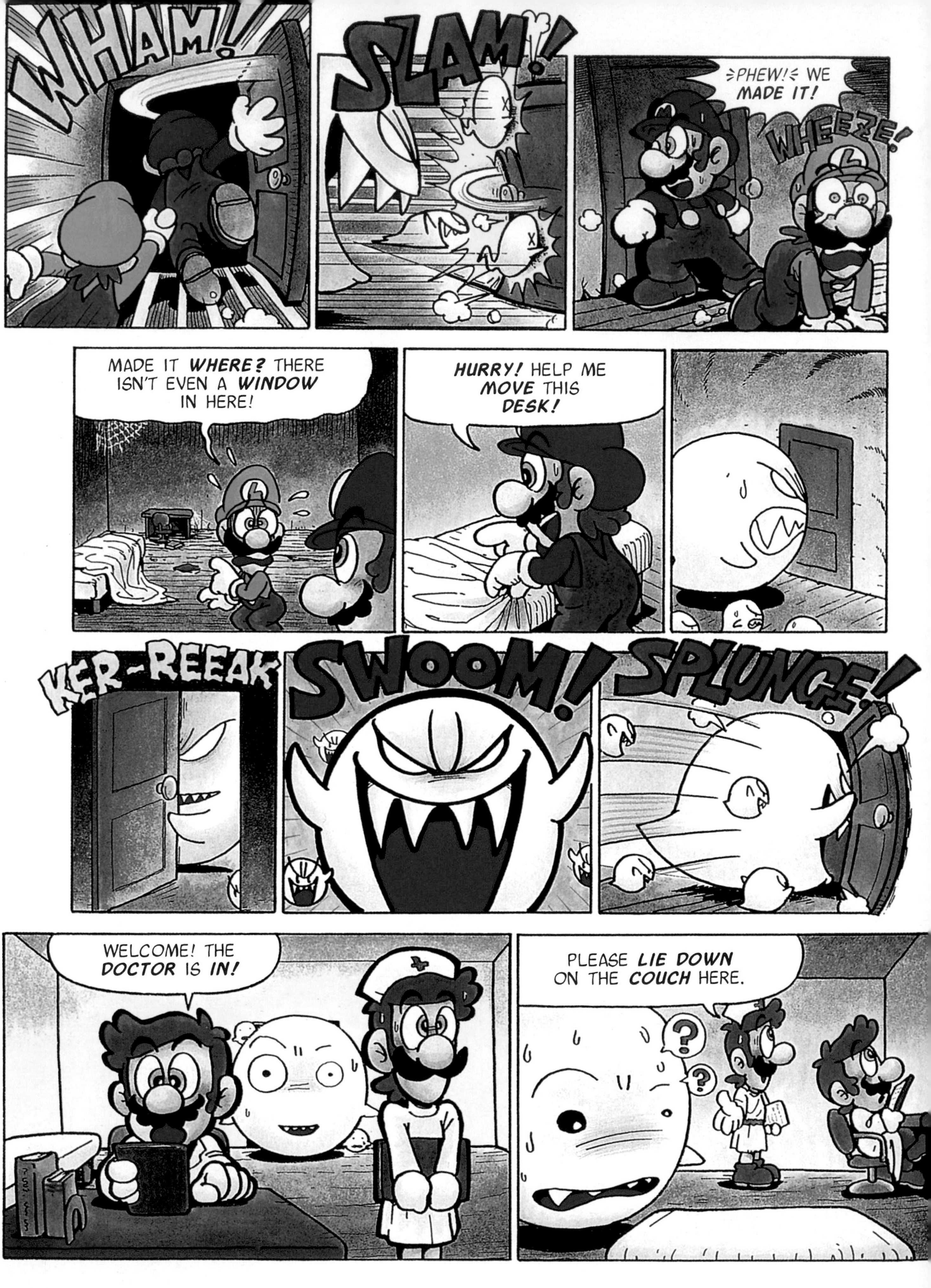
WHAM!
SLAM!!
PHEW! WE MADE IT!
WHEEZE!
MADE IT WHERE? THERE ISN'T EVEN A WINDOW IN HERE!
HURRY! HELP ME MOVE THIS DESK!
KER-REEEAK
SWOOM!
SPLUNGE!
WELCOME! THE DOCTOR IS IN!
PLEASE LIE DOWN ON THE COUCH HERE.
?
?

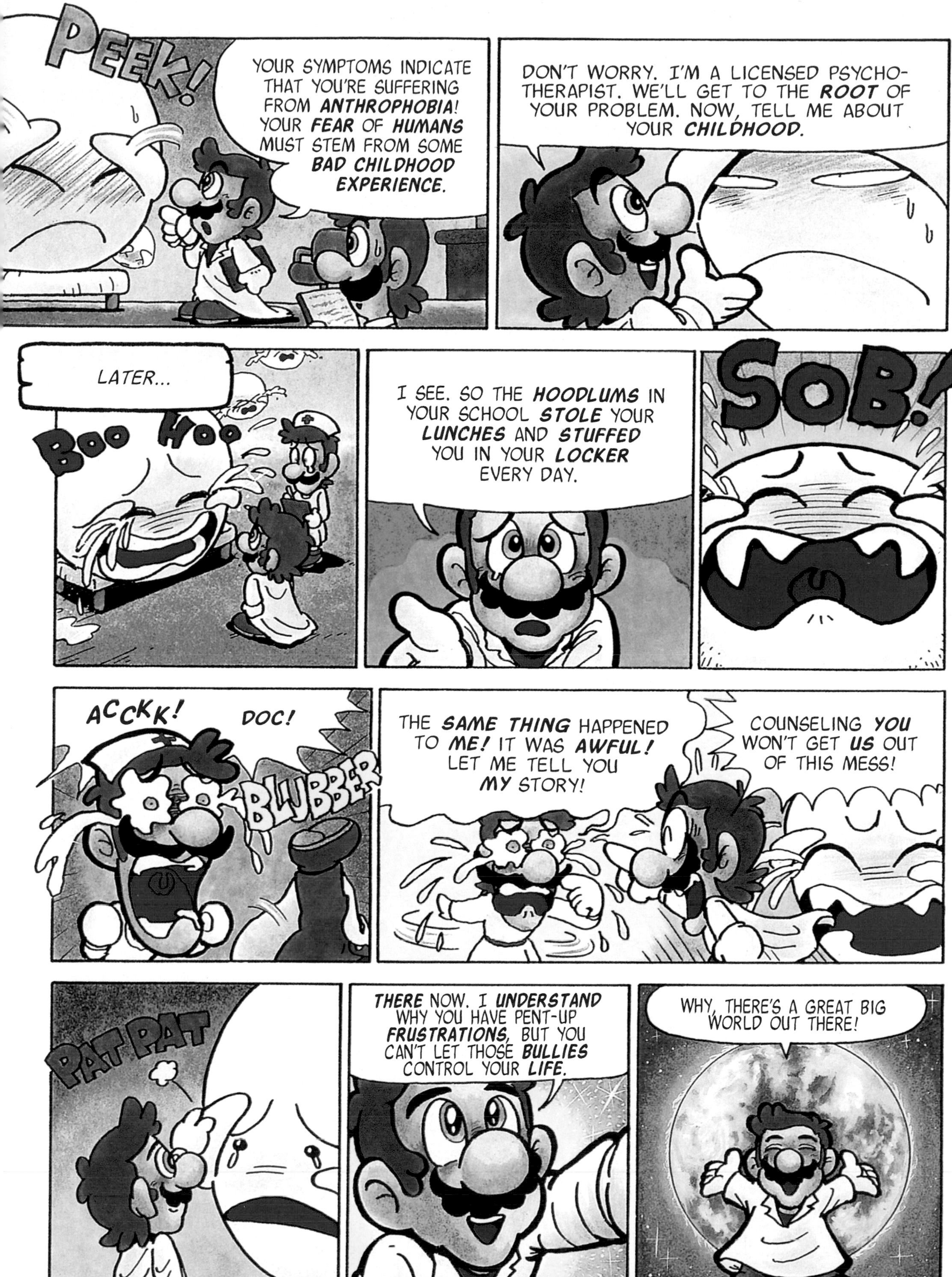
PEEK!
YOUR SYMPTOMS INDICATE THAT YOU'RE SUFFERING FROM ANTHROPHOBIA! YOUR FEAR OF HUMANS MUST STEM FROM SOME BAD CHILDHOOD EXPERIENCE.
DON'T WORRY. I'M A LICENSED PSYCHO-THERAPIST. WE'LL GET TO THE ROOT OF YOUR PROBLEM. NOW, TELL ME ABOUT YOUR CHILDHOOD.
LATER...
BOO HOO
I SEE. SO THE HOODLUMS IN YOUR SCHOOL STOLE YOUR LUNCHES AND STUFFED YOU IN YOUR LOCKER EVERY DAY.
SOB!
ACCKK!
DOC!
BLUBBER
THE SAME THING HAPPENED TO ME! IT WAS AWFUL! LET ME TELL YOU MY STORY!
COUNSELING YOU WON'T GET US OUT OF THIS MESS!
PAT PAT
THERE NOW. I UNDERSTAND WHY YOU HAVE PENT-UP FRUSTRATIONS, BUT YOU CAN'T LET THOSE BULLIES CONTROL YOUR LIFE.
WHY, THERE'S A GREAT BIG WORLD OUT THERE!

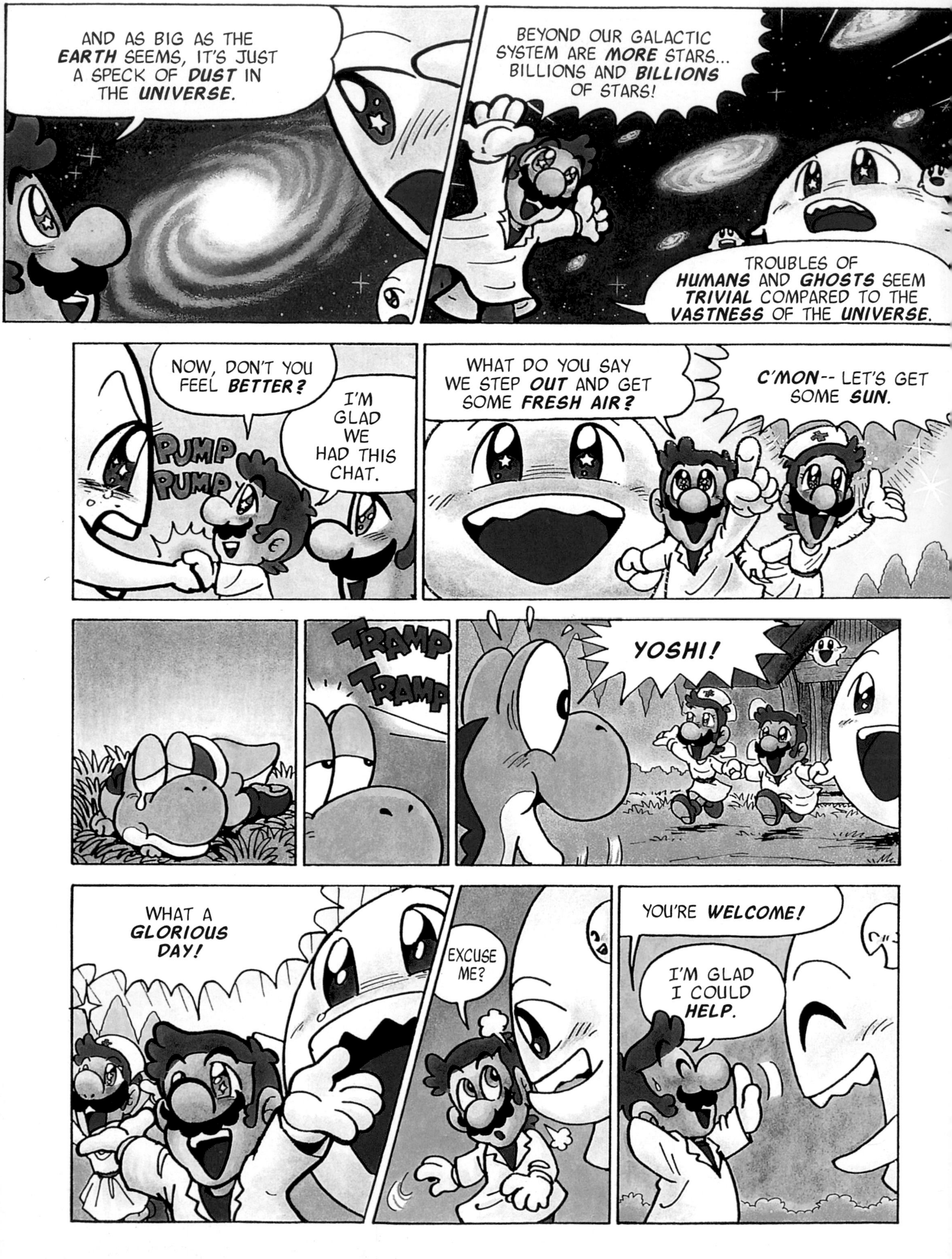
AND AS BIG AS THE ***EARTH*** SEEMS, IT'S JUST A SPECK OF ***DUST*** IN THE ***UNIVERSE***.
BEYOND OUR GALACTIC SYSTEM ARE ***MORE*** STARS... BILLIONS AND ***BILLIONS*** OF STARS!
TROUBLES OF ***HUMANS*** AND ***GHOSTS*** SEEM ***TRIVIAL*** COMPARED TO THE ***VASTNESS*** OF THE ***UNIVERSE***.
NOW, DON'T YOU FEEL ***BETTER?***
PUMP PUMP
I'M GLAD WE HAD THIS CHAT.
WHAT DO YOU SAY WE STEP ***OUT*** AND GET SOME ***FRESH AIR?***
C'MON-- LET'S GET SOME ***SUN***.
TRAMP TRAMP
YOSHI!
WHAT A ***GLORIOUS DAY!***
EXCUSE ME?
YOU'RE ***WELCOME!***
I'M GLAD I COULD ***HELP***.

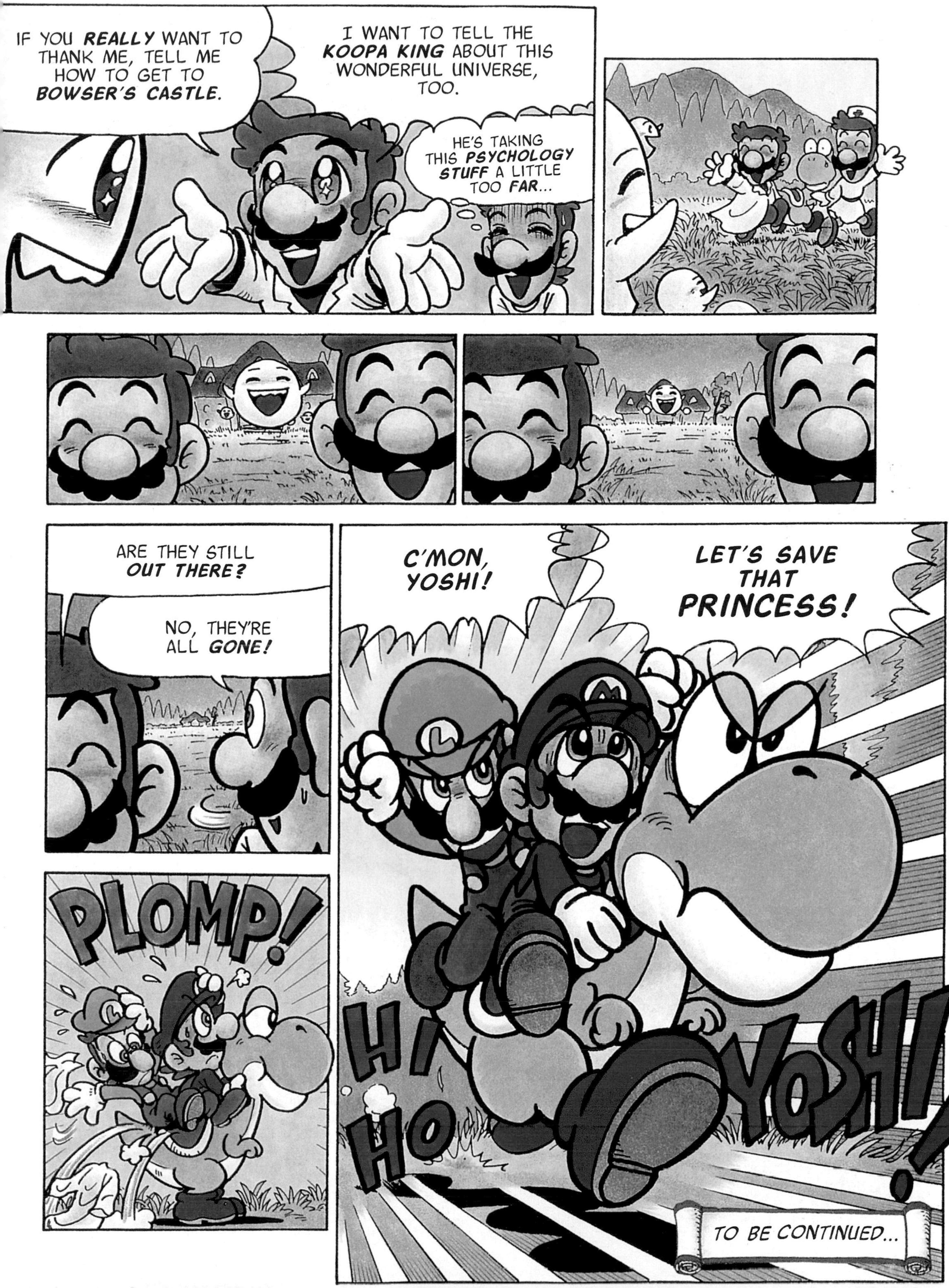
IF YOU REALLY WANT TO THANK ME, TELL ME HOW TO GET TO BOWSER'S CASTLE.
I WANT TO TELL THE KOOPA KING ABOUT THIS WONDERFUL UNIVERSE, TOO.
HE'S TAKING THIS PSYCHOLOGY STUFF A LITTLE TOO FAR...
ARE THEY STILL OUT THERE?
NO, THEY'RE ALL GONE!
C'MON, YOSHI!
LET'S SAVE THAT PRINCESS!
PLOMP!
HI HO YOSHI!
TO BE CONTINUED...

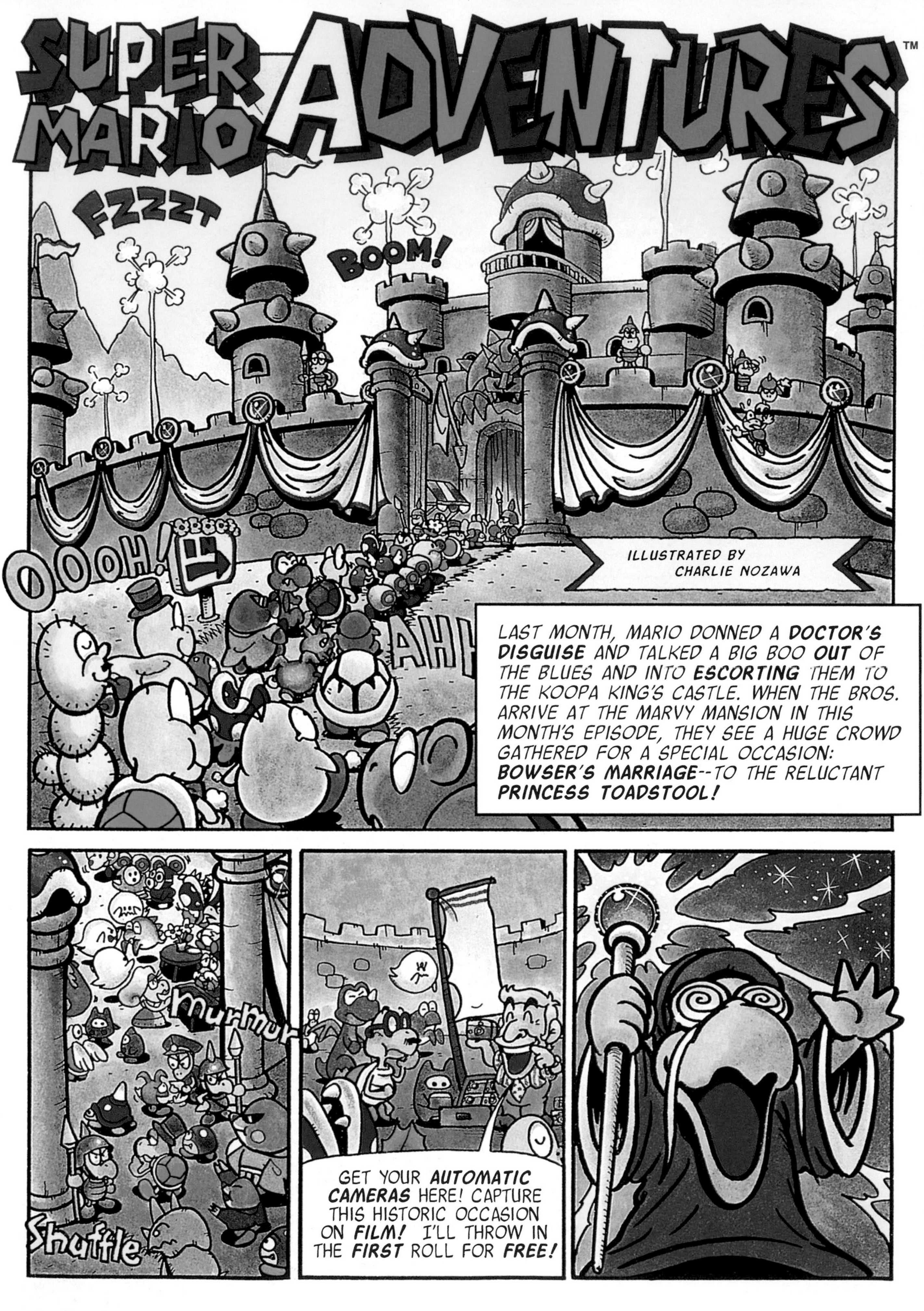
SUPER MARIO ADVENTURES™
FZZZT
BOOM!
OOOH!
ILLUSTRATED BY CHARLIE NOZAWA
AHH
LAST MONTH, MARIO DONNED A **DOCTOR'S DISGUISE** AND TALKED A BIG BOO **OUT** OF THE BLUES AND INTO **ESCORTING** THEM TO THE KOOPA KING'S CASTLE. WHEN THE BROS. ARRIVE AT THE MARVY MANSION IN THIS MONTH'S EPISODE, THEY SEE A HUGE CROWD GATHERED FOR A SPECIAL OCCASION: **BOWSER'S MARRIAGE**--TO THE RELUCTANT **PRINCESS TOADSTOOL!**
murmur
Shuffle
GET YOUR **AUTOMATIC CAMERAS** HERE! CAPTURE THIS HISTORIC OCCASION ON **FILM!** I'LL THROW IN THE **FIRST** ROLL FOR **FREE!**

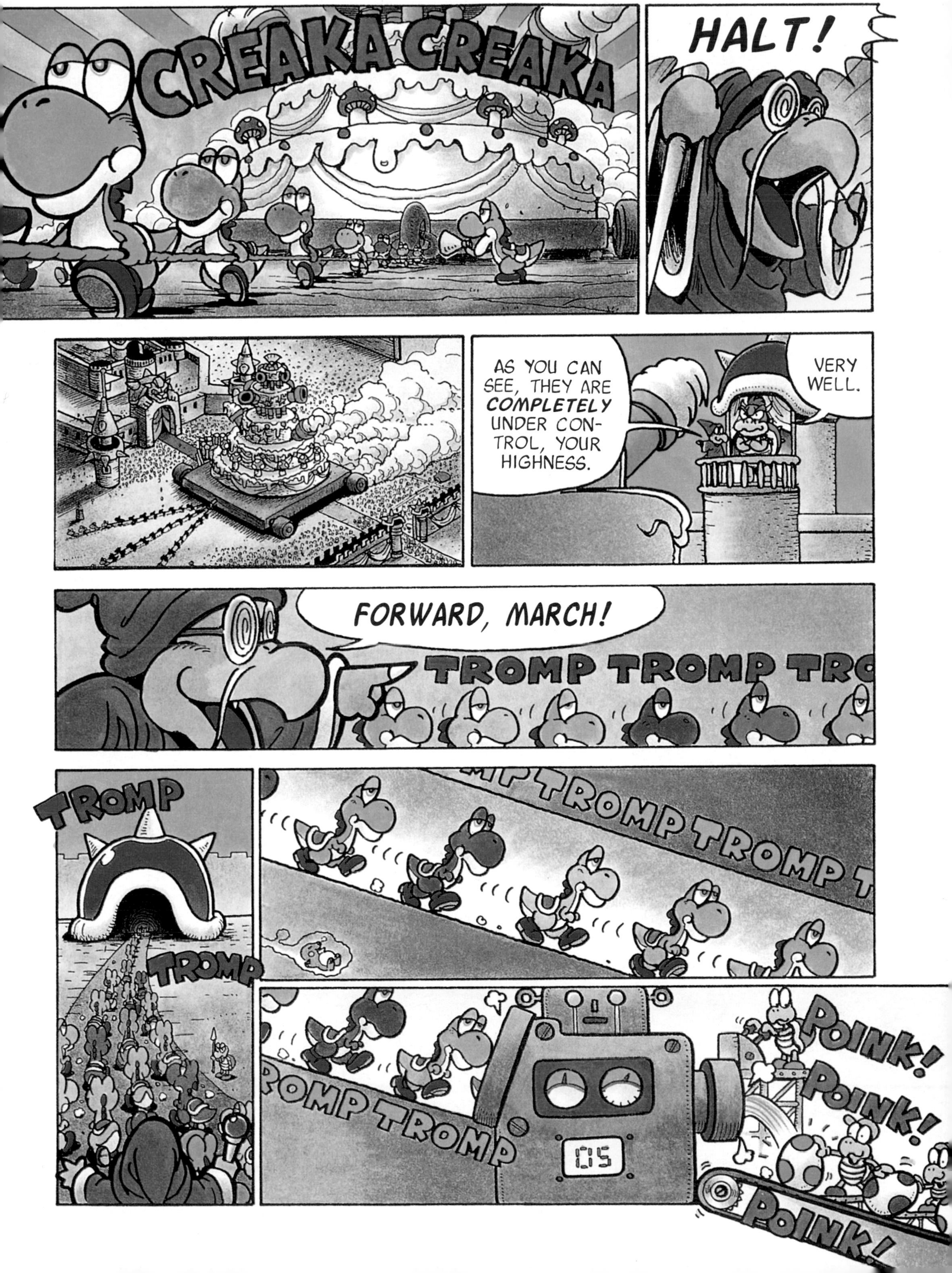
CREAKA CREAKA
HALT!
AS YOU CAN SEE, THEY ARE ***COMPLETELY*** UNDER CONTROL, YOUR HIGHNESS.
VERY WELL.
FORWARD, MARCH!
TROMP TROMP
TROMP
TROMP
TROMP TROMP
TROMP
05
POINK!
POINK!
POINK!

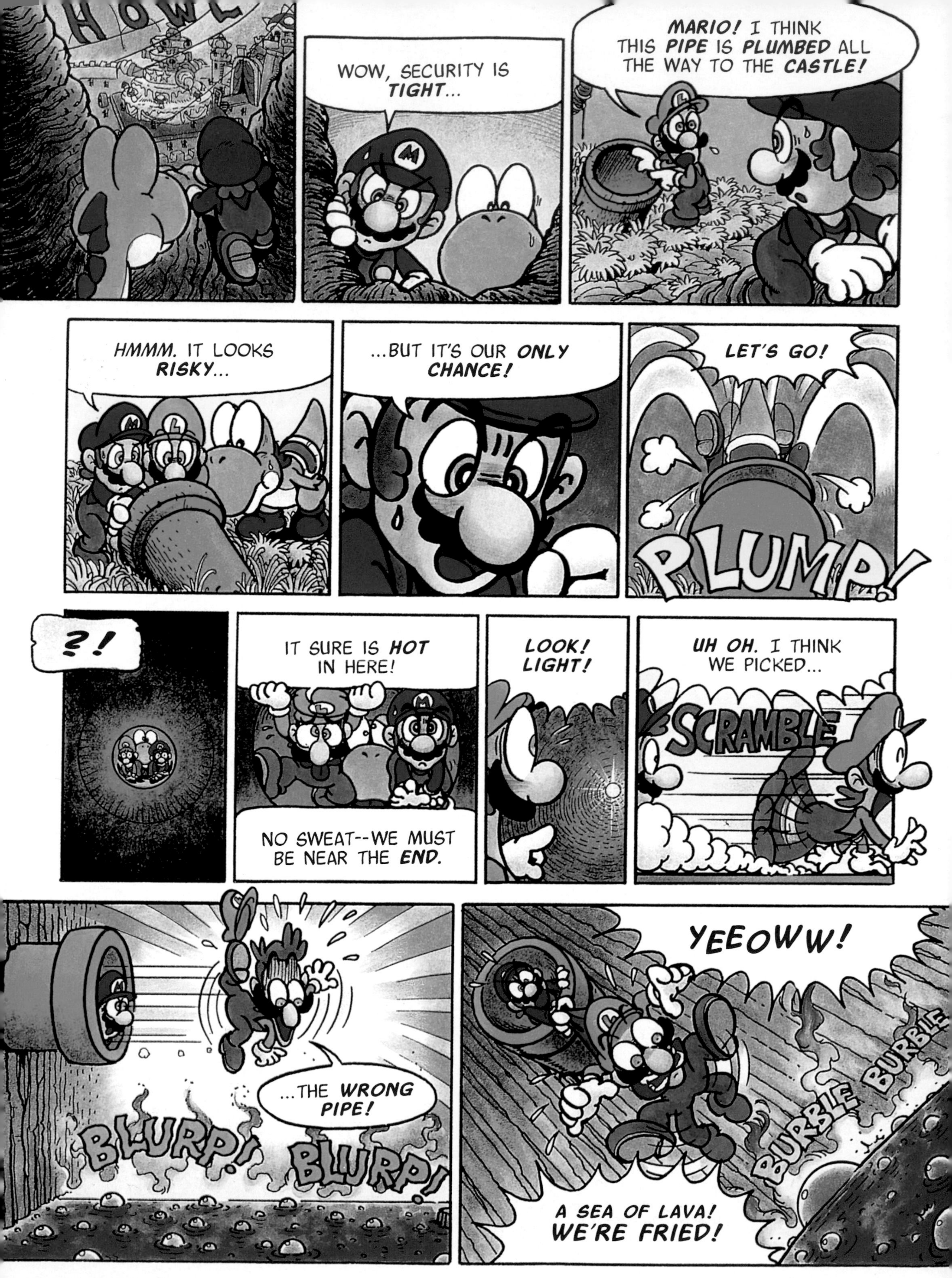
HOWL
WOW, SECURITY IS TIGHT...
MARIO! I THINK THIS PIPE IS PLUMBED ALL THE WAY TO THE CASTLE!
HMMM. IT LOOKS RISKY...
...BUT IT'S OUR ONLY CHANCE!
LET'S GO!
PLUMP!
?!
IT SURE IS HOT IN HERE!
NO SWEAT--WE MUST BE NEAR THE END.
LOOK! LIGHT!
UH OH. I THINK WE PICKED...
SCRAMBLE
...THE WRONG PIPE!
BLURP!
BLURP!
YEEOWW!
BUBBLE
BUBBLE
A SEA OF LAVA! WE'RE FRIED!

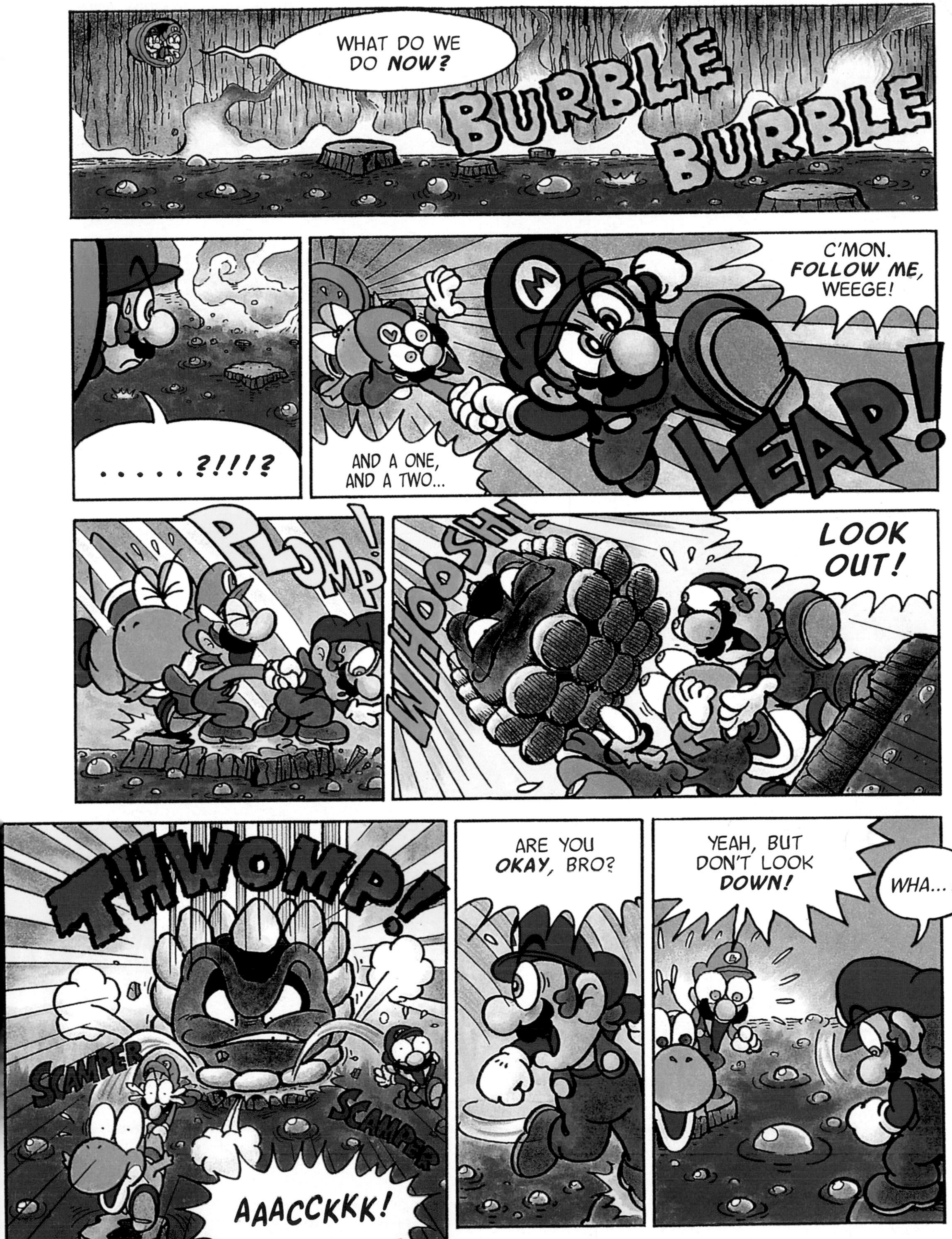
WHAT DO WE DO NOW?
BURBLE BURBLE
. . . . . ?!!!?
AND A ONE, AND A TWO...
C'MON. FOLLOW ME, WEEGE!
LEAP!
PLOMP!
WHOOSH!
LOOK OUT!
THWOMP!!
SCAMPER
SCAMPER
AAACCKKK!
ARE YOU OKAY, BRO?
YEAH, BUT DON'T LOOK DOWN!
WHA...?

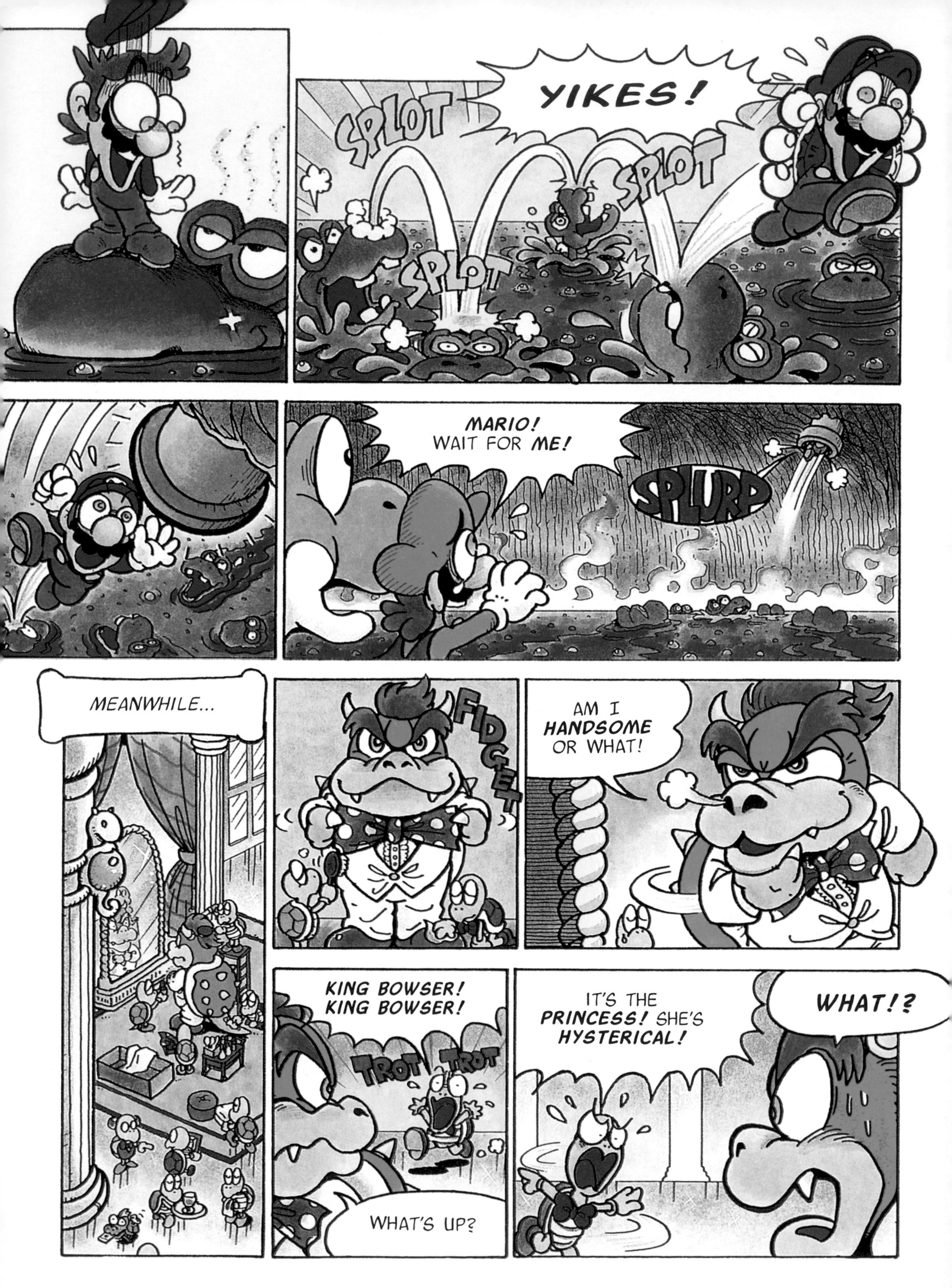
YIKES!
SPLOT
SPLOT
SPLOT
MARIO! WAIT FOR ME!
SPLURP
MEANWHILE...
FIDGET
AM I HANDSOME OR WHAT!
KING BOWSER! KING BOWSER!
TROT TROT
WHAT'S UP?
IT'S THE PRINCESS! SHE'S HYSTERICAL!
WHAT!?

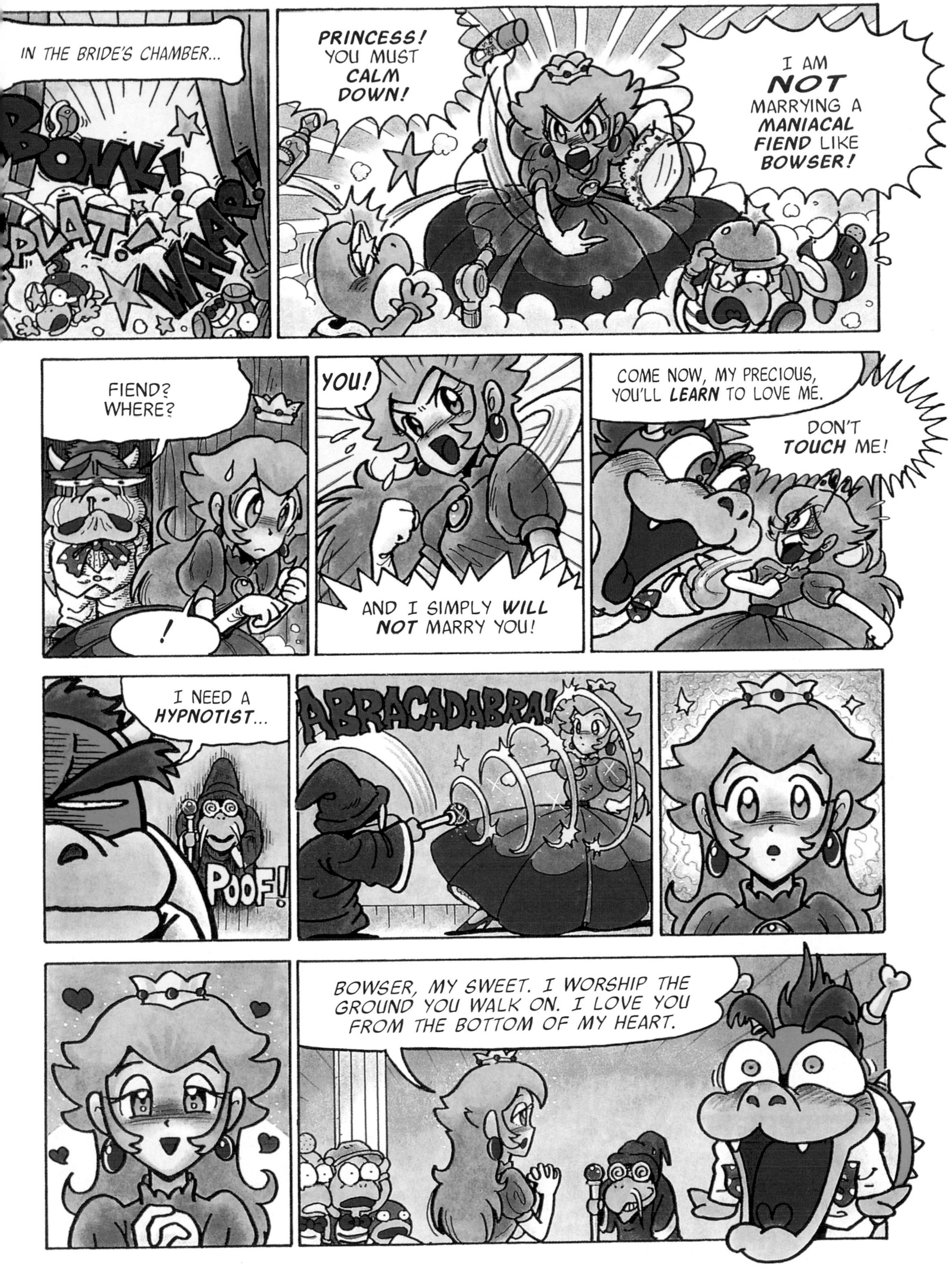
IN THE BRIDE'S CHAMBER...
BONK!
PLAT!
WHAP!
PRINCESS! YOU MUST CALM DOWN!
I AM NOT MARRYING A MANIACAL FIEND LIKE BOWSER!
FIEND? WHERE?
!
YOU!
AND I SIMPLY WILL NOT MARRY YOU!
COME NOW, MY PRECIOUS, YOU'LL LEARN TO LOVE ME.
DON'T TOUCH ME!
I NEED A HYPNOTIST...
POOF!
ABRACADABRA!
BOWSER, MY SWEET. I WORSHIP THE GROUND YOU WALK ON. I LOVE YOU FROM THE BOTTOM OF MY HEART.

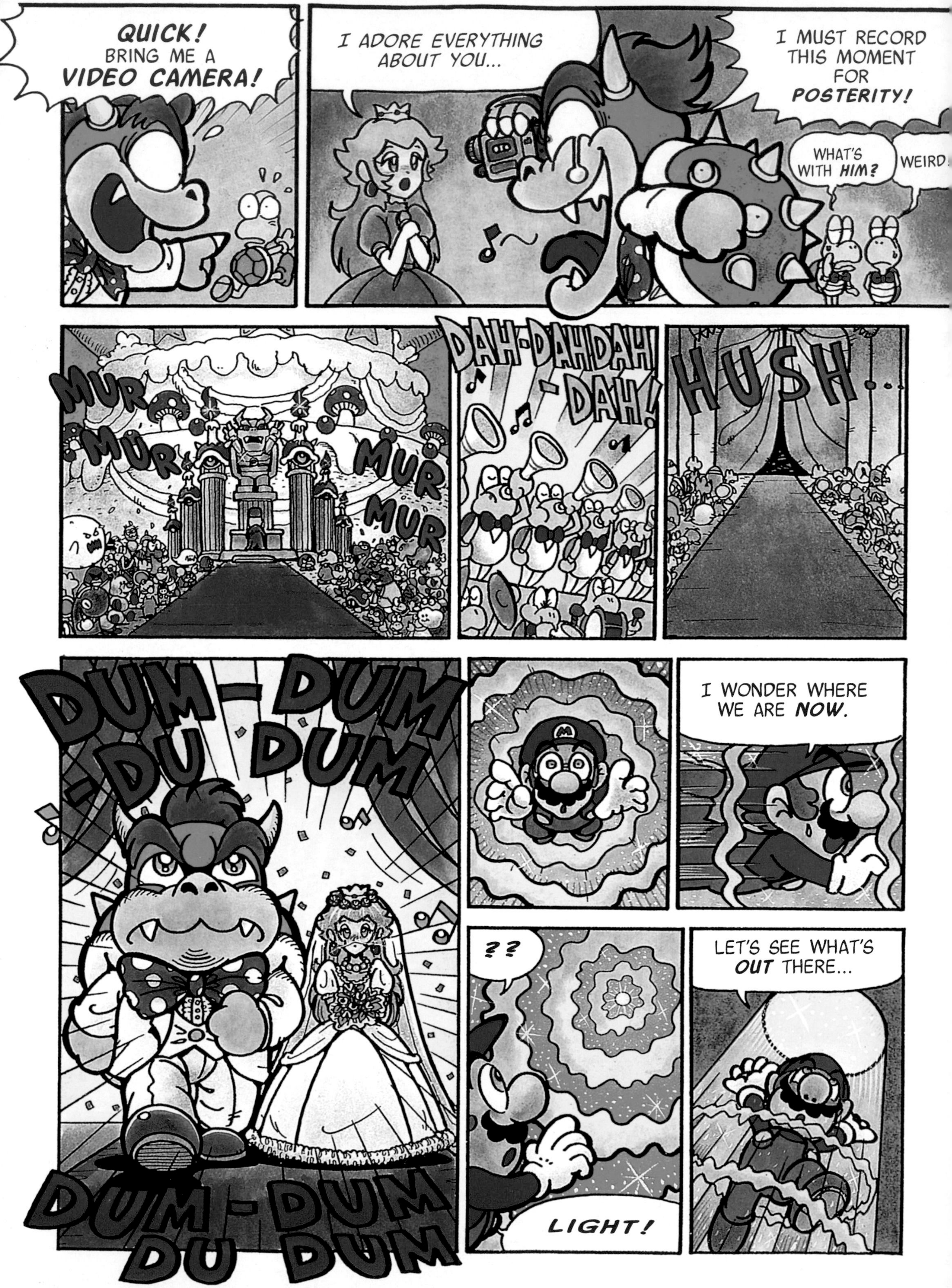
QUICK! BRING ME A VIDEO CAMERA!
I ADORE EVERYTHING ABOUT YOU...
I MUST RECORD THIS MOMENT FOR POSTERITY!
WHAT'S WITH HIM?
WEIRD.
MUR MUR
MUR MUR
DAH-DAHDAH-DAH!
HUSH...
DUM-DUM-DU DUM
DUM-DUM DU DUM
I WONDER WHERE WE ARE NOW.
??
LIGHT!
LET'S SEE WHAT'S OUT THERE...

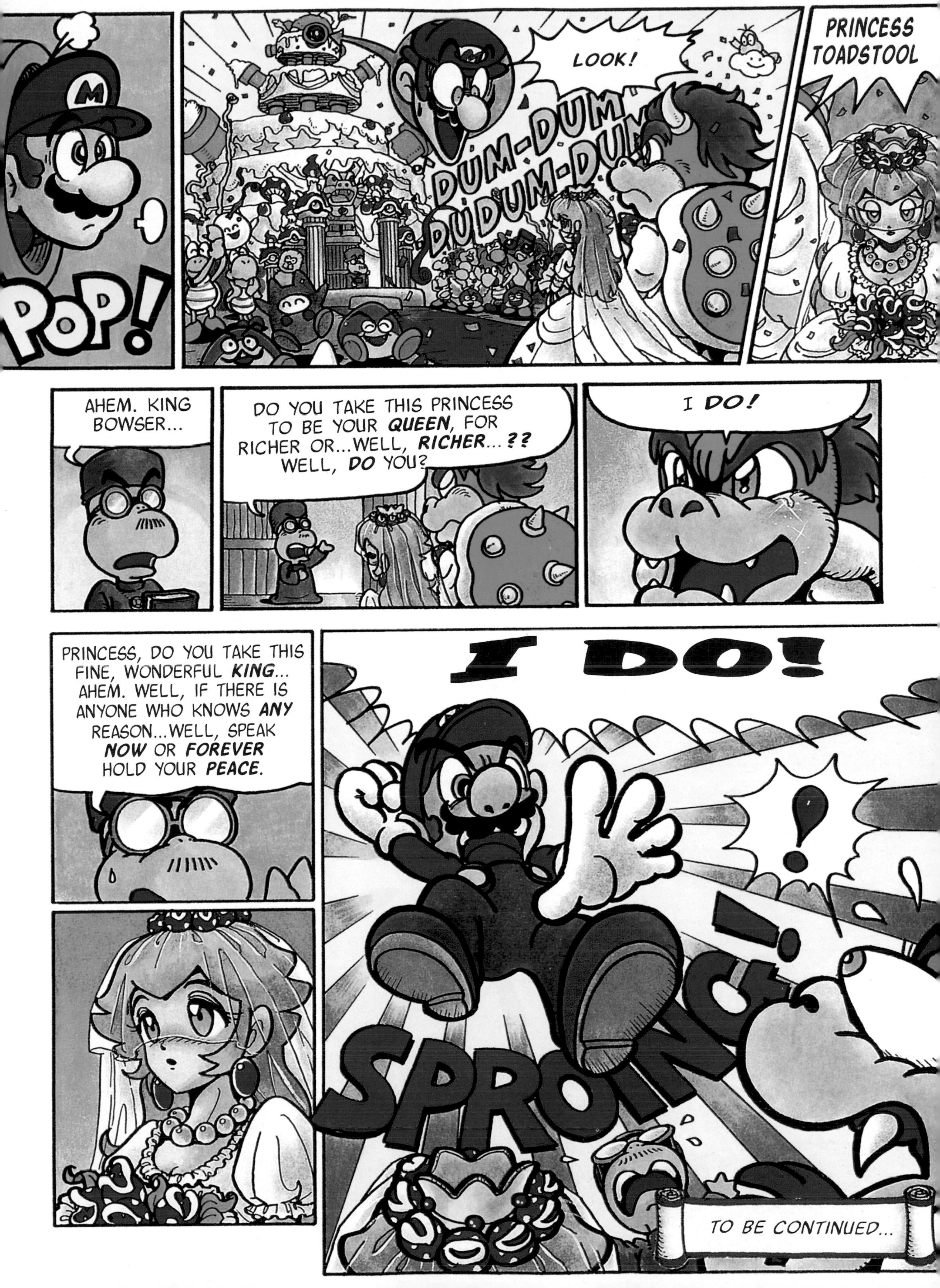
POP!
LOOK!
DUM-DUM DUDUM-DU
PRINCESS TOADSTOOL
AHEM. KING BOWSER...
DO YOU TAKE THIS PRINCESS TO BE YOUR QUEEN, FOR RICHER OR...WELL, RICHER...?? WELL, DO YOU?
I DO!
PRINCESS, DO YOU TAKE THIS FINE, WONDERFUL KING... AHEM. WELL, IF THERE IS ANYONE WHO KNOWS ANY REASON...WELL, SPEAK NOW OR FOREVER HOLD YOUR PEACE.
I DO!
!
SPROING!
TO BE CONTINUED...

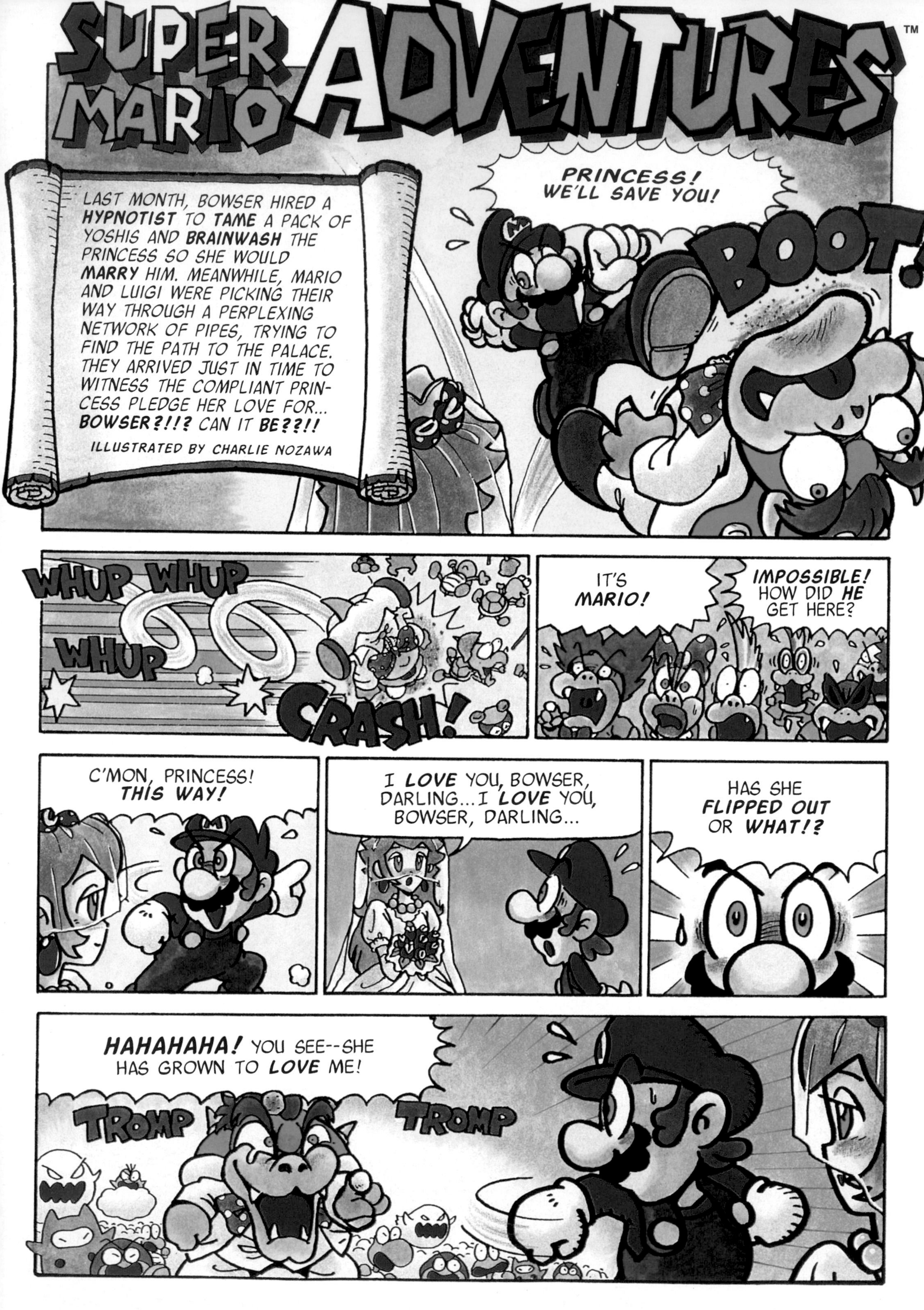
SUPER MARIO ADVENTURES™
LAST MONTH, BOWSER HIRED A **HYPNOTIST** TO **TAME** A PACK OF YOSHIS AND **BRAINWASH** THE PRINCESS SO SHE WOULD **MARRY** HIM. MEANWHILE, MARIO AND LUIGI WERE PICKING THEIR WAY THROUGH A PERPLEXING NETWORK OF PIPES, TRYING TO FIND THE PATH TO THE PALACE. THEY ARRIVED JUST IN TIME TO WITNESS THE COMPLIANT PRINCESS PLEDGE HER LOVE FOR... **BOWSER?!!?** CAN IT **BE??!!**
ILLUSTRATED BY CHARLIE NOZAWA
PRINCESS! WE'LL SAVE YOU!
BOOT!
WHUP WHUP
WHUP
CRASH!
IT'S *MARIO!*
IMPOSSIBLE! HOW DID *HE* GET HERE?
C'MON, PRINCESS! ***THIS WAY!***
I *LOVE* YOU, BOWSER, DARLING...I *LOVE* YOU, BOWSER, DARLING...
HAS SHE ***FLIPPED OUT*** OR ***WHAT!?***
HAHAHAHA! YOU SEE--SHE HAS GROWN TO ***LOVE*** ME!
TROMP
TROMP

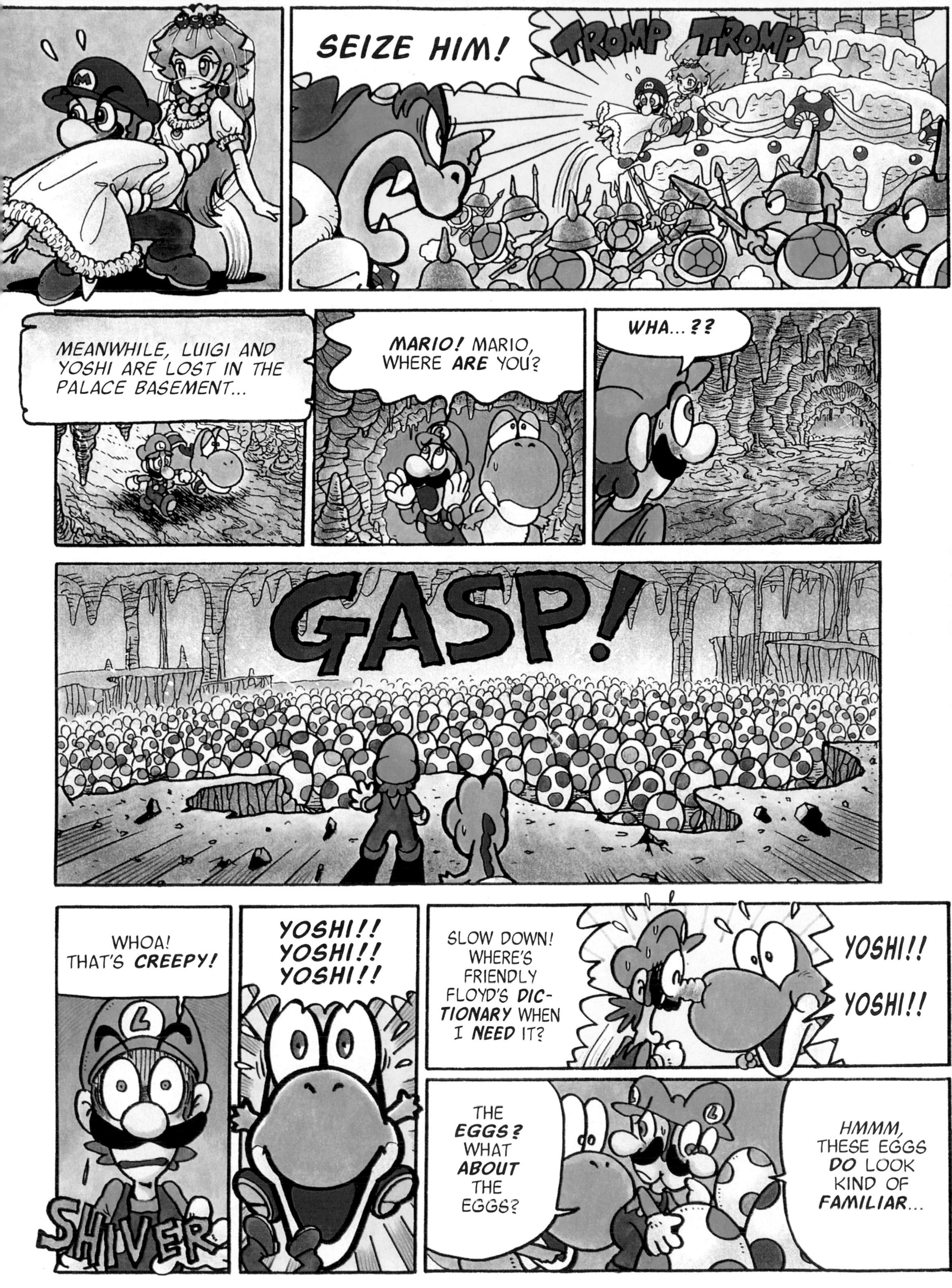
SEIZE HIM!
TROMP TROMP
MEANWHILE, LUIGI AND YOSHI ARE LOST IN THE PALACE BASEMENT...
MARIO! MARIO, WHERE ARE YOU?
WHA...??
GASP!
WHOA! THAT'S CREEPY!
SHIVER
YOSHI!! YOSHI!! YOSHI!!
SLOW DOWN! WHERE'S FRIENDLY FLOYD'S DICTIONARY WHEN I NEED IT?
YOSHI!!
YOSHI!!
THE EGGS? WHAT ABOUT THE EGGS?
HMMM, THESE EGGS DO LOOK KIND OF FAMILIAR...

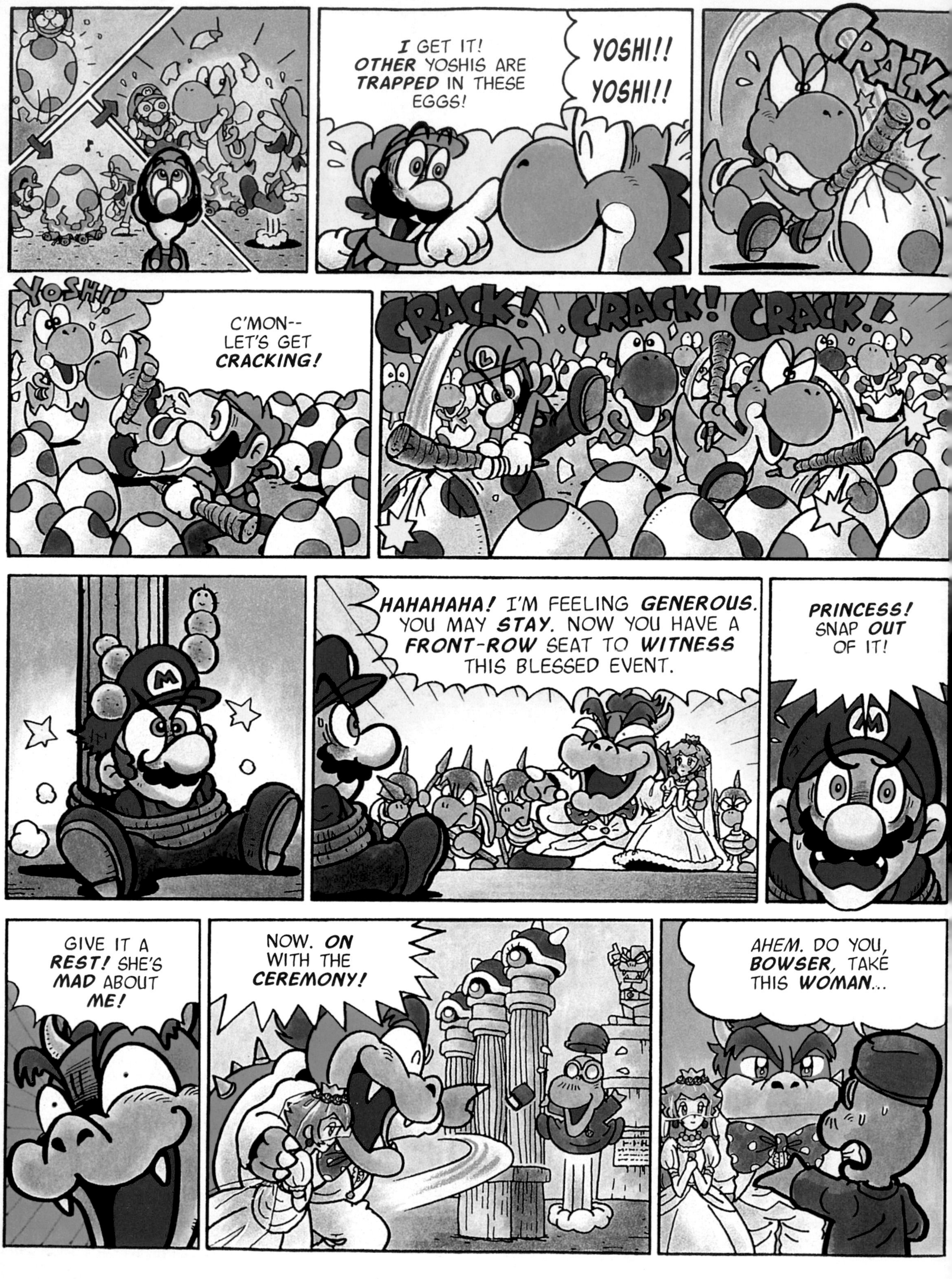
I GET IT! OTHER YOSHIS ARE TRAPPED IN THESE EGGS!
YOSHI!! YOSHI!!
CRACK!
YOSHI!
C'MON-- LET'S GET CRACKING!
CRACK! CRACK! CRACK!
HAHAHAHA! I'M FEELING GENEROUS. YOU MAY STAY. NOW YOU HAVE A FRONT-ROW SEAT TO WITNESS THIS BLESSED EVENT.
PRINCESS! SNAP OUT OF IT!
GIVE IT A REST! SHE'S MAD ABOUT ME!
NOW. ON WITH THE CEREMONY!
AHEM. DO YOU, BOWSER, TAKE THIS WOMAN...

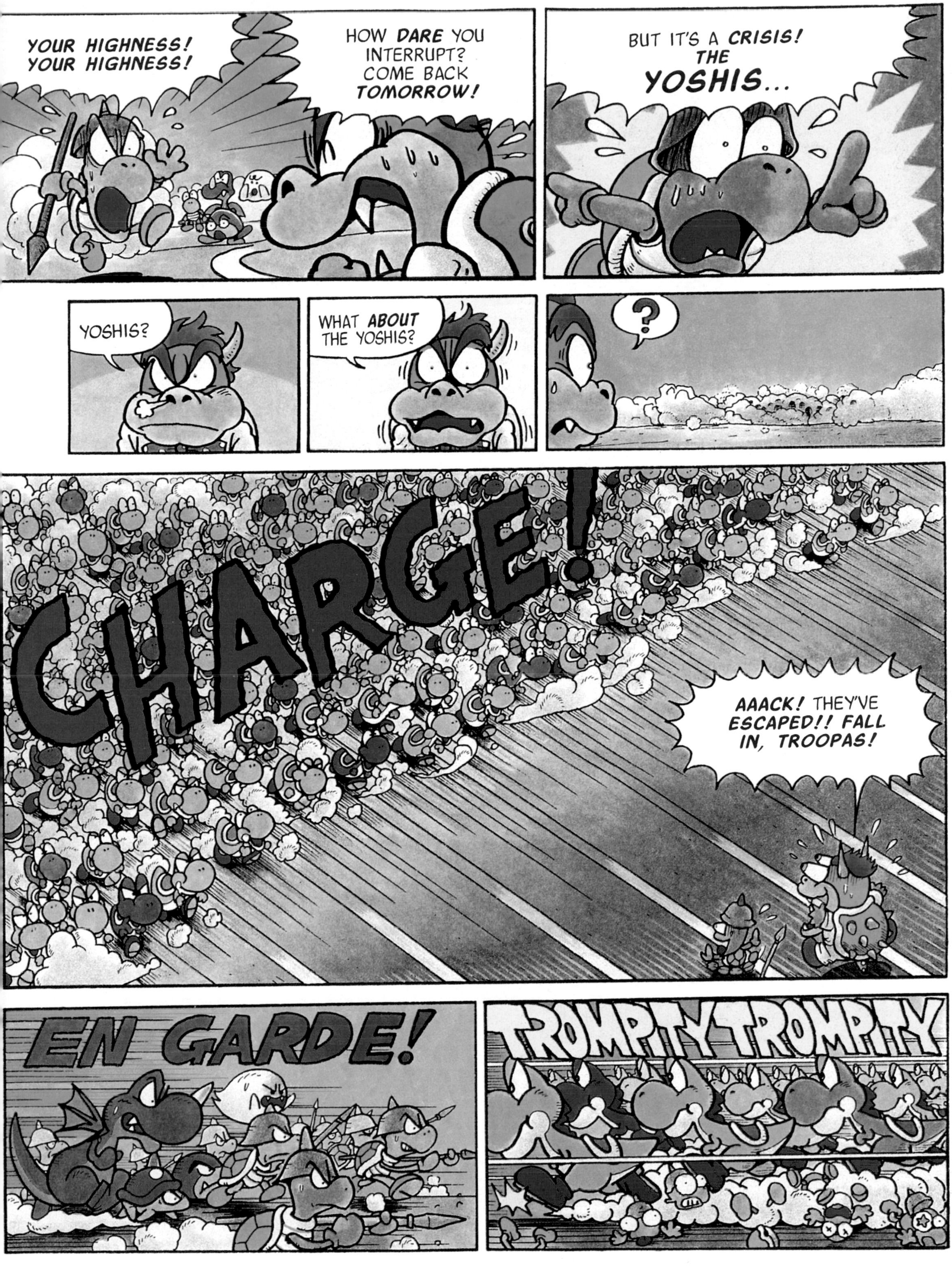
YOUR HIGHNESS! YOUR HIGHNESS!
HOW DARE YOU INTERRUPT? COME BACK TOMORROW!
BUT IT'S A CRISIS! THE YOSHIS...
YOSHIS?
WHAT ABOUT THE YOSHIS?
?
CHARGE!
AAACK! THEY'VE ESCAPED!! FALL IN, TROOPAS!
EN GARDE!
TROMPITY TROMPITY

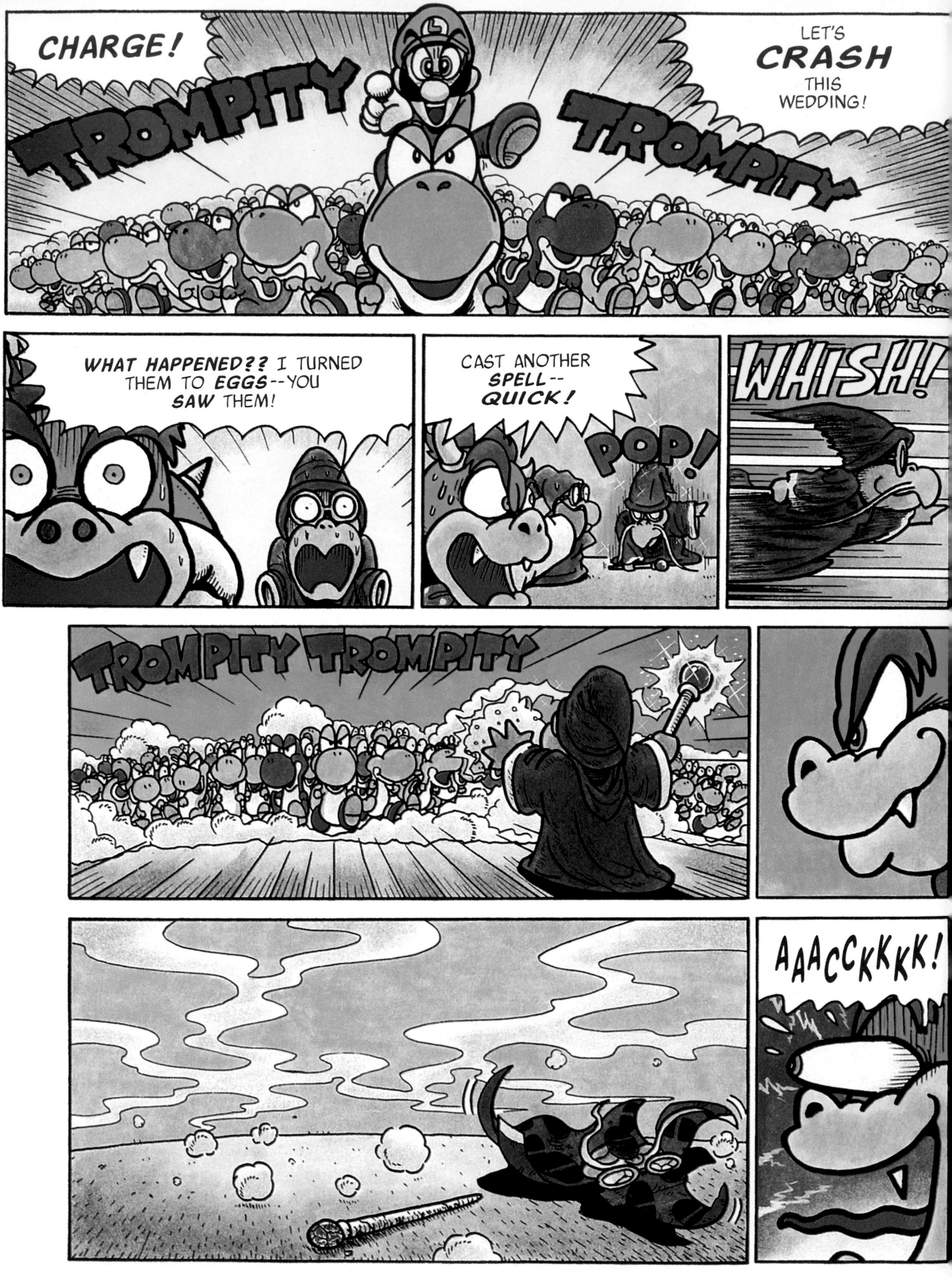
CHARGE!
TROMPITY
TROMPITY
LET'S CRASH THIS WEDDING!
WHAT HAPPENED?? I TURNED THEM TO EGGS--YOU SAW THEM!
CAST ANOTHER SPELL-- QUICK!
POP!
WHISH!
TROMPITY TROMPITY
AAACCKKKK!

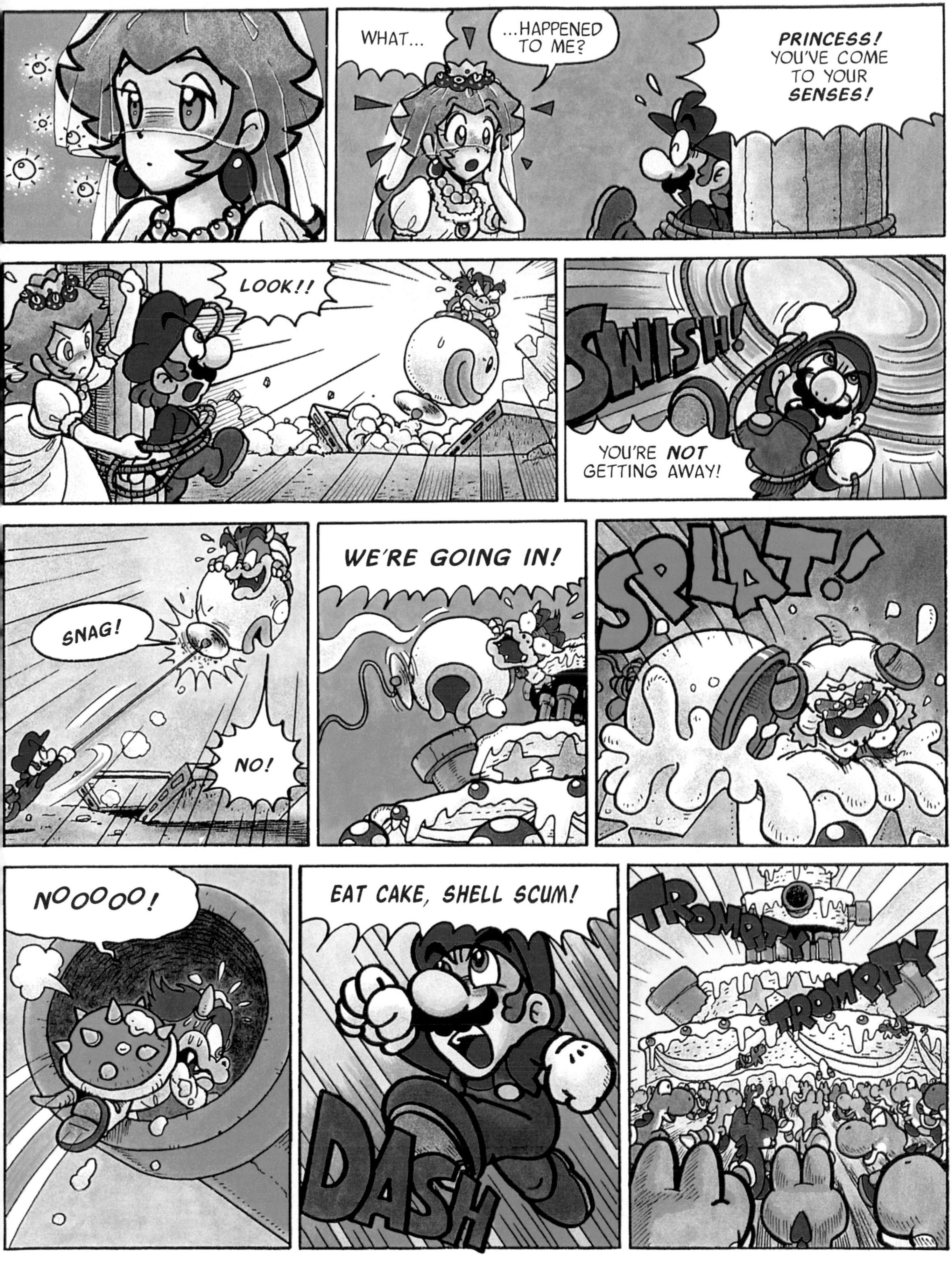
WHAT...
...HAPPENED TO ME?
PRINCESS! YOU'VE COME TO YOUR SENSES!
LOOK!!
SWISH!
YOU'RE NOT GETTING AWAY!
SNAG!
NO!
WE'RE GOING IN!
SPLAT!
NOOOOO!
EAT CAKE, SHELL SCUM!
DASH
TROMPITY
TROMPITY

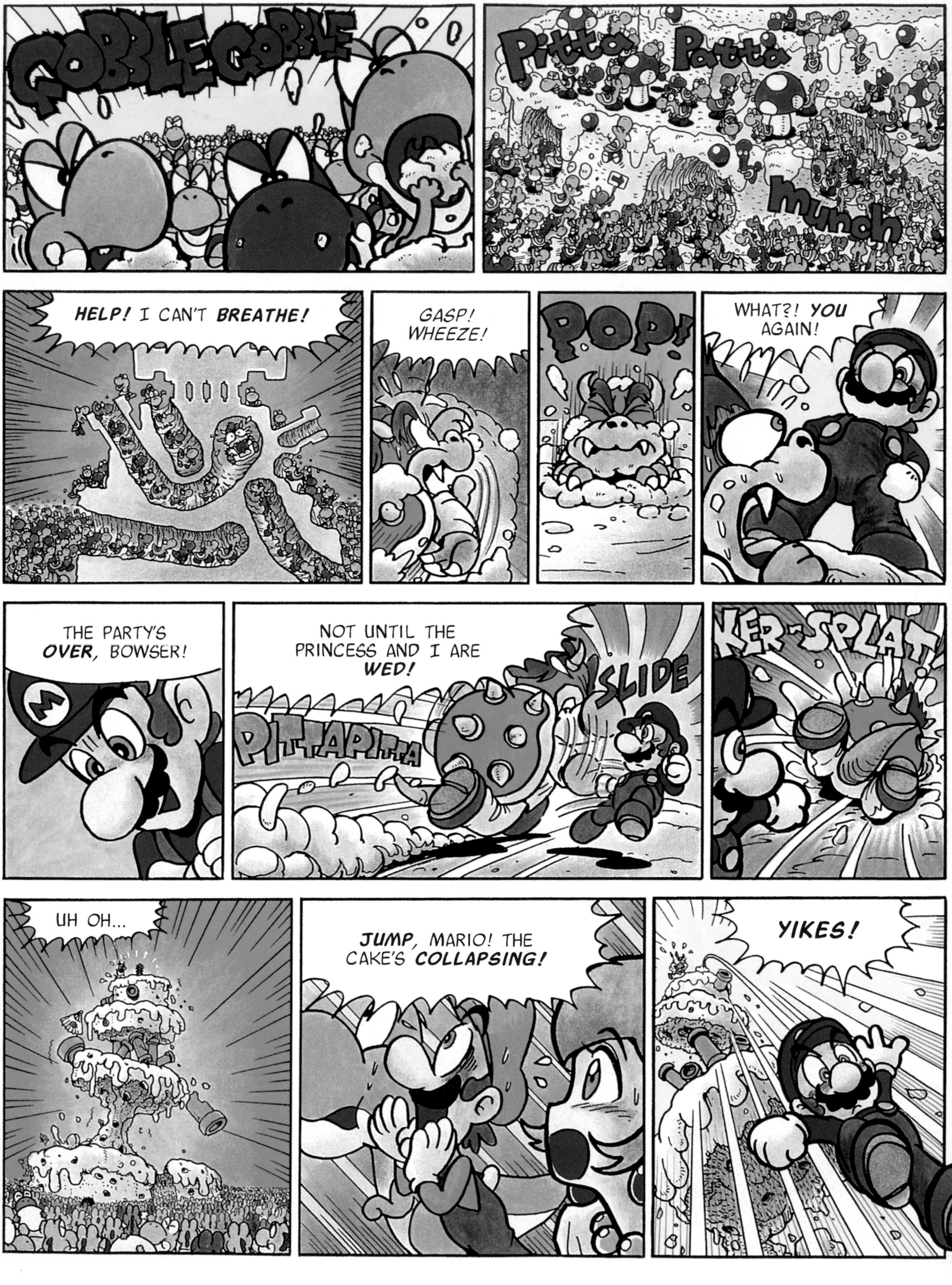
GOBBLE GOBBLE
Pitta Patta
munch
HELP! I CAN'T BREATHE!
GASP! WHEEZE!
POP!
WHAT?! YOU AGAIN!
THE PARTY'S OVER, BOWSER!
NOT UNTIL THE PRINCESS AND I ARE WED!
SLIDE
PITTAPITTA
KER-SPLAT!
UH OH...
JUMP, MARIO! THE CAKE'S COLLAPSING!
YIKES!

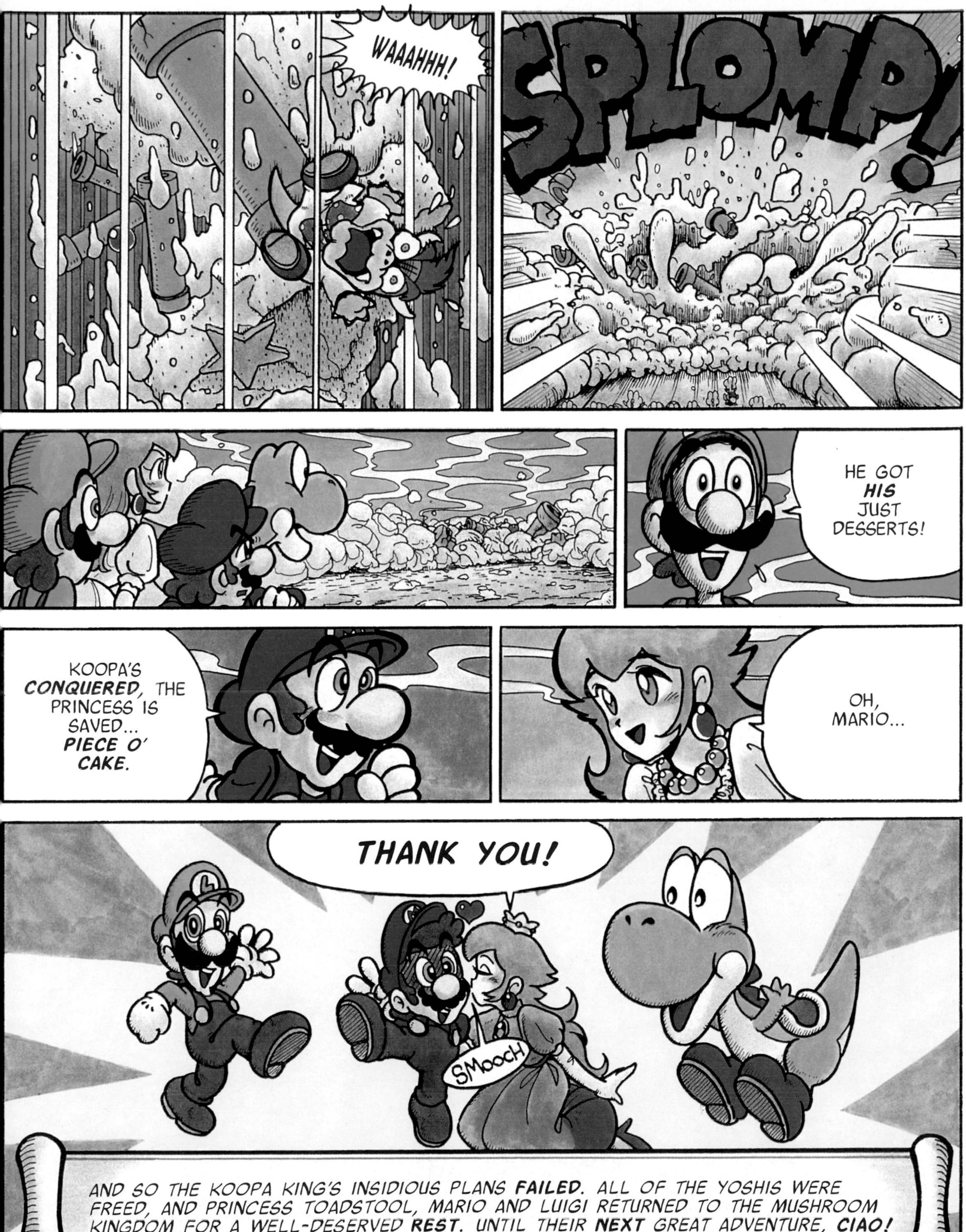
WAAAHHH!
SPLOMP!
HE GOT HIS JUST DESSERTS!
KOOPA'S CONQUERED, THE PRINCESS IS SAVED... PIECE O' CAKE.
OH, MARIO...
THANK YOU!
SMOOCH
AND SO THE KOOPA KING'S INSIDIOUS PLANS FAILED. ALL OF THE YOSHIS WERE FREED, AND PRINCESS TOADSTOOL, MARIO AND LUIGI RETURNED TO THE MUSHROOM KINGDOM FOR A WELL-DESERVED REST. UNTIL THEIR NEXT GREAT ADVENTURE, CIAO!

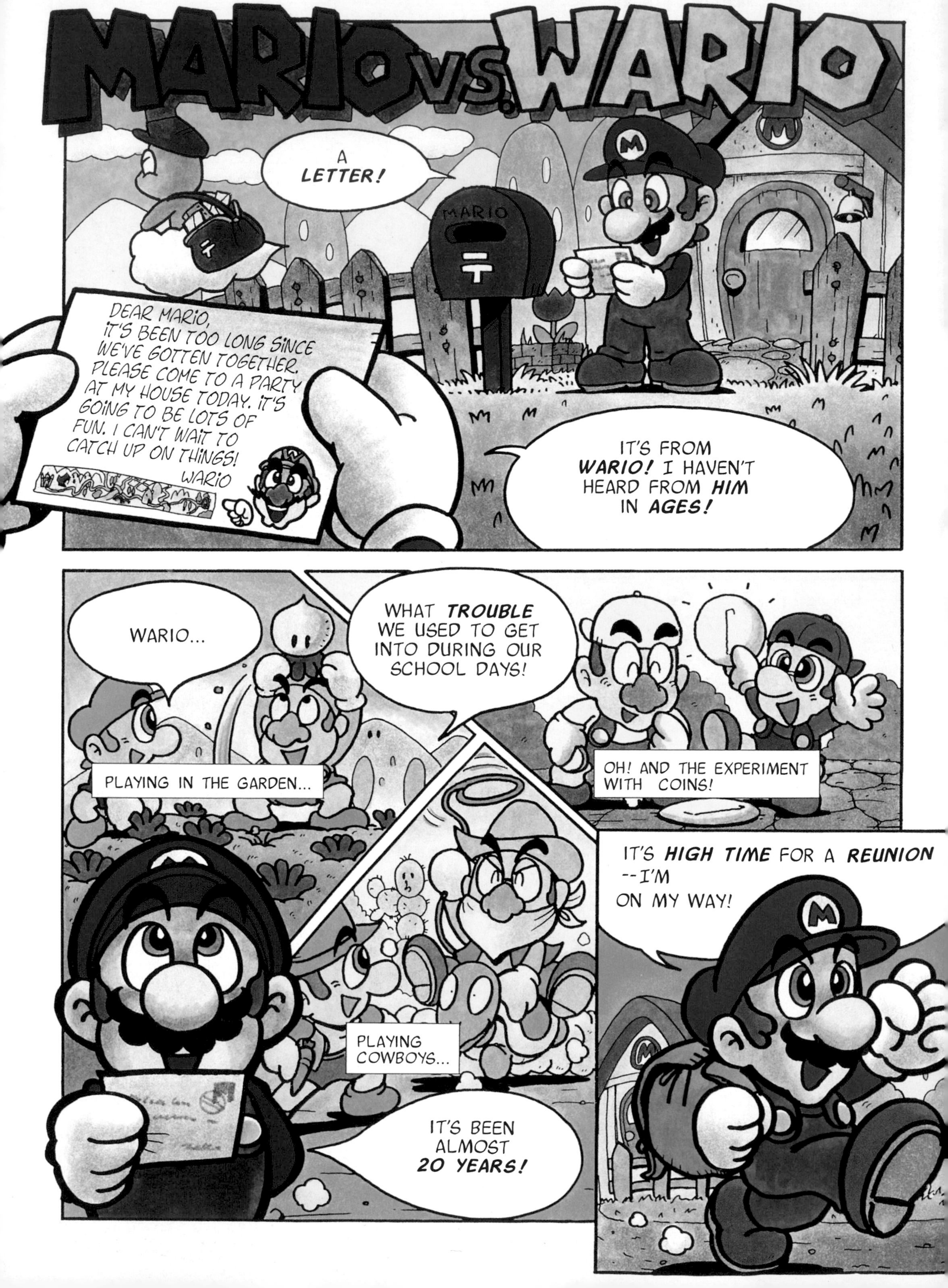
MARIO VS. WARIO
A LETTER!
MARIO
DEAR MARIO, IT'S BEEN TOO LONG SINCE WE'VE GOTTEN TOGETHER. PLEASE COME TO A PARTY AT MY HOUSE TODAY. IT'S GOING TO BE LOTS OF FUN. I CAN'T WAIT TO CATCH UP ON THINGS!
WARIO
IT'S FROM WARIO! I HAVEN'T HEARD FROM HIM IN AGES!
WARIO...
PLAYING IN THE GARDEN...
WHAT TROUBLE WE USED TO GET INTO DURING OUR SCHOOL DAYS!
OH! AND THE EXPERIMENT WITH COINS!
PLAYING COWBOYS...
IT'S BEEN ALMOST 20 YEARS!
IT'S HIGH TIME FOR A REUNION --I'M ON MY WAY!

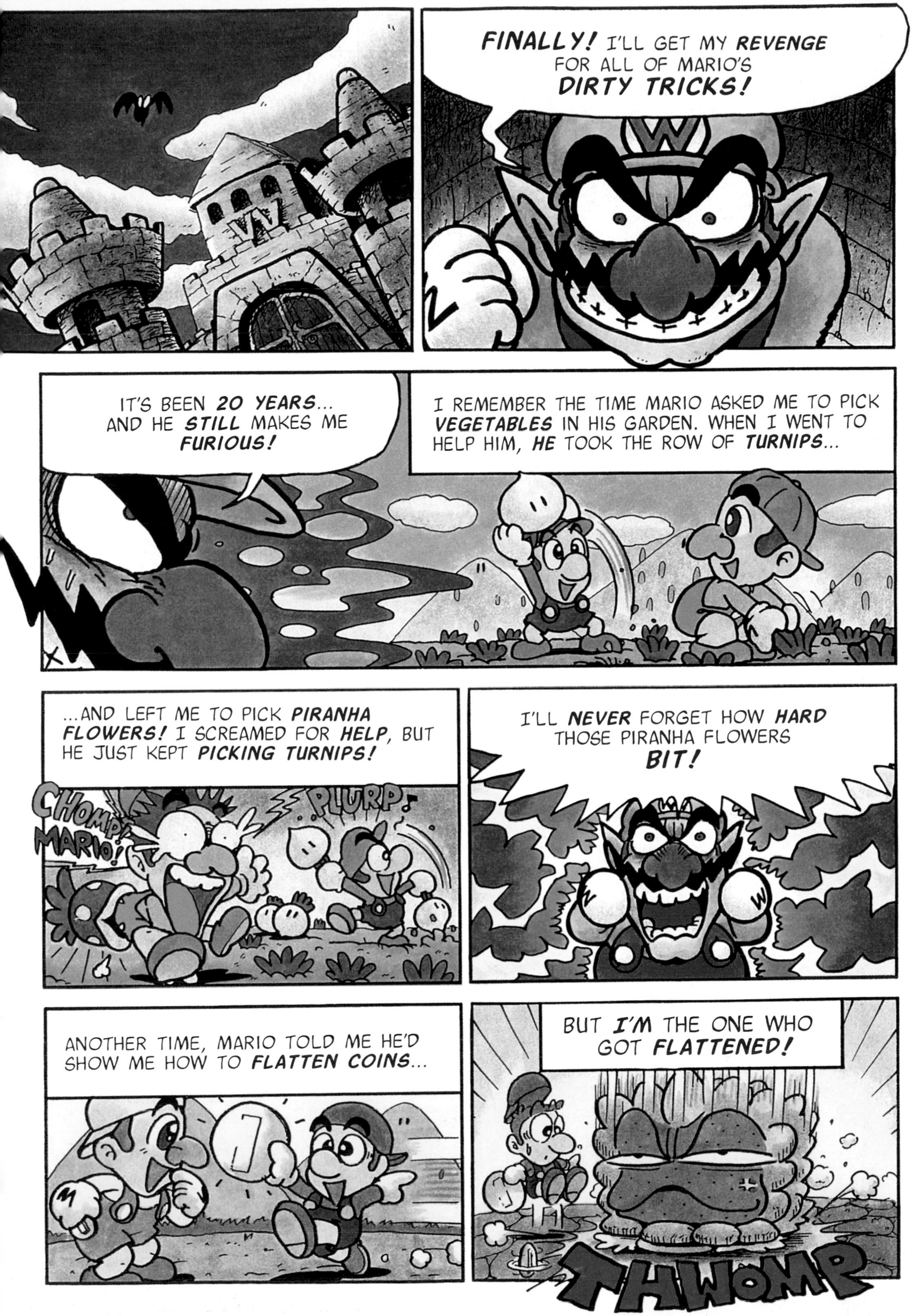
FINALLY! I'LL GET MY REVENGE FOR ALL OF MARIO'S DIRTY TRICKS!
IT'S BEEN 20 YEARS... AND HE STILL MAKES ME FURIOUS!
I REMEMBER THE TIME MARIO ASKED ME TO PICK VEGETABLES IN HIS GARDEN. WHEN I WENT TO HELP HIM, HE TOOK THE ROW OF TURNIPS...
...AND LEFT ME TO PICK PIRANHA FLOWERS! I SCREAMED FOR HELP, BUT HE JUST KEPT PICKING TURNIPS!
CHOMP!
MARIO!
PLURP
I'LL NEVER FORGET HOW HARD THOSE PIRANHA FLOWERS BIT!
ANOTHER TIME, MARIO TOLD ME HE'D SHOW ME HOW TO FLATTEN COINS...
BUT I'M THE ONE WHO GOT FLATTENED!
THWOMP

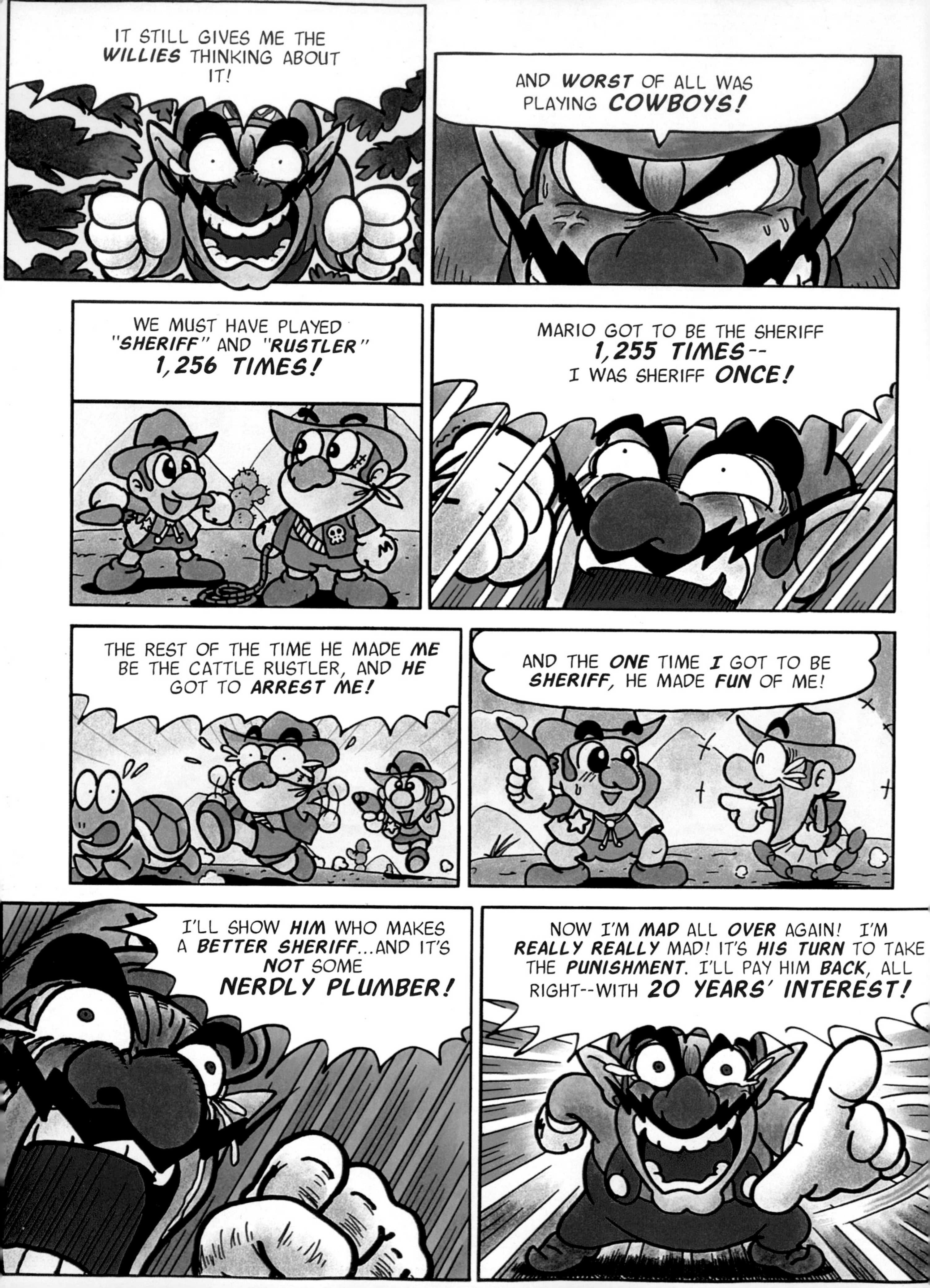
IT STILL GIVES ME THE WILLIES THINKING ABOUT IT!
AND WORST OF ALL WAS PLAYING COWBOYS!
WE MUST HAVE PLAYED "SHERIFF" AND "RUSTLER" 1,256 TIMES!
MARIO GOT TO BE THE SHERIFF 1,255 TIMES-- I WAS SHERIFF ONCE!
THE REST OF THE TIME HE MADE ME BE THE CATTLE RUSTLER, AND HE GOT TO ARREST ME!
AND THE ONE TIME I GOT TO BE SHERIFF, HE MADE FUN OF ME!
I'LL SHOW HIM WHO MAKES A BETTER SHERIFF...AND IT'S NOT SOME NERDLY PLUMBER!
NOW I'M MAD ALL OVER AGAIN! I'M REALLY REALLY MAD! IT'S HIS TURN TO TAKE THE PUNISHMENT. I'LL PAY HIM BACK, ALL RIGHT--WITH 20 YEARS' INTEREST!

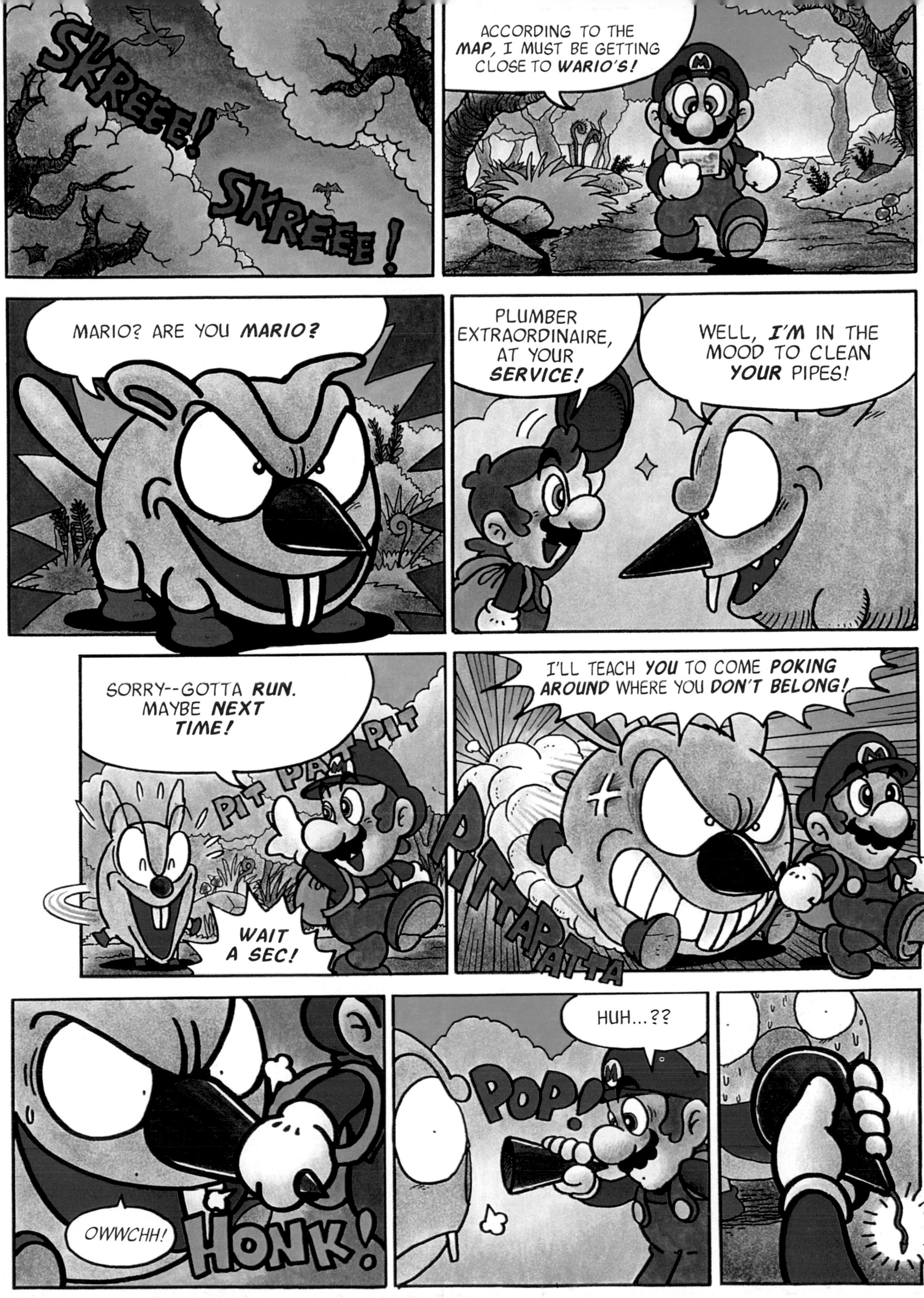

SKREEE!
SKREEE!
ACCORDING TO THE MAP, I MUST BE GETTING CLOSE TO WARIO'S!
MARIO? ARE YOU MARIO?
PLUMBER EXTRAORDINAIRE, AT YOUR SERVICE!
WELL, I'M IN THE MOOD TO CLEAN YOUR PIPES!
SORRY--GOTTA RUN. MAYBE NEXT TIME!
PIT PAT PIT PIT
WAIT A SEC!
I'LL TEACH YOU TO COME POKING AROUND WHERE YOU DON'T BELONG!
PITTAPATTA
OWWCHH!
HONK!
HUH...??
POP!

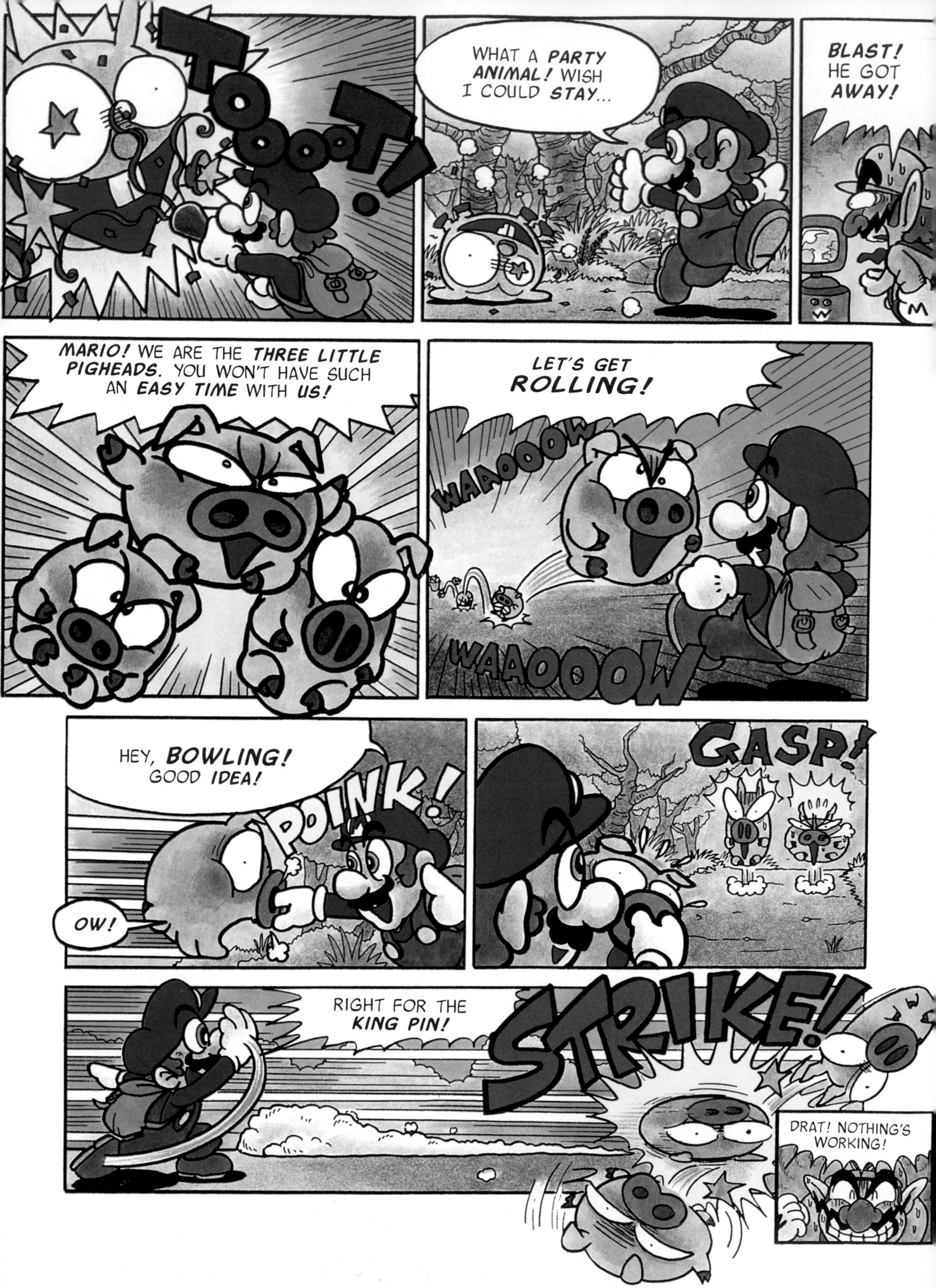

TOOOOT!
WHAT A PARTY ANIMAL! WISH I COULD STAY...
BLAST! HE GOT AWAY!
MARIO! WE ARE THE THREE LITTLE PIGHEADS. YOU WON'T HAVE SUCH AN EASY TIME WITH US!
LET'S GET ROLLING!
WAAOOOW
WAAOOOW
HEY, BOWLING! GOOD IDEA!
POINK!
OW!
GASP!
RIGHT FOR THE KING PIN!
STRIKE!
DRAT! NOTHING'S WORKING!

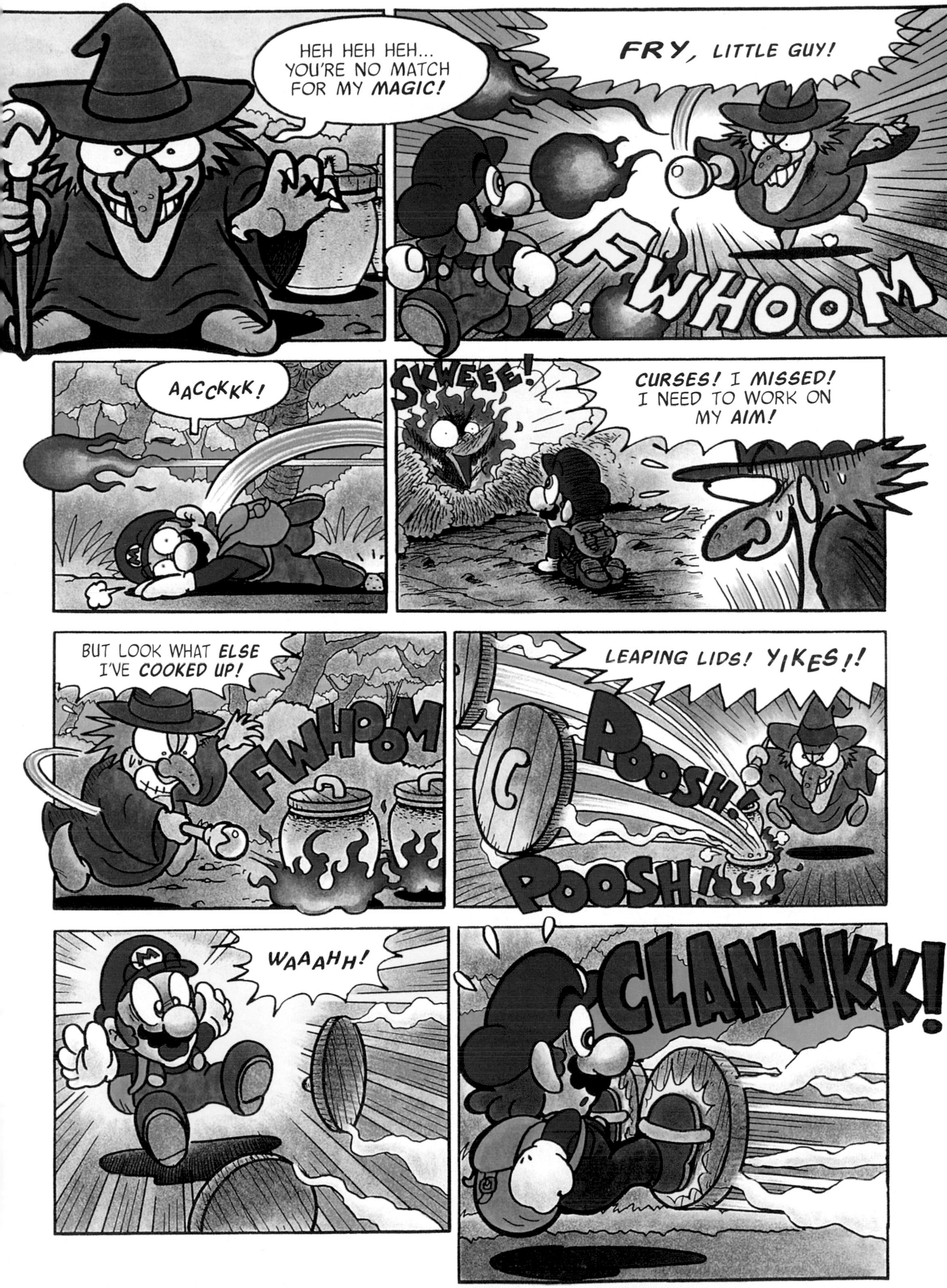
HEH HEH HEH... YOU'RE NO MATCH FOR MY MAGIC!
FRY, LITTLE GUY!
FWHOOM
AACCKKK!
SKWEEE!
CURSES! I MISSED! I NEED TO WORK ON MY AIM!
BUT LOOK WHAT ELSE I'VE COOKED UP!
FWHOOM
LEAPING LIDS! YIKES!!
POOSH!
POOSH!
WAAAHH!
CLANNKK!

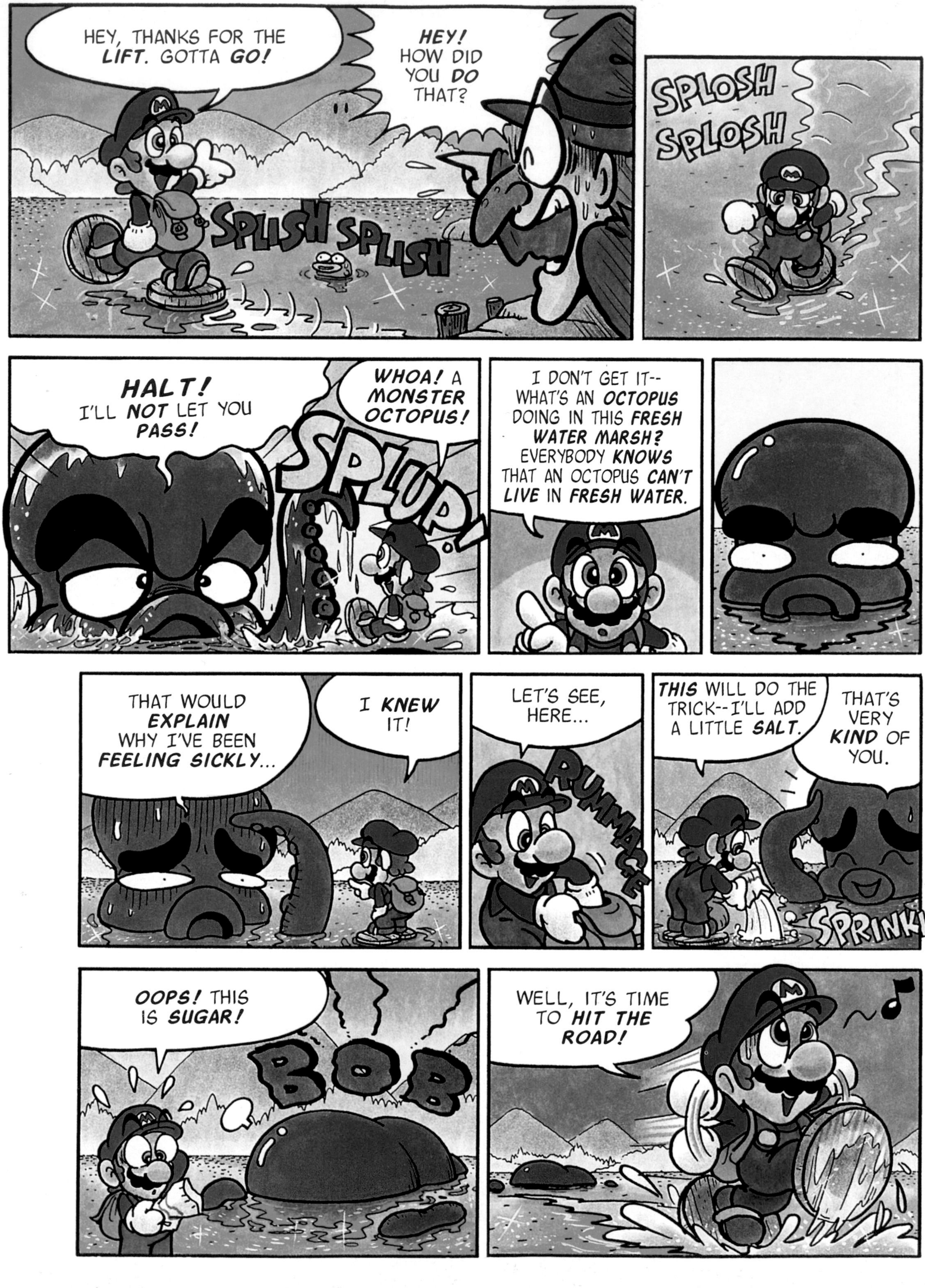
HEY, THANKS FOR THE LIFT. GOTTA GO!
HEY! HOW DID YOU DO THAT?
SPLISH SPLISH
SPLOSH SPLOSH
HALT! I'LL NOT LET YOU PASS!
WHOA! A MONSTER OCTOPUS!
SPLUP!
I DON'T GET IT-- WHAT'S AN OCTOPUS DOING IN THIS FRESH WATER MARSH? EVERYBODY KNOWS THAT AN OCTOPUS CAN'T LIVE IN FRESH WATER.
THAT WOULD EXPLAIN WHY I'VE BEEN FEELING SICKLY...
I KNEW IT!
LET'S SEE, HERE...
RUMMAGE
THIS WILL DO THE TRICK--I'LL ADD A LITTLE SALT.
THAT'S VERY KIND OF YOU.
SPRINKLE
OOPS! THIS IS SUGAR!
BOB
WELL, IT'S TIME TO HIT THE ROAD!

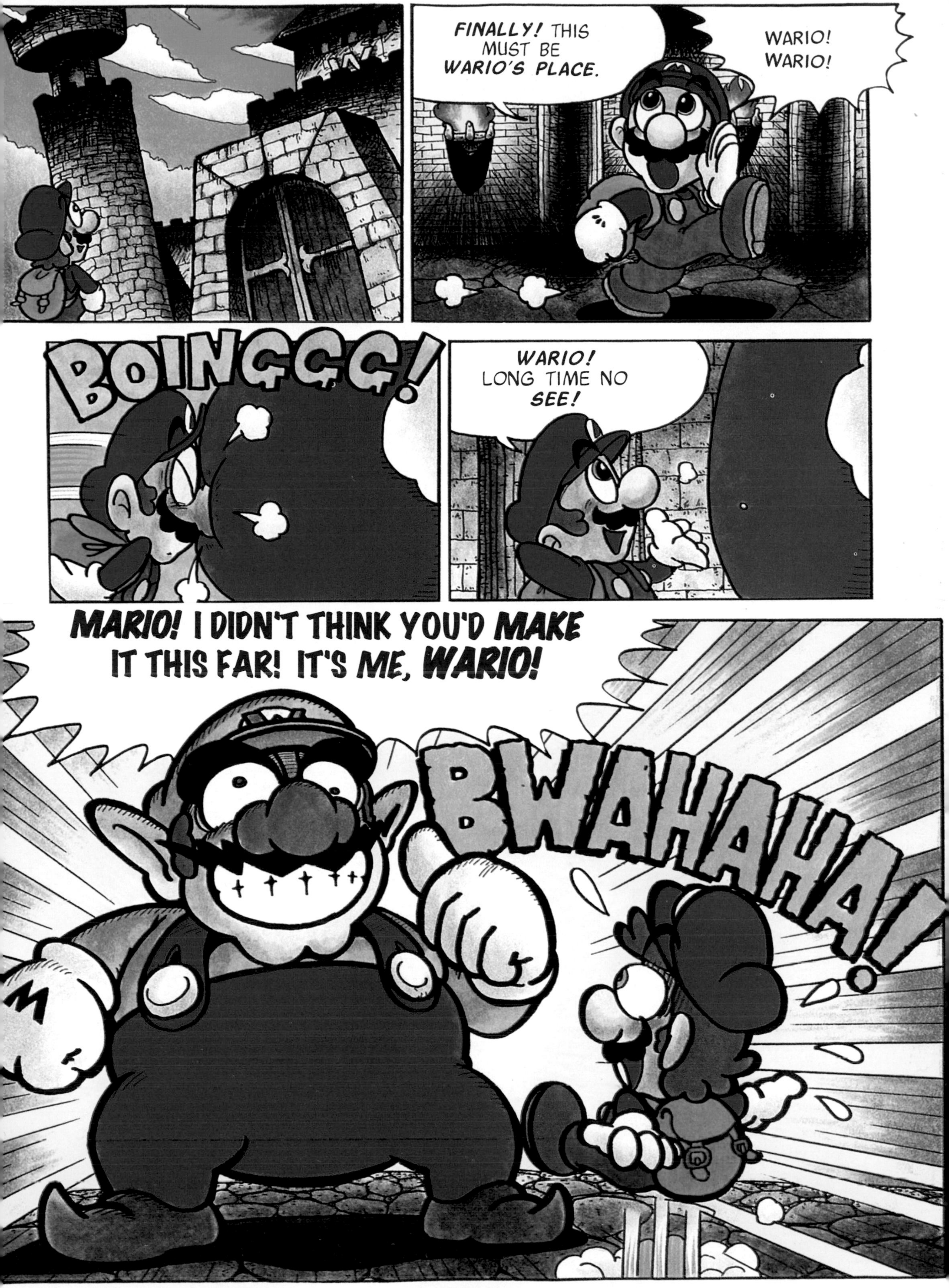
FINALLY! THIS MUST BE WARIO'S PLACE.
WARIO! WARIO!
BOINGGG!
WARIO! LONG TIME NO SEE!
MARIO! I DIDN'T THINK YOU'D MAKE IT THIS FAR! IT'S ME, WARIO!
BWAHAHA!

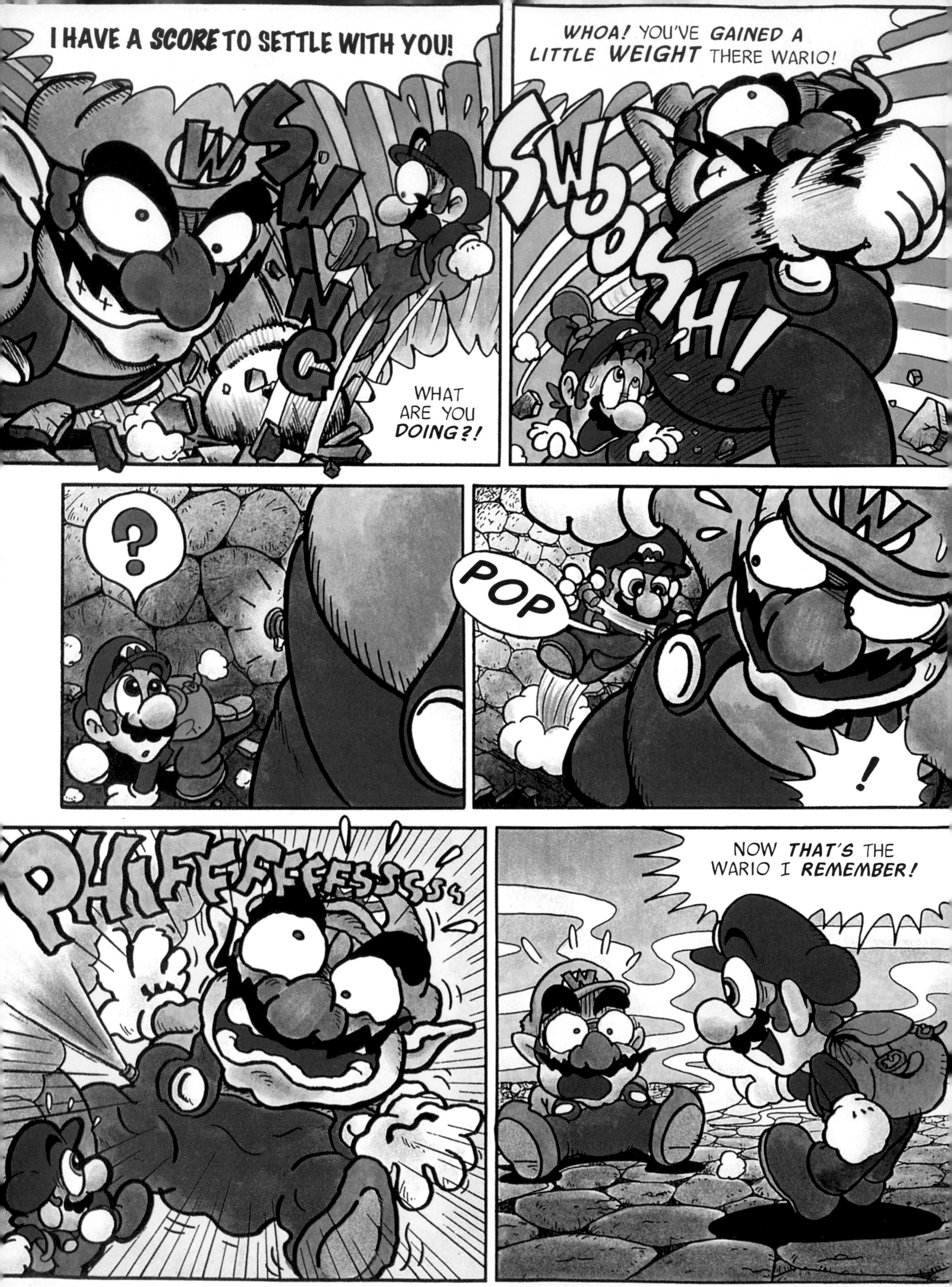
I HAVE A **SCORE** TO SETTLE WITH YOU!
SWING
WHAT ARE YOU ***DOING?!***
WHOA! YOU'VE ***GAINED A LITTLE WEIGHT*** THERE WARIO!
SWOOSH!
?
POP
!
PHIFFFFFFSSSSS
NOW ***THAT'S*** THE WARIO I ***REMEMBER!***

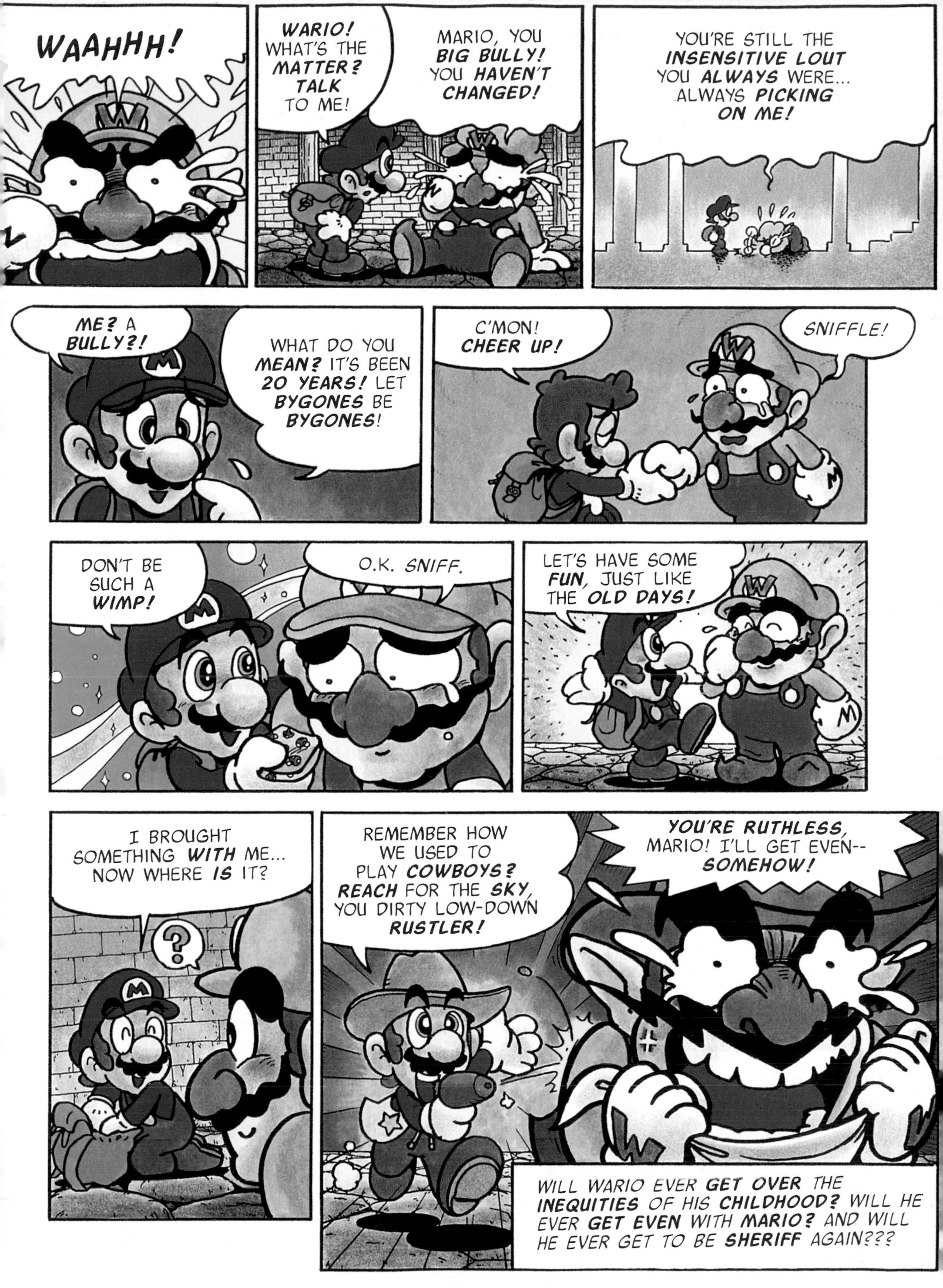
WAAHHH!
WARIO! WHAT'S THE MATTER? TALK TO ME!
MARIO, YOU BIG BULLY! YOU HAVEN'T CHANGED!
YOU'RE STILL THE INSENSITIVE LOUT YOU ALWAYS WERE... ALWAYS PICKING ON ME!
ME? A BULLY?!
WHAT DO YOU MEAN? IT'S BEEN 20 YEARS! LET BYGONES BE BYGONES!
C'MON! CHEER UP!
SNIFFLE!
DON'T BE SUCH A WIMP!
O.K. SNIFF.
LET'S HAVE SOME FUN, JUST LIKE THE OLD DAYS!
I BROUGHT SOMETHING WITH ME... NOW WHERE IS IT?
?
REMEMBER HOW WE USED TO PLAY COWBOYS? REACH FOR THE SKY, YOU DIRTY LOW-DOWN RUSTLER!
YOU'RE RUTHLESS, MARIO! I'LL GET EVEN--SOMEHOW!
WILL WARIO EVER GET OVER THE INEQUITIES OF HIS CHILDHOOD? WILL HE EVER GET EVEN WITH MARIO? AND WILL HE EVER GET TO BE SHERIFF AGAIN???

SUPER MARIO ADVENTURES™

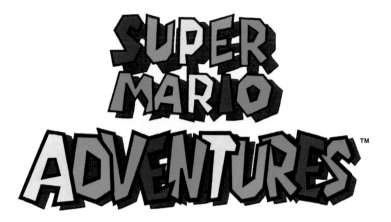

ABOUT THE COMICS

The first twelve comic episodes presented in this book originally ran as a series in *Nintendo Power* magazine, beginning in January 1992 (Volume 32) and running through December 1992. The final episode, which was printed in the first issue of 1993, introduced Mario's alter ego and tormented childhood playmate, Wario. The comics don't follow the storyline of any particular game. However, they do incorporate many characters from the games and even introduce some new ones.

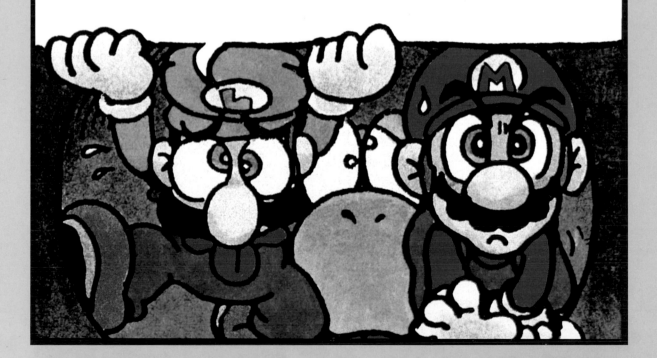

WE ARE THE MUSHROOM KINGDOM'S PLUMBERS EXTRAORDINAIRE!
THE SUPER MARIO BROTHERS, WHAT A PAIR!
DO YOU HAVE PROBLEMS WITH YOUR PIPES?
IS YOUR WATER RUNNING RIGHT?
ARE THE FITTINGS SCREWED DOWN TIGHT?
IF THEY AREN'T, DON'T DESPAIR! THE SUPER PLUMBERS WILL BE THERE!
AND THERE'S NO PIPE WE CAN'T REPAIR!
AND I HAVE A PERSNICKETY, PARTY-PLANNING PRINCESS EXPECTING PLUMBING-- BY TONIGHT!
EH, NO PROBLEMO!
A PIPELINE JOB BY TONIGHT? I CAN'T START A JOB THIS BIG ON AN EMPTY STOMACH.
WE'LL FASTEN
FITTINGS IN NO

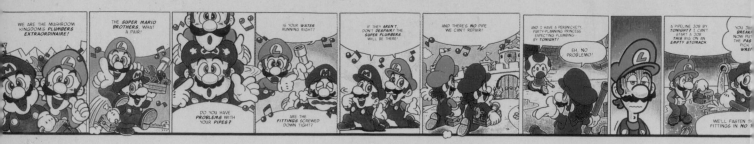

ABOUT THE AUTHOR

Charlie Nozawa, the artist who created the comics, is known in Japan by the pen name Tamakichi Sakura. His most notable works include *Shiawase no Katachi (Shapes of Happiness)* and *Oyaji no Wakusei (Dad's Planet)*.

Kentaro Takekuma dreamed up the scenario. He is best known for co-authoring *Even a Monkey Can Draw Manga*.

C'MON, WEEGE, IT'S EASY! JUST MATCH THE COLORS.
THIS RED PIPE'S CONNECTED TO THE RED PIPE
...AND THE BLUE PIPE'S CONNECTED TO THE BLUE PIPE...
...AND THE YELLOW PIPE'S CONNECTED TO THE...
YELLOW
HMMM. IT LOOKS RISKY...
...BUT IT'S OUR ONLY CHANCE!
LET'S GO!
PLUMP!
IT SURE IS HOT IN HERE!
NO SWEAT--WE MUST BF NEAP THE FND.

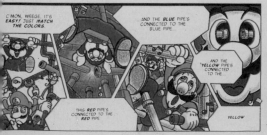

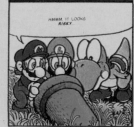

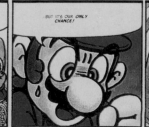

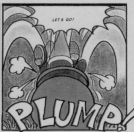

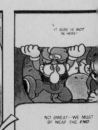